MURDER, NEAT

Dear Ethelle, Enjoy the murders, thefts, + general criminality!

MURDER, NEAT

A SleuthSayers Anthology

Love, Eve Fisher

Edited by
Michael Bracken
and Barb Goffman

LEVEL
SHORT

First published by Level Short 2024

Copyright © 2024 by Michael Bracken and Barb Goffman, Editors

All rights reserved. No part of this publication may be reproduced, stored or transmitted in any form or by any means, electronic, mechanical, photocopying, recording, scanning, or otherwise without written permission from the publisher. It is illegal to copy this book, post it to a website, or distribute it by any other means without permission.

Individual Story Copyrights © 2024 by Respective Authors

These stories are entirely works of fiction. The names, characters and incidents portrayed are the work of the authors' imagination. Any resemblance to actual persons, living or dead, events or localities is entirely coincidental.

Michael Bracken and Barb Goffman assert the moral right to be identified as the editors of this work.

First edition

ISBN: 978-1-68512-566-0

Cover art by Level Best Designs

This book was professionally typeset on Reedsy.
Find out more at reedsy.com

Last Call

It's said no one ever dies as long as they're remembered. Here's to our late SleuthSayers Paul Marks, Fran Rizer, and Bonnie (B.K.) Stevens.

Contents

Praise for Murder, Neat	iii
Introduction	iv
LYRICS AND MUSIC	1
By Mark Thielman	
THE ATONEMENT OF MICHAEL DARCY	15
By David Dean	
SHANKS'S SUNBEAM	22
By Robert Lopresti	
THE COLONEL	33
By Janice Law	
BOURBON AND WATER	39
By John M. Floyd	
WHEN LILACS LAST IN THE DOORYARD BLED	45
By Joseph D'Agnese	
BAD WHISKEY	63
By Jim Winter	
A FRIENDLY GLASS	70
By Elizabeth Zelvin	
WHEN YOU WALK INTO THE ROOM	87
By Steve Liskow	
SHUFFLE OFF TO BUFFALO	103
By David Edgerley Gates	
BAR NONE	110
By Michael Bracken	
THE MOB, THE MODEL, AND THE COLLEGE REUNION	116
By Melodie Campbell	

ROOM OF ICE	128
By Stephen Ross	
TWO FOR ONE	141
By Art Taylor	
FLESH WOUNDS	159
By O'Neil De Noux	
NOT YO' MAMA'S IPA	166
By Kristin Kisska	
NOBLE ROT	179
By Robert Mangeot	
RAZING THE BAR	192
By Leigh Lundin	
THE CATHERINE WHEEL	199
By Brian Thornton	
BAD INFLUENCE	216
By Eve Fisher	
THE BAR	231
By R.T. Lawton	
DEEP TIME	237
By Lawrence Maddox	
GOLDEN PARACHUTE	251
By Travis Richardson	
NEVER HAVE I EVER	264
By Barb Goffman	
Contributors	274
About the Editor	279
About the Editor	281

Praise for Murder, Neat

"Simply put, the SleuthSayers are the finest authors of short crime fiction working today. For readers, this collection will be a joy. For aspiring writers, it's a chance to belly up to the bar and let the best in the business show you how it's done. Not to be missed!"—Edgar Award finalist Joseph S. Walker

"Twenty-four SleuthSayers walk into a bar, and mixologists Michael Bracken and Barb Goffman pour enough top-shelf crime fiction to guarantee you many happy hours of reading pleasure. Bottoms up!"—Josh Pachter, editor of *Happiness Is a Warm Gun: Crime Fiction Inspired by the Songs of the Beatles*

Introduction

Pull up a stool. The bartender will be here in a minute. What's your poison?

Sorry. Probably not the best metaphor for the occasion.

I invited you here to tell you about a book. The one you're reading, as it happens. It's a long time coming; you could say it's fifteen years in the making.

No, wise guy, it didn't take that long to find a publisher. Cut it out, or you can pay for your own drinks. Speaking of which, here's the man with the magic. Beer for me, thanks.

Okay, back in 2007 James Lincoln Warren had an idea. You know James? Great mystery writer. He wanted to promote the short story form so he concocted a blog named *Criminal Brief*. Seven writers, each speaking up one day of the week. I was The Man Who Was Wednesday. And we wrote about short stories.

Mostly. When it's a few hours before deadline, believe me, you can get desperate for a subject. For instance, I wrote a piece called "What My Cats Would Read If Cats Could Read." Not exactly in the strike zone.

The blog was very popular but after running it for three years—and he set up every piece himself, complete with illustrations—James suffered a sudden attack of sanity and decided to retire from the blogging mines.

But by then, a few of us had developed a taste for the thing, and so we—John M. Floyd, Janice Law, Leigh Lundin, and yours truly—decided to start our own establishment. However, we decided that the once-a-week grind was too much, so we added more members so we could each appear fortnightly.

And so *SleuthSayers* was born in 2011. It is still going strong, averaging well over two thousand readers a day. We are committed to writing about mystery fiction, often—but not necessarily—about short stories. (I believe I have somehow avoided commenting on feline literacy.)

Of course, over ten years, contributors come and go: we've had about forty regulars. But our rule is that *SleuthSayers* is like the Mafia. Once you're in, you're in for life. So some of the stories in this book are by former bloggers.

Oh, yes. About this book. The stories in *Murder, Neat* all take place—at least partly—in drinking establishments. This makes sense because booze has always had a place in crime fiction, all the way from a certain cask of Amontillado to the bottle of cheap bourbon that all private eyes seem to be awarded on the day they get their license.

The other thing all these stories have in common is this: they are all top-shelf concoctions from masters of the art.

The twenty-four stories you are about to enjoy include the work of authors who have won or been nominated for a wine cellar full of crime-fiction awards: the Edgar, the Agatha, the Black Orchid, the Macavity, the Shamus, among others.... I count more than one hundred fifty such honors in the crowd.

The editors who had the privilege of herding all these geniuses are Michael Bracken and Barb Goffman. Not only are they both excellent (and prize-winning) authors of shorts, but between them, they have edited thirty-seven prior anthologies, scoring more prizes and nominations than you want to sit through.

Speaking of sitting, let's get you a refill.

I don't want to be one of those barroom bores, so let me just say I think you will find plenty to your taste in these pages, whatever your taste may be. There are frothy cocktails and high-proof liquor, as well as beer by the mug, pint, and pitcher.

One bit of advice: if you imbibe several of these stories in one sitting, please call for a ride home. We don't want you driving under the influence.

Here's mud in your eye.

—Robert Lopresti
Bellingham, Washington

LYRICS AND MUSIC

By Mark Thielman

> *Outside those hospital doors*
> *I could barely catch my breath.*
> From: "God Needed an Angel"
> Lyrics and Music by Jimmy West

On the lacquered bar, the sweaty mug slid between his hands like a puck on a shuffleboard table. Waves of beer lapped at the sides of the glass. Jimmy raised the mug and tossed back the bottom third. He pushed the empty across the bar. "Fill me up again, would you, Alison?"

The bartender finished drying the mug she held in her hands. "You know that Matthew doesn't like you having more than one before you go on stage."

Jimmy grunted. "What's he gonna do, run me off? I've been begging him to fire me for years."

"No, he'd fire me. Then Matthew would hire somebody else, somebody who wouldn't break the rules for you. What would you do then?"

Jimmy leaned back on his stool. His eyes ran over the familiar beer signs. "I'd write you a song."

Alison smiled and rested her elbows on the bar. "Tell me about my song."

"You'd get a tender love song, Alison Carter."

"Jimmy West, what would my song's title be?"

Jimmy looked at her face. Even in the dim light of the Wagon Wheel, she had the prettiest brown eyes he'd ever seen. He chewed on his lip as he thought for a minute. "I'm Drinking Bottled Beer Since My Bartender Got Canned."

Alison's smile broadened. Those eyes grew brighter. "It might be worth getting fired for."

Jimmy scowled. "No one would ever hear it. Nashville won't touch me till I get out of this contract."

Alison let Jimmy smolder in private for a moment. Then, she looked both ways before refilling his glass. She pushed it across the bar.

Jimmy wrapped both hands around the mug. "Why do you treat me better than I deserve?"

"Same reason I feed scraps to that flea-bitten old dog that lives by the dumpster."

Before Jimmy could reply, Alison spun on her boot and walked to the far end of the bar. A young man in starched Wranglers and a pearl-snap shirt stood, his eyes moving back and forth between Alison and Jimmy.

Alison fixed him with her best smile. "Help you, cowboy?"

Seeing how she looked at him, Jimmy felt a twist in his stomach.

The young cowboy didn't answer. Instead, he took a tentative step toward Jimmy. "Ain't you—"

"I used to be," Jimmy said and looked at the kid. He had a square jaw, broad shoulders, and an unlined face. His clear blue eyes would attract women like flies. Jimmy glanced over at Alison.

She saw the blue eyes too.

Jimmy wanted to blacken one of them.

"My daddy says I might not be here today if it weren't for your ballads. He says they made Momma want to dance," the kid said.

Jimmy glanced over at Alison. She watched him with eyes narrowed to slits. He took the hint and resisted the temptation to say anything ugly. Instead, he nodded, acknowledging the remark. "Which is her favorite?"

"She likes 'Leaving in the Morning,' but her favorite is 'God Needed an

Angel.' May I get your autograph for Momma?"

Before Jimmy could say no, Alison pushed a clean napkin and a pen over to him.

Jimmy picked up the pen and started writing. He wagged his index finger, motioning the boy to come closer. "Here's some trivia," he whispered. "Tell your momma that the song was supposed to be 'God Needed an Angle,' but old Jimmy got too drunk to spell." He pushed the napkin across the bar.

The young cowboy looked at him wide-eyed. Then, he carefully folded the paper.

"Son, it's a napkin, not the flag," Jimmy said.

The kid put the autograph into his shirt pocket and snapped it shut. "Thank you, Mr. West." He backed away from the bar, his eyes never leaving Jimmy. Alison trailed him to the end of the bar.

"Next time, get him to buy a drink before you sign something. This is a business."

Jimmy looked to see Matthew Titan standing behind him.

"Jimmy West, you're a cash cow for this bar. Look at the people coming in on a Wednesday. But to be a cash cow, you've got to make us some cash."

"Matty," Jimmy said. He watched the man stiffen. Jimmy knew full well that the boss hated to be called anything but Matthew or Mr. Titan. That's the thing about wanting to be fired, Jimmy thought; it gives a person liberty. "Matty," he repeated. "If I'm the cash cow, how come you get all the money, and I get all the bull?"

Matthew's face tightened. The Budweiser sign hanging over the bar accentuated the redness in his face. Standing there, he reminded Jimmy of the devil. The devil at the Wagon Wheel. Jimmy made a note to tuck that away for a song title.

After a moment, Matthew regained control and sneered. "'You got the cash, and I got the bull.' That's a good line, Jimmy. You should write that song up. We could use another hit."

Jimmy felt his face flush and his fists clench.

Matthew stepped closer, his smirk inches from Jimmy's face. "Think carefully about which hand you're gonna punch me with, Jimmy."

Jimmy felt the warm breath of every exhale.

"You break a finger, and you can't play guitar. You can't work. I still don't let you out of your contract, but you don't get paid." Matthew's lips disappeared in a fake smile. "But I'm sure you can live comfortably off your investment portfolio for quite some time." He grunted a laugh. "Or dumpster dive with that old dog."

They stood face-to-face. Jimmy felt the muscles at the back of his jaw twitch.

"Think about it," Matthew said.

"Dripping testosterone makes the dance floor slippery," Alison said. She'd come from behind the bar and pushed herself between Matthew and Jimmy, wedging them apart. "Slip and fall is a liability risk. Gets both of you sued." Alison cocked her head toward the door. "Matthew, why don't you go greet your new customers?"

Matthew followed her eyes. A half-dozen bikers pushed their way through the door.

"Don't let him drink anymore. He's starting to show bad judgment," Matthew said to Alison before hurrying across the bar.

Alison and Jimmy watched him mingle with the new arrivals.

"Them crow's nest beards and vests kinda stand out in here," Jimmy said.

Alison nodded. "The Wagon Wheel crowd usually breaks down along Resistol versus Stetson."

"They might liven up the place."

Alison and Jimmy watched as one biker peeled away from the rest. He and Matthew disappeared down the hall leading to the owner's office.

"I coulda taken him, you know," Jimmy said.

Alison shook her head. "He's got twenty years and twenty pounds on you."

"But I'm armed with the strength of the virtuous."

Alison grunted and walked down the bar to wait on a customer.

For 12 long hours, I held her hand,
At the bed, I knelt by her side. [1]

"Why did you sign such a dumb-ass contract?" Alison asked.

Jimmy stood by the bar during his break. He nursed a glass of water. "Can't you pour me something a little stronger than this? You know what water does to my stomach."

Alison shook her head and then cocked it in the direction of Matthew. "Boss's orders. Don't change the subject."

He threw back a swallow and grimaced. "Why do you want to hear that old story? I've told you fifty times if I've told you once."

"I keep hoping that if you say it a little different, you'll hear a way out."

Jimmy took a deep breath. "I met this woman once. She was pretty enough if you kept the lights off and the blinds drawn."

Alison grunted. "Chivalrous as ever, Jimmy West."

Jimmy raised his index finger to forestall any further comment. "But what she lacked in looks, she made up for with her profound bad judgment."

"You mean by falling for a guy like you?"

Jimmy nodded. "Pretty clear evidence of diminished mental capacity."

Alison clasped her hands over her heart. "And you two fell in love."

"Well, she was only nasty when she was sober, so that didn't present a problem too often."

Alison grunted again.

"Despite her disagreeable nature, I got used to having her beside me in the pickup. We traveled around as I worked my circuit. Just living life on the road. I managed to scratch out a couple of cry-in-your-beer tunes people seemed to like. Life was pretty good."

Alison smiled. "Anything else good happen?"

Jimmy shook his head. "Nothing worth talking about."

"Then you got married."

Jimmy shook his head. "I didn't want her taking half my stuff when she sobered up and left." He saw the look she gave. "I had two guitars, and I needed them both." Jimmy picked up his water glass and sipped. Setting it down, he picked up a napkin. "Then, one day, she got sick and couldn't shake it. We went to the hospital, and they diagnosed the cancer." He leaned in across the bar. With his index finger, he motioned for Alison to draw closer.

"This may come as a surprise to you, but the insurance benefits of itinerant musicians are rarely written up in your finer business magazines." Jimmy looked down, studying his water glass. His eyes widened as he realized that he had been twisting the bar napkin into a tight roll. Small bits of torn paper floated down on his jeans.

"I'm sorry, Jimmy."

He looked up and smiled. "I hope, Alison, that this will serve as a cautionary tale. Do not allow yourself to become involved with a musician." Jimmy leaned back on his barstool to give her a full view of his upper torso. "Even a smoking-hot one."

He saw her eyes shift over to look at the young cowboy she'd been talking to earlier. The kid sat at a table with a pair of buddies. He hadn't been back to the bar.

"Do not allow yourself to become involved with a musician unless your alternative is a starch-shirted cowboy wannabe. Even a musician is better than that."

Alison stabbed him with a smile. "Quit changing the subject."

"Not much more to tell. This young entrepreneur, Matthew Titan, came along. He was opening a new club and wanted me to be his house act. He offered me some upfront money to sign an open-ended contract and the rights to my songs. Well, I needed cash for medical bills, and the hospital here has a good reputation for fighting cancer. Besides, everyone knew that traditional country music was getting kicked to the curb. I was going to be washed up anyway, so I signed the contract and took the money."

Alison patted his hand. "I'm sorry."

Jimmy shook his head. "Don't be. If I had it to do all over again, I'd do it all over again. The old battle-ax died as comfortable as I could make her." Jimmy's eyes clouded, and he again studied his drink.

Alison busied herself, putting glasses away at the other end of the bar. After allowing Jimmy a minute to compose himself, she made her way back to where he sat.

He smiled again. "If I'd known that neo-traditional country music would come along and sponsor a revival of the old songs, I might have negotiated a bit more strenuously."

Alison looked at him. Her eyes asked if the retelling had given him any fresh ideas.

Jimmy shook his head. "I'm stuck here. I bring enough business through the door that Matty can cook his books and launder the Diablo's Disciples's meth money." He cocked his head toward the table of bikers who'd come in earlier. Jimmy saw Alison's eyes glance at them before returning to her young cowboy sitting two tables away. He knew she didn't need to look. He had told her about the operation when he'd first sensed it beginning. Jimmy had urged her to quit, but Alison had refused. They both knew enough to know who to be careful around.

"I can't reason with him," Jimmy said. "Matty's a crook. A crook thinks everyone else is a crook. No lawyer will take my case on a contingent. They'll only look at it if I pay them by the hour, which I can't do. So I can't bust the contract. And the record labels won't take a chance on a new song if they fear they'll end up in litigation. Them companies don't need to dredge up some has-been songwriter. The internet has made it too damn easy to find fresh talent."

"But people want to hear more of the old stuff."

"They'll have to hear it from someone besides me. I got nothing left to lose. When I try to get out, you know what Matthew Titan says?"

Alison waited. She knew the punch line.

"Not a damn thing. He just laughs."

Jimmy watched her study the look in his eyes. She took a step back from the bar. "Don't go and do nothing stupid, Jimmy West."

He pushed away from the bar, leaving behind a half-empty water glass and the shredded scraps of a napkin.

Although I knew this time would come
I felt alone and scared to death. [1]

Jimmy's dressing room had barely enough space to hold him and his guitar. The guitar would probably have to move to the hall if Jimmy wanted to change clothes. One advantage of a job you don't care about, Jimmy decided, was that he felt no pressure to dress for success. He wouldn't wrestle himself into a Nudie suit bedazzled with rhinestones and embroidery for the Wagon Wheel gig, even if he could afford one. Tonight, he'd taken the stage in his Wranglers and a Houston Astros jersey. Jimmy rarely used the room for dressing. More often, this was the place he came to drink.

Jimmy pulled the pint of Black Eagle bourbon from his back pocket and tossed back a swallow. The final set had gone well. The Wagon Wheel's crowd had swelled over the evening. Many had taken to the dance floor. The guitar had stayed tuned, and nobody had gotten nasty. One advantage of being a has-been is that everyone knows the songs you're singing. The crowd had helped on the chorus and left the verses to him.

He took another pull from the bottle. Jimmy had surprised the crowd with a couple of tunes, new songs he'd been picking at. He'd debuted "Rehab is for Quitters," a dance tune he called a Texas Twelve-Step. The boss had thrown an angry look at the stage when he heard Jimmy playing a song joking about methamphetamine. Then the Disciples had begun laughing and Matthew had relaxed, Jimmy's revenge had gotten lost in whoops and applause.

The crowd had fallen silent when he crooned "God Needed an Angel" for the finale. One man had even dared to shush the Disciples. Jimmy swallowed more whiskey and remembered the final ballad. He'd strummed and sang. Looking out across the audience, he'd watched the crowd swaying. Most of the crowd, anyway. The young cowboy had disappeared from his table. Jimmy had finally spotted him sitting at the bar, huddled close to Alison.

When the song finished, the audience erupted in applause. For a moment, Jimmy remembered every reason why he had allowed this life to grab ahold of him.

As Jimmy walked off stage, Matty reached out his arm and shook his hand. He'd drawn Jimmy close. "I like the new stuff," Matty had said, just loud enough for only Jimmy to hear. "You'll keep this place full for years." He'd given Jimmy a snake's smile before releasing his grip.

Jimmy's good feeling had disappeared.

He swallowed some more bourbon and paced the floor. Three steps to one wall before he spun on his boot, stumbled, threw a hand out to catch himself, and then took three steps back. He drained the pint bottle and dropped it.

The Black Eagle bottle lay face up on the cushion of the room's one chair.

"I've got to go ffff-ix this," he said to the label. "This ssss-ituation has become intolerable."

The label made no reply.

A thought seeped into Jimmy's head. "The Label Made No Reply" might make a pretty good song title. He found a red pen and then fumbled about, looking for a blank sheet of paper to scribble down some notes. He ended up writing the title on his forearm.

Pausing, Jimmy studied his arm. The marks were hard to read. He hoped they'd be enough to jog his memory. Jimmy added a few additional comments to help him remember. He'd get to work when he awoke. Most of his serious writing occurred at the breakfast table.

Jimmy stopped, remembering Matthew's phrase about new songs keeping him in business for years.

He threw the pen across the small room.

Jimmy needed to see Matthew and make him tear up the contract. This might be the best time. Matthew would be in a good mood after the successful night. He might even have knocked back a cocktail or two. Perhaps the liquor would make him more amenable to reason. Jimmy smiled. "This time will be different," he said aloud. No sooner were the words out of his mouth than he realized how naïve they sounded. Matthew wouldn't let him go voluntarily. He'd have to be forced into making some changes. Jimmy might have to get rough. He looked at himself in the mirror, narrowing his eyes and scowling. He drew a breath and pushed out his chest. Alison's words rang in his ears. Matthew was bigger, stronger, and younger. Jimmy exhaled, fogging the image in the mirror. Through the haze, the grizzled face looked back. They both knew he couldn't take Matthew in a fair fight.

Digging in his guitar case, Jimmy found the picture of his beloved. He paused. "Would things have turned out differently if I'd have married you like I shoulda?" He looked at the picture, studying again the curves of her face. Then, he carefully set the picture aside. "Focus on a problem you can solve," he said and continued rummaging. There, beneath picks, a pack of steel GHS strings, and a tuning fork, Jimmy found his bone-handled stockman knife. He unfolded it and scraped his thumb across the razor edge of the blade.

Jimmy faced the mirror. "I might bury the tip in the desk, stick it between his fingers, just to get his mind right." He looked for the whiskey bottle. Finding it empty, he returned his attention to the mirror. He waggled the knife. A spot of light bounced off the polished blade and dotted the wall. "If you got to nick him a little, stay away from the right arm. You don't want to get any blood on the contract when he writes 'canceled.'"

He traced an S in the air with the knifepoint before lowering the blade. Jimmy slowly shook his head. He knew it wouldn't be that easy. He stared into the reflected eyes of the mirror. "Jimmy, you old fool, if you go in there, only one of you is coming out. You ain't bluffin' Mattie. A crook thinks everyone's a crook."

Jimmy stood at the mirror staring. Pursing his lips, he blew a long, slow breath. He nodded. "Do what you got to do. Leadbelly and his guitar twice played their way out of Angola State Prison." He closed the blade and shoved the knife down into his pocket. "Damn shame to cut my leg open walking down there."

He took one more deep breath, then checked the Black Eagle bottle one last time. He would love to have one last drink. He leaned over and dropped the bottle into the trash can. Straightening up, he felt the world spin slightly. "You need to move, Jimmy." He turned off the light and stepped out into the hallway.

Keeping his left hand on the wall to steady himself, he pushed his right hand down into his pocket. Clutching the handle, he walked toward Matthew's office. As he neared, he felt his pace slow. Jimmy forced himself to quicken his steps. He couldn't afford to think too much about what he had to do. The door stood just around the corner. Jimmy tightened his grip on the knife.

A man dressed in black, from his facemask to combat boots, jumped in front of him. He pointed an assault rifle at Jimmy. "Get down on the ground now!"

Jimmy dropped to the linoleum floor. Old beer smells filled his nose.

The man jerked Jimmy's hand from his pocket. He quickly bound both wrists behind his back. "Clear," he said into his radio before continuing down the hall. The raid jacket he wore had POLICE stenciled in bold white letters across the back.

Jimmy West was not so drunk that he could not immediately begin cursing his run of bad luck. Although he'd kept his voice down while talking to the mirror, somebody had obviously overheard him. In a minute, they'd search him and find the knife. Jimmy kicked the floor in disgust. Later today, he'd be lying in jail with a hangover. "Jimmy, you've got to stop livin' a country song."

Before he could berate himself any further, two more masked men came down the hall. The taller one stopped when he saw Jimmy prone on the floor. He pointed to Jimmy. "Get this man up and outta those cuffs."

"But LT, we've not identified…"

"Don't you know who that is?" The lieutenant asked. "Y'all have just cuffed up Jimmy West. He's a country music legend."

The other officer looked at Jimmy.

"Get his hands out of those cuffs now before he injures one. The lawsuit could bankrupt our department," the lieutenant ordered.

As the officer helped Jimmy to his feet and freed him from the flex cuffs, the taller man peeled back his face mask.

Jimmy looked in the lieutenant's blue eyes.

"How is the wrist, Mr. West?" He held Jimmy's arm in his hand and examined it with an experienced eye.

Jimmy squeezed and relaxed his fingers before rotating his wrist. "Not too sore to sign another cocktail napkin, son."

The lieutenant smiled. "Only when I'm working undercover, Mr. West."

Alison and another officer came around the corner. They wore latex gloves and carried a sheaf of paper. When she saw Jimmy being attended to, she raced to his side. "Daddy, are you hurt?"

I stood before the nursery glass,
The day she changed my world.
God needed an angel,
So he gave us a little girl. [1]

At the ambulance, Lieutenant Johnson insisted that the EMT check Jimmy's wrist again. The lieutenant and Alison both huddled around him.

"Let me repeat myself: I'm fine," Jimmy said.

"Drunk but fine, Daddy."

"I had the good sense to take something proactively for the pain."

The lieutenant looked to the EMT, who nodded. "I thought he had some nasty scratches on his forearm, but they turned out to be red ink. They cleaned up with an alcohol swab."

Jimmy looked to Alison. "He agrees…alcohol fixes things."

"I just need to make sure you're OK, sir," the lieutenant said. "I don't think you'll be working here anymore. The Wagon Wheel is closed effective immediately."

"But I'm still under contract," Jimmy said.

"I don't know who'll be around to enforce it. Matthew Titan is looking at some serious time in the penitentiary for money laundering and drug dealing," the lieutenant said.

"But can't he still sue? He might need the money more than ever."

"He'll have trouble finding proof. We found your contract in a desk drawer underneath a kilo of methamphetamine. That contract just became evidence in a criminal case."

Jimmy pointed to the Wagon Wheel. "He had a kilo in there?"

The lieutenant shook his head. "Matthew had a kilo in his office. And five more in the storeroom."

A uniformed officer appeared at their side. "LT."

"Excuse me," Lieutenant Johnson said before following his officer.

Jimmy stood beside Alison, looking at the Wagon Wheel. "What kind of worthless father lets his only daughter work in a dive like this?"

She looked at him. "The kind who never had a choice in the matter."

He nodded. "You know I went a little off the rails after your mother died. I never could quite find my way back home."

Alison didn't say anything. They stood side by side, quietly watching the police carry evidence out of the Wagon Wheel.

Jimmy broke the silence. "What kind of idiot boss keeps a kilo in his office?"

"The kind of boss dumb enough not to lock his door just before a police raid."

Jimmy looked at her, slack-jawed.

Alison winked. "When Brad said they were about to move, Matthew was busy."

"Brad?"

"Lieutenant Johnson. He's called me a couple of times, mostly for intel."

"Mostly?"

"He tipped me that they were coming so that you and I'd be safe. With Matthew busy, I saw my opportunity to fix your problem, so I relocated a little of his methamphetamine."

"But what about evidence?"

Alison flipped the white towel at her waist. "I carried it with my bar mop. No fingerprints. I figured you'd be safe. Nobody'd be threatened by a broken-down old crooner."

Jimmy straightened up, "This broken-down old crooner can take care of himself."

"And what would you have done?"

Jimmy exercised his right to remain silent.

Alison smiled. "Matthew won't be claiming any ownership of a contract that ties him to a prison sentence just shy of a million years."

"I really can get out of here?"

"Get yourself to Nashville and start writing some hits, Jimmy." Alison looked across the parking lot and watched Brad Johnson directing his officers. "You never know when you might need to pay for a wedding."

[1] From: "God Needed an Angel"
   Lyrics and Music by Jimmy West

THE ATONEMENT OF MICHAEL DARCY

By David Dean

Clutching the tumbler in trembling, speckled hands, the ugly little man lifted the glass of amber liquid from the tabletop. Then, noticing tiny concentric ripples widen to its rim, threatening to spill over its sides, he set it down again in frustration. After a few moments, seeing that none of the few patrons scattered about the room were paying him the least attention, he dipped his shaggy head down to the glass and slurped from its edge.

From beneath his eyebrows, he saw a blond, heavy-set woman who had seated herself with a younger couple, watching him over their shoulders. Whiskered, pockmarked cheeks flushing with shame, he sat up straight and stared at the tabletop.

After a few moments, the drink calmed him, and he felt confident that he could hold the tumbler and not have to lap from it like an animal. When he looked back up, the woman was smiling and chatting with her young friends. He was forgotten.

Having warned himself that nothing would be the same, that things could not be the same after so many decades, he was still stunned to find that everything had, in fact, changed. The bar of his younger days was unrecognizable.

It had been a fixture of Elizabeth, New Jersey, since the fifties. Not a tourist destination, as nowhere in Elizabeth was such a place, but a neighborhood bar that had served the simple drinking needs of the local Irish. In the late seventies and early eighties, when he had been a frequent customer, it had been a long, narrow saloon with a few Formica-topped tables and aluminum-legged chairs, their cracked plastic backing and seat cushions brittle and split. Dominating the dim room had been the bar itself, the fly-specked mirror behind it festooned with St. Patrick's Day decorations that were left to gather dust and drop off when the tape dried out.

The old man could see that the back room that had once served as his mob's de facto headquarters had been converted to a dining room separated from the bar by swinging doors. He assumed there was an actual kitchen back there somewhere, as the finger-smudged jars of pickled eggs and beef jerky were no longer displayed, nor were bowls of salted peanuts on proffer. They would not have fit in now, just as he did not. He ran long fingers across the shamrock with its signature drop of blood tattooed on his neck—the brand of Elizabeth's Irish mob. Faded with years, the kelly green and crimson colors were as pale as smeared crayon.

Risking it, he picked up the half-full glass with one hand and brought it to his lips, finishing it off with a gulp. For the briefest of moments, he had the urge to slam it down onto the tabletop and cry, "Sláinte!" like he had done in his youth. But that would have startled the customers, and he didn't want to draw any attention to himself.

What kind of bar was this, anyway, he wondered. Is this what he'd heard called a "Fern" bar—whatever that was—or might it be an upscale pub? In Rahway Prison, the young guys would sometime bring him up to date on such things, but after a few decades he had found that it was like listening to tales of foreign lands or life on distant planets—interesting, but meaningless.

Setting the empty tumbler down gently on the table, he looked up to find the blond woman having left her own and leaning on the bar. Whatever she was saying, she had the full attention of the sleek young man behind it. He nodded once, set two tumblers on the bar, filled them with Irish whiskey—the same brand Michael was drinking—and made to pick them up, but she stopped him with a gesture. Nodding once more, he slid them to her, each with a paper coaster, and she took them up.

With the ease of long practice, despite her weight and a limp, she turned and made her way to Michael's table without spilling a drop and set them down. Pulling out a chair, she settled across from him.

It was the limp that brought her into focus, and the old man felt a wave of shame and terror wash over him, even as he felt his heart swell to bursting. He bent his head to stare at the tabletop and clasped his hands together to stop their shaking.

"You shouldn't have come here, Michael," she said with the faintest of lilts. "I knew you the moment I laid eyes on you, despite all these long years, and I'm that hurt you didn't recognize me. Have I changed that much?"

"Yeah," he answered after a long, stunned moment, his voice hoarse. "You have, Maggie."

"I can see prison hasn't improved your manners. You never knew how to speak to a girl."

"I thought you'd gone back to Ireland—that's what I was told. I had no idea you still worked here," Michael went on, seeing her in his mind's eye as she had been, slender and leggy, her blond hair natural and shoulder-length, her full lips framing a laughing mouth. "I never would've come if I'd known, I swear it."

"You're not to blame for not knowing, Mikey. I just come back a few years ago."

"I'm so sorry, Maggie," he whispered, tears sliding down his gaunt cheeks toward his pointed chin. "You'll never know how sorry. I always wanted to tell you, to beg your forgiveness, but you wouldn't see me—you sent back my letters."

She nudged his glass closer to him with her own. "It's on the house."

Swiping at his eyes with a sleeve of his worn denim shirt, he glanced at her through the tendrils of unwashed hair that partially concealed his face. "You own the place now, Maggie?"

"Bought it after old man Kirwan died. Seamus Tyrrell put me onto the deal. We're partners."

"I knew his dad growing up. We did time together." Michael sniffed. "I heard his boy's the boss of my old mob now. S'that true?"

Maggie took a sip of her whiskey. "Yeah, it is—Seamus killed Bandy Lynch and promoted himself to the vacancy. He blamed him for having his pa murdered there in Rahway. Was that your doing, Michael?"

"Nah. I was done with killin' after what happened, Maggie. Lynch sent word for me to do the job, but I didn't have that in me no more. Besides, I never believed Tyrrell was ever a rat. He weren't no rat that I could see." Michael downed the drink, then nodded at the empty glass. "That's the real thing. I've had nothin' but prison piss for years."

"Why are you here, Michael? If you didn't know I was back in the States, what brought you back? I can't imagine the parole board gave you the nod to visit here."

Shaking his greasy head, he answered, "They got me stashed in a halfway house up in Hackensack. I don't know nobody there, Maggie, and I'm too old to get work. I just couldn't quit thinkin' about home, ya know. I just wanted to come back for a quick visit—to see someplace familiar, maybe somebody I used to know. Not that I expected anyone to recognize me after all this time. I didn't even want them to." He took a deep, shuddering breath. "I can't believe I'm lookin' at you, Maggie—that you're here. Can you ever forgive me for what I done?"

"Has God forgiven you?"

"I confessed it so many times that the priest told me to stop doing it. He said it was wrong to keep confessing a sin that you was forgiven for the first time. But I didn't feel forgiven because I kept thinkin' 'bout you, Maggie—about how much I hurt you and how much you must hate me."

"Hate you?" Maggie's faded blue eyes grew distant with memory. "I loved you, Michael, always had from the moment we met. After a very long while, I forgave you—but how could I put it away from me—what you done? What atonement could you possibly make that would be enough?" She paused to study his face for a moment. "But here you are all the same."

Calling their goodbyes to Maggie, the young couple strolled out as the sleek bartender washed up some glasses. He caught Maggie's eye and held up five fingers.

She waved an assent, and the bartender, drying his hands on his towel, slipped out a door at the back.

The place seemed smaller to Michael than he remembered it and much quieter.

"It was a beautiful day," he began in a soft voice. "I remember it. Every day, I remember that morning. I was so happy to think that you loved me—ugly, little me—and you so beautiful.

"Then I seen him coming out your door, and I felt cold, and the day turned gray as ash around me." His face darkened, his voice growing ragged. "He was a good-lookin' fella—the kind of guy I could see you being with—blond hair, tall like you, smiling and laughing as he left." Michael's grip on the empty glass tightened, the tendons in his large, wide hands rising like cables beneath the skin. "I went away from there, but the next day I come back and watched and waited. And he came out again. Still laughing. Still smiling."

"I didn't know why you were keeping away, Michael, why you weren't answering my calls. You should've asked me. You should've trusted me."

"I didn't have no trust in me, Maggie. You know how we lived then. I was in with the Irish, and nobody could be trusted. It gets to you—always lookin' over your shoulder, waitin' for the police to nab ya, some other mob to kill ya, maybe somebody in your own gang to betray ya. I didn't know nothin' else then. And you so beautiful…me so…so…so, on the third day—"

"You shot him to death as he came out of my house—one bullet for each day you'd seen him."

Michael could still see the good-looking man backing away from the bullets, hands held up as if to stop them, blossoms of red erupting from each wound. No longer handsome, he collapsed into the doorway to lie amongst the trash and debris that had collected there.

"I didn't know he was your brother, Maggie. You never said he was over here. I'd never seen him before. It wasn't till later that I heard he was on the run from Ulster—wanted for some bombings, they said."

"That was a lie. Timmy wasn't involved in nothing like that. He was a good boy. Do you think he could've done something like that after what had happened to me—my leg sliced open by a car bomb as I was walking home from school? Timmy cried over my leg more than I did. He was a gentle, sweet boy."

"I never cared about the limp, Maggie...or the scar—you was always the most beautiful girl in the room—I couldn't even see nobody else when you was there. I'm so sorry for what I done."

"Timothy wasn't wanted by the police at all, Michael. It was a mob back in Derry had put the black mark on him. They thought he was an informant. That's why I was hiding him over here. I was afraid to tell even you, cause I wasn't sure that the Elizabeth Irish wouldn't finish the job for them. There was still strong connections across the pond back then. Like you said yourself, no one knew who to trust in those days. It's no different now, is it?"

"I wouldn't know, Maggie."

Smiling a little, she reached across the table and ran a veined hand down his scruffy, hollow cheek. "In some ways, Michael—in spite of all the things I know you've done—you was always such an innocent." She looked into his bloodshot green eyes for a moment. "I should 'a told you. That's a mistake I'll take to my grave. Trying to protect my brother, I killed him, I reckon."

Taking her hand away, she finished her own drink.

Two men in business suits came in and sidled up to the bar, speaking loudly, as if they had been drinking already. Michael started at the commotion, noticing in the same moment that the bartender had returned to his post.

Having glanced round to see them, Maggie said with a slight smile, "It's 'bout that time. The end of a workday to be celebrated."

As if in confirmation, three young women in brightly colored, impossibly tight dresses entered the bar, taking a table to themselves. One shook droplets of moisture from her curly hair. Michael thought they looked as if they were coming from a party instead of a day at work.

"I better go, Maggie."

"Yeah," she agreed after a moment, "there's nothing for you here anymore, Michael—and you and I can't go back—we never could."

Pushing away from the table, Michael stood. "I'm glad that you forgive me, Maggie. It means the world to me."

She nodded.

"And thanks for the whiskey."

"Godspeed, Michael."

"Godspeed, Maggie."

He felt lighter on his feet than he had coming in, the bright day beckoning through the stained glass inset of the door. The unexpected had happened. Perhaps now he could go forward again—toward what, he didn't know.

Stepping out into the fresh air of a day just cleansed by a shower, he blinked at the watery daylight, even as he felt with a shock of pain both his arms pinioned by strong, young hands, his small frame hustled forward by two men.

A square, tough face leaned into his own, saying, "Remember my pa, ya little bastard? Well, you can bet your life I do."

Michael recalled Maggie speaking with the bartender, him stepping out for a few moments.

He thought of denying it, but the pale, merciless eyes of Seamus Tyrrell stripped him of any hope.

As Maggie had said, there was atonement to be made, and for Michael, it was contained within the dark rectangle of the open sliding door of a panel van, the engine running, the driver grinning like the devil.

SHANKS'S SUNBEAM

By Robert Lopresti

"That was a good morning's work," said Leopold Longshanks. "I think we've earned some lunch."

"Excellent," said Connor, grinning. "I'm starving." Being in his early twenties, thirty years junior to Shanks, he had provided the physical labor that morning while Shanks contributed mostly management skills.

They had come to Manhattan that day because a struggling theater group had given its final death rattle, and the company director, a friend of a friend, had told Shanks he could carry off any of the group's equipment he wanted as long as he rescued it from the storage unit before the rent came due.

Not that Shanks personally needed color scrollers, roll-up banners, or side-loading arbors (or even understood what most of them were). Such doohickeys were seldom required in his profession, which was writing mystery fiction. But he served on the committee that ran a theater in his hometown, and the board president, who happened to be his wife, had deputized him to glom onto the goodies.

Connor was the theater's new handyman, so it was natural that he come along. They (mostly Connor) had filled the rented truck to capacity and were now strolling toward a tavern in Greenwich Village, a place where Shanks had joyfully acquired several pounds of excess weight in his younger years.

"What's the best hamburger you ever had?"

Connor blinked and named a fast-food chain.

"Ha! Prepare to be astonished. The stuff they serve here is—"

"Shanks!"

The shout came from halfway down the block, but that booming baritone was crystal clear. Shanks winced. They turned and saw, as he knew they would, a shorter-than-average man with curly red hair graying at the temples. He wore heavy-framed glasses and an unfashionable white turtleneck.

"A little ray of sunshine," Shanks muttered. "Hello, Proctor."

They waited outside the tavern until the smaller man caught up. "It's been years, Shanks. What brings you to the big bad city? Is this your son?"

"Just a coworker on an errand of mercy. Connor Davins, this is Proctor Ade."

"Are you headed to lunch? Can I join you? My treat."

Shanks sighed. "Why not?"

***

After settling into a quiet corner table at the tavern, Ade and Connor ordered beer. Shanks chose mineral water.

Ade gave him a suspicious glance. "Don't tell me you've gone on the wagon. So many of my friends seem to have lost the true path."

"Not exactly. But this is the first time I've driven a truck in a decade."

Shanks explained their mission to the city. He didn't go into a lot of detail because Ade's eyes began to glaze over, as usually happened when the topic was not publishing or himself.

"Plus driving in the city," Shanks continued. "I figure I need my wits about me."

"You should have told me," said Connor. "I could have driven."

"I've seen you behind the wheel. Enjoy your beer."

"It's amazing anyone can get anywhere in the streets of Manhattan," said Ade. "If you put a car chase in a novel about this town, they would label it science fiction."

"Proctor is an author too," Shanks told Connor. "A very successful one."

Ade gave out a mild snort. "Successful, me? Don't I wish. Do you read mysteries, Connor?"

The young man shook his head. "Mostly graphic novels."

"Well, of course." Ade sighed. "That's why our incomes are collapsing. Young people today can't read without pictures."

"And before that, it was television," said Shanks. "Before that movies. Or radio. We old codgers always have some competition to complain about."

"There are two kinds of people in the world," said Ade, finger raised like a prophet. "People who read mysteries and people who don't know what they're missing."

"Speaking of missing," said Shanks, "I'm searching desperately for a sirloin burger with steak fries."

After they ordered, Shanks asked Ade what he had been up to, which led to a lengthy discourse on a movie deal for one of his novels.

"The studio actually bought the book, would you believe it? Not an option. They bought the rights to the damn thing, free and clear."

Connor's eyes were wide.

"They had an Oscar-nominated director lined up to shoot it and a Golden Globe-winning screenwriter working on the script. Then you know what happened?"

Connor shook his head, making his ponytail wave frantically.

"The director and the writer broke up. They'd been sleeping together, and one of them went back to his wife. Now the studio has lost faith in the damn thing—whatever that means. Is Hollywood a religion now? And remember, they *bought* the damn book, so I'm screwed."

"That's Tinseltown," said Shanks, who hadn't heard so much as a whisper from the West Coast in years. "Always a fresh way to burn you."

"Speaking of burning," said Ade, with a smile for the waitress who was delivering their lunch, "I hope they didn't overcook these things."

They didn't. Shanks ate his first few bites in delighted silence before Ade cleared his throat.

"By the way, I have a question for you."

"Oh?"

"You were on the Best Novel committee for that award this year, weren't you?"

A small alarm bell rang in Shanks's skull. "I was indeed."

"I was surprised by some of the nominees. Not the usual suspects."

"You mean you were surprised your latest book wasn't among them."

Ade shrugged as if that were a mere trifle. "Well, there were a lot of better-known authors with books out this year who didn't get a mention."

Shanks drowned a steak fry in a puddle of ketchup. "That's a good thing, isn't it? It shows the field is growing, that the bench is deep."

Ade nodded. "Very true. If they *were* the best books."

"Oh, Lord. Can't we eat in peace, Proctor?"

The other man leaned forward, putting his tie into his plate. "You were the only man on that panel of judges. And I notice that most of the nominated books were written by women."

"Three out of five. You can't have an even split with five, can you?"

"I'm sure you fought hard for whatever books you thought were best, Shanks, but was it a fair fight? I mean, four women ganging up against you?"

Connor seemed to have lost all interest in his lunch, miraculous considering his usual appetite. He watched the conversation like a tennis fan.

"I see what you're doing," Shanks said. "You're pretending to be sexist"—which was giving the man a huge benefit of the doubt—"to try to get me to break my promise."

"Promise?" said Connor.

"The judges sign a pledge not to discuss the process. But Proctor is hoping I'll rush to defend my fellow judges and explain what went on. Not gonna happen."

Ade leaned forward. "Just tell me how many ballots my book appeared on during the first vote."

Shanks sipped mineral water, pretending it was a fine imported beer. Alas, imagination could only take you so far. "How are you getting along with your new editor, Proctor? It must have been a shock when Greenberg packed it in."

Ade sat back, scowling. "So you're keeping secrets."

"I'm keeping a promise."

The red-haired man looked around for sympathy. "Not that it does you much good to get nominated. Last time I received a nod I was up against a book by the writer who was getting the lifetime achievement award that year. There's some advice for you, Connor. Never be nominated against the person whose whole life work is being celebrated. You don't stand a chance."

Connor nodded, wide-eyed.

"There are two kinds of people in the world. Those with good luck and those with bad, and you are looking at the poster boy for the latter kind. I really thought this might be my year. I thought—" He shifted in his seat. "Whoops."

Ade pulled out his phone and stared at the screen. "Have to take this. Be right back."

Shanks shook his head. Time to eat.

"Is he right?" asked Connor.

"Almost certainly not," said Shanks. "What do you have in mind?"

"I mean about the women giving most of the…whatcha…nominations to women whether the books were the best or not."

"Come on, you heard me say I'm pledged to secrecy."

"But you can tell *me*."

"Really?" Shanks was interested in the logic. "How do you figure?"

"Because I'm not involved! I don't know any of the people, so there's nobody I could tell about it anyway."

"I see." Shanks pulled out his wallet and fumbled for a credit card. "If I tell you, would you promise to keep it secret?"

"Sure."

"So did I."

Connor thought about that, frowning. And then: "Why the credit card? Proctor said it was his treat."

"True, but he's going to stiff us." Shanks tucked the card into his shirt pocket for easy access.

"How do you know?"

"Just watch. Ah, speak of the devil."

Ade shifted into his seat, shaking his head. "That was the new editor you were asking about. He'll be the death of me. He's complaining because my latest book doesn't resemble anything currently on the bestseller list. He called it *fresh*, which he intended as an insult."

"They do like a track record, don't they? But you should be enough of a brand name—"

"I wish! Now, if I wrote a series, like you, or—" Ade's eyes went crafty. "That reminds me. Fiona Makem has a very successful series going, doesn't she?"

"Her Irish mysteries, yes. What about them?"

"And she chaired that Best Novel committee."

Shanks frowned. "What of it?"

"Oh. Nothing much." Ade smirked. Definitely a smirk. "I just heard she may not be asked to judge anything in the future."

Now he had Shanks's full attention. "Oh? Why is that?"

Ade pulled out his phone. "I suppose the news will spread soon enough. I received this email the other day. Anonymous."

He tapped the screen. "Ah. Here it is. Give a listen."

And he began to recite.

"If Dublin is the heart of the Irish nation, O'Connell Street is the pulsing artery, except that analogy doesn't work, because arteries don't run *inside* the heart.

"So what does one call O'Connell Street? The main drag? A channel through history? A place to buy overpriced coffee and baguettes?

"Start at the river and admire the statue of Daniel O'Connell, who led the fight to liberate Irish Catholics two hundred years ago.

"Look north, and you can see the Spire, Ireland's millennium project, an impossibly thin streak of silver, soaring one hundred and twenty meters into the air. Some tourists walk right past it, their minds refusing to accept what they are seeing. The spire stands on the site of a monument to England's hero, Lord Nelson, blown up by anonymous patriots in 1966.

"Next comes the General Post Office, center of the Easter Rising..."

Ade smiled. "Does that sound familiar?"

"It does," said Shanks, with a frown. "It's the opening of Fiona's latest novel, isn't it? *Clubbed in Dublin*. This is just before her detective hears a woman screaming for help."

Ade turned to Connor. "Your friend has quite the memory, doesn't he?"

The young man nodded.

"But the text is not quite the same. She changed a few words, here and there."

"Changed them from what?" Shanks asked.

Ade waved his phone. "This is a photo of a page from a tourist pamphlet, all about O'Connell Street. Looks like Ms. Makem couldn't be bothered to take another trip to refresh her memory."

Connor's eyes widened. "She ripped off the pamphlet? Is that legal?"

Ade smiled. "Well, nobody goes to jail for plagiarism, kiddo. But it's not good for an author's reputation. Publishers tend to cancel contracts for fear of lawsuits."

"Wow. She could get sued?"

"Been known to happen." He shrugged. "Honestly, I doubt the author of some obscure tourist rag would bother, but you never can tell—"

"Can you send me a copy of that email?" Shanks asked.

"Sure. Let's see if I have your address in my contacts list. Ah! Here you go."

"When I was in school," said Connor, "they used to warn us against plagiarism in term papers, but I never understood it. Why does writing a footnote make it OK?"

"Well," said Ade, professorially, "footnotes are how you acknowledge your sources. It means you didn't steal; you only borrowed."

"Do they put footnotes in novels?"

Shanks was ignoring them, studying the image Ade had sent him. It showed what appeared to be the outside of a cheap tourist pamphlet, looking to be eight pages long. The cover had the title: VISIT O'CONNELL STREET! INTRODUCTION... The text that Ade had recited followed.

The back cover featured a photo of the Parnell Monument at the north end of the street. Beneath that was the information about the publisher.

"May I interrupt?" said Shanks.

"Of course," said Ade, with a wave of his hand. He sipped beer.

"I'm looking at the last page of this pamphlet. No author listed. But I see what I suppose is the publisher: Liffey Banks Printer. June 2001."

Ade nodded. "Yes. Ever been to Dublin, Connor?"

"No. That's in Ireland, right?"

"Yes. It's the capital, and the River Liffey runs right through it. Hence the name of the printer. I believe there is also a traditional tune called 'Liffey Banks,' so the printer might have had that in mind."

Shanks put down his phone. "Have you checked to see if the company is still in business?"

"Good question. The web came up with nothing. Not a surprise after almost twenty years. I don't suppose publishers are more enduring there than they are here."

"No surprise at all," said Shanks. He swallowed mineral water. "I'm afraid I'd have to give you a D, Proctor. Maybe with practice, you could get your grade up to a D-plus."

Ade frowned. "What the devil are you talking about?"

"I mean the story you just told us." He waved at his phone. "Fiona didn't steal her text from that pamphlet."

"Oh? Then how do you explain it?"

Shanks cast an eye toward the tavern's gloomy ceiling. How, indeed, without inviting a charge of slander? Proctor Ade was known to be a swift hand with a lawsuit.

"Let's put it this way. Someone went to a lot of trouble to print up that pamphlet page and send it to you from a dummy account. I don't know who that person was—"

He looked Ade straight in the eye with an expression that said: *Oh, yes, I do.*

"But he made a big mistake."

Ade glared back. "And what was that?"

"The date on the pamphlet. When was the last time you visited Dublin?"

"I don't know. A long time ago."

Shanks nodded. "Cora and I were there a few years ago, and I lost track of how many Dubliners gleefully told us that the Spire, which was the country's big millennial project, didn't get built until three years after the Millennium. It was installed in 2003."

Ade was frowning. "So?"

"So a tourist pamphlet published in 2001 wouldn't be talking about it in the present tense. This pamphlet is a phony."

"Does it say 2001? Are you sure?" He looked at his own phone, then dropped it on the table.

"I hope," said Shanks, spacing his words carefully, "that you haven't forwarded that message to anyone yet. Anyone but me, I mean. It would be embarrassing for you to have to explain how you were fooled."

He wanted to tell Connor to shut his mouth, which was dangling dramatically.

At last, Ade sighed. "You know what your problem is, Shanks?"

"No, but I've always wondered."

"You don't know how to take a joke. Whatever idiot sent that picture didn't fool me for a minute. I just wanted to see if you spotted the clue that it was fake."

"Ah," said Shanks. "Is that it?"

"Obviously." Ade hit a button on his phone. "This was merely lunch conversation."

"I'm glad."

"I just deleted the picture, and I suggest you do the same."

"You know what? I think I'll keep it. Just in case the forger thinks about trying a second edition. You know how dishonest some people can be."

The red-haired man rose abruptly. "Excuse me. I need to lose some beer."

As Shanks finished the last bite of his burger, he noticed Connor staring at him. "That was amazing!"

"Glad you enjoyed it."

"He made the page up, didn't he? Just to get that woman in trouble."

"There's no proof of that."

Connor snorted. "What a stinking bastard. I know he's your friend, but—"

"Not a friend. Just someone who would make a bad enemy."

"I got some bad news, then. I think you made him your enemy today."

"I hope not." Shanks shrugged. "I didn't feel like I had a choice, though."

"Sure. Since that writer woman is your friend."

"I hope I would have done it for anyone. As you get older—"

The waitress had arrived, bill in hand.

"Thank you very much," said Shanks, producing his credit card. "By any chance, did my friend tell you we were in a hurry, so please rush over the check?"

"He did." Her smile faltered. "Is that okay?"

"Absolutely."

When she left, Connor shook his head. "He ripped you off, just like you said."

"Well." Shanks scratched his bald spot. "It didn't exactly require a psychic to predict that."

The waitress came back with his card and paperwork, followed almost immediately by Ade. "Oh no. This was supposed to be my treat. I'm so sorry."

"You can get it next time."

Connor rolled his eyes.

* * *

As the two men walked back to the truck, Connor judiciously admitted that the burger had been even better than the ones served at his favorite fast-food boutique.

After a few minutes of silence, he added, "That Ade guy is a creep. But I guess he's got good reason."

"What do you mean?"

He waved an arm dramatically. "All that bad luck he told us about. The movie deal that crashed. His editor retiring. And…"

"Connor." Shanks sighed. "Did you ever see a movie called *Silver Targets?*"

The young man's face lit up. "You kidding? Those flicks are great! I've seen all five."

Shanks's bushy eyebrows rose. "Five? I had no idea. I lost interest after the first sequel. But they were based on one of Proctor Ade's novels. He's made so much money off those films that he owns a brownstone near Central Park, and I forget how many acres of ranchland on Maui. Or is it Molokai?"

Connor stopped in his tracks. "You're kidding! But he griped for ten minutes about a movie deal that went south."

"The one that got away, yes." Shanks unlocked the truck, and they climbed in. "And all that whining about awards? He's received almost every major prize in our field at least once."

"I don't get it, Shanks. Why is he always complaining?" Connor tugged at his ponytail. "And if he's rich, why is he so cheap? And, and bitter?"

Shanks started the truck. "Because the truth of it is, there are three kinds of people in the world."

"Three? How do you figure?"

"Type one says the glass is half-full. Type two says the glass is half-empty."

"And type three says—"

"The glass is all mine," said Shanks. "And no one else deserves even a sip."

THE COLONEL

By Janice Law

Every evening, the Colonel arrived to drink at The Huntsman, a modest brown-shingled tavern nicely situated on the state road between the two nearest towns. Unlike most of the men who favored this watering hole, the Colonel was a rich man who could have drunk good liquor at home. That he did not do so might have been an item for speculation in another circle, but not here, for he had a password, *Anzio*.

Today, Anzio is a pretty Italian beach resort, but in those days, it evoked hard fighting and uncertain leadership, and dreadful casualties taken in miserable conditions. Many of the regulars had their own passwords, *Saipan*, *Omaha Beach*, and *Riva Ridge*, and their own reasons for spending long hours at The Huntsman. They came for the company of men who did not need explanations or offer excuses and for Joseph, the barman, who poured generously, and for separation from a world, so long desired, that had proved foreign and almost intolerable.

The Colonel came for those things, too, but in smaller doses. He always sat at the same booth, a little distance from the others, with whom he had the one big thing in common, but many smaller ideas, mannerisms, and circumstances setting him apart. That was all right: *Anzio* covered a lot of ground. Still, it might have surprised the company to know that the quiet Colonel spent every night planning how to murder his wife.

Her name was Blanche, Baby to her friends, but the Colonel, who had been besotted with her as a boy and married her as soon as he graduated from college, thought of her now as Blanche of the White Hands, a *belle dame sans merci*. This was a fancy way of separating the woman he intended to kill from the Blanche he had known and loved, back before he had a password to places like The Huntsman and to even darker places in his heart, back before he became, in his own imagination, The Knight of the Sorrowful Countenance.

Oh, she'd been the perfect girl! Giddy and energetic, she danced all night and was ready to ride at dawn. Blanche swam, sailed, and skied with perfect grace, and she was a good sport who loved a party, a picnic, a night on the town. Sometimes, the Colonel remembered happier days and felt that his heart, frozen as it was, would shatter within his chest.

Nonetheless, he spent his evenings planning obsessively to kill her because the war had so wounded him that all the things he had once enjoyed now filled him with dread. And worse, Blanche had had what they called *a good war*. She'd joined one of the women's services and hied off to Washington, where her good looks, good connections, and good spirits secured her a liaison job with some hush-hush outfit. About her war work, Blanche was perfectly serious.

But underneath, she appeared unchanged, still full of life and fond of what might be called reasonable risks. The Colonel guessed that his old friend Marcus fell into the latter category. Blanche and Marcus became an item quite soon after the Colonel returned, burdened with the great indifference that clouded everything. To do her justice, Blanche had tried to reach him, although patience was not her strong suit. But her gaiety and even her kindness failed to touch the Colonel, who had withdrawn to some deep and secret place and who wanted to die.

He sometimes thought that he should be grateful for the affair, because while her virtues had failed, her betrayal kept him going. He could honestly say that Blanche of the White Hands had given The Knight of the Sorrowful Countenance a reason to live. Soothed by the murmur of his fellow drinkers, he sat every night in the tavern, pondering the removal of both his wife and his former friend.

He had certain requirements: It must be done at night; that was essential. And on that night, he must be seen elsewhere. While death might have a pleasing finality for The Knight of the Sorrowful Countenance, the thought of prison and disgrace was unbearable. The Colonel had experienced considerable frustration before he realized that The Huntsman, situated a mere ten minutes along the state road, could supply his alibi.

To forward this plan, he took pains to establish himself at the tavern as a creature of habit. Whether Blanche liked it or not, every night, the Colonel rose from the table immediately after dinner, taking time only to change out of his evening clothes. He arrived at The Huntsman no later than nine-thirty and ordered a double Scotch and soda. After an hour or so, he took a break outside to "clear his head," a sacred interval that neither heat nor cold nor rain prevented. Best, though, were the cold, clear nights like this one, when the Colonel might stay out half an hour or more, contemplating the stars or walking along the dirt side road and listening for night noises.

His routine was so well established that when the Colonel walked out with a wave to Joseph, the others nodded or lifted a hand or ignored his departure. But this time, he did not light a cigarette and stare at the night sky. This time, he hurried to his Jaguar, parked, as always, at the very back of The Huntsman's lot. He eased the car onto the road and drove with his lights off until he had cleared the hill above The Huntsman.

Then the Colonel floored the gas, for, although he was normally cautious driving back from the tavern, the road was empty on this special night, and the moon was up and bright. He flew down the highway, not even braking to enter the smaller town road, and arrived almost instantly at the dirt road to his farm, where he switched off his headlights again. The Colonel felt his heart beating, felt the adrenaline, felt life returning.

Oh, how much he had changed, that only this night drive restored him. But best not to think of such things, not on the eve of battle. When the Colonel rolled down his window, he saw the long grasses at the roadside sparkling with frost, and the cold air revived him so that he remembered to avoid the gravel drive with its distinctive crunch and parked behind the stable instead.

He stepped out into silence and felt a rush of panic. What day was it? What day? Wednesday. Midweek. Cook's day off. All right. She would return from the city Thursday morning. The other domestics were safe in the apartments above the free-standing garage. The Colonel felt his breathing return to normal. He would walk to the back of the house and enter through the kitchen. The door would be unlocked, of course, for any disturbance was unthinkable to Blanche. The Colonel smiled at that thought.

Inside, he moved silently down the corridor, past the laundry and the cook's rooms. Jessie had been his mother's cook, and he felt a twinge. It would never do to endanger her. But Wednesday was her day off, thirty-six hours in the city, and, as was proper, he had taken that into account. The Colonel felt better at this evidence that he was not changed so very much. He could not be seriously altered if he had considered the old cook.

In the big kitchen, he went straight to the vast professional range and turned on the oven and all the burners. The Colonel had made sure there was plenty of gas, having waited until the recent propane delivery. He left through the butler's pantry, easing open the door to the dining room, just below the bedroom where Blanche of the White Hands would be with Marcus. With almost hallucinatory detail, the Colonel saw him arising in the night to return to the city. Marcus would switch on the bedside light to admire his still beautiful lover while he had a cigarette, a little cap for the pleasure of the evening. He would smile at her and reach for his Camels and his handsome silver cigarette lighter, a present from his old friend, her husband—then Wooosh!

The Colonel thought he could count on that, but just in case, he lit the candles on the dining room table before leaving. He had a bad moment when he stumbled on the terrace. Luckily, there was no sound, but it wouldn't do to be careless, not now, though he was desperately anxious to be away. At the same time, he seemed incapable of haste, drifting across the lawn in the brilliant moonlight, a long, slow progress before he reached the safety of the big spruces and so to the road and the stable where the Jaguar waited. Inside the car, he felt momentarily that he would collapse with exhaustion, with battle fatigue. Battle fatigue on the domestic front, he thought, and started to laugh. Not a good idea.

The Colonel made himself drive slowly away, the car dark on a dark and silent night. At The Huntsman, he found he had almost burned his fingers with his dying cigarette. He was surprised to realize that he had only been gone a matter of minutes and wondered at the amazing elasticity of time.

He collected another double Scotch before reclaiming his seat in the tavern. But now, everything was different. Now he was alert, all ears for the sound of sirens, surely audible, if not from their village to the west, from the bigger town in the east. The engines would scream up the twisting valley road, trailing bad memories in their wake. The Colonel could imagine it all. He was well acquainted with fire and screams and earth-shaking destruction.

But as the minutes passed, he gradually began to lose the serenity he had felt outside, watching his cigarette smoke drift toward the stars. He checked his watch. Forty-three minutes had passed since his return. Too long, he thought, too long, and he was beginning to tap his fingers on the table, the nervous tic that so annoyed Blanche, when the tavern's phone rang. He sat up straighter. Perhaps the fire department from the village had answered the call, perhaps the wind was from the east tonight and the sound had not carried, perhaps this was the fatal, official notification. The Colonel could hardly keep still.

Joseph was on the phone, nodding, his face impassive. The Colonel knew that his voice would be calm and sympathetic, for the barman was the soul of tact. He hung up, wiped his hands, and stepped over to where the Colonel sat. Though Joseph spoke barely above a whisper, the regulars exchanged knowing glances; the Colonel's sharp and formidable wife often left messages for him.

"That was the missus," Joseph said. "I assured her you could drive home."

The Colonel closed his eyes for an instant lest Joseph, kind and perceptive, should glimpse his soul. Then he stood up, seemingly alert, with not a hair out of place. "Thank you, Joseph. You did the right thing," he said.

Of course, he could drive. He drove every night without trouble, and there was no need to summon George from his bed. Disturbing George would have been Blanche's stated concern, though a late call for the chauffeur was always fine if it kept *her* from inconvenience.

The Colonel nodded to Joseph and the group at the bar, then walked, still straight, but cautious and conscious of every step, out the door. Overhead, the stars were very high and cold, and he shivered in the December wind as he stood beside the Jaguar. With a stab of despair, he realized that his imagination, more treacherous than even his faithless wife and friend, had deceived him. He was tempted to speed into the night and end present misery, before he had another thought. This was Wednesday, and Marcus would not have been visiting but sleeping in his own city apartment.

Though it was distressing to have forgotten so crucial a detail, the Colonel nonetheless smiled as he got into his car. He had certainly proved it could be done, and Friday or Saturday night, he would do it. Marcus would visit, and everything would unfold, the Colonel thought, just as he envisioned it, for at The Huntsman, anything was possible.

BOURBON AND WATER

By John M. Floyd

The middle-aged man and woman sat facing each other across a tiny table in the darkest corner of the bar. It was almost midnight, with only a few other customers in sight. The bartender, a scruffy guy with a gray goatee and a ponytail, sat motionless on a stool behind the counter, staring at his cell phone. The woman was staring into her drink.

"I had a crazy dream," she said. Her voice was low, almost a whisper.

The man tilted his head and studied her a moment with his left eye. The other was covered by a black patch. "Last night?"

"Just now. It was the funniest feeling—I must've zoned out or something." She rubbed her forehead. "It was so…real. You know how authors say they can sometimes picture everything about their characters, not just how they look and talk and think, but even their history, their life stories? I felt I could see all that too, about these people in my dream."

She fell silent again, listening to the pounding of her heart. From the far side of the room, she heard the scrape of a chair and footsteps as someone rose and stumbled to the restroom. She took a long breath. The images still lingered in her mind.

"Tell me about it," the man said.

She focused again on her drink. "Two people, a woman and her husband." She had a thought, looked up at him, and smiled a little. "He looked a little like you, without the eye patch. Same color hair and a strong face. Stoic."

"Arrrrrrr," he said. "All pirates are stoic."

The smile lingered a bit and then faded. "Her name was Sue Ellen," she said, solemn again. "Like J.R.'s wife in that old show—"

"*Dallas.*"

"Yeah. But this woman was Carter, Sue Ellen Carter, and in my dream, she was at some kind of resort on an island." She paused, raised her head, and looked around. "Maybe it was here or close to here." Somehow, that thought scared her. "But no, it couldn't have been…"

"Go on," the man said. "I'm listening."

"That's how it started. She was in a vacation cottage on an island with her husband." She stopped again, remembering. "It's the weirdest thing. It's as if I was there, in her body. I watched as she set a suitcase down on an unmade bed, opened it, reached inside—"

***

—and took out the little .32 automatic. With practiced ease, Sue Ellen ejected the clip, checked it, slapped it into place, and put the gun back underneath the folded clothes. She and her husband, Frank, had purchased it after landing the previous night and taking a taxi into town on the way to the resort, an errand that required time as well as caution. She found herself longing for the old days when you could carry a weapon onto a plane inside checked luggage with no worries and no hassles. Times had changed.

Sue Ellen heard the shower turn off in the bathroom. Seconds later, the phone on the bedside table rang. She answered it, listened to the accented voice, and hung up. "Strange," she said.

Frank stuck his head out the door. "Who was that?"

"Somebody at the front desk, where we got off the bus. He said…the oddest thing. He said my mother's on her way here."

"What?"

She turned to look at him. "He told me to go to the main building. Mommy's coming."

Frank disappeared again into the bathroom. "That makes no sense, Sue

Ellen. The building where we came in is half a mile inland, and your mother doesn't even know we're here. I bet she hasn't left Atlanta in ten years. And why would someone else call her Mommy?"

"Don't worry about it—I must've heard him wrong. I can't understand half of what anybody says here, anyway." She sat down on the bed beside the suitcase and yawned. Behind her, outside the window of the bungalow, palm fronds swayed in the sea breeze.

"Well, we won't be here long," he called.

She snorted and thought, *Long enough*. Vacationing at a place like this was one thing; coming here on an assignment was another. She wouldn't relax until their target was dead and they were on their way back to the States. And they hadn't even made contact yet. "What time are we supposed to do this group swimming deal?" she asked.

"Snorkeling. Just after lunch, I think."

The guy they'd been hired to eliminate was supposed to be a part of the group activities, he and his girlfriend. Frank and Sue Ellen had studied photos of them both. The plan was to meet them on the outing and invite them to have drinks tonight at the bar, at which time Sue Ellen would drop quick-dissolving tablets into their drinks. The girlfriend would get the sedative, and the target would get the poison, both of which wouldn't take effect until later. By the time the girl woke up, and the guy didn't, the two Carters would be packed and ready to take the morning shuttle to the airport. The alternate plan involved the gun in the suitcase and would be necessary only if the poison didn't work as it should or if Sue Ellen wasn't able to get it into the guy's drink. If they were forced to take that approach, the girlfriend would probably have to die also, so there'd be no witnesses. Too bad, but such things happened. One way or the other, the job would get done, the Carters would collect the second half of their fee, and the world would continue to spin on its axis. They hadn't really needed this job, but it never hurt to pad the accounts a bit. Both of them had retirement on their minds.

"I'm not too sure," she called out, "about this snorkeling thing."

She heard him chuckle in the echoing bathroom. "Who knows, you might like it."

"Will it be cold?"

"Warm as bathwater," he said. "Difference is, it has fish in it."

"Ugh." She studied the still-open suitcase. "Hey, do you remember where I packed that bottle of bourbon?"

"Bourbon? It's nine in the morning."

"I bet it's happy hour back home."

"Check my bag."

Sue Ellen stood and crossed the small room, vaguely aware of a deep, dull rumble that seemed to come from the walls themselves. Probably the air conditioning. This was supposed to be a swanky resort, but their bungalow looked old as Methuselah's grandfather. Then she paused, frowning. "Funny thing is," she said, "he called me by name."

"Who did?"

"The desk clerk, or whoever it was, on the phone. He said, all excited and out of breath, 'Sue—Mommy's coming. Go to the main building.'"

"That *is* strange." Frank came into the room half-dressed, his hair damp. He started to say more, then looked at the window and froze. Sue Ellen saw him and followed his gaze. Her jaw dropped; her eyes widened.

Extending from one end of the horizon to the other was a huge white-topped wave. It looked like a towering blue wall, moving steadily closer. The roaring was louder now. On the golden stretch of beach, people were screaming and running. An absurd thought flashed through Sue Ellen's mind: *No snorkeling today.*

"He didn't say 'Sue, Mommy,'" Frank murmured, staring. "He said 'tsunami.'"

At last, she found her voice. "What…what can we do?"

He turned, his face pale, to focus on her. "You can find that bottle," he said.

* * *

"And I did," said the woman in the bar. She looked across the table at her husband. She'd spoken those words through her fingers, because moments ago, she had clapped her hand over her mouth. "That was me, wasn't it? I'm Sue Ellen Carter. I'm the woman in the dream."

He took her other hand, squeezed it tenderly, and said, "You found the bottle and gulped about a third of it at one pull, and I drank most of the rest, and we stood there and held each other and watched the wave come in."

"Yes. I know that now." She swallowed, the sound loud in the quiet, gloomy bar. "It's the last thing I remember."

Frank stayed silent for a long time, gazing into her eyes. She could see how pleased he was and relieved as well. Finally, he took a deep breath of his own and said, "That was a month ago and a hundred miles away. They tell me most of the island was wiped clean."

"But we made it," she said dazedly.

He nodded. "A lot of people didn't. We got separated, you and me, and were swept inland, almost to the main gate. Something hit you on the head—a tree, a car, a picnic table, part of the bungalow, something—and you lost your memory. We and other survivors were taken to a hospital on the mainland, and when you and I recovered, physically at least, I convinced one of the doctors to set us up here."

"And…your eye?"

He touched the black patch. "Healing. It was a close thing, though."

She shook her head. "I can't believe this." She gingerly touched her left temple, where the bandage had been. "I've been—what? Out? All this time?"

"In a way. You've been functional, just not…normal. As I said, memory loss."

"But—what about our…"

"Assignment?" He cast a quick look around and lowered his voice. "Done. Target's drowned, girlfriend's missing, client's happy. Our mission was accomplished, just not by us."

She stared at him, still a bit stunned. Before she could reply, she heard someone behind her clear his throat, and turned to see the man behind the bar hold up a shot glass and raise his eyebrows. *Need a refill?* Both she and Frank shook their heads, and the bartender went back to looking at his cell phone.

She focused again on her husband, trying to get her thoughts back on track. She realized she could hear the distant murmur of surf and that, this time, it was no dream or memory. There was a beach here, too, somewhere. Nearby.

A seaside bar in the tropics. What a place to wake up from a dream.

"So...will we get paid?" she asked before she realized how silly it sounded.

"No," Frank said. "They think we're dead too, Sue Ellen. Everybody does, except the few people I had to bribe to keep it that way. Good thing is, we got half the fee up front. No one's looking for us."

"But we also can't go back. Right?"

He shrugged. "No need to. We can access our investments from anywhere."

"So...we *are* retired."

"You can call it that. A little earlier than planned."

She felt herself smile. "Lost in paradise?" she said. Instead of answering, he took a sip of his drink and smiled, too. His look said there was no better place to be lost.

She swallowed again and thought about that awhile. She couldn't help remembering—actually *remembering* now—her pre-tsunami views on things like visiting here versus being sent here. She'd never had any views on *living* here. Fate was indeed a strange thing.

Frank was right. Early retirement didn't sound bad at all.

"Maybe I'll learn to snorkel," she said.

WHEN LILACS LAST IN THE DOORYARD BLED

By Joseph D'Agnese

The engravers were the second group of patrons to arrive each weekday afternoon when Pfaff's, the rathskeller under the old hotel, opened for business. They took the seats vacated by curmudgeonly printers dashing out of the basement to jump horse-drawn omnibuses bound for Franklin Square downtown, where magazines such as *Harper's* and *Leslie's* were printed.

Young Thomas Nast arrived soon after, taking his customary seat under the sidewalks below Broadway, where the massive hogshead barrels were stored. Nast preferred one table in particular, not too close to the gaslight chandelier but not so far that the lamp's meager yellow glow was blocked by the curves of the vaulted brick arches. He sipped his brew and sketched away, his pencil catching and preserving the forms of actors and actresses and stagehands and the penurious penny press scribes who began to fill Pfaff's two underground rooms with their chatter.

The illustrator's pencil circled back a couple times to the large figure sitting alone at one of the small tables in the front vault. From the rakish tilt of this man's ridiculous hat and voluminous cape, Nast pegged the shadowy figure as none other than Ponder, the theater critic. Back to the wall, Ponder hunched over his notebook, eyes straining to peer through minuscule blue lenses. He was pushing sixty and three hundred pounds, and his opera cape draped him snugly.

Heavens, he made the scribe's art seem so tortuous! A poser, wasn't he? Had he not once bragged that he never had to actually see a Broadway show to know what he thought of it? Yes! All the great Ponder needed was the playbill to tell the world what he thought of the newest opera mounted at the Fellow's or the Astor Place or, for that matter, the minstrel act at Niblo's.

Similarly, Nast did not have to *see* Ponder to draw Ponder. You sketched the waiters whirling around him. You sketched the handsome, obsequious actor in his crisp tweeds, fawning over Ponder. Or later, the lissome lady in red bending to whisper into the great man's ear. As Nast's pencil danced, Ponder's ponderousness alone threatened to fill the page.

When he was being honest with himself, Nast could admit to his own issues in that department. Why, his girlfriend, Sallie, called him Roly-Poly in their most intimate moments. And Nast had once drawn a cartoon of himself as a pig!

A plate of oysters and a bowl of turtle soup later, when Nast had occasion to turn his pencil back to the critic, he noticed that there was not much new to sketch. The pencil in the critic's hand, his notebook, his hat, his cape, the bottle of Pfaff's cheapest champagne, and the delicately etched coupe glass by Ponder's wrist—all of it hadn't moved in an hour.

It was just that way long after Nast departed, emerging from the cool basement into the humid summer heat to pay a call on Sallie before heading home to his mother on William Street. And it was that way still when dear Pfaff raised the lamps in his back room and shooed the lingering night owls to the long table up front, the better to start cleaning the joint.

Night after night, these bohemians would leave poor Pfaff shaking his head. Always they were wanting to stay later. Always they cajoled him into keeping the tavern open just a little while longer. They drank, they ate, and then wheedled him to mark their charges on their tabs until Friday! It was madness to run a business this way. But the stolid German tapster did it, secretly fearing he that would be lost without the literary sort who had made his locale legendary throughout the nation.

And *this* fellow, in the corner by the barrel…

"Mr. Ponder," Pfaff said, bowing curtly. "Soon I close… Mr. Ponder? Your champagne is not good? I see you do not drink—"

That's when he spotted the blood.

The critic had been silenced at last.

* * *

That's how it was in Manhattan, 1859. You could die, and no one would ever know. So many died, and so often alone, that a popular weekend pastime had emerged. One dressed in one's Sunday best and visited the city's various morgues in search of missing acquaintances and loved ones, hoping to spot them before they were consigned to potter's fields or the tables of dissectionists.

Friday morning at the morgue in the Tombs on Centre Street, the unclothed remains of Eustace Ponder peered up into the living eyes of another man.

—*Heavens, Ponder*—

the living man thought

—*your bulk, your body, like waxed marble*

—*unmatched, the sheer size of you*—

—*against your wit*

It was always this way. The words tumbled out, struggling to form themselves in the living man's mind.

—*Stop it*

The living man was tall and ruggedly built, but sadness was etched into his limbs. He was still grappling with the recent loss of a newspaper job across the river and the cheerless silence that had greeted the second edition of his magnum opus. His father had died four years ago, only days after the son had coaxed his first edition of poetry into the world.

Death, joblessness, a parade of frivolous affairs, and lost love had thinned the poet's mop of hair and shot gray through his beard. Death dogged him everywhere. His poetry suffered. The words came miserably or not at all.

He had just turned forty but looked decades older. But he did himself no favors. His workman's shirt, open at the collar, revealed a thatch of equally gray chest hair. In his hands, he clutched a shapeless felt farmer's hat.

"How did it happen?" he asked. It was a booming voice, suitable for declaiming poetry in darkened saloons. A voice that echoed off the marble and plaster walls.

Detective Ronk was shorter and younger, with pale-pink cheeks and lovely blue eyes. Firm arms and chest beneath his woolen jacket. He swiped a hand under his waxed mustache and sniffed, his nose crinkling at the pervasive scent of decay.

"That's the confusing bit," said Ronk. "If you'll step around, ah, *sir*, you can see the wound where the knife entered." He pointed unhelpfully. "Yes, you'll have to, ah, roll him. Stabbed in the back, so to speak. Right between the ribs. Quick and dirty. Probably nicked the heart or the membrane surrounding it. He would have bled quickly. The blood was copious, but his…ah, cape contained it well. His clothes were drenched."

"So far…I see nothing confusing," said the poet.

Ponder's appearance transfixed the poet. The man who had seemed so plump in life appeared deflated. His face, particularly, looked gaunt, the line of his jaw positively skeletal. Had he lost weight prior to death?

"There's conflicting evidence," the detective said. "He ordered a bottle of champagne upon arrival at five p.m. A champagne *demi-sec*, whatever that means. Pfaff himself opened the bottle for him, poured a bit, which your Mr. Ponder here swallowed in one gulp. Pfaff poured a second glass and left the bottle. Mr. Ponder was there all night till closing. Never touched the rest."

"I sense you are about to sow confusion with your next words, Detective. I await them. Urgently."

"The contents of the bottle were found to be laced with five grams of arsenic. Enough to kill a man forty times over."

"Goodness!" yelped the poet. "Stabbed…*and* poisoned?"

"That's what muddles it, yes. What remains of the beverage adds up exactly to one bottle, minus one drink quaffed. No arsenic in the glass, just in the bottle. And the wrappers of three different pharmacies found in his cape."

The poet's eyes clenched in seeming agony.

"Did you know him, sir?" Ronk asked.

"Everyone knew Ponder," said the poet. "You could not walk Broadway and say you didn't."

And the poet walked Broadway. Ceaselessly. He had become a semiprofessional *flaneur*, a walker in the city. Brooklyn was his home, but the great Mannahatta held his heart.

The corners of his mouth drooped, but his mind raced:

So…Ponder patronized several shops, buying rat poison at various locales to avoid arousing suspicion. There was certainly no shortage of chemists or pharmacists in the area. Three alone on Broadway between Bleecker and Houston, six if you counted all the way to Fulton Street.…

That's what the poet did on those long, jobless summer afternoons. He walked and counted. Daydreamed. Chatted up the occasional newsboy, omnibus driver, haberdasher, lavender bouquet hawker, or oysterman. Lower Broadway was the poet's special domain. There were fifteen theaters and lecture halls in that neighborhood, not counting Mr. Barnum's castle, a museum of dubious Egyptian "antiquities," and a phrenological publishing house and exhibit hall. At least six daguerreotype or ambrotype galleries, including one operated by Mr. Mathew Brady. One infirmary. Thirty-odd hotels and boardinghouses that were handy for impromptu assignations. Fifty-three beer and oyster saloons—

Ronk cleared his throat, breaking the poet's reverie. "If you don't mind, I fail to see why Mr. Pfaff asked you to speak on his behalf, Mr.—"

"Whitman. Walter Whitman. Of Brooklyn, late of Long Island. Once of Ryerson, Classon, and now North Portland Avenue. Pfaff has little English, while I'm afraid I suffer from an abundance of it."

"Oh! You're an attorney, Mr. Whitman?"

The poet chuckled.

"A physician?"

Whitman laughed again while Ronk perused a long list of names in his notebook. "I see you were not among the patrons questioned last evening.

That's good. And good old Pfaff does not count you among the patrons yesterday. Also good. Eliminates you entirely from the scope of the inquiry. I gather you don't frequent the establishment?"

"I do, my dear young man," the poet responded. "But since I make a point of staying sober and closing my tabs each night, I find it necessary to make my appearances brief and infrequent."

The detective shook his head. "Probably for the best, I'd say. I detest drunkards. Odd establishment, Pfaff's. Frequented by men and ladies alike. *Unescorted* ladies, if you receive my meaning." His lips curled slightly. "You're a theaterman, I take it?"

Whitman knew better than to speak the truth. In his four decades, he had learned to cloak his secrets in the threads and manner of a country bumpkin. But his canny mind was something else. Mannahatta had enlarged it. Pfaff's—and its media-savvy clientele—had taught him how to self-promote, how to shrewdly edit and present himself on the world's stage.

He had a notion about this flatfoot. And so he held up his hands, displaying his calluses. "I'm a builder of houses. A setter of type. A printer. A real estate investor, sir, in the great city of Brooklyn."

"Ah, a tradesman then," Ronk said. "Of entrepreneurial turn."

"Former newspaperman, to boot."

The detective's features sank. "Police reporter?"

"Hardly. Politics and the like."

"Good. I hate police reporters," said Ronk. "Politics! Well, you'll have a lot to write about there...."

Unfortunately, that was one arena where Whitman was still a naïf. The era's politics were a quagmire. Whitman had blundered horribly, cranking out editorials in which he'd called for the licensing of prostitutes and widespread acceptance of premarital sex for women. They had been, ahem, his *final* editorials for the staid, conservative daily paper.

Whitman trailed the dashing, daft Ronk out of the morgue and through the building's cavernous corridors. Lighting in the Tombs was dismal; the walls wept hideous, calcified tears squeezed out by damp.

"Glad I am, sir," Ronk said, "that fine upstanding people—the reformers, the Republicans—mean to take the city back from the patronagists. We did it with the department. We can do it with Tammany. Say! If you know Brooklyn, then you know the biergartens of Williamsburg, I'll wager. My mother was German, sir. My father, good Anglo-Dutch. That's how I know old Pfaff. I suspect he's worried about the fine. The beat coppers who answered the call last night wrote him up for keeping the tavern open past license. But I gather he's no stranger to fines with *that* clientele. Ah, Pfaff! Good stock, Germans. Hard workers. *Business*people. Not like the filthy, corrupt Irish—"

Ah, there we go, thought Whitman ruefully.

"I take it you're familiar with his exciting new beverage, sir? It's called… *lager*."

Whitman was lost in thought, as always.

Dear Ponder. Why were you about to off yourself? And who got to you first?

* * *

Whitman was no stranger to editorial operations, but *Leslie's* offices were a revelation. He was accustomed to seeing writers and editors standing at their composition desks, crafting pieces in longhand. The sheer number of them, however—arrayed in long rows in an upper-floor loft lit by arched cast-iron windows—boggled his mind. A room bedecked with tweed, linen, and whiskers, perfumed by sweat and tobacco.

—*Makers of words*
—*fashioners all*
—*high in your factory of sense and idiom*
—*alter my…*

The boyish Nast was tucked in an alcove behind pebbled-glass windows. A nineteen-year-old badger in a waistcoat perched behind a drawing table. It was a delight to hear his voice, flawless English shot through with the German accent he'd never been able to shake, though he'd emigrated when he was just a boy of six. "Eight o'clock!" he sputtered. "Eight o'clock in the morning, he came banging on Mother's door. 'You couldn't wait till I was at the office, Officer?' No! He had to conduct his interview on our front porch and me in my stockings!"

His long legs folded under a stool, Whitman dandled Nast's sketchbook on his lap. The floor was covered with pencil shavings and curls of wood, remnants of visits from the engravers who etched Nast's illustrations into blocks of wood. "You showed him these pictures you made at Pfaff's yesterday?"

"No! They get nothing from me. They don't fool me with their reformist nonsense. Who fought the Municipals in that riot two years ago, hmm? It wasn't me. It was the same Metro coppers riding us now. Giving more words to a policeman, Whitman, is as bad as handing them rope. They will always find a way to fashion testimony into a noose."

Flipping through the newsprint pages of Nast's book, Whitman felt as if he'd stepped into the twin vaults under Broadway once again. There were the chandeliers. The bar and its gleaming bottles. Rotund Pfaff in his apron. The handsome waiters in their crisp white—

"There is truth in what you say, Tommy. And it is far more alarming than you can conceive. They suspect a woman for the deed. Witnesses say they saw one stop by his table. She was in a red dress."

"*Ja.* I saw her," Nast snapped. His fingers gestured at the sketchbook. "She's right there."

Whitman produced his own bound notebook, stuffed with scraps of paper. He carried it with him everywhere. Besides failed poems, the book contained the names and ages of his lovers. A book of beauties, a precious trophy that he would have hidden in a second if police had shown up at his door at eight o'clock on a Friday morning in July.

"Since you've been so kind to share your creations," Whitman said, "allow me the same courtesy. Two clues. One: a note written in Ponder's notebook, just under the review he was writing of the new show at Astor Opera. Right below it, in a painful scrawl, he wrote these words…" Whitman held up his notebook and intoned. "*'I I I I love you.*' That's the entire message. No punctuation."

"Four eyes?" Nast said.

"Does that mean anything to you?"

"No. But he was dying! He writes a farewell note, and he makes a botch of the job."

Whitman winced. "It eludes sense, Nast. If a man is dying, he stutters in his *speech*, not his writing."

"Ah. Well, you're the writer. You would know."

"There's more. Here's what the police found tucked into the same inside pocket as the arsenic wrappers. Puzzled them immensely. Do you know it?"

On a scrap of blue accounting paper, Whitman had drawn what appeared to be an American dollar coin. But only a pie slice of it. A quarter, to be precise. The stars, Liberty's head, and her flag were on the obverse. On the reverse, the angry eagle's head and beak.

"You have the makings of a fine illustrator," Nast said, drawing closer. "Ha! I can't believe it! I always thought it was a legend."

"Tell me!"

"The Brotherhood of the Dollar! You know how hard it is for a writer to earn the dollar, *ja*? Well, some of the earliest bohemians who gathered at Pfaff's first place, the one he kept at Third before moving down to Bleecker, commemorated their bond in just this way. They cut a dollar into fourths and pledged that they would always gather at least once a year at whatever venue Pfaff operated to reassemble the dollar and drink a toast to their confraternity. I don't know how often they actually met—or if they ever did. Back then, I was too young to frequent the place. But I can tell you that as soon as the new Pfaff's opened, there were far more bohemians than you could count. A new breed. And they fancied *themselves* the first bohemians of New York! Of the first four, I know one of their number died. Leichsenring, the comic writer. Dissolution by alcohol, of course. He may have never made it to the second Pfaff's. And now Ponder. That leaves two."

"Who were they?"

"Who can say? This whole bohemian posture smacks of fatuousness, Whitman. This isn't Europe. We are not the avant-garde. We're New Yorkers, eking out a poorly paid trade with our minds and fingertips. We mean nothing. We *are* nothing. Dust to dust."

Sorrow seized Whitman's breast. "You are wrong, Tommy. Wrong. The bohemians mean something. We are brothers and sisters of a trade. Culture-makers of a great dawning *American* republic. And we uplift each other."

He longed to say more, but shyness halted his tongue.

—*Without you, Pfaff's*

—*Your taps, your brass, your glass, the tavern's glow*

—*Mr. Brentano's newspapers, foreign and domestic, strewn across your malt-soaked tables*

—*Without the jests and gibes*

—*My soul is winnowed to…*

"Well," Whitman continued, "the detective imagines the snipped coin is the mark of a murderous cabal of radicals. Or a spurned lover. And so we come to *her*." He pointed to Nast's notebook image of the woman looming over Ponder's table. "Witnesses said she wore red, a suggestive color, which may have bewitched the detective's mind."

"She *did* wear red," said Nast.

"Who is she?"

"No idea. I, too, took her for a lover."

"*Ponder's* lover?" Whitman said, nearly spluttering. *You have a lot of growing up to do, Nast.* "I think not. This sketch of yours… I can't make out her face."

"Nor could I. She wore a veil."

Whitman exhaled deeply. "Was it red?"

* * *

Leda Halleck Mulloy, possessor of the city's largest and most scandalous collection of ladies' hats and veils, did not appear terribly shocking when Whitman found her in her dressing room at Laura Keene's Theatre on Broadway, south of Pfaff's. The walls crawled with garish posters and cast-off wardrobe. Open jars and sticks of grease paint tainted the air with their lardish stink. The lamps flickered, casting a warm glow over the auburn beauty. She curled like a cat in an overstuffed chair, breastfeeding her infant daughter. Whitman sat cross-legged on a tufted pillow at her feet.

—*Give suck, succulent mother!*
—*Suck on babe*
—*Daughter of a great metropolis, in your lap one day the teeming hordes—*
—*No, that doesn't work....*

"She looks happy," Whitman said, eyebrows rising in wonder. "Good appetite?"

"Oh, yah! Quite enamored of me teats. In that respect, she takes after her father," Mulloy quipped.

"Which one?"

Mulloy cackled and snapped, "Piss off, Walter."

For months, the city's penny press had devoted reams of ink to Mulloy's brazen out-of-wedlock pregnancy, her refusal to name the child's father, and her near-obscene decision to continue her profession in her condition. Shocked audiences showed up in droves to watch her perform while hiding her bump under her layers of clothing. Only weeks before delivery, she'd raised the stakes—and filled her impresario's purse—by reprising her most famous role: Lady Delilah in *Scarlet Vengeance*.

In nineteen sold-out performances, Delilah once again trod the boards and exacted her revenge on the six—count them, six!—men who had ruined her and her sister's good names, dispatching each mustachioed cad in diabolically creative ways. In the show's over-the-top climax, just as coppers were breaking down the door, Delilah shucked off her blood-spattered clothing and disappeared out a window, dressed only in a sheer body stocking and the trusty hat and crimson veil that so magnificently hid her identity. Murder, sex, and faux nudity had never been so titillating.

Whitman's own purse had been too light of late to take in the "baby" shows, but he'd caught one of the original shockers years back, when he was gainfully employed. Something told him that Detective Ronk, for all his posturing, had seen the show. Indeed, the spectacle had likely tainted his view of the Ponder case.

"Correct me if I'm wrong," Whitman said. "In the past, you have routinely 'donated' your cast-offs to some of Pfaff's...ah, *masculine* clientele."

Mulloy laughed so hard that the infant began to cry. She soothed the baby, clasping it closer. "The pretty boys, you mean?" she said. "The pretty *little* boys. They're the only ones who can fit into a dress me size. Oh, Pfaff's! What would we do without it? What other establishment in town would allow such things? Who would ever allow a *persona non grata* like meself in for a bite of dinner and a drink?" She closed her eyes in a parody of ecstasy. "Is our sweet little sanctum done for, do you think?"

"Not if we can clear up Ponder's murder to the satisfaction of the police. Now, look, Leda—"

She dug her one free hand into her waist. "By the way, I'm still waiting for the return of me bloomers, Mr. Whitman! I thought you looked fetching in them that night. Looked tidy tucked into your boots."

Some weeks back, he'd indulged in a bit of outré theater himself. The tavern regulars had given him a standing ovation when he'd bellowed one of his poems while wearing a pair of Mulloy's flouncy leggings. "Alas, I'm afraid you won't be seeing that article again."

He couldn't risk his mother finding them in his bedroom. The fabric was quickly relegated to cleaning paintbrushes at the family's latest Brooklyn dwelling.

Clearing his throat, Whitman said, "Speaking *recently*, though, have you given any garments to any of the young lovelies? A dress *or* a veil?"

"Well, come to think it," she said, "I should have thought it strange, considering it was him who died."

"Him?"

"Ponder. His Theo had some of me dresses. Wore them mostly when the two of them were alone. I gather Ponder fancied a bit of dress-up."

"Were they *together*? I thought it was business between them."

"You miss things, Walter, when you don't come 'round much to Pfaff's. Theo came knocking at the stage door close to me performance Thursday, begging for a veiled hat. Don't know why he couldn't wait. Ponder was always out late. It would be hours before he'd be back to the boardinghouse where he kept Theo."

"Which house?"

WHEN LILACS LAST IN THE DOORYARD BLED

* * *

Whitman's amorous exploits in lower Manhattan had taken him to many homes, but he couldn't recall if he'd ever been to this particular brownstone on Great Jones, not far north of Mulloy's theater. On the sidewalk, before ascending the stoop, he buttoned his shirt and affixed a cravat to his neck, donning just enough respectability to bluster past the landlady.

The door at the end of the topmost hall was answered with a crack at the jamb, terrified eyes, and the smell of fear and hashish in equal measure.

"I'll stop if it bothers you," Theodore Bastone said, puffing as he paced the Heriz rug in his small but exquisitely furnished quarters. "I find it soothes the nerves. Unfortunately, it also stokes one's appetite."

Strategically draped silks blunted the gas lamps' glare and reddened the walls. Whitman felt as if he had entered a seraglio, though the meaning of the word had eluded him until this very second.

Theo was a small but wiry fellow in his twenties. Green-eyed, thick-haired, with a sweetly turned chin. Loose hips that swiveled easily in woolen trousers. Even if Whitman had never seen him once garbed in Leda Mulloy's castoffs, he would have had no trouble picturing Theo in them now. A wig, rouge, and a fine crayon pencil would have completed the effect, transforming a handsome fellow into a lovely lass.

"Have you not eaten?"

"I cannot leave this room! Not by day. At night, when the mistress of the house has turned in, I scurry out like a rat to scrounge up food south or north of here. I dare not show my face at her table. Or at any of my usual haunts, Pfaff's least of all! I cannot think how you found me! If *you* could, can the police be far behind?"

Whitman folded himself onto a leather ottoman. "The police have no idea of your involvement, Theo, because they cannot conceive of the right questions to ask. For one thing, they're looking for a woman, not a man."

"But Pfaff is on the line, no? If they make *his* life hell, he'll surely remember something about seeing me in a dress from time to time."

"Pfaff's a working stiff, Theo. A widower with a small boy to care for.

Waiters and bills to pay. He's too exhausted to entertain such notions."

"I hope so. Poor fellow! He has no idea what that place means to us. Where will we go if he runs us off?"

"A city of eight hundred thousand," Whitman cooed. "There are places for us all."

"You believe that?"

"Sincerely, yes. Now just tell me. Tell me all of it!"

"Ponder's people are from New Orleans," Theo began, his voice a torrent of emotion, "and he has a decent patrimony that he was able to dip into when the pain started. There were a half dozen physicians until we found an upstanding one who didn't just peddle nostrums. The news is bad. Morgagni's pancreas. Cancer of the viscera, I gather. Months to live, or up to a year. It terrified Eustace. 'I've seen how it goes,' he says. 'All the Ponders are snuffed out by it.' His mother, I take it, and her father as well. His mother's brother slit his throat to be free of the pain. Eustace set his sights on arsenic because it's all he knows. But what does a critic know about poisons?"

"It's an atrocious end," Whitman said, quietly noting Theo's inability to use the past tense. "Not something you can do quietly in a darkened saloon. Morphine would have been better."

"Exactly what I told him. See, I worked over at the Alms House Hospital at Bellevue for a few years before I got sick of it. A diener first, in the morgue. Then a nurse."

Whitman's eyes perked up. "A nurse?"

"The pay's just as bad as carving up the dead." Theo's eyes twinkled mischievously. "I much prefer live bodies. The pay's better. But Ponder doesn't know of such things. That's what draws me to him. So regal! Such bearing! An opium den was beneath him."

Funny, the turn of some minds, Whitman thought. He himself would never have applied the word *regal* to Ponder. Pompous, perhaps. An insufferable ass, even.

"He bought his poison slowly," Whitman said. "To avoid being noticed. Then?"

Theo bit his lip. "It was a matter of getting up the nerve. He went several nights in a row to Pfaff's. 'No place else I'd rather be at the end,' he says. He gets the notion to buy the sweetest drink possible. To kill the taste."

"Arsenic is tasteless," Whitman mused.

"Exactly. But you try arguing with a man who thinks opera is high art. Three nights on, he can't even bring himself to drop the powder into his drink."

"And on the fourth?" Whitman said.

"I told him I wouldn't go. I couldn't watch. But I also could not sit still, waiting. So I went to Pfaff's and found him there among the barrels. He'd dropped the poison into the champagne but could not bring himself to…to…"

Theo began weeping. Perching the cigarette on a nearby bureau, he mopped his glistening cheeks with a handkerchief.

"He looks up at me. 'I'm lost, Trio,' he says. 'If I can't do it, it's Mother's fate for me.' That's when I knew, Walter. If I did not help him, no one could. But I also knew I could not be seen…seen…as *myself*."

"You had not gone to the saloon in your finery, then?"

"No. I haven't worn those publicly in some time. I went just as you see me now. But when I left the tavern, I knew I needed to enhance my disguise. I hit up Leda for the veil, came home, and changed. I planned on stealing a knife from my landlady's set, but I hadn't counted on her locking up the silverware at night. All I had was a razor, though I didn't much fancy slitting his throat. It would be too terrible. Too public. When I got back to the saloon and saw that face of his—so noble and sad—I realized I needed a quick whiskey to get my head on straight. At the bar, I saw a waiter set down his oyster knife. Too short. Another waiter came by and set down the remains of a steak dinner. One drink and the steak knife—that's all I needed. I slid behind Eustace. 'Trio?' he said, 'That you?' I bent and kissed him once on the cheek, then shoved the knife…s-s-shoved it…"

Bastone's face fell into his hands. The last of his cigarette dusted the carpet.

"He's lost weight, but he's still a big man. I knew the third intercostal space was my only chance of getting near the heart. He did not cry out! He was so brave! I was up the block before I realized I still had the knife. I stuffed it in my purse. Luckily, my dress was red...."

Whitman held up a hand. "He called you Trio?"

Theo looked puzzled. "Why, yes. My nickname. Trio. Three. Monsieur Petite Trois. He called me that the first time we were together. Back when he was just a customer. Before we became close."

"Why three?"

"It's a play on Theo, isn't it?" he said, as if it were obvious. "A reference to my three-piece." Sensing Whitman's lingering confusion, Theo gestured impatiently at his own crotch. "My bells and whistle?"

"Ah...oh...*right*," Whitman said, surprised to feel himself blushing. He raised his notebook. "You have resolved the final mystery in my mind. Now allow me, young man, to relay Eustace's final message to *you*. He wrote '*I I I I love you*.' The Roman numeral three, then *I love you*."

Overcome, Theo sank to the bed, tears dropping to the quilted satin coverlet. Whitman watched him weep until he himself could stand it no longer. He rose and braced himself on the doors of Theo's open wardrobe. Eyes fluttering over Theo's collection of wigs and feminine dress, Whitman wiped away his own tears.

Later, Whitman asked, "Where are the clothes you wore that night?"

"Outside. Hidden behind the privies. I—I didn't know what to do with them. They're covered in blood."

"That's *why* I need them. And some money, if you can spare some."

"Money's not an issue. Eustace is generous...*was*. But why? I don't understand."

"You don't need to. Come to think of it, I'll need another dress. One that will accommodate me. Do you have such a thing?"

Theo's eyes flicked upward, suddenly serious. "With those shoulders? I have just the thing! High-waisted. Diaphanous. It will stretch. But, why on earth for?"

***

Detective Ronk's fingers caressed his shot glass tentatively, waiting for the waiter to disappear into Pfaff's inner vault. "Bottoms up, sir!"

They downed their whiskeys, Whitman shuddering to stave off the burn.

Ronk mopped his muscular mustache with a thick cloth napkin. "The attendant in the cloakroom at the Hoboken Ferry station noticed the valise had not been collected when he came on Monday morning. The night prior, he had accepted it from a tall woman in a brown dress whose features were obscured by a red veil. Red, sir. Mark that well. The same woman purchased a train ticket to Philadelphia. But none of the conductors recall her boarding the train."

"And the contents of the valise?" Whitman said.

"That is the damning evidence, sir. A red velvet dress. White lace at the collar and wrist. All heavily stained with blood. Tucked into a lady's reticule was a blood-encrusted steak knife and three equal slices of a dollar coin. You'll recall Mr. Ponder had such a slice of silver in his possession."

"My, my! Was his the fourth piece, I wonder?" Whitman asked, cocking his head. He resisted the urge to gesture. His hands were still sore from wielding his late father's cold chisel on the dollar coin. "But what does it mean for the case? This wretched assassin goes free?"

"I've dispatched word to Philadelphia. This she-devil is their problem now. Although I can't speak for the alacrity and might of their department…"

Ronk waxed on. Whitman's thoughts turned to the column of smoke he'd sent heavenward that morning in the rear yard of his mother's home. A fire stoked by his castoff disguise. Pity to lose such a lovely dress.

He was mulling still when the disheveled Pfaff appeared at his elbow. "You fix?" Pfaff said, indicating the narrow staircase between the barrels where Ronk had ascended to Broadway only minutes ago.

"I fix," Whitman chuckled.

Pfaff heaved a sigh of relief. "You bohemians. Such trouble you bring me."

Whitman clapped his hands once, wincing, and fluttered his fingers like the wings of a dove. "Poof," he said. "All gone."

Pfaff nodded. "You read tonight, yes? I have shell steak. Very tender. Mustard sauce. Very good. *German* mustard. Greens from Brooklyn. Crispy, in oil and garlic—"

—I eat you, Brooklyn.

—I swallow you whole

—The crunch of you, so preferable to Mannahatta—

"I'm sorry," Whitman said. "It sounds delicious, but I don't have the specie."

He was nearly shouting. In the two vaults under the sidewalk, the voices in Pfaff's had grown loud.

Pfaff patted Whitman's shoulder. "This, my treat."

"Well, in that case—"

"Wine? Champagne? Kir? Cassis? For you, anything, Mr. Walter. You are good fixer."

"Just lager, thank you," Whitman said.

His heart was light, his soul lighter still. He leaned back against the cool stone wall of the basement, his keen eyes glancing past actresses to alight instead on the beautiful young men who lurked in the shadows. Lurking there, at least for now.

Maybe, just maybe, the words would come again.

The very thought of it aroused him. The day was hot, and so was he.

"Oh, Pfaff?" he sang out. "The beer is cold, yes?"

"Always!"

BAD WHISKEY

By Jim Winter

"This is my beloved son," the man shouted, holding an open black Bible in one hand and waving his free hand as he spoke, "with whom I am well pleased." He closed the Bible. "My friends, our Lord and Savior came to the river to be baptized before our Heavenly Father."

Leon rested a hip against the old Chevelle, a 1969 model with an engine that purred but a body on the verge of quitting. That morning, he felt like the car. His heart still beat, but the rest of him wanted to lie down and die. And then he happened upon the riverside baptism.

"The Lamb of God invites us to be baptized," the preacher continued. "To go into the water in the name of the Father, the Son, and the Holy Ghost. He not only invites us, he commands us. Who here accepts the invitation and heeds the command of Christ?"

"I do," said Leon. "I accept." He had no idea he would say the words until they left his lips. He marched down to the side of the stream, between congregants in ill-fitting suits and plain, loose dresses. "I wish to be with Jesus."

The preacher came up out of the water. "What is your name, brother?"

"Leon. My name is Leon."

"And Brother Leon, have you confessed your sins before the Lord?"

Had he? Hell no, but no time like the present. "Preacher, I have sinned. I have whored. I have gambled. I have provoked and engaged in violence against my fellow man. And I have had a thirty-year love affair with the bottle. Is that confession enough?"

"And do you renounce your sins? Do you renounce the ways of the devil and his angels?"

He stumbled as he stepped forward and swallowed hard before he spoke. "I do."

"And do you accept Jesus Christ as your personal Lord and savior?"

"Hell, yes."

The preacher ignored his blasphemy. "Then come into the water, Brother Leon, and be cleansed by the precious blood."

Leon did as he was told, handing his cell phone and his gun to a woman standing at the river's edge. He waded out into the stream with two men as the preacher followed. The men tipped him backward into the water as the preacher blessed him in the name of the Father, the Son, and the Holy Ghost. He shook the preacher's hand, told him he felt like a new man, then took back his phone and his gun.

Still soaking, he climbed into his Chevelle and drove off. Half a mile down the road, he pulled the half-drunk fifth of Jim Beam from under his seat and pulled on it. "Thy will be done, Lord."

***

He kicked open the door to Thea's apartment. She sat there in that silly hippie dress she always wore, playing with her tarot cards like a game of solitaire. Her expression told him she expected him.

"Been drinking again," she said. "I can smell it over here."

"We're done, Thea," he said. "I've been baptized. I've turned my back on this life."

She laughed. At him, not with him. "What? You passed some traveling preacher's revival meeting on the riverbank and decided you wanted to be right with Jesus? Jesus doesn't care about you."

"Don't toy with me."

She rose from the table, a card in her hand. "You won't leave me. We're tied together." She held up the tarot card. It was the Lovers. "You. Belong. To me."

He slapped the card out of her hand. "I'm through with that devil shit."

"Doesn't smell like it." She sniffed his breath. "Smells like Jim Beam. Did you drink that on the way back from getting right with God?"

He grabbed her wrists. "Don't toy with me."

She looked him up and down, then at the hands with an iron grip on her wrists. "Is that what you want, Leon?" She pressed closer. "Are you going to punish me? Show me what a real man you are?" She now pressed against him. He could feel her nipples hard against his chest. "You don't do anything I don't want you to do." She kissed him. "If you truly are right with God, Leon, then let me go and leave me. Otherwise..."

He pushed her back onto the couch and climbed on top of her.

* * *

He awoke two hours later, he and Thea naked and wrapped up in each other. She lay with her head on his chest, her eyes closed. Over on the table, a fresh bottle of Jim Beam sat with a single shot glass. He extracted himself from her. She mumbled and made halfhearted attempts to keep him at her side. In the end, she rolled over and began snoring.

He padded over to the table and poured himself a shot. Then another. Then another. She left a pack of cigarettes, Kool Menthols, of course. It did not matter. He needed nicotine and didn't care if it tasted like mint-flavored ash. He lit one and drew a card from her tarot deck. The Lovers came up. The card seemed to mock him as he stared at it.

You don't do anything I don't want you to do.

He'd tried to tell her they were through. Instead, he'd thrown her down on the couch, ripped off her stupid hippie dress, and proceeded to do whatever he wanted to do with her. Then he'd dragged her into the bedroom and had her every way he could before collapsing from exhaustion. She'd laughed at him the entire time.

You don't do anything I don't want you to do.

He still held the lighter. A smile formed on his lips. "Did you want me to do this?" The card caught fire and blackened as he dropped it in the ashtray.

Nature called, and he heeded the summons. Her phone lay on the back of the toilet. The screen displayed six messages, all from a man named Rory. The last suggested she discreetly come to his place that night.

Leon put the phone down, found his clothes in the living room, and fished out his gun. The P-390 felt comfortable in his hand. He walked into the bedroom and pumped three rounds into Thea, the first into that pretty head of hers.

"Did you want me to do that, bitch?" He dressed, grabbed the bottle of Beam, and headed out to the car. His poker game started at six sharp.

Rory would sit in tonight.

***

"I fold," said Leon for the third time that evening.

They sat in the back of a bar, five men, all chain-smoking. Leon had a bottle of Bushmills next to him. It apparently did not contain the luck of the Irish, as he had been bleeding chips for an hour or so. Someone told him Bushmills was Protestant whiskey, but that suited Leon. He had been dunked by a Baptist preacher that morning.

Rory, bearded, gray, and fat, pulled the chips to him like a waiting lover. "Come to Papa." His laugh came out as smooth as the gravel in the bar's parking lot. Groans followed from around the table.

"I swear," said Dave, a long-haired Deadhead type, who probably had worked at the bar when it opened in the early seventies, "he's cheating."

"On my wife, maybe," said Rory. That prompted laughter all the way around the table. Even Leon joined in.

He is cheating.

Leon looked around. He could have sworn he heard Thea's voice from behind him.

Barry, the current bartender, who locked up the shop every Sunday evening for the game, stared at Leon. "You act like you saw a ghost."

You did, Thea whispered in his brain. *You were inside me. Then you killed me. Now I'm inside you.*

Leon shook it off. "Possum crossed my grave. Whose deal is it?"

"Yours, old man," said Barry, who had at least five years on him.

He started to deal the cards. One of them slipped from his hand and fell face up. It was one of the tarot cards, Death. Only Death did not have a skull face. It had Thea's. She winked at him. *I'm even in the whiskey bottle, Leon. You want to maintain that buzz, you'll have to drink me to do it.*

Sure enough, he could see her silhouette in the smokey amber of the whiskey bottle. He chalked it up to hallucination. "Maybe I should switch back to Beam."

"Maybe you shouldn't buy weed off Dave," said Rory. Everyone laughed. Except Dave.

Dave raised the bird. "Fuck you guys and the horses you rode in on."

"Cole fucked a horse once," said Barry, wagging his eyebrows at the cook in the greasy apron. "He lost a bet."

"And his virginity," Rory added.

Cole shrugged, which disturbed Leon. It meant the story was true.

Leon took the cards and reshuffled. They looked like a normal deck now. He tossed out five cards to each player. Before looking at his own hand, he noticed Dave had a halo around his head. At first, he thought maybe he'd caught a glare from the light behind the man. Only Dave sat in the dark. He shook his head.

"Not holding your liquor so well, Leon?" said Rory. The rest of the table laughed.

He's laughing at you, Thea said in his head. *He's had me. Now he's cheating you out of your money.*

Leon did not even look at his hand. He threw down his cards. "Is there some sort of problem, Rory?"

Rory simply grinned that insipid grin of his. "I don't seem to be the one with the problem, Leo."

Normally, the name "Leo" made him see red, but that had been a figure of speech. This time, he really saw red. Rory was no longer Rory. He looked like the devil.

Go on, Thea's ghost whispered in his head. *Kill him. You know you want to. You know I want you to. Then it'll be just you and me.*

Leon upended the table, sending cards, chips, money, and drinks flying everywhere. The others yelped and swore. Devil Rory just laughed. "So, you know, don't you? My, but she's a screamer." He cocked his head, looking Leon over. "You killed her, didn't you?"

Kill him.

Leon didn't wait, drawing the P320 and pumping five rounds into Rory's chest. Rory, however, fired a single bullet from his .38 straight through Leon's heart.

And laughed.

The world went black.

* * *

The woman patted him on the cheek. Dark-haired with one of those New Agey crystal necklaces, he thought he recognized her. "Thea?"

She laughed. "No, I'm Sarah. I'm the barmaid. What happened to you, Leon? You passed out at the poker table."

"But we…I…you…?" His head thumped back on the couch. "Why does my head hurt?"

Barry came in. "Oh, good. He's awake. Leon, buddy, Sheriff Crenshaw wants to talk to you."

"Sheriff…. Wha'?"

Barry let out a long sigh. "Get some coffee into him. He's still not fully back yet." He knelt so that Leon could see his face fully. "I don't know what shit Dave put in that whiskey, but he was trying to roofie poor Sarah here."

"Almost worked," she said, "but I don't drink on duty. If Barry's paying me, I'm on duty."

"Randy's got a pot going in the kitchen." Barry stood. "I'll tell Crenshaw you're still waking up. He's going to want to talk to you." The bartender left.

Sarah helped him sit up. "You OK, buddy? You look like you've seen a ghost."

The cobwebs started to clear in Leon's head. "You're not Thea."

She laughed. "That crazy old lady who lives in the swamp? Used to be married to the preacher man over at Antioch Baptist? Not even related."

"I could have sworn your name was Thea, and we... Well..."

"I'm not Thea. Just another hippie chick stuck in a podunk southern town." She fingered the necklace. "Was I good?"

Leon could not bring himself to tell her the entire sequence of events, especially as they had faded from memory. "I'm sorry, Sarah. What did he put in that whiskey bottle, anyway?"

"It's Dave," she said. "So, who knows? I got high with him once. Woke up on the hood of my car topless, clutching some sort of roadkill. Head hurt like a mother for about three days after that."

"Did he...?"

"He's still alive, so that's a no to that."

He pushed himself off the couch and stumbled toward the door. Sarah grabbed his arm and guided him back. "Let's get some coffee into you, shall we?" She guided him to the chair at Barry's desk. Luke Bryan blared from the front of the house singing about margaritas. The thought of a margarita made his head hurt. "Sarah, you got a smoke? That'll clear my head faster than coffee."

She frowned. "I haven't smoked in a while, but I keep an emergency pack on me." She dumped out her purse on the desk and rummaged through the contents. Sarah kept the usual things in her bag: Kleenex, spare change, wallet, cell phone, and bottle of Advil. One other item made Leon's blood run cold.

A Tarot deck fell out of the purse, the Lovers card slipping off faceup.

Sarah tapped a crumpled pack of Camels and shook one out for him, offering him a light in the process. He kept staring at the Tarot card. Slowly, he raised his eyes to Sarah.

She winked at him. "Bad whiskey will make a man do anything I want."

A FRIENDLY GLASS

By Elizabeth Zelvin

The Chat Gris was the most convivial bar in Sainte-Marie-sur-les-Remparts, whose residents, both French and expat, considered it the crown jewel of the Alpes-Maritimes. The village, still ringed by its original medieval wall, had not yet been discovered by tourists when I got thrown out of the youth hostel in Nice for trying to sneak in after curfew one balmy summer night in 1962. I hitched a ride in a *camion* to the foot of the *remparts* and got even luckier when Alain, French heaven on a motorcycle, came along right after the truck dropped me off. He knew exactly where my college roommate's mother's writer friend lived, at the top of the hill on a winding, cobbled village street.

Eleanor lived in the South of France because her novels were too steamy for Kansas City, according to my roommate, or, her mother's version, because she drank too much. She couldn't simply move to New York, like so many other hard-drinking novelists, because she had to put an ocean between herself and her own mother in order to write at all. In any case, she'd taken to life in Sainte-Marie like a duck to *sauce à l'orange*.

"If you get as far as Nice, Julie," my roommate said, "you must go and look her up. You can show up on her doorstep any time. She'll be thrilled to see you. And you'll love Sainte-Marie. It's bursting with painters and poets and actors. You might have a friendly glass with the next Oscar winner in the Chat Gris—or trip on the cobbles and realize the old guy with knobby knees you've just knocked over is Picasso."

Eleanor greeted me at the door with kittens draped around her neck and riding on her feet.

"Welcome, Julie, *bienvenue à Sainte-Marie!* I'm cat-sitting," she said. "Please tell me you're not allergic. They're my friend Vanessa's. She has dozens. These are the ones that aren't sick. Vanessa danced at Covent Garden and the Ballets Russes long, long ago. Now she lives in a cave."

"A wine cellar?" I was trying very hard with my French.

"Not a cahv," she said, "a cayve, a medieval cellar carved out of the ramparts. They're solid rock beneath the village as well as around it. Was that Alain Colbert's motorcycle I heard dropping you off? Such a nice boy and a *good* painter. He'll be at the Chat Gris checking up on his wife. She has a tendency to dance on the tables. I'll take you there."

The delectable Alain, with his soaring black brows, sharp cheekbones, and aquiline nose, had a wife.

***

The Chat Gris was the place to *prendre un pot* with Eleanor's friends. We went there every night.

"A pot?"

"Not a pot," she said, "a poe. *Un pot, un verre.* A friendly glass. It's a way of saying, 'Have a drink with me.'"

The Chat Gris was more than a bar, and the word bistro didn't do the food justice. The place was suffused with ambiance. Low ceilings, age-blackened beams, and heavy oak tables all looked as if they had grown in place. Each pool of candlelight and intimate dark corner lay in the perfect spot. The regulars sat at a long central table on wooden benches worn to a smooth gloss by generations of use.

I quickly learned that when it came to friendly glasses, *un* did not mean "one." *Un pot* was two or three or as many as your friends would buy you.

"It's rude to count," Quentin said one evening when I'd been there a couple of weeks. "And one gets home on one's feet like a gentleman. *N'est-ce pas,*

Harry?"

Quentin was a middle-aged English expat. Harry was his bulldog, who looked just like him. Vanessa, the dancer, sat on my other side. She was ancient, all wrinkled skin on twig-like bones, and had a kitten in every pocket of her flowing garments. Vanessa let them sip *pastis* off her fingers. Harry had his own beer in a dish on the floor.

Halfway down the long table, Eleanor chattered away with a group of locals.

"I wish I spoke French fluently," I said.

"Dear Eleanor," Quentin said. "She reminds me of Chaucer's Prioress, who speaks the French of Stratford Atte Bowe."

I was trying not to stare at a couple across from Eleanor, a man with the face and body of a Greek god and a woman it was equally hard to look away from.

"I haven't seen those two before. Who are they? They look so familiar."

"They should," Vanessa said. "That's Jacques Morel and Madeleine Marchand. He's the greatest living French actor, and she's the sex goddess of French cinema. They're married."

"Sex goddess?"

"She's what they call a *belle laide*," Quentin said. "The French don't care about young and pretty the way you Americans do."

An ugly beauty. It made sense in French and even more sense the more I looked at Madeleine Marchand. I wrenched my eyes away from the sex goddess. The man sitting next to her was equally striking.

"Who's the one who looks like a panther?" I asked.

"That's Ricardo Granato," Vanessa said. "He's a fashion designer. Ballet past, haute couture present, selling out to cinema in the near future, they say. The woman next to him is called Lilas. She models. I don't know why people make a fuss about her. She's nothing but a coat hanger, only less animated."

Vanessa went on, but I stopped listening because I saw Alain come into the room. I had already met Angélique, his wife, and Paul Travert, the partner who shared his *atelier*. With them was a very young man I hadn't seen before.

I half raised a hand in greeting. Alain's eyes lit up, and he steered the little group toward our end of the table.

"*Salut, Julie! Quentin, mon brave! Et la belle Vanessa!*"

Alain kissed Vanessa's hand and kissed Quentin on what Eleanor called "all three cheeks." One *bise* left and right might be enough for the chilly Parisians, but in the South of France, they kissed three times. He did the same to me. Paul, thin-lipped and very French in a cravat and beret, shook hands all around.

"You must meet my friend Colin," Alain said, "who is also *artiste* and wishes an *apprentissage* with me."

Colin was enormous, with streaks of paint in his shoulder-length blond hair. Big paint-stained hands and outsize shoes suggested that he hadn't finished growing. He grinned at me and gave Vanessa's withered cheeks a hearty triple *bise*.

"Sir." He pumped Quentin's hand. "*Enchanté, Mademoiselle Julie.*"

"Colin escapes from England to live with us," Alain explained. "He is but fifteen and too young to drink in that sad country, but in France, we believe that if you are old enough to desire a thing, you are old enough to possess it. Right, Colin?"

"Don't listen to Alain." Colin did his best to turn a blush into a laugh. "When he's not being a clown, he's a superb artist and a brilliant teacher."

It never got any easier seeing Angélique. She had a cloud of golden hair falling in waves to her waist, and she carried herself like Lady Godiva, as if both her clothing and any other women present were simply not there. Her face saved from perfection by an appealing gap between her front teeth. I had yet to see her dance.

"Colin, you must entertain *la petite Amerloque*," Angélique said.

I longed to call her a Frog in return, but not in front of Alain.

She turned away and began greeting other drinkers and diners with great animation. Alain's lips tightened as he looked after her.

"*Laisse tomber, Alain,*" Paul said quietly.

Colin squeezed in onto the bench between me and Vanessa. He ordered a bottle of wine.

"Have you tried much good Bordeaux yet, Julie?" he asked. "The '59 Lynch-Bages will be a great wine in 1979, you know. What do you think of Sainte-Marie so far? How long are you planning to stay? Have you been to Vence yet? It has wonderful museums. We could go together—it's not far. Doesn't being in France give you the most remarkable sense of freedom? It does me. Anything could happen!"

He clinked his glass with mine.

"*Cul sec!*"

I knew what that toast meant literally, though I'd never heard it. It was remarkably vulgar. I bet Colin wouldn't have made it if he hadn't been far from home and three or four drinks ahead of me already. My new friends were determined to make sure I enjoyed myself that evening. Quentin told me stories of his travels throughout Europe with Harry as his sole companion. Vanessa reminisced about the ballet, dropping the names of bygone greats. Eleanor introduced me to Madeleine Marchand, whose allure was even stronger at close quarters. For the five seconds, she held my hand in hers, it felt as if she cared about me more than anyone else in the world. Jacques Morel smiled at me kindly. Ricardo Granato, absorbed in his conversation with Angélique, ignored me. So did the model Lilas.

"Don't mind them," Eleanor said. "Everyone knows that Angélique is a *garce*. Alain was a fool to marry her."

"Can't he divorce her?" I asked.

"Honey, you can't go making yourself miserable," Eleanor said. "I'm not sure he wants to. Besides, he'd have to catch her cheating. If he beat her, *she* could divorce *him*. French laws."

"Alain would never beat her," I said, "even if she is a *garce*."

"She wouldn't divorce him anyway," Eleanor said. "His paintings are going to be worth a fortune someday."

The Chat Gris got rowdier and rowdier. A guitarist from Granada played flamenco, his fingers fluttering on the strings. His buddy began a passionate Andalusian song, the melody pouring out in a flood of garlic breath. Everyone began to clap to shouts of *"Olé!"* Someone brought out castanets.

"Give me those!" Angélique clambered up on the heavy table. Clacking the castanets expertly, she tossed her long golden hair and began to dance.

"Arriba! arriba!"

The clapping intensified.

"Angélique, you're drunk!" Alain sounded furious. "Get down from there."

"You can't make me!" The gap between her teeth made her smile look both lascivious and defiant. "Paul! Come up here and dance with me."

Alain's studio partner, very drunk himself, stumbled up onto the table and clumsily mimicked Angélique's movements.

"Jacques! Ricardo! How about you? I know you know the dance!"

I looked around for Eleanor. She had settled into a dark corner with two tough-looking Frenchwomen and a bottle of Armagnac.

"I'm leaving," I whispered in her ear. *"Ciao."*

The night air cooled my flushed cheeks. I could smell lavender and rosemary.

I heard footsteps on the cobbles behind me.

"Julie," Alain said. "Let me walk you home."

I suddenly felt happy.

We walked in silence. At Eleanor's door, he kissed me on the lips. Then I watched his back recede through the medieval arch, down the stone steps, and along the cobbled street toward the Chat Gris.

* * *

"What does *cul sec* mean?" I asked. Eleanor and I were in her kitchen, eating flaky croissants and drinking *café au lait* from cups the size of soup bowls. "I know *sec* is 'dry.'"

"Bottoms up," she said. "But be careful where you say *cul*—it actually means 'asshole.' Anatomically. For name-calling, use *con*."

I took a bite of croissant and a mouthful of creamy coffee and moaned with pleasure.

"Was it Faust who sold his soul to the devil for a perfect moment?" I said.

"Eleanor! Julie!" Colin burst into the kitchen. "Angélique is dead!"

"What?" Eleanor spewed coffee.

"Dead!" I said. "What happened?"

"She was poisoned," Colin said. "It's all over the village."

"When?"

"Last night in the Chat Gris," he said. "A dozen people saw her collapse and die."

"Oh God, Colin," I said, "were you there?"

"No, I've just heard," he said. "She was still dancing when Vanessa and I left. I was pissed, but she was legless."

"Do they have a suspect?" Eleanor asked.

"The police think Alain killed her," he said.

"They would," Eleanor said. "They're French. They always think it's the husband!"

"He was furious with her," Colin said. "Everyone could see that."

"But he left," I said. "He was with me."

"Julie!" he said. "Don't lie for him."

"He's right, dear," Eleanor said. "If you tell them you were lovers, you'll be handing them a motive."

"That's not what I meant," I said. "He walked me home. Nothing happened." One kiss was nobody's business.

"He went back," Colin said. "Everyone saw him there."

"Let's hope no one noticed that he left to walk you home," Eleanor said. "If you tell the French police that nothing happened, they won't believe you."

"I still don't believe he killed her," I said. "Alain *wouldn't*."

I couldn't feel sorry that Angélique was dead. Everyone knew she was a *garce*. Plenty of people must have wanted to kill her.

"Last night, Angélique was all over Paul Travert," I said. "And she seemed to know Jacques Morel and Ricardo Granato pretty well. If she was having an affair with Morel, would Madeleine Marchand have been jealous?"

"Good question," Eleanor said. "You know that *very* famous movie star who killed herself? Morel made a film with her in Hollywood last year. It's common knowledge around here that they had an affair."

"Americans and the French have such different ideas of what a sex goddess is like," I said. "What did Madeleine do?"

"She sat it out here in Sainte-Marie," Eleanor said. "When the storm blew over, she was waiting for him."

"She might react differently if he did it again," Colin said. "I don't understand infidelity."

"Ah, youth," Eleanor sighed.

"Are Granato and Lilas a couple?" I asked.

"Were Pygmalion and Galatea?" Eleanor said. "Granato is an old friend of Morel and Marchand. He's been coming to Sainte-Marie for years. Lilas is a recent addition to the *ménage*."

"Do you think we can get into Alain and Paul's atelier?" I asked. "Or will the police have it locked up?"

"I suppose the *flics* may have let Paul go on working," Eleanor said.

"Were Paul and Angélique close?" I asked.

"I believe they were," Colin said. "Her darkroom is in a cellar below Paul's side of the studio. I often heard them nattering away from Alain's side."

"Why, dear?" Eleanor asked.

"I have questions for Paul," I said. "I didn't know Angélique was a photographer."

"An excellent one," Eleanor said. "She exhibited."

"Don't 'photographs' make you think of blackmail?" I said. "I'd like to have a look at her darkroom."

"I'll come with you," Colin said.

"What kind of pictures did she take?" I asked as Colin and I started down the street.

"Portraits. Art photos," he said.

"Does that mean nudes?" I asked.

"Not necessarily," he said. "Landscapes with figures. Like paintings, only photos."

"I hope Eleanor doesn't mind my being so snoopy," I said. "She's been so good to me."

"Like Vanessa to me," Colin said. "I can't go to art college until next year, and my parents only agreed that I could stay in Sainte-Marie if I found a respectable place to stay. I told them an elderly English gentlewoman invited me to her home."

"Could she have a blackmailable secret?" I said. "Could you ask? Gently?"

"I'd hate to upset the old darling," he said. "She wouldn't *kill* someone."

"Neither would Alain," I said. "*Please,* Colin. If she hasn't done anything, you have nothing to worry about."

We found Paul alone in the studio. The police had searched the whole place thoroughly, including Angélique's darkroom. There, they had found cyanide—a fixing solution used in developing photographs—the same poison that had killed her.

"They will accuse me next," he said. "But I loved her. Never would I kill her!"

"Did she love you?" Colin asked.

"She loved no one," he said. "She loved to tantalize, to lead a man on and dance away. I was under her spell, but I knew I was not her only lover."

"You've had an exhibition on," I said. "The studio was open to the public?"

"Yes," he said. "*Le tout* Sainte-Marie came to see our work."

The darkroom was unlocked. Anyone could have taken the cyanide.

"What did the *flics* do with Angélique's photographs?" I asked.

"Nothing yet," Paul said. "They ask me to sort them. There are thousands. Angélique was not well organized. The *flics* wish to see the men in these photos. The jealous husband, you see."

"It sounds like an enormous job," I said. "Let us help. We can work down there while you set the studio to rights. They've made quite a mess."

Colin and I spent hours going through the photos. Angélique was a good photographer. I stole one of Alain, rich in subtleties of light and shadow on the dramatic planes of his face against the ramparts. Hardest to look at were their wedding photos, presumably taken by someone else. The bride wore a filmy chiffon dress and flowers in her hair. Alain looked at her adoringly. Angélique looked with adoration at her own bare ivory shoulder.

"What will the police think when we give them these?" I showed Colin half a dozen I'd just picked out. "To me, they scream, *He cares, she doesn't.*"

"I think they'll just see wedding pictures," Colin said. "What do you make of this?"

He handed me a photo of Angélique, Jacques Morel, and Madeleine Marchand having a picnic in a field of flowers, beautifully grouped as if in an Impressionist painting.

"It's very emotionally charged," I said. "I wonder who took the picture."

"Angélique might have taken it herself by time-lapse," he said, "except she looks so caught up in the moment. Or Ricardo Granato, if they're all such mates."

"Who's doing what to whom?" I asked.

The poses were fluid. None of the figures touched. I looked for signs of physical threat, entreaty, or blatant seductiveness in their stances and expressions. Were Morel and Angélique smoldering at each other? Was Madeleine glaring? What if Morel and Angélique were having an affair, and that was the moment Madeleine found out? Or was that the moment a spark between Morel and Angélique caught fire, right under Madeleine's nose? What about whoever took the picture? Granato? Lilas? What did that moment mean to them?

Back at Eleanor's, I found her beating eggs for an omelet.

"What's Quentin's story?" I asked. "Why does he live in Sainte-Marie? Is he a lord? A remittance man? A criminal? Why doesn't he ever talk about England?"

"Ask him yourself," she said. "Even better, leave him alone."

"But if Alain didn't kill Angélique, someone did," I said. "What if she was a blackmailer?"

"You think she blackmailed Quentin?" she said. "For heaven's sake!"

I invited Quentin to lunch at my favorite outdoor café. It had a view of golden green-terraced vineyards sloping away beyond the ramparts.

"Do you have a dark secret, Quentin?"

"Only an embarrassing one, my dear," he said as we scraped up the last of our *pots de crème*. "You see, I had a famous father. He wrote children's books that are beloved in every English nursery. Unfortunately, he named me after his main character, who was a lovable but accident-prone hedgehog. I do mean *every* nursery. I was a laughingstock at school, and it didn't stop when

I grew up. I'm afraid it kept me from making much of myself in life. Then Papa died, leaving me a great deal of money. I crossed the Channel, vowing never to return."

"French children don't read the hedgehog books?" I asked.

"As Papa's sole heir," he said, "I was able to withdraw the French-language rights and buy up the remaining unsold copies. Today, you won't find a single story about that bloody hedgehog in all of France."

If Quentin was telling the truth, Angélique wasn't blackmailing him. I would see Colin at the Chat Gris that evening. I bet I could talk him into getting Vanessa to tell him *her* dark secrets.

***

The following afternoon, I was drinking an *apéritif* at the café when Colin rushed up, overturning a small wrought iron chair in his haste.

"Julie! Can you come? Vanessa is in a state, and I don't know what to do!"

"Should we get a doctor?" I trotted to keep up with his long strides. "Shall I go get Eleanor?"

"No, just come."

We threaded our way through a narrow alley and down a flight of steps.

"*Attention!*" he said. "Don't trip." The ancient stones were concave with wear. "I should have known one can't get Vanessa drunk halfway."

"I shouldn't have asked you to pry."

"I wanted to know as much as you," he said. "And it's I who gave her two bottles of Chateau de Laubade Armagnac. If I'd drunk as much as she did, I'd be out cold."

"So she's conscious?"

"She's crying and talking nonstop. She's wretched, Julie, and I blame myself."

We found Vanessa sitting on the stone floor of her dungeon-like cellar.

"I was never in the bloody ballet," she sobbed. "I danced in seedy cabarets when they would have me. But mostly, I was just a *pute*. Nothing but a tart, and that's the ugly truth."

Colin and I cleaned her up and got her to bed. He stayed to keep watch while she slept it off. I went back to Eleanor's and poured out the whole story to her, curled up at her feet as I sobbed out my feelings of guilt into her lap.

"It's all my fault, Eleanor. I never should have started asking questions. and I *never* should have twisted Colin's arm into trying to find out if Vanessa had any secrets. Colin thinks it's his fault, but he's still just a boy, and I knew he'd do whatever I asked. I'm sorry. I'm so sorry! She could have died!"

Eleanor stroked my hair.

"You made a mistake, the way we all do when we're young. And you're not responsible for an impressionable boy's case of puppy love. Vanessa's a tough old bird. If drinking hasn't killed her yet, it wasn't going to this time."

"Did you know about her past?"

"She used to hint, but she never made it sound sordid," Eleanor said. "She would show me presents men had given her, expensive trinkets and jewels she said were real. And I had no idea she was never a ballerina at all."

By the time I got back to Vanessa's, she was sleeping. Colin and I kept apologizing to each other until we both realized we were beginning to sound ridiculous and were almost ready to laugh at ourselves. Then we talked quietly until Vanessa woke up, much restored and ready to talk.

"Angélique found out all about me, you see," she told us. "I wasn't just an artist's model. I was a pute, and when I needed money, I'd do anything. There were photos, many photos. Once I was paid, I never gave them another thought. Half the time, I was out of my head on morphia or absinthe when they were taken. She found some of the most degrading at a bookstall in Paris. My dignity was all I had left. I had to keep her quiet. I couldn't give her money—I never had any—but I could give up my mementos. All of them. Jewels from lovers, from the good years. Souvenirs from the ballet. I always loved the dance. That much was real."

"Darling Vanessa," Colin said. "I hate to think how you've suffered."

"Your past doesn't matter to us," I said.

"It matters to me," Vanessa said. "I don't want anyone to know. But tormenting people gave her pleasure."

"She deserved to die," I said. "We'd understand if, well—"

"I wouldn't poison anyone," Vanessa said. "I had the most beautiful Maltese cat, Bluebell, who was poisoned, and she died such a pitiful death. Let us forget *la garce* once and for all. She was vicious, but she was *small*. Off with you, children. I don't need a minder. *Il fait beau*, so enjoy the day."

So, Colin and I went to look at modern art in the neighboring village of Vence, where we ran into the model Lilas. We invited her to *prendre un café* and encouraged her to gossip about Morel, Marchand, and Granato. Maybe she got bored being silently decorative and appreciated our rapt attention.

"Madeleine and I are old friends," she said. "We were very close in Paris in the old days. Morel I met later, and through them Granato, who made my career."

"And now you're a couple?" I asked.

"You Americans always want a fairy tale," Lilas said. "Granato and I are professional partners. Jacques and Madeleine, now, their drama has a happy ending. They are about to fly off to Hollywood together—into the sunset, *n'est-ce pas*? They will sign a contract for three films with one of your big American studios. I am furious with them. Granato is angry too. But they are determined. Ever since the War, we poor Europeans must surrender to your mighty American dollar."

"I'm not American," Colin said.

"And I was a student until a couple of months ago," I said. "I have very few of those mighty dollars."

Then we talked about art, the two of them popping intelligent comments back and forth and me struggling to keep up until it was time to return to Sainte-Marie.

"We shouldn't have changed the subject," I said later. "But Americans hate to be accused of being rich—'ugly Americans' using money to dominate Europe."

"And we British hate to be accused of being American." Colin laughed. "What did we learn about 'who did what to whom' from that conversation?"

"Lilas and Granato are not a couple," I said. "Lilas and Marchand know each other from way back. And Morel and Marchand must be reconciled for real if they're making movies together in America."

"Lilas is angry at them for going," he said, "and so is Granato, if you believe her."

"Maybe they're angry because Morel and Marchand have made up," I said. "Maybe Lilas was having an affair with Morel. Or Marchand was having an affair with Granato. Or both."

"How does Angélique fit in?" Colin asked.

"Say Angélique was having an affair with Morel," I said, "and he ended it so he and Marchand could make up and take this Hollywood deal. Angélique wouldn't have liked that."

"She'd have felt humiliated," Colin said. "What if she threatened him?"

"Morel's a famous actor," I said, "married to France's sex goddess. What do you suppose she had on him? Could she have had an affair with Granato?"

"At the same time?"

"Or before," I said. "He might have told her something about Morel."

"Granato might have had an affair with Morel," Colin said. "It hadn't occurred to you? You are such an American."

I didn't like being called an American any more than Colin did, even though I was one—not in the South of France by a good-looking fifteen-year-old boy.

"Americans are very fond of morality," he said, "even in the film world. Europeans don't think that superstar of yours, poor girl, did anything terribly scandalous, but she shocked the American public with not much more than scanty clothes and outrageous statements. I wonder if that studio contract would have come through if Angélique had sent photos of Morel with a male lover to the gutter press."

"The whole gang of them were buddies with Angélique," I said. "They could have taken the cyanide from her darkroom."

"We should talk to Madeleine Marchand," he said. "If anyone knows Morel's secrets, it's she."

"I'm in awe of her," I confessed. "What will I say?"

"Tell her how much you admire her acting," Colin said.

"And gradually work around to who her husband's been sleeping with and did he murder that *garce* who got killed?"

"Think about it," he said, "while I look in on Vanessa."

I made my way to the ramparts. I had the spectacular sunset to myself. *Le tout* Sainte-Marie was proceeding from an *apéritif* to *un verre encore*. The French do make drinking sound classy. I was too scared for Alain to think about anyone else. I'd heard that French justice was based purely on logic and hard evidence. It sounded pitiless. My mind dissolved into wordless longing. Twilight gathered. *Le crépuscule*, a lovely word.

Lights winked on in the valley. A warm breath stirred my hair.

"All alone?" Madeleine Marchand murmured.

She put her hand on my cheek and turned my face toward hers. Her fathomless eyes gazed into mine.

"Tu permets?"

If she'd been asking permission to cut my throat, I couldn't have moved or looked away. I had the crazy thought that she was going to kiss me. Instead, she boosted herself onto the wall. Her shapely legs dangled an inch away from mine. I heard a cowbell clang in the valley, sleepy birds, the clatter of French housewives preparing dinner.

"Alors, ma petite Américaine? A quoi penses-tu?"

"I was thinking about Alain Colbert," I said. "He'll be convicted of killing his wife, and he didn't do it. You people still use the guillotine, don't you?"

"Hardly ever, nowadays."

She lit a Gauloise, one of those vile black cigarettes that reeked of the darkness and a glamour I'd thought I could find in France without being touched by it.

"Prison, then," I said. "It's not right. He should be painting."

"You don't think it was a crime of passion?"

"Maybe," I said. "But not Alain's."

Madeleine Marchand blew smoke out her nostrils and gazed at the deepening lavender sky.

"A *crime passionelle*," she said, "occurs in the heat of the moment. To poison, one must plan. Angélique had much allure, but she was greedy and vindictive. What she had, she must keep, even when she no longer wanted it—lovers, possessions, information. And having no generosity or creativity herself, she was rapacious of the gifts of others."

"People can be passionate about their ambitions," I said, "no matter how much they have already achieved. I heard that you and Monsieur Morel plan to go to Hollywood."

"The contracts were not yet signed," she said. "The heads of the American studios are prudish, ridiculous when it comes to their so-called morality. They would have dropped us if Angélique had approached them with her photos."

"Compromising photos," I said.

"Of Morel with me and Lilas. Of Morel with Granato and with Granato and me. Of me with Lilas and of me with Angélique."

"Too many people know about those photos now," I said. "Did you take the cyanide?"

Madeleine shrugged with that *panache* the French have perfected.

"I asked Angélique what value she placed on friendship," she said. *"La garce*, she laughed and said, 'Je m'en fous.'"

"What value do *you* place on friendship, Madame Marchand?" I asked.

"So formal, *ma petite*?" She laughed and brushed her forefinger across my lips. "Friendship, a little. Love, a little more. Reputation, *je m'en fous*."

Was she telling me she didn't care if we went to the police about the photos? She'd as good as told me she'd taken the cyanide from Angélique's darkroom. They'd find her fingerprints if they checked thoroughly enough.

"The freedom of the artist to create," she said, "*ça, alors, tu as raison*. You are right; that is the only thing that truly matters in the end. For that alone, I will admit that, yes, I offered her a friendly glass."

She gave me the breathtaking smile that had made millions of moviegoers fall in love with her. Only French words could do justice to that smile: *seduisant, intriguant, ravissant*. Though I was sure she was a murderer, that smile seduced, intrigued, and ravished me.

"I grow bored, child. *Je m'en fous de tout*. Alain with his talent, you with your innocent heart, you cannot imagine such a state. But you can raise a glass to me. *Tchin tchin*."

The vial was at her lips before I could stop her. She had saved a little for herself.

WHEN YOU WALK INTO THE ROOM

By Steve Liskow

The woman walked into St. Pauli Gurlz dressed like she didn't plan to leave alone. Her Mets jersey was buttoned one button above showtime, her faded cutoffs matched her light-blue eyes, and the frayed spots on her butt showed milky white skin…and no underwear. She ignored the men who watched her approach the bar and dug into her purse.

She looked back at the band, which chose that moment to take a break, maybe to get in tune.

"Hi." Sandy felt a new expression on her face. "Um, not to be judgmental, but you're dressed like the meter's running, and we're really not that kind of place."

"I just moved into the neighborhood." The woman had hair the color of patent leather, clearly dyed, and teeth that belonged in a toothpaste ad. She was Sandy's five-six, with cheekbones most of the men in the place could shave with. "I figured this was a good way to meet guys in a hurry."

Jimmy, the other bartender, finished making a margarita and put it next to the taps where Dee, the barmaid, could deliver it. His long hair covered the missing ear from Afghanistan, but he still had the physique to be a bouncer on the rare occasions that was necessary.

"Um, yeah," Sandy said. "But there are friends, and there are friends. Most of the friends here are guys you'll want to talk to the next morning without blushing."

The woman drew a ten from her purse. "Will you let me buy a beer, or should I leave now?"

Sandy rolled her eyes. "Sorry. It's just that this is a working-class neighborhood. Some of the guys might see you and…um, misunderstand."

"I know 'working class,'" the woman said. "I grew up there and got married there and got divorced there. Now, I'm moving on. Sort of. Now, may I have a Blue Moon?"

"It's Wednesday," Sandy said. "We run a special on St. Pauli Girl every Wednesday. Two bucks until nine o'clock."

She waited until the woman looked at her again. "My sister and I own the joint, and we're the St. Pauli sisters."

"You own this place?" The woman's eyes flashed to Jimmy, who was busy at the tap again. He nodded at her before turning his attention back to filling the glass.

"Yeah," Sandy continued. "Jimmy's just the eye candy. We took it over from my dad when he and Mom moved to Arizona."

"OK, what the hell, give me a St. Pauli Girl."

Sandy made change. "If you just moved in, are you going to be a regular? If you are, I should know your name and get used to what you like."

The woman's eyes seemed to laugh at her even though the rest of her face was less cheerful than kidney stones.

"If you don't like the way I dress, you definitely don't want to know what I like."

"To drink," Sandy said. "To eat. We have the best short-order cook on the East Side, and our carrot cake makes divorcées moan."

"Carrot cake? You look like a shot and beers joint. Don't take that as a bad thing."

"I don't. Dee's and my grandfather opened this place after World War Two and called it 'Old Grandad's.' Our father took it over when Grandad was seventy-three. Then he won the Powerball and moved to Arizona with our mom. Dee and I were both in night school and working here anyway. We finished our MBAs and took it over. Changed the name, added to the menu."

"To 'St. Pauli Gurlz.'" The woman toasted Sandy and sipped.

Sandy grinned. "You gotta have a gimmick, right? What do you want me to call you? I'm Sandy."

The woman took time to swallow. "Crystal."

She looked back toward the bandstand, where the musicians huddled around the drummer.

"These guys play every night?"

"They're auditioning," Sandy said. "We do an open mic on Tuesday. A poet, a couple of comics, five or six musicians, none of them all the time. It's a fun night. Lots of people show up to listen. We're trying to find live bands for Saturday."

Crystal looked at the band again. The keyboard player scrolled through a tablet. The guitar player stepped down off the platform and approached the bar. When he saw Crystal, his smile was bigger than the drummer's cymbal.

"Hey," he said. "Can I get you something?"

"Not just yet. What do you guys call yourselves?"

"Friendly Spirits." The guy handed Sandy a ten and ordered four St. Pauli Girls before he turned back to the newcomer. "What do you call *your*self?"

"Crystal," she said. "Waterford."

Sandy saw the guy not get the joke.

"Where'd you come up with that name?" Crystal asked.

"Well, we're playing in a bar, so it fitted in. It's from Rocky and Bullwinkle, you remember them?"

Crystal kept her face neutral. "Maybe from the History Channel."

"Ha, good one. I'm Jackson, as in Jackson Daniels."

Crystal raised her eyebrows as though she suspected she had stepped into an alternate universe. Jackson picked up speed and momentum.

"You have any requests, let me know, and we'll play them for you."

Crystal tilted her pilsner glass at him. "Thank you. I'll keep that in mind."

Jackson returned to the bandstand. Sandy's sister, Dee, appeared with a tray under her arm.

"Two bacon burgers, two fries, and a margarita."

Sandy slid the order through the pass-through to Charley, the short-order cook. When she turned back, Dee was studying Crystal, standing near the bandstand while the guys at the table behind her checked out her fashion statement.

"Uh, who's the newbie? And does she have any concealed weapons, too?"

"Her name's Crystal." Sandy reached for a glass. "She says. I think she was playing Jackson, though."

"Okay, so she's not totally stupid."

"Hard to tell," Sandy said. "Walking in here flashing her talents like that."

Dee nodded. "If she likes to dance, we might have to break out the fire extinguisher."

Friendly Spirits clinked beer bottles, and Sandy made the margarita. By the time she salted the rim, the band was tuning up, which she considered progress. They began playing again, and two guys at the table immediately flanked Crystal. She joined one of them on the dance floor, a space slightly larger than a pool table. She danced the way she dressed.

Dee picked up the margarita.

"Does she know about what happened three weeks ago? And the week after that?"

Sandy watched the girl shaking all over. "Think we should tell her?"

Three weeks before, a woman had been assaulted two blocks away after leaving another bar. She couldn't describe her attacker well enough so police could even narrow down suspects. A week later, another woman was attacked, probably by the same guy. St. Pauli Gurlz wasn't a meat-market joint, but even fewer unescorted women had shown up since then.

"With luck, she's got her car parked out back. Maybe Jim or Charley can walk her out when she's leaving."

"If she doesn't find a friend before then."

"Yeah, there's that." Dee headed toward a booth with her tray. Sandy ran a cloth over the bar. St. Pauli Gurlz had been non-smoking for years, but the old wood showed decades of cigarette burns under the fresh shellac. It resembled an old knotty pine basement.

Charley hit his bell and slid the burgers into the pickup window. Crystal was dancing with the other guy from the table now and making more friends by the minute. When the band finished the song, she let someone pull out a chair for her and almost vanished in the cloud of testosterone. By the time the band finished their second set, she was drinking her third St. Pauli Girl. It was almost nine, so her next one—if Sandy would serve her another—would cost five dollars instead of two.

A few minutes later, she passed the bar on the way to the restroom. When she returned, she caught Sandy's eye again.

"The guys at the table were telling me a woman was attacked near here."

"Three weeks ago." Sandy tried not to look at the girl's chest. "Another a week after that."

"The police don't have any leads?"

"The women didn't even see the guy until he grabbed them."

Crystal's eyes seemed to get deeper and darker. Maybe it was the beer. Sandy went on.

"The second one was a regular here. She was somewhere else the night she was attacked, but she hasn't been back since."

"That sucks."

"Yeah. That's why I made a thing about how you're dressed."

Jackson Daniels appeared again.

"Yo, Crystal. Can I get you another beer?"

"I'm filling up, Jack, thanks."

"How about a shot, then? I'm getting shots for the guys. We're all friendly spirits, see? Like I'm Jackson Daniels. Guess our other names."

"Do I need a number two pencil?"

"The keyboard player's Johnnie Walker," Jackson went on. To go with his other skills, he had terrible comic timing. "The drummer's Mark Maker, and our bass player is Glen Fiddich. He's Scotch, get it?"

"Scottish." Crystal rolled her eyes. "You came up with your names late at night when you were all wasted, didn't you?"

"You're good." Jackson moved closer, and Crystal stood straighter.

"Move. Your. Hand." Her voice dropped an octave and was so soft Sandy barely heard it.

"Hey, lighten up. You're pretty, and I'm pretty good. Let me buy you another drink. Maybe we can get together after."

Crystal turned her face toward Jackson's. "Do you like being able to play guitar?"

Dee slid between the two and gave Jackson time to think about it.

"A grilled cheese and two St. Paulis. I told the table I'd give them all the special rate."

Sandy looked at the clock. "One minute left. I'm on it."

She turned back to Crystal. "I don't think you need another drink for a while."

"Hey," Jackson said. He held up two tens.

"A Jack, a Johnny Walker, a Mark, and a Glen."

Crystal slid around him and returned to the table. Sandy looked at the artful gash in her cut-offs, just below the jersey. If *she* had an ass like that, maybe she'd show it off too.

"Back off, Jackson. She's new to the neighborhood, and the guys at the table told her about the women who were attacked."

"Oh. Yeah. Heard anything more about that?"

"Not a word."

She poured the shots and put the glasses on a plate. Jackson dropped his money on the bar.

"Keep the change, OK?"

He picked up the plate and returned to the bandstand. Crystal talked to a guy in an Alan Jackson tee, a regular who drank Coors and liked buffalo wings. Trevor. Crystal could do a lot worse, even at that table. Trevor was even bigger than Jim, the bartender, but he was housebroken.

Charley appeared in the pass-through window.

"What, nobody's hungry?"

"Dee's working the crowd," Sandy said. "Maybe the band is killing everyone's appetite. I don't think so, though. They'd be drinking more to make up for it."

"Yeah, probably. I'll say this for those guys, they're not terrific, but they're not crazy loud, either."

"True, that." Sandy watched the band members clink their glasses and drink, then Jackson brought the empties back to the bar.

"What do you think?"

"Not a lot of people are dancing, are they?" Sandy looked toward the minuscule dancing space.

"Not really. I wish we'd get a few more requests, too."

"How long have you guys been together?"

"About three months. We're still learning a bunch of songs, but it's easier with tablets."

Sandy realized everyone except the drummer had one clipped to his microphone stand.

"The night's still young. Well, maybe not. It's a work night. People will start leaving in another hour or so."

"Yeah. Our last set'll be over about quarter of."

Jackson eased over to Crystal and said something. Trevor looked up at him, and he went back to the bandstand. He and his mates huddled together and swiped their tablets again.

Charley rested his forearms on the counter of the pass-through. His face glistened from the heat, and his eyes were big and brown as a burger. He nodded toward Crystal.

"The new girl dance with anyone yet?"

Jim watched Crystal as though he was afraid she'd shatter.

"Two, maybe three of the guys at that table."

He frowned, then took a drink order, making the drink mostly by feel, his eyes never leaving the table near the band.

Two more guys came up for refills: a tequila and a Guinness.

Jackson leaned into the mic.

"OK, we've got a request for this song, a real golden oldie. Hope you like it."

Nobody had approached the band. Did someone ask Dee to pass it on? No, she hadn't talked to them, either.

The band stumbled through an intro that Sandy didn't recognize; then the keyboard player began singing "Crystal Blue Persuasion."

The song was older than anyone in the bar, and Sandy couldn't remember who sang it. Trevor escorted Crystal two steps onto the tiny floor, and she put her arms around his neck.

"Damn," Jim said.

Dee bustled over. "Charley, two carrot cakes, I'll get the coffee."

"Gotcha." Charley disappeared.

The band took the song slowly as they figured out the changes, and Trevor took advantage of that. By the time the song finally ended, Crystal's head rested on his shoulder, and his arms held her close. They held hands on the way back to the table, Jackson's eyes following them every step of the way.

Charley put two wedges of carrot cake on the pass-through counter, and Dee delivered them to the booth along with the coffee. Sandy eased to the far end of the bar.

"Jim, what's up with you and the new girl? You look like she's the puppy you wanted for Christmas, and someone else got her."

He shook his head. "She reminds me of someone."

Sandy looked toward the table again. "Someone famous, you mean? Or just because she's hotter than Charley's buffalo wings?"

"I'm not sure. Just...familiar somehow. I could almost swear I know her, but her name wasn't Crystal."

"Well, I don't think this one's name is Crystal, either. She told the band guy her last name was 'Waterford.'"

Jim snorted.

"You're kidding."

"Nope. And he didn't get it. Where do you think you know her from? In the service? School?"

He adjusted his hairnet. "That's what's bugging me. I'm not sure. But something about her—"

"Don't tell her that. It sounds like a cheesy pickup line."

"Yeah, I know. About one step up from 'Nice shoes.'"

Two guys returned to the bar, and Jim refilled their beers. The band was trying to get people up on the dance floor, which would accommodate about four couples if they stood still. Jackson caught Dee's eye, and she went over to him. She returned to the bar as the band moved into a ragged attempt at

Garth Brooks. She rolled her eyes at Sandy.

"He wants another St. Pauli Girl for Crystal," Dee said. "I told him it was a bad idea."

"Go ask her if she wants it. I'm guessing Trevor will be pissed."

"Ya think?"

"Just do it. If Trevor doesn't say anything, he's gonna lose points in my book."

Sandy didn't mention that Trevor was one of the guys she was hoping would hit on her eventually. You'd think the job should make her look better with every beer, but it didn't seem to work that way. Crystal looked too much like her meter was running, though. If Trevor wanted her, Sandy might cross him off her list.

Dee hunkered down between Crystal and Trevor, her lips moving. They all looked toward Jackson, now singing earnestly with a drawl that became him only slightly better than a tutu. Crystal's lips moved, and Sandy could read her lips from twenty feet away. Trevor's face suggested that he agreed.

When the band took another break, Jackson moved near the table behind Crystal. Before he could say anything, Trevor stood up and punched him in the face. He staggered back, then shook his head and raised his fists.

"Oh, crap." Jim leaned into the pass-through window. "Charley, out here."

Charley appeared in seconds and followed Jim into the ring of patrons watching the two men. When they cleared a path, Sandy saw Trevor standing over the musician, who was on his hands and knees as though he was looking for his teeth.

"Okay," Jim said. "Party's over. Both of you need to leave."

"But..." Trevor turned to argue, and Jim slapped the sawed-off baseball bat against his palm. He and Trevor were about the same size. Charley didn't have a bat, but he was even bigger.

"I'm with the band." Jackson's words seemed to come through a sponge. When he looked up, his nose was bloody, and one eye already looked swollen. His lips resembled sausage links.

"We need him," the keyboard player said. He stood on the edge of the crowd as though he'd been trying to pull his buddy back. Obviously, he failed.

"Really, guy," he went on. "If you toss him, we'll have to pack up and leave early. Look, I'll buy the other guy a beer. I know Jackson's kind of a jerk, but…"

Trevor flexed his hand and looked at Crystal. She didn't look back at him.

"Listen," Trevor protested, "he started it. This sucks."

"Sorry," Jim said. "We're a peaceful place. If we want fights, we get them on cable. Today's Wednesday, so I don't want to see you in here again until next Saturday. Got that?"

Trevor looked at Crystal again. "Can I wait until the lady finishes her drink?"

Crystal's face turned red. "I think I'm going to be a while, Trevor. Drive safe."

The room turned so quiet Sandy heard ice melting in everyone's drinks. Trevor stared at Crystal with his mouth and eyes wide open, then reached over and pulled his flannel off the chair.

"Can I have some ice, at least? Put on my hand?"

Jim stepped behind the bar and scooped ice into a plastic bag. He handed it to Trevor, and they watched him slink out the door and pass the window on the way to the parking lot. Jim looked back at Jackson.

"You started this, so you're out too."

"But what about us?" the keyboard player demanded.

Jim shook his head. "If you can play as a trio, do it. Otherwise, you're done. By the time you pack up, Trevor will be long gone."

"But…"

Jackson looked toward Crystal. She turned away from him and walked to the ladies' room. He looked back at Jim.

"Can I have some of that ice too? Christ, I think my teeth are all loose."

Sandy scooped more ice into another bag and handed it across the bar. Charley and Jim returned to their places, and the crowd slowly settled back into their booths and tables. Friendly Spirits turned off their amps and unplugged their cables.

"Maybe they can write a song about this," Dee said softly.

"Sure," Jim agreed. "Maybe change their names too, so nobody knows it's about them."

Sandy looked toward the restrooms. "I'm going to see if the girl's all right."

Crystal stood in front of the mirror, her fists clenched and her purse next to the sink.

"Are you OK?"

"I'm sorry. I didn't want…I didn't mean—"

"Testosterone does that sometimes. But I must admit, you didn't help."

"I probably won't be back here either."

"You don't have to stay away," Sandy said. "But maybe next time, cover up a little more?"

Crystal bit her lip.

"You mind if I stay here awhile?"

"I'll tell you when they're all gone, all right?"

"Thank you."

Sandy returned to the bar, where Jim was swamped with drink orders, many of them for Johnnie Walker, Jack Daniels, or Glenfiddich, but a fair number of St. Pauli Girls, too. When the band disappeared with the last of their equipment, she returned to Crystal, standing near the wall-mounted blow dryer.

"The band just loaded the last of their gear," she said. "Did you and Trevor even get each other's digits?"

Crystal shook her head. "If they're all gone, I should go too."

"You don't have to leave yet."

"I should. That was all my fault."

Sandy found herself liking the woman more. She led the way out, speaking back over her shoulder.

"It's not your fault that you look the way you do. You could use a few fashion tips, though."

"Let me think about it, okay?" Crystal glanced at her purse, then at Jim, standing by the beer taps. "What do I owe you?"

"You're all set." Jim came over and looked down at Crystal.

"Would you like me to walk you out? Make sure you're okay?"

"No, it's all good. I'll be fine. Really. Thank you."

He didn't push it, and Sandy decided not to push it, either. She held the door near the bandstand and watched Crystal's cut-offs disappear into the parking lot. There were still enough customers that when Jim announced last call, he and Sandy were busy. Charley waited a few minutes for final orders, then turned off the grill and started cleaning up the kitchen.

"That band," one of the regulars said to Jim. "You gonna have those guys back?"

Jim shrugged. "Did you like them? If you did, we can probably get them back. I'd wait a couple of weeks, though."

"Wait longer."

The people with him nodded in agreement. They paid and left, and Jim raised the remote to turn off the three TV sets. Charley rinsed out his scouring pads and block and washed his hands.

Dee and Sandy took rags to mop tables and booths while Jim counted the money. He'd barely started when someone pounded on the back door. Charley went to open it, and two patrons appeared, their eyes wide.

"There's someone dead out here," the taller one said. "It looks like the guy who was fighting."

"Trevor?" Sandy demanded. "Or the guitar player?"

"The big one. He's out in the parking lot. We've called nine-one-one."

Sure enough, they already heard sirens in the distance. Red and blue flashers bounced off the mirror behind the bar.

The body lay face up in a parking space sixty feet from the building, and the police flashers and spotlights made him look like garish artwork, which was the only reason Sandy didn't throw up. She could see blood on his face, and his shirt was pulled open, so another circle of blood showed on his stomach. It was about the size of a baseball. Sandy was glad to stay behind the tape, so she couldn't see any details.

The officers guided Jim over to look. He nodded slowly.

"Trevor," he said. "I don't know his last name."

The first cop held a wallet. "We've got it. He was in your bar tonight, right?"

"Uh, yeah. He got into a fight with the guitar player, and we kicked them both out."

"What time was that?" The cop guided Jim back away from the body, and Jim looked at the others before he answered.

"About ten. The band was pissed off because it meant they were going to have to stop playing early. I said fair was fair, so they packed up."

"Did they all leave together?"

Jim shook his head. "No. Trevor left first. The band had to pack up their stuff. They must have been twenty or thirty minutes later."

"What was the fight about, do you know?"

"A woman," Sandy said. "She was pretty, and she came on to both of them. Actually, she seemed more interested in Trevor, but the guitar player wouldn't let it go."

"So, who threw the first punch?"

"Trevor," Sandy said, and the others agreed.

"But the other guy asked for it," Jim said.

"So maybe the band ganged up on him when they left?"

Sandy shook her head.

"He left long before they did, like Jim said. And if there were four of them, they wouldn't have stabbed him, would they? Just beat him up?"

The cop looked back at the body. An ambulance eased back behind the building, along with another police van. More flashing lights bounced off the buildings, and the sound echoed louder than the band had inside. Men got out of the van with cameras and tape measures, and two EMTs opened the back door of the ambulance.

"Do you know the woman?"

"She'd never been in before," Sandy said. "She sounded like she might come back another time, but I warned her not to dress quite so…slutty."

"You didn't happen to get her name, did you?"

The crime technicians started taking pictures of the body, moving to a different angle for each shot.

Sandy cleared her throat.

"Crystal," she said. "Crystal Waterford."

The cop raised his eyebrows.

***

Two months later, the nights were cooler, and dusk came sooner. Tuesday was open mic night, and a new girl showed up to read her poetry. She wore a baseball cap above a black T-shirt and black jeans that did nothing to hide her figure, even with a denim jacket over the tee. Her hair was the color of good single-malt scotch, a braid through the back of her Mets cap.

Sandy barely listened to the woman's poetry, but everyone clapped when the woman was finished. She nodded shyly and left the stage to meander over to the bar. Eric, the emcee, plugged in the next performer's guitar and adjusted the microphone for him. Then, he went to his board and started playing with volume levels.

"Could I have a Blue Moon?"

Sandy tried not to stare too closely.

The woman traced an ancient cigarette burn on the bar with her fingernail. She had pale blue eyes and amazing cheekbones. Sandy tilted a pilsner glass under the tap and brought it to the woman.

"Crystal?"

The woman shook her head. "Diane."

She sipped her beer and watched the guitar player talk into his microphone. "I look like my cousin Laura. She used to come in here a lot."

Sandy felt goosebumps move up her back. "She hasn't been here in a few months."

Jim heard the conversation and joined them. "If Laura's your cousin, you probably know…"

"I do. I guess they didn't catch the guy. Is that right?"

"Nope." Jim looked at the woman more closely. "There haven't been any more attacks, though. Not after those two. Your cousin was the second one."

Diane sipped her beer and looked back at Jim. The guitar player started his first song, and everyone stopped talking until he finished. He thanked everyone for the applause, then began retuning his guitar for his second song.

"I liked your poetry," Jim said softly. Sandy saw him struggling to act nonchalant.

"Thank you." Diane sipped her beer again. "I heard something else happened here a few weeks ago, too."

"That was even worse," Sandy said. "They haven't found whoever did that, either."

"That sucks too."

Diane tapped her nails on her glass in time with the guitar player's song.

"Someone told me your sister's name is Dee," she said. "And you're Sandra. So you're Sandra Dee."

"Our mom and dad met when they were surfing. They loved the Gidget movies."

Diane eased back to a table with another girl, one of the regulars, who wrote her own songs and a guy Sandy thought was her boyfriend. Maxine and Ben. Maxine liked pinot grigio, and Ben drank Rolling Rock.

Sandy saw the same look on Jim's face that she suspected was on her own. She watched him peer at the table.

"Is she carrying the same purse?"

"It might be." Jim shook his head. "If it is, she probably got rid of the knife, though." He wiped a spill from the bar in front of him. "Or maybe we're both really crazy."

"If we're not…" Sandy didn't want to say the rest of it. No more attacks since someone stabbed Trevor in their parking lot six weeks before. She remembered holding the door for Crystal, or whatever her real name was, but she didn't watch her drive away. If she'd been out in the parking lot…

Diane rested her chin on her hands and watched another singer. Two different guys came up to talk to her, but they returned to their own tables after a minute or two. When everyone had played their first set, Diane returned to the bar and held up her glass to Jim.

"Can I have another Blue Moon?"

Jim put her glass in the sink and picked up a clean one. "You know, if you come back on Wednesday, we have a special on St. Pauli Girl. Two bucks until nine."

"I heard. Maybe I'll do that."

Jim topped off the new glass and put it on a coaster before he spoke again.

"You looked good with black hair, but blond makes you ten times more beautiful."

Diane looked at him over the top of her glass while she sipped. Then she licked foam off her upper lip.

"Hated it. I went into five bars, one every night, before I ended up here."

The goosebumps moved down Sandy's arms, and her hands felt cold.

"I'd say you finally got lucky," Jim said. "But that's a really bad way to put it."

"Once in a blue moon." Diane raised her glass to him, and she smiled.

"I think I'm going to be even luckier tonight."

Sandy watched Jim beam.

SHUFFLE OFF TO BUFFALO

By David Edgerley Gates

When the heat was on, it was common practice among some in our trade to absent themselves from their regular environs and rusticate awhile in more temperate climes. I'm not talking about the weather, mind, but the ebb and flow of moral vigilance and the hasty alarm of the powers that be.

As it happens, I was on my way upriver as companion to a fine broth of a boy named Gerry Tyrone, himself having attracted the unwelcome attentions of the Italians, and it was thought best to get him out of the city for the time being. This was in the wake of the Five Families gang war in 1948, when the Mafia clans had settled a bitter dispute betwixt themselves with brute violence and no small cost in political capital.

Why not throw him to the wolves? you might ask. Piece him out to Frank Costello or Joe Bananas in return for goodwill or future favors. A ready answer is that such would countenance betrayal. A more thoughtful one is that Young Tim Hannah, who bossed the Irish mob on the West Side, wasn't one for short-term gain. He played a deeper game.

"Mickey," he told me, "keep the lad safe from harm."

He meant long enough to see if his investment matured.

* * *

We left Grand Central in the early morning on the milk run. Yonkers, Tarrytown, and Croton, where the overnight passenger trains changed over to steam, and up through Peekskill to Poughkeepsie and Hyde Park. We got off at a whistle-stop called Hudson, about an hour south of Albany.

This was a diversion, mind, in the event we'd picked up a tail, but nobody appeared to have taken any interest. The plan was that we'd cool our heels, and come five o'clock that same afternoon, I'd put Tyrone on the Lake Shore Limited as it passed through.

We repaired, then, to a place on Front Street called Foley's, kitty-corner to the red-brick train station. It was a homely sort of place, with a pressed-tin ceiling and an enormous mirrored back bar, all beveled glass and Gothic detail carved out of mahogany. They had Genessee lager and Utica Club on tap, with pickled pigs' feet and hot cherry peppers for the bold.

The saloon owner was one of our tribe, a certain Charles Francis Foley, known familiarly as Chuck, which gave rise to the inevitable joke of Chuck You, Foley. He bore it with pained good humor. Foley had managed this refuge for years, since before the war. It should be said that Hudson itself was always considered neutral turf. The last gangland murder in the town had been the killing of Legs Diamond almost twenty years before. They say it was ordered by Dutch Schultz, but not without the blessings of the Albany machine, and surely it meant they were hand in glove.

These days, there was naught but scrupulous somnolence.

* * *

He was an Ulsterman. The name gave him away. Centuries of Tyrones, in the North. I'd had a bellyful of Fenians, and thankfully, he was none of that stripe, but he seemed melancholy, a common Irish affliction.

We were seated in the back, at a corner table, with the wall behind me, where I could see both doors. An old habit, not easily forsaken.

"Can they find me?" he asked.

"If they mean to kill you, they will," I told him. "The question is how much importance they attach to it. Who benefits from your death?"

"It would redress an injury."

I nodded. Both the Italians and the Irish have a long memory for grievance. Still, insult can usually be redeemed, if not entirely forgiven. "Shame the devil," I said, smiling.

He hesitated, looking down at his hands.

It was suddenly alarmingly obvious. "What was her name?" I asked, pricking up my ears.

"Nicoletta," he stammered. "Nicoletta de Luca."

There was a lieutenant in the Gambino family named de Luca, a Calabrese, not Sicilian. "Aldo de Luca's daughter?"

Gerry didn't meet my unbelieving gaze.

Aldo Quattrocchi, they called him, because he wore heavy prescription glasses with darkened lenses. Tyrone had knocked up the daughter of a Mafia *capo*. No wonder there was a price on his head.

"She—"

She'd led him on, I was certain he was about to say, but he thought better of it. My fury would have curdled cream.

The tavern keeper, Foley, came over to our table to tell me I had a phone call. I got up and went behind the bar. Foley stepped through the batwing doors into the kitchen to afford me some privacy, and I picked up the receiver.

It was just above noon, and Tyrone and I were alone in the pub. I spoke my name a second time, but nobody answered. There was only the windy sigh of an open connection.

I was a step behind, and it was my aggravation with Tyrone that had dulled my wits. I put the telephone receiver down gently on the wood, not hanging up, and slid the .38 Super out from under my arm. I glanced at Gerry, who sat morosely, staring at his shoes, and I moved further down the bar, away from him. I wanted to put more distance between us and provide two separate targets.

They came through both doors, of course, one apiece, the front entrance and the side, to catch us in a cross fire. I had but one advantage. The upper half of the doors were frosted glass panels, and their shadows printed on the glass ahead of them.

I dropped the thumb safety and shot the guy directly in front of me just as he opened the side door. And pivoted to my left, toward the front, to acquire the second shooter.

A right-handed man will fire more accurately, tracking from right to left, turning his upper body with the gun. Swinging your arm to the right gives you less control, and the guy coming in the front door made that mistake, snapping a bullet wide.

I put the first shot through the knot of his tie, the slide slamming back with the recoil, and the second center chest.

Spent brass chimed on the floor.

It all happened very fast. BLAM. Beat. BLAMBLAM. The time it took for the Colt to cycle a round.

Gerry Tyrone was only just climbing to his feet, which was exactly the wrong reaction, when he should have been flat on the floor. I hissed at him to get down.

I picked up the phone and held it to my ear. I heard a man breathing. "Foley?" he asked softly. I hung up.

* * *

I caught him in the kitchen before he could run out the back and pinned him to the floor. I put the muzzle of the gun in the soft part of his throat, under the jaw.

"*Who*, you daft barstid?" I demanded.

Foley stared up at me, terrified.

"You sold me out. Who paid you to punch the kid's ticket?"

"Magaddino." He almost choked on the name.

Jesus, Mary, and Joseph. "Why?" I asked him.

"I had no choice, Mickey. They'd have killed me, sure."

"Not *you*, you bloody foolish man, why Magaddino?"

Foley looked puzzled. "He brokered the peace," he said.

I sat back on my heels. There was an inevitable logic to it. Up along Lake

Erie, the Magaddino crew held the reins. Stefano Magaddino, known as the Undertaker, kept court in Buffalo, but he had influence as far as Cleveland and Detroit and trafficked across the border to Toronto and points north, up the St. Lawrence into French Canada. If the Five Families needed somebody who commanded respect and had no designs on their own territory, Don Stefano was well-credentialed. He'd been in power since the early days of Prohibition and kept himself insulated from the downstate rivalries and quarrels so he could be called on to arbitrate disputes. It also put him in a position to ask and return a host of favors.

The problem was that I now had two of his torpedoes dead on the floor of Foley's saloon, the smoking gun still in my fist.

* * *

We drag the dead men into the kitchen. Foley gets to work with a mop and pail. Blood can be a stubborn bastard. A surprise, you'd think, that the racket didn't attract a lot of attention, but down here, there was only the station and the train tracks, and beyond that, the river, the current oily and slow. The wrong end of a dilapidated little town.

"Draw the blinds and lock up," I told Foley.

He moved slowly, like an old man. He knew he was living on borrowed time.

"The phone call," I said. The phone call was a signal.

"A voice, only."

"If you had the wit, Foley, you might live through the afternoon," I said. It wasn't strictly true, but I wasn't above giving him false hope. "Was it a trunk call or local?"

He took too long to think about it.

"Call the exchange," I said.

The local exchange would connect everybody through a town switchboard, some of them still using party lines. It was a rural phone system, not the big city. But a long-distance call still had to be placed with a toll operator. It was a laborious process. It left a broad footprint and a paper trail.

He picked up the phone.

I looked across at Tyrone. I suppose when your dick leads you astray, it's hard to imagine mopping the blood off the floor after. I had little sympathy for him.

"Marjorie," Foley said when the switchboard operator answered. "I had a phone call here at the bar, oh, twenty or so minutes ago. It would have been from out of town."

He listened.

He looked over at me and covered the receiver with his hand. "Niagara Falls," he said in a stage whisper. "She says it was person-to-person."

I held out my hand for the phone, and he gave it to me.

"Marjorie, love," I said. "What was that number?"

* * *

We waited out the shank of the day, Foley drowning his sorrows, Tyrone with a case of the fidgets. I wouldn't have minded a wee taste of Bushmills malt meself, but I needed a clear head.

Approaching five o'clock, we heard the train whistle down the valley. I could see Foley imagined it to be his own Last Call. I didn't disabuse him, although I no longer had any appetite for it. The need was gone. I'd decided Foley might in fact prove more useful among the living.

Tyrone gathered himself up, looking altogether cheerful. I thought it misplaced or inappropriate.

I was of two minds, I suppose, but leaning toward malice.

The three of us crossed the street to the depot. Foley was a little unsteady, but I couldn't trust him to his own devices.

I held him upright as the train pulled in, and he got teary-eyed as we handed Tyrone aboard. It made for good theater. Like a young lad being sent off to the battlefields of the Marne, I didn't wonder. Gerry was ticketed through to Chicago. He had a sleeper reserved. The train bumped into motion.

Foley raised his hand in a forlorn wave. Tyrone's last look at the two of us on the platform was one of placid disdain. He'd made a successful exit. We were left on the empty stage.

I walked Foley back to the saloon, staggering and weepy.

"I'm not going to kill you now, Foley, for Christ's sake," I said. "Are ye daft? There's no practical reason for it. Not in the grand scheme of things."

He blinked at me, not ready to believe it.

"Where's the whiskey?" I asked him.

He went down the bar to get it.

I lifted the telephone handset and jiggled the hook, and the switchboard answered. "Marjorie," I said. "Would you place that call for me, please?"

There were clicks and static as the long-distance relays chattered, and then the connection was made, and somebody picked up in Niagara Falls. They chose not to speak.

According to the timetable, the Lake Shore Limited was scheduled to pass through Buffalo the following morning at 1:30 a.m., and the train would wait in the station for ten minutes, should anyone care to meet it. I had the number of the berth on the sleeper ready to hand and read it off the slip of paper.

There was a long pause, the stale air hollow and crisp, and they hung up.

I put the phone down. Foley poured me a drink.

I don't know if Young Tim Hannah had meant to trade Gerry Tyrone for preferment or advantage, for pocket money or a better man's life, but I was more than happy to trade him for my own.

BAR NONE

By Michael Bracken

Donnie Brewster slapped a crisp five-dollar bill on the bar top and said, "Give me a Jack and Coke."

I pushed the five back. "I can't. Your brother said to stop serving you."

"Johnny ain't the boss of me," he said as he pushed the five in my direction.

"But he's the boss of me." This time, I left the five where it was and stared into Donnie's eyes.

"Fuck." Donnie licked his chapped lips. "Glass of water, then. On the rocks."

I scooped ice cubes into a tumbler, topped them off with water, and placed the tumbler next to the five.

"How about a Jack chaser?"

I pocketed the five. "How about you drink the water and I don't tell Johnny you were here?"

He glared at me for a moment. "One of these days," he said, "my brother will get what he deserves."

Then Donnie downed the water, pushed himself to his feet, and walked out.

Joyce Klim, a middle-aged blonde I'd hired that morning to replace Andrea Johnson, had watched the entire exchange from the far end of the bar. "What was all that about?"

"That's the owner's younger brother. If you let him, Donnie will drink himself stupid," I explained. "Then he'll pick a fight with a guy twice his size, a fight he'll lose if we don't break it up."

I showed her the cut-down doubled-barreled shotgun on the shelf under the cash register and pointed to the hole in the ceiling over the pool table. "Johnny did that the last time his brother was in trouble. Me? I would have let the fight continue until Donnie learned his lesson."

By then, Bar None had been open for ten minutes, and we were interrupted by our first customer not related to the owner. Carl Linstadt, a silver-haired gentleman who held down the stool at the far end of the bar beneath the flickering Budweiser sign, settled into place and held up one finger. I popped open a bottle of Bud, carried it to him, and asked, "Why you drinking tonight?"

"I'm drinking to remember what I drank to forget last night." He upended the bottle and downed half of it. Then he asked, "Who's the new babe?"

Joyce hadn't been a babe since George H. W. Bush lost his re-election campaign, but from Carl's end of the calendar, she looked like a spring chicken. I introduced Carl and Joyce and left them to get acquainted while I moved to the other end of the bar to finish emptying off-brand tequila into a Jose Cuervo bottle.

The Bar None, a little place in the middle of fuck-all nowhere, opened at four today, like every afternoon, and our regulars drifted in over the next few hours, keeping Joyce and me busy enough that we didn't have much time to talk. She had worked at some of the best and some of the worst watering holes in the county, so she caught on quickly, and I never saw her shorting the till—a bad habit that had led to her predecessor's dismissal despite frequent after-hours hookups.

Carl Linstadt was the last customer to stagger out of the Bar None at two a.m. the following morning, leaving Joyce and me to cash out. Because we shared the single register, we both counted the cash and compared it to the total on the Z tape. Once satisfied, I put the cash in the safe, popped open a pair of Buds, and carried them to the table where Joyce sat. I handed one to her and said, "You did good."

"Like this every night?"

"Pretty much. Fridays and Saturdays are busy. That's when Johnny comes in and works with me behind the bar."

She looked around. "What about cleanup?"

A husband and wife with suspect green cards came in at eight every morning to give the place a thorough cleaning, so I told Joyce not to worry. "Finish your beer and head home. I'll lock up after you leave."

After Joyce drained her beer, I walked her to her car. Then I stood in the pool of yellow light from the single bulb over the rear door and watched as she drove away. Back inside, with front and rear doors dead-bolted, I returned to the office and opened the second, hidden safe. I drew out a thousand dollars in small bills, added them to that evening's take, and rejiggered the books to represent better sales than we'd actually had.

I did this three hundred and sixty-five days a year, skipping only February 29th every leap year, and I had been doing it ever since Johnny Brewster hired me to manage the Bar None. I never asked where the extra money came from, and he never once offered to tell me.

* * *

Johnny rolled into the Bar None at seven Friday evening and promptly joined me behind the stick. I introduced him to Joyce, but there wasn't time for casual conversation. We were busier than usual, and orders were already backing up, which is never a good thing in a place that relies on a steady stream of alcohol to keep customers satisfied.

With Johnny's help, we caught up and soon had everything operating like clockwork. We even managed to replace Carl's Budweiser bottles as he drained them, never leaving him without beer long enough to smack his lips. Business peaked around midnight and then slowly tapered off as the new day crept across the clock.

I wasn't prepared when Andrea showed up moments before closing time. Only Carl remained at the bar when she stepped up, took one look at Joyce, and said, "This your new piece of ass?"

"Excuse me?" Joyce said.

I stepped around the end of the bar and grabbed Andrea's arm. "What are you doing here?"

"Jesus, Tim," she said. "You threw me over for a two-bagger?"

"You need to leave."

"Not before I get my final paycheck."

When I fired Andrea, I told her I would mail her check. I hadn't yet. It was on the desk along with mine and Joyce's. I dragged her down the hall to the office, put the check in her hand, and shoved her backward out the rear door, directly into the arms of Donnie Brewster.

He had a canvas shopping bag in one hand and a blue woolen ski mask atop his head that he was in the process of pulling over his face. He stumbled, pushed Andrea to the ground, and pulled a Smith & Wesson from his waistband. He pointed it at me.

"What the fuck?"

"Back up," Donnie said. I could smell alcohol on his breath and knew he had been somewhere drinking himself stupid. He tugged at the ski mask, finally pulling it over his face. "Inside."

Andrea grabbed Donnie's leg, and he kicked her arm away.

I reached for the door, intending to pull it closed.

Donnie still had the revolver trained on me, and he shook his head. "Don't."

I stepped backward, Donnie stepped inside, and the wind blew the door closed behind him, leaving Andrea outside.

"The second safe," he said. "Open it."

"There's no—"

"Don't be a hero," he said. "It ain't your money."

He was right. It wasn't.

I backed into the office and opened the second safe. We'd had a recent delivery, and it contained $28,000. The regular safe contained another few thousand, and I put it all in his canvas shopping bag.

As Donnie stepped out of the office and was backing down the hallway, I heard a commotion out front, a commotion I later learned was Andrea telling Johnny about the robbery happening in the back half of the building.

Then Johnny stepped into the hall and leveled the bar's cut-down double-barreled shotgun at Donnie.

"Don't!" I shouted. "It's your—"

Johnny didn't hear me finish the sentence. The shotgun roared.

"—brother!"

Gutshot, Donnie fell backward against the door. The roar of the shotgun in such a confined space deafened me, but I saw Donnie squeeze the revolver's trigger twice before his weight falling against the door caused it to open behind him.

Both shots caught Johnny in the chest, and he dropped to the hallway floor.

Donnie fell through the open door to the ground outside, and I saw the canvas shopping bag open beside him, loose currency fluttering away in the wind. Joyce, Carl, and Andrea stepped into the hallway behind Johnny's body.

"The money!" I shouted, even though I couldn't hear myself. "Get the money!"

They saw where I was pointing, and soon, they were chasing hundreds of small bills across the parking lot, using their cell phone flashlights to aid them.

Several minutes later, when we were reasonably confident they had collected all the loose currency, I divided the money between them.

"Take it," I said, "and get the fuck out of here. We were already closed before this happened, and y'all don't know a damned thing about it."

They didn't argue, and a few minutes after the last car pulled away, I dialed 911.

The sheriff took my statement and made me repeat myself several dozen times, but I kept my story simple and consistent. Two men in ski masks had entered through the back of the Bar None and had forced me to open the safe. Johnny had been out front and had heard what was happening. He shot it out with the two robbers, killing one. The other got away. No, I didn't see the getaway car. No, I didn't know the dead man in the ski mask was the owner's brother. No, I didn't know how much was taken, but it couldn't have been much because we hadn't cashed out the till.

* * *

Several weeks later, I opened my apartment door to face two sharp-dressed men. They invited themselves inside and questioned me about my employment prospects.

I didn't have any.

They looked at each other, and then one said, "We have a bar in Texas that needs a manager."

THE MOB, THE MODEL, AND THE COLLEGE REUNION

By Melodie Campbell

The smell of stale beer met me at the door. You might think a place called The Tap Room sounds just like a small-town sleazy bar where they serve cheap brew in not very clean draft glasses, and you'd be right. My eyes tried to adjust for the low light and dark walls, but I knew the way through this dive, like the intervening years had never happened. Even the soles of my shoes still stuck to the floor. Designer shoes now, of course.

The Tap Room hadn't changed in three decades. Too bad I couldn't say the same for the rest of us. A quick sweep of the room told me that, for the most part, women fare better than men when it comes to the aging game. We gals owe a lot to hair dye, whereas most of the men in here would have no use for such a thing now.

I looked around for familiar faces. Mainly guys of a certain age, which was situation normal for such a place, although the gents here today hailed from Wall Street instead of Main Street. The room went quiet as the same gents stared at the two of us, trying to put names to faces. John was a known quantity, so of course, the eyes were on me.

I looked pretty good today, at least as good as it gets. Still warm enough in September for sleeveless, and the green jungle-print dress that clung to my body suited me, with a sheen that accentuated my curves. The deep V surplice neckline was trademark "di Marco," as my agent would say. My dark hair, still long, was behaving for once, even after the exercise it had been subjected to.

In any case, I had my share of attention at this moment. One man leaped up from a crappy wooden table and lunged our way. The body was the same as I remembered—several inches over six feet and lanky. The eyes still had that predatory look to them. I watched as they went wide with surprise.

"What the—"

I smiled sweetly. "Hi, Nigel," I said. "You remember John, of course."

"O'Connell. When the fuck did you two get together?" He didn't sound pleased, which would make John a tad smug. OK, downright gleeful.

Nigel had a few inches on John, yet I'd bet on the latter in a fight. Funny how that description came so quickly to me after all these years. I hadn't seen a prize fight since my mother's cousin left the ring and upended the family tradition of fixing. But that's the way I thought of John, as the man who would never back down. Good thing, with my family.

We had stopped several feet inside the doorway, where he had draped his strong arm across my shoulders. It was a clear sign of possession, and for once in my life, I didn't mind.

"Good to see you too, Lurch." John bared teeth like a crocodile. I left John's arm to give Nigel a swift hug.

"He rescued me from despair after my husband died two years ago." I said it quietly so that only Nigel would hear it clearly. "First on the scene, so to speak." That was a lie. Sometimes, it's smarter to lie, I've found.

Nigel grunted and pulled out a chair for me. I sat on it and watched as John pulled out another for himself.

"Taking Care of Business" was playing on the ancient sound system. I had to smile. Competition was the fuel that fed most of the men in my past, be it classmates or family. Nigel had tried to date me back at school when we had all been so young. Funny idiom, those innocent words "date me." A more accurate phrase would be "fuck the hell out of me," and Nigel had made it clear in the last few years that even though we were decades older, his goal hadn't changed.

"Guys, you remember Donna di Marco." Nigel waved a hand at the table. "Mark, Jeff, and Randy." Mark stood up and gave me a big grin. As John's golfing buddy, he'd been in on our romance, of course. Jeff and Randy just nodded and gaped. It made me wonder what was going through their minds. Best I not know, probably.

I moved to blow off the awkwardness. "Hiya, boys," I said with my biggest smile. "Long time no see. Can someone order me a Rickards Red? A person could die of thirst around here."

That picked up grins all around, and I prepared to watch the primeval antics of males beckoning for more beer. Then I sat back to listen to these past-their-best-before-date guys launch into their latest corporate exploits.

There are many different circles of hell, and for me, one is the college reunion. I hate class reunions. Weird shit always went down at these things, endless questions that threatened to expose my past, and for years I had avoided them. It was only to please John that I had agreed to go. We were a burning hot item, he explained. And we'd graduated in the same commerce class, so what excuse could I possibly give for not going with him?

Except I knew I shouldn't go. Call it clairvoyance, call it witchery, call it the old Sicilian evil eye. Whatever you want to label it, I had it, and the Fates were telling me this was not a place for me to be today.

My business class had few women in it, and not many classmates took their wives along. The testosterone level at these five-year get-togethers was off the chart. One-upmanship played at championship levels, just like back in the seminar rooms. Every freaking person had letters pasted after their name—CEO, CFO, COO—whereas I was merely a youngish widow with a posh waterfront condo, a sketchy past, and an on-and-off-again modeling career.

Speaking of which, I could see Nigel staring down the cleavage that balanced the ample hips below. If I wasn't careful, soon I'd be modeling plus-size.

My bottle of beer arrived without a glass. It was that sort of place. Damn the calories. I slugged back half of it in one go.

"I thought you only used to date blondes," Nigel said to John with a sly glance to me.

"*Fanculo*," I shot back clearly and precisely.

"What?" said Nigel.

"It means 'the hell you say' in Italian," I replied. It doesn't.

"Didn't know what I was missing," said John. "She's whiskey in a teacup." A slow smile spread across his face. I knew that smile, and I knew what he was thinking, as we had just passed the last few hours in a biblical way. Yes, I said hours, and I felt just peachy. But a girl doesn't talk about those things in mixed company.

John is a great guy. I don't know how I missed him in first year. Oh, yes, I do. Much easier to sleaze free beers at the Clark Hall pub, which was full of lonely engineers eager for the sight of anything female. I eventually married one of them.

But as I said, John rocks. We'd been dating—haha, euphemism—for five months, and I was pretty sure I wanted to hitch my wagon to his BMW. From what I have discerned, he has only one fault, and that is IBS. *Europe from Toilet to Toilet* is the book he might write someday. This will explain why he was in the can when the lone gunman busted in.

I always try to get a seat facing the door. If that isn't possible, I look for a corner, as per the family training. Just like the old cowboys in Western films, I like to see what's coming at me.

In this case, I didn't like what I saw. My size-'em-up instinct immediately went into overdrive: *five foot eight, 145 pounds soaking wet, weak shoulders, easy peasy lemon squeezy for takedown.* I was the first to see him push through the doorway and possibly the only one to instantly recognize his lamentable vocation. Kid was a textbook loser, no more than a punk. His brown hair was curly, his dark eyes wild above the surgical mask left over from Covid times. Funny, that. Little did we guess what use those masks could be put to after the pandemic.

Bugger, he had a real gun; now that just wasn't fair. I hadn't thought to bring one. In his other hand, he held one of those reusable shopping bags. I squinted to read the words on it. "Bruno's Fruit Market." Jesus. My uncle's store! He wouldn't appreciate the advertising.

I waited wearily for the television cliché, for him to say "this is a stickup—nobody move."

He used a variant. "Everyone put your wallets on the table, and no one will get hurt."

"Slay me now," I muttered. "No one says that in real life."

For a few seconds, no one moved. Nobody said a word. "Money for Nothing" wailed away on the sound system, filling the silence with irony. Then, gradually, hands went into pockets, and wallets and billfolds came out onto tables.

"Do you want our watches, too?" said a shaky tenor voice from another table.

"Ian, shut up!" said a companion.

"Oh, for...," I started. "He doesn't want your watches. No one wears watches anymore except you guys." Jeesh. Get with the century.

For a moment, I wondered what to do. As the lone female, I had a large purse, not a wallet. The one thing I did not want to do was open it up and pick through all the crap. Not yet, anyway. So, I turned to the robber and said, "Would you like me to gather up all the wallets and bring them close to you?"

He hesitated, seeming to weigh up the idea. Then he pointed to the counter beside the cash register. "Put them in this here bag." He put the shopworn thing down on the counter and gestured with the gun.

It was a Walther, I could see now. Hardly a gun at all. Really, things were deteriorating in the grab-and-run trade. I slung my purse across my body and rose to my feet.

Nobody stopped me. Not a single man said, "Donna, you're putting yourself in harm's way. Let me do that." Nope, the testosterone level in the room had dropped to bunny poop. No heroes at this table now that John had left the room. And it was a good thing he wasn't there because I had no doubt he would have put his foot in it. And that wouldn't do at all because I had a plan.

I moved from table to table, collecting all the wallets and billfolds from the Wall Street buccaneers. When my hands were full, I placed the crap on the counter and went back to collect more. I took care to look into the eyes of the men I knew from way back. I smiled sweetly, watching them flinch as I did so. Too bad none of them had any real cojones. They could take care of business, sure, but it took an average-size gal from the wrong side of the tracks to take care of *this* business.

On my final trip back to the counter, I looked straight at the gunman. He was watching me with equal intensity, and the hand holding the pistol was shaking slightly. I got this creepy feeling of déjà vu. But that was silly because I was pretty sure I'd never done a job in a dive like this before. With effort, I jerked myself back to the plan.

"Oh! I feel dizzy. I think I'm going to faint." I let myself fall so that one arm clung to the bar, and the other flung out and gripped the gunman's left arm.

"*Porca vacca!*" said the gunman, shifting his weight to keep us upright.

That voice! That expression! I got this cold feeling. Really cold. Like I was back in the cradle of the family, and that cradle was about to fall from the goddamn trees.

"Tony? Is that you?" I whispered to the gunman in Italian.

The grip shifted. "Aunt Donna?" said a strained voice in the same dialect. "What the fuck are you doing here?"

"Language!" I barked.

"Sorry," said Tony.

"Shit, Tony. Uncle Vince know you're doing this?"

"Jesus Christ!" muttered the gunman. "You can't tell anyone."

"Oh, for heaven's sake." Why me? Why the freaking hell did I have to be born into this family?

"What's she saying?" came a voice from the floor.

"I'm trying to talk him down," I announced in English.

This would have to be quick. People were watching and starting to whisper, and I couldn't go on speaking Italian forever. "Shut up and let me get you out of this," I hoarsely whispered to Tony. "Just follow along."

Tony stood like a stone, with about the same intelligence.

"Oh, *please* don't take me hostage!" I cried in English, throwing myself back against him.

It took a moment for him to catch on. "You're coming with me," he said, deepening his voice. I felt his left arm close around my chest.

"Watch the hands," I whispered sternly in Italian.

"Sorry," he whispered back, obviously not sorry.

"Nobody follow us and she won't get hurt," Tony announced to everyone, waving the Walther for good measure.

"Don't forget the bag," I whispered in Italian.

"Shit," he said, looking confused. With his left arm around my chest and the gun in his right hand, he was out of arms.

I gritted my teeth. It was pathetic, really. As usual, I had to think of everything, and it wasn't even my job. "I'll carry it! Don't hurt me!" I pleaded. I pushed away from him, picked up the bag of loot from the counter, and fell back, waited for him to reposition his arm around me. It was a bit of a monkey show. Good thing the onlookers were all old guys who were half blind.

Together we wiggled toward the back entrance, Tony trying to look like he was forcing me and me trying to keep his hands off my boobs.

"Please don't follow us," I pleaded. It was a pointless request. Not a single body in that room had any intention of breaking rank. If lemmings could sit in chairs—lethargic lemmings with no aversion to the color yellow—they couldn't do better than to ape this gang.

The Beatles were pounding out "You Really Got a Hold on Me" on the sound system. We kept up the act, me whimpering convincingly, him growling like a demented pug, all the way out the push door and down the concrete steps. I shook off his arm as soon as we were on flat ground and shoved the bag at him.

"A *Walther*, Tony? Where did you get that useless excuse for a pistol?

"Some guy—"

I threw up my hands. There was always "some guy." "For Gawd sake, it's embarrassing, that's what it is. Get yourself a real gun…a Glock like the rest of us."

"Sorry about that, Aunt Donna," he said sheepishly. "Didn't want to go to the family."

I did a quick inspection of the area, noting the pile of cigarette butts close to the stairs. No smokers outside at the moment, which was a good thing, because I wasn't finished.

I pointed my finger right at his nose and kept going. "And about that. Are you goddamn crazy, going freelance?" I yelled in Italian. "Do you know what the aunts would do to you if they knew?" If you think the men in our family are crazy, wait until you meet the women.

"Sorry, Aunt Donna," he said again, transferring the bag from one hand to another. "Blew through my allowance at school. Needed some ready cash, and I knew that the Tap would be full of those homecoming geezers—"

"Can the excuses until later. Let's get out of here." I scanned the immediate vicinity, then walked farther down the back laneway, which appeared to be empty. "Wait a minute. Where's your car?"

"Uh—don't have a car." He sounded sheepish.

I stopped and turned, then said slowly and precisely, as if talking to a toddler, "You didn't bring a getaway car?"

He shrugged. "Brought a bike."

"A motorcycle?" Ducatis were big in the family. Couldn't see one of those, either.

"Nope. A bicycle."

My temperature shot up about ten degrees.

"A getaway bicycle? What is this, preschool?" I flung my arms. "How are we going to blow this pop stand on a bicycle? Me on the handlebars?" Jesus, how were they training burglars these days? I'm sorry, but Uncle Vince was going to hear about this, freelance job or not. He needed to take better control of this generation.

"Uh oh," said Tony. He then commenced running around in circles like a chicken minus a head. "It's not here!"

"What's not here?" Without a car, we'd have to make a run for it. Or at least, I would. He could take the bike. But I was wearing heels, dammit. Of all the rotten days to dress like a lady…

"The bike!" yelled Tony, throwing the bag of loot to the ground. "Some fucking prick stole my bike!"

"Stole..." Now, he had my full attention. I rolled my eyes in disbelief and launched into lecture mode.

"You nincompoop! You didn't even lock it? Didn't they teach you anything?" I continued yelling and flapping my arms. "Flaming hell, Tony, did it not occur to you that you might not be the only thief on the block?"

Jesus, the young are trusting.

There was a suspicious silence. He pawed the pavement with the toe of his boot. "Couldn't lock it. Had to break the lock."

Of course, he did. I whacked my hand to my forehead. Then I aimed for his head and made it in one.

"Ouch!" he yelled, leaping back.

"Where'd you steal it from?" I said.

"Back of the Seven-Eleven. An hour ago."

I moaned dramatically. I *knew* this day was going to be a shit show. Why didn't I listen to myself? Dweebs swiping bicycles, only to have them re-stolen an hour later. Uncle Vince would have a coronary. First rule of burglary is to keep your booty close. Did nobody teach these kids anything? Or were they flipping through cell phones the whole time instead of listening to the veterans?

Pathetic. A complete lack of ethics in the younger generation, that's what it is. I blame the internet.

"Can't even report it stolen to the cops," Tony grumbled.

"Report it—" I was starting to hyperventilate. "If I end up being interviewed by the cops because of this—" I didn't need the cops looking into my background. Which was pretty much the same as Tony's background. And if word got out on the street that I'd engineered my own hostage-taking minus a car, we'd be the laughingstock of the crime world.

Thank God I had managed to get Tony out of the bar, at least. No worries about my old classmates risking their butts to rescue me, as predicted. I could imagine them on their phones, frantically contacting financial institutions to report those stolen cards. Taking care of numero uno.

This hostage thing could have been a good plan under the circumstances. But with no getaway car, I had to think fast. We could both sneak away in opposite directions, maybe. And I could turn up later unharmed. Yes, that seemed to be the best option. I'm pretty sure it would have worked.

Except the door burst open, "Rumble in Brighton" blared from the indoor speakers, and John charged out.

"Let go of her!" he yelled, leaping the steps in one jump.

I stood like a dope with my mouth open. Oh, my Gawd, John was going to be a hero. "Son of a bitch," I mumbled in Italian. "Tony, hit him with the gun handle."

"Huh?" said Tony, equally stunned.

"*Cazzo!*" I said, still in Italian, knocking the gun out of his hand. "Do I have to do everything in this family?"

"What?" said Tony as John charged him.

John hit him like a steamroller, and down they went. The bag went flying. John was bigger by a country mile, but Tony was surprisingly wily and managed to get a knee up where it shouldn't. I cringed, hoping there wasn't too much damage. I had a personal stake in that package.

This was turning into a first-class street fight. I let them roll around for a while, stirring up the dusty gravel, just to make it look good. Then John got in a good punch, and when it looked like he was going to pulverize the kid, I moved in fast.

"Look out, John—he's got a Taser!" I yelled. Of course, he didn't. I did. I pulled the old-school Taser from my purse and shot John from behind as cleanly as I could, exactly where my cousins had trained us: make the body drop but do the least damage. John collapsed with a small "eeep." I caught his arm as he fell to ease his way to the ground. We both kind of slid down in a slow-motion heap, me still holding the Taser and landing with a thud on my butt.

A few moments passed. The Taser slipped neatly back into my purse. I put my head down on John's chest to check for a heartbeat. Still ticking. Then, I scanned the area for spectators. Still clear.

"Pick up the gun, but leave the bag and get out of here," I hissed at Tony.

My nephew hesitated. "Please don't tell Mom," he pleaded. Then he took off like a track star.

I watched him clear the corner and disappear. I shuffled over on my bum, dragging my shoulder bag along with me, and reached with both arms to cradle John's head in my lap. Just in time. The door flew open again, and a bevy of class bozos spilled out.

Nigel led the pack. He sauntered over, bent his lanky frame a mite, and spared a glance down at John. "He dead?" Nigel said hopefully.

"He'll be OK," I said to the assembly. "Got hit with a Taser, that's all." I leaned down to kiss John's forehead. The moans stopped, and his gray eyes opened.

"Don't try to talk yet," I cooed to him. Damn straight, he better not talk. I had to get my story straight first.

A crowd had gathered around me. Not the sort of crowd that gently lifts you off the ground. More the sort of crowd that gawks.

I figured it was time to take charge. "Did you see it? John took down the gunman by himself!" I cried out.

I watched the others take in the scene. The disturbed gravel. John, on the ground. The bag of stolen wallets and billfolds lying close by. Me, with my dress hiked up and top awry, showing a little too much. Purse hanging from my side. I reached for it and closed the zipper.

Low chatter filled the air. I ignored it and instead looked down at John to give him my most adoring smile. "You really are my hero."

His face twisted in confusion. He tried for a feeble grin and made to sit up.

"Someone help me here," I said to the men. Mark rushed forward to help John sit up. The rest of them set about pawing through the shopping bag of wallets like piranhas in a feeding frenzy.

"Did you see it?" I said breathlessly. This was where sleight of hand came in. They hadn't seen it, of course. But I'd taken Psych 100 back in the day. If I gave a good enough story, many would chime in and retell it as if they had.

I launched into a good-enough story.

John watched with dazed eyes as I related his heroics. Even I was impressed by what he hadn't done.

A few minutes later, the rest of the guys trickled back into the bar. Mark paused at the door, looking back to see if we were coming. When we didn't move, he flicked the doorstop down to keep the thing open for us.

John and I sat on the warm pavement, my arm still around him. "How are you feeling?" I asked him.

He put a hand up to his temple. "My head hurts."

I nodded in womanly concern. "Now you know why I hate class reunions," I said darkly. "I told you this was a bad idea."

The sound system belted out "Witchy Woman."

ROOM OF ICE

By Stephen Ross

Tim felt the knife in his jeans pocket. A switchblade. He'd bought it with the five pounds an aunt had given him for his fifteenth birthday. She'd told him to get a haircut. His forty-fifth birthday was in a week, and he still had the knife. It had served him well. A lad should never be wanting for a weapon when a kerfuffle was to be had.

He took another mouthful of his beer. It was just after eight o'clock, a Tuesday night in November 1999. He was seated at an old wooden table in the Fox and Hounds, Dulwich, London. The beer was cold in his throat, the glass wet with condensation. The room was warm with people and an open fire that gently cooked a pair of logs. Music played, piped in over dusty speakers bolted to the wall near the ceiling. Background jazz.

Finally, the old man walked in. He nodded a hello to the landlord, who sported a walrus mustache and who was pulling a pint for a chatty Liverpool bird. There were eight drinkers in the pub, not counting Tim and the old man. Eight drinkers huddling in the warmth from the winter's night outside. Quiet conversation, a few laughs.

The old man took off his coat. He slung it over the back of the chair at the table between Tim's and the fire. He wore a powder-blue shirt and brown slacks. He looked different up close. Seen from across the street the previous few days, the old man had appeared sprightly. From five feet away, he appeared crumpled. A face of creases, thinning gray hair. His eyes encircled by sagging red skin.

He sat down and smoothed the wrinkles out of his shirt sleeves. His wristwatch was the only sign of wealth that never came from Woolworth. The landlord brought him a glass of ruby port, his usual. They exchanged a few pleasantries, and the landlord left him to it. He sipped on the port. His fingers were bony. His nails clipped.

Tim felt the outline of the knife in his pocket. He studied the aged skin of the old man's neck.

The old man noted the man seated at the next table.

Tim had a confident, knowing smile and blue eyes. He was middle-aged, chubby, with a bald head and dark, unshaved jaw. Few of his checked-shirt buttons were done up; there was a faded *Star Wars* T-shirt. The overshirt's sleeves were rolled up, making part of a tattoo visible on his right bicep. He looked the type of fellow you wouldn't want to pick a fight with.

The old man nodded a polite acknowledgment.

"I know who you are," Tim said.

The old man nodded. "Yes, I am William Evers, but I haven't been William Evers for some time. I quit the business a few years ago."

"I know that was your acting name. I know your real name is Percy Badger."

"Indeed, it is."

Tim leaned toward the old man. He spoke in a whisper. "You're going to give me ten thousand pounds."

Percy Badger studied the younger man. "I haven't seen you in here before."

Tim sat back. "I'm only staying the night." He pointed upward.

Percy nodded. "One of the landlord's comfy rooms, no doubt."

"I've seen most of your films," Tim said. "I like the old Hammer horror ones you did back in the fifties and sixties."

Percy smiled. The gruff man was a fan. "Those were the days," he said. "I did four Hammer horror movies. I never got top billing. I was always the young man. The leading lady's brother or the office clerk sent to investigate an insurance claim."

"I liked *Room of Ice*."

Percy glowed. "That was my favorite. Technically, I had the lead, but Chris Lee was in it. My star never shone as brightly as his. He's still working too. I heard he's off down to New Zealand to do a film of *Lord of the Rings*."

Tim shook his head. "That's a book, innit?"

"Yes. I did a radio adaptation twenty years ago for the BBC. For the life of me, I can't remember who I played: Bilbo or Gandalf."

"Whatever happened to Karen Peak?" Tim asked.

Percy stared at Tim and put down his glass of port. His smile evaporated. A strain of seriousness appeared in the skin around his eyes. "I don't know what happened to her."

"She was an attractive actress."

Percy nodded. "I haven't heard her name for many years. She disappeared, you know."

"Yeah. I read all about it on the internet a month ago. She used to be your girlfriend."

The old man nodded. "She was. For a time."

"She disappeared in 1959."

"That sounds about right."

"The year you made *Room of Ice*."

"Was it?"

"Yeah. The internet has all the information."

Percy shook his head. "My memory isn't what it used to be. I've asked my doctor about it, but he only offers me half-truths. Maybe the other half is just too bad to know. Karen was in the first Hammer horror movie I did. I played her brother. Peter Cushing had her locked up in his laboratory in Kent and was injecting her with monkey glands."

"Karen Peak was also in *Room of Ice*," Tim said.

"Was she?" Percy shook his head. "I don't remember her in that one."

Tim insisted, "You told me she was."

Percy studied the stranger sitting at the table next to his. "Do I know you?"

"In a way. I was in *Room of Ice*."

"Really?"

"Yeah."

"I don't remember you."

"You wouldn't. I was a kid. Five years old. I was only in one scene with you and had no dialogue. My name wasn't even in the credits. I was one of the two little boys."

Percy shook his head. He didn't appear to remember.

"My mother worked for the catering firm at Hammer," Tim said. "They needed two small boys to play the children of the villagers. My mother grabbed me and the boy who lived next to us. She got us into the picture."

Percy sat back and drank some more port. He didn't take his eyes off Tim. "This pleasant little meeting of ours on this pleasant Tuesday evening didn't happen by accident, did it?"

Tim shook his head. "I've been planning this."

Tim drank another mouthful of his beer. "I never saw *Room of Ice* at the end of 1959, when it came out. It had an X rating. To be honest, I forgot about it. I grew up. Started an apprenticeship as an electrician. I got into trouble, so I joined the merchant navy and went to sea. Twenty years, I did, on the waves. Rose to third mate. Sailed around the world many a time. And then I got into trouble. I didn't see *Room of Ice* for the first time until a year ago in a hotel room in Spain."

"Did you like it?" Percy asked.

"Yeah. I said I did. And there was something about the film that made me remember you."

"What was that?"

Tim finished his beer. "I have a couple of things upstairs I want to show you."

"What have you got upstairs?"

"I have a prop from *Room of Ice*. I'd like you to autograph it."

Percy nodded. The gruff seaman was a fan with memorabilia.

* * *

Tim led the way up a narrow set of creaky stairs with 1970s carpet.

Percy followed with his coat over one arm and his glass of port in his hand.

"Are you a collector?"

"What do you mean?" Tim asked.

"Do you collect movie memorabilia?"

"No."

Tim led the way down the passageway to his room. He unlocked the door, and they went in.

Tim's hotel room was modest but tidy—a double bed, a dresser, two wooden chairs, a twenty-four-inch television set on caster wheels, and a window with a view out to the street in front of the pub. It was raining. The streetlights glistened in the dark.

Tim shut the door. He went over to the bed and picked up the dirty yellow object that lay on it. It was big but lightweight, three feet long, with a fat end that tapered down to a thin end.

"It's an icicle," Tim said, presenting it to Percy.

Percy recognized it at once. "It's one of the stalagmites." He laid his coat on the bed and stood his glass of port on the dresser. He took the stalagmite and studied it with delight. "The whole roof of the set was covered in the things. We were always bumping our heads into them. They're made from papier-mâché." He laughed. "We all stole one at the end of filming."

"I found it clearing out my mother's attic," Tim said. "I remembered the yellow—all the icicles were painted bright yellow."

Percy nodded. "The film was shot in black and white. Yellow looks like a brighter, more vivid white on black-and-white film stock."

Tim handed Percy a ballpoint pen.

"Where would you like me to sign it?"

"On the base."

Percy tipped up the stalagmite. "What's your name?"

"Tim Cleare."

Percy wrote a short, cheerful message to Tim and signed it with his stage name. He carefully placed the object back on the bed.

Tim pulled out his knife. He flicked the switch, and the blade spat out of the handle with a dull clank. "Don't raise your voice," he said. "Don't scream. Sit in that chair by the window."

Percy didn't blink. He didn't say a word. His two wide-open eyes stared at the knife blade. He sat in the chair.

"Don't get out of the chair," Tim said. "Don't try for the door. I can kill you in one second."

Percy nodded.

Tim unplugged the aerial cable from the back of the television set and then wheeled it across the room to the length of its power cable. He parked it three feet in front of Percy, facing him. He then went and fetched the duffel bag that stood on the floor in the corner.

He never let go of the knife.

He opened the bag and took out a laptop computer. He stood the laptop on the top of the television set and lifted the screen. He turned it on, and it powered up. He took out a cable from the bag. He plugged one end into the laptop's VGA socket and the other into the video-in socket in the back of the television.

"What are you doing?" Percy asked.

"We're going to watch *Room of Ice*."

"Why?"

"Because after we've finished watching it, you're going to give me ten thousand pounds."

"Why in the Dickens would I do that?"

Tim turned the television on. A screen of static came to life.

"Because if you don't, I'll kill you."

Percy nodded; he understood. The gruff man was twice his size and had a knife.

Tim selected the AV channel on the television set's front control panel. The television screen changed to a bright red. He moved the pointing stick at the center of the laptop's keyboard and then clicked some buttons. At once, the black-and-white logo for Columbia Pictures appeared. The movie's soundtrack, a mournful violin, came out of the laptop's tiny speaker.

Percy watched as the camera panned across a rugged black-and-white coastline.

Tim dragged the other chair across the room and put it next to the television set, facing Percy, and he sat in it.

The title *Room of Ice* appeared.

Tim studied Percy; his eyes were on the screen. The camera tracked up a lonely road toward a large Gothic house. It stood on a cliff next to a rugged coastline. Waves crashed on the rocks beneath it. The names of the principal cast appeared—Christopher Lee, William Evers.

"My scene appears twenty minutes in," Tim said proudly.

Percy nodded.

Tim reached into his jeans pocket and pulled out a packet of cigarettes and a plastic cigarette lighter.

He never let go of the knife.

He lit a cigarette.

"I hung around the set for a week," Tim said. "No school. It was a great lark. Because I was a kid, I guess, they let me wander anywhere I wanted. One day, I wandered into your caravan, and I saw you strangle Karen Peak."

Percy stared at Tim.

"All the stars of the film had little caravans for dressing rooms," Tim said. "There was a row of them behind the studio building. I walked up the little steps, opened the door, and walked into yours. I didn't know whose caravan it was. I didn't know anyone was in there. I was looking for one of those little Bush transistor radios to steal. I saw you strangling Karen Peak. She was on her knees on the floor, and you were standing over her, gripping her neck."

Percy shook his head. "I don't remember this."

"You saw me and yelled. You yelled at me to get out. So, I left."

Tim stood up and fetched the ashtray from the top of the chest of drawers. He sat down again. He put the ashtray on the floor at his feet.

"I didn't know at the time who you were or what you were doing. I was five. That night, I asked my mother who the woman with the big blue eyes and big blond hair was. She told me Karen Peak, and that she was a famous actress. The next day, you came and found me. You did. You took me to one side and told me that you and Karen, the actress, were rehearsing a scene for the movie. You said that movies were all about pretending. Nothing is real, you said. Do you remember telling me that?"

Percy shook his head.

"I was in my thirties before I realized what I'd actually seen you do."

"I remember we were always cautious when there were children in our movies," Percy said. "We were making horror pictures at Hammer. Some of them were quite gruesome."

"Karen Peak isn't in this film," Tim said. He glanced at the screen. A much younger Percy was knocking on the door of the old house. He looked intent. He wore an Edwardian suit and clutched a sheath of papers. "I've watched the film nine times. Her name isn't in the credits, and there's no one in the thing who even remotely looks like her. There's no scene where you strangle anyone. No one strangles *anyone*."

Percy shivered, as if ice cubes had been inserted into his veins. "Good God, man! You think I murdered her?"

Tim nodded.

"Is that what this is all about?"

"Yeah, it's all about you giving me ten thousand quid."

"They cut her scenes," Percy exploded. "I remember now. That's why I couldn't recall if she was in the movie or not. We shot scenes. She was meant to be in it, but after her disappearance, the studio cut her character and all her footage."

Tim stared at Percy; his confidence had been dented.

"Her character's name was Kathleen," Percy said. "After she disappeared, the plot was changed. They rewrote large blocks of the script. Scripts change all the time. Not everything filmed winds up in the final movie."

"What's your proof?" Tim asked.

Percy threw it back at him. "What's *your* proof I murdered anyone? A childhood memory from almost half a century ago and some things you read about on the internet?"

Tim had no answer. The confident smile he'd started the evening with had vanished.

"You want proof?" Percy snapped. "I still have the script, the original script. I kept all my old scripts. I keep everything. I can show you. I can show you the scene. Karen meant everything to me. She was the love of my life. I went off the rails after she disappeared. I didn't work for nearly two years."

"I saw you strangle her," Tim said, clinging to his memory.

"You saw two actors rehearsing. Come back to my house. I'll show you the damn script. I'll show you the physical pages. You can hold them in your hands. And then you can get this lunacy out of your head."

***

Percy drove his late-model Audi through Dulwich in the night. Tim admired the smoothness of the ride, the dashboard's elegant finish, the glow of its lights. The windscreen wipers silently swiped light rain. Few other cars were on the road.

"Why do you need ten thousand pounds?" Percy asked.

"I have some debts," Tim answered. "Some hard-arses from the North are leaning on me."

"How did you get into that mess?"

"It happens."

"My house is five minutes away. Tell me."

Tim shrugged. "After I left the merchant navy, I started cleaning cars for a rental company in Hackney. And then, about six months ago, me and my friend came up with this deal where he'd rent a car, drive over to the continent, pick up some, you know, chemicals that are on the government's prohibited imports list."

"Heroin?"

Tim shook his head. "Cocaine. He'd hide it inside the car. He'd come back over the channel, drop the car off, and I'd clean it." He stressed a point. "We didn't deal the stuff. We just took the money upfront from the dealers and did the purchase and the transit. It was becoming a nice little earner."

"What happened?"

"Two weeks ago, my friend got caught at Folkestone coming off the ferry. Sniffer dogs. Damn things crawled right under the car."

"Bad luck."

"It happens."

"I could lend you a few bob," Percy said. "I couldn't go to the full ten thousand, but I could help you out."

Tim looked across at Percy. He had no idea what to say.

"Instead of a life of crime, you should be collecting movie memorabilia," Percy advised. "There's a fortune to be made in that."

They stopped and waited for a set of traffic lights to change.

"I recognized there was a market way back in the early 1960s," Percy said. "People love things from movies. Everyone wants a piece of the artifice. So, I started keeping things—costumes, props, scripts, anything I could walk away with. You know, they tailor-made several dozen shirts for Sean Connery when he did that first James Bond picture. And afterward, they just gave them all away to the crew, who wore them to work, and then probably just threw them away when they wore out. Imagine if you had one of those shirts today in mint condition? People pay absurd amounts of money for that kind of thing. That stalactite of yours back at the hotel is probably worth at least five hundred pounds. More, now that I've autographed it."

Tim was impressed. He'd had no idea. "Where would I sell something like that?"

"On the internet. People in America, they're the best buyers. They'll pay through the nose for memorabilia, especially from older movies."

Percy looked across at Tim and smiled. "I think I might have something in my collection that might help you out. An old prop that might make you a few pennies and maybe even give you a few spare."

"Is it from *Room of Ice*?"

"No, *Star Wars*."

That caught Tim's attention.

"They filmed that here at Elstree in '76. I had a week's work on it with Peter. He played Tarkin. We're in the Death Star scenes."

Tim nodded lovingly. He could remember every line of their dialogue.

Percy's Audi turned into Hambledon Place.

They drove along the leafy street, slowed, and turned in through a gateway.

They drove up a cobblestone driveway and parked in front of a stately two-floor pale-brick house. Its white wooden window frames were trimmed with red bricks. It reminded Tim of the houses he saw in a copy of *Country Life* once while waiting for the dentist.

* * *

Tim sat in a fat leather armchair and smoked. He watched Percy go through every book, film script, and wad of paper on his bookcases—it was a room of dark wood bookcases, with three leather chairs, a fireplace, and a drinks trolley. Tim had never sat in a library inside someone's house before. Percy's library was bigger than his bedsit in Shoreditch.

Tim wondered if Percy had read all the books.

"The memory is a curious thing," Percy said. "It so easily plays tricks on us."

Tim couldn't argue. "Have you read all these books?"

"Most of them."

Percy gave up the search. "I was sure it was here in the library. It must be up in the attic with the others."

They climbed the stairs to the second floor. The staircase walls were lined with framed photographs of Percy. Each picture was of him and another famous actor or other luminary. Tim recognized a few: Julie Christie, Rita Tushingham, Mick Jagger. Some he didn't know. One was of Percy and Alfred Hitchcock standing and smiling together at Tower Bridge.

"Were you in *Frenzy*?" Tim asked. He had seen a few Hitchcocks.

"Yes. I was. One of those blink-and-you'd-miss-it parts. A fake nose and wig, and three lines of dialogue."

They went up a narrow flight of stairs from the second floor, through a door, and into the attic. The attic was ten times the size of Tim's bedsit. It was windowless and dimly lit and packed full. It was a warehouse of cinema. Costumes hung on racks, movie scripts and books filled shelves, and props of all descriptions lay cluttered: a bicycle, a policeman's helmet, a sundial, a zebra-skin rug, a bust of a Roman emperor, a mannequin wearing a red kimono. And, in the corner, Tim spied another of the yellow icicles from *Room of Ice*.

"Every time I run short of cash," Percy whispered confidentially, "I flog a few pieces off. I do so using a false identity." He grinned. "To hell with the taxman. He's got his filthy mitts on enough of my lucre over the years."

He and Tim traded knowing nods.

Percy picked up a large, solid-looking black cross. It was a Latin cross, two feet long, a foot across, made of plain wood, with no ornamentation. "This is one of my favorite props. I doubt I'll ever sell it."

"What's it from?"

"Ken Russell's *The Devils*."

"I never saw it."

"It was a good movie, if somewhat offbeat. Typical Ken Russell. Vanessa Redgrave and Oliver Reed were the leads."

"What's this thing you've got from *Star Wars*?" Tim asked. He was eager to find out.

Percy smiled. There were several large trunks lined up against one of the walls. "Come and see."

He opened one of the trunks. Inside lay a bunch of clothes neatly folded and stowed in plastic bags.

"No, this is just costumes." He hesitated, looked around, and then said, "I think it's that one."

He went over to a green trunk and unlatched it. He lifted the lid. "Yes, this is the one."

Tim walked up.

"How about that?" Percy asked proudly. "What do you reckon that's worth?"

Tim looked in the trunk. At first, he didn't recognize the large object wrapped in plastic. When he realized exactly what it was—the mummified body of a woman with blond hair—he also realized hers wasn't the only mummified body in the trunk. He didn't have time to count them before Percy struck him over the head with the wooden cross from the Ken Russell movie.

***

The next night, after eight o'clock, Percy Badger walked into the Fox and Hounds, Dulwich. He took off his coat and took his usual seat at the table by the fire. The landlord brought him his regular glass of port.

TWO FOR ONE

By Art Taylor

Standing at the stove, Sandra pretended that her boyfriend, Wylie, was admiring the curve of her hips, but she knew he wasn't. At the table, he studied his *Dine-A-Mate* book instead while she sliced prosciutto to sneak into his eggs. She'd tell him it was bacon—*a bacon-and-cheese omelet, just like you like it.* And at worst, he'd tell her, *Tastes like you oversalted, hon.* Slowly, without him knowing it, she would expand his horizons, spice up their lives, and this Sunday morning routine would change—all their routines, even Wylie himself.

"How about Mexican?" Wylie flipped through the paperback-sized book—half-price offers, special discounts, scattered freebies. "I'm in the mood for something spicy."

Sandra laughed inside at the irony.

Dine-A-Mate is Dine-A-Mite! the book's cover announced. *Thousands of dollars in savings! A year of opportunities awaits!* Wylie was a believer. The book had earned a permanent place on the table at her apartment.

"Look," he said, "here's a two-for-one at Shanghai Garden."

"Shanghai is Chinese, not Mexican," Sandra said.

Mexican and Chinese were Wylie's idea of exotic cuisine—the extent of his culinary horizons. In the next room, the morning news droned on the TV, and the Sunday paper sat on the sofa, an after-brunch read, a weekly try at the crossword. For nearly as long as they'd dated, this had been their routine: Wylie spending Saturday night at her place, Sandra cooking brunch the next morning, the TV on, the paper standing by. Early on, Sandra had invited Wylie over for a home-cooked meal one Wednesday, and that quickly became custom as well. She learned quickly that deviations from routine didn't sit well with Wylie, leaving him unmoored, irritable, and tense.

As Sandra flipped the omelet, she felt irritable, too, wishing for something different, *anything* different. A romantic bed-and-breakfast some spur-of-the-moment Saturday, an extravagant champagne brunch one Sunday with Wylie feeding her strawberries, or for Wylie to stand up right now, slide against her, wrap his arms around her, send one single meal off in some new direction.

"Chinese can be spicy, that's all I meant," Wylie said—his tone clearly stung. "Either way, a good deal."

Sandra knew he'd add that. Each of their twice-a-week "nights out" was now motivated by some new bargain, scheduled around the coupon's stipulations: Thursday night only, 6 p.m. seating only, take-out only.

"Another coupon down," Wylie announced after each dinner.

And it wasn't just food. They'd also gone bowling at four different alleys, visited the planetarium, played twilight golf under giant spotlights—each outing carefully curated, purposefully planned.

"Wylie," she'd asked him months before, driving home from an afternoon at the regional speedway, "where do you *want* to go? Where are *we* going?"

And she had watched his grip tighten around the steering wheel, heard his heavy sigh.

"Shanghai's fine," she said finally, giving the pan a quick jiggle, sliding the omelet onto the plate. "Whatever you want will be fine."

* * *

Sandra worked as a receptionist at a law firm in downtown Raleigh, and on Friday mornings, she browsed through the newspaper between calls, looking for new ways to lure Wylie away from *Dine-A-Mate*. In recent weeks, she had been drawn repeatedly to an ad for the new Royal International

Buffet.

Alaskan King Crab Legs! Peking Duck! London Broil! Chilean Sea Bass!—each entrée was encased in a starburst. Drawings of the Eiffel Tower and the Taj Mahal, the Leaning Tower of Pisa, and the Golden Gate Bridge stood in each corner of the ad. *Visit the world on our 70-foot-long buffet! Chefs of all nationalities! Kids buffet for tiny travelers! Elegance and sophistication!*

Elegance and sophistication? She knew better. A buffet was a buffet. But that wasn't the point.

"I saw this new restaurant," she told Wylie on their regular Wednesday. "Want to try it one night?" She handed him the paper.

They'd finished the steaks she'd pan-fried with a little Marsala sauce. Capers and green peppercorns and a hint of Dijon—though she'd called it pan gravy for Wylie's sake. Last Wednesday, she'd added a single finely minced porcini mushroom into a quick pasta sauce, even though Wylie claimed an aversion to "funguses." Another Wednesday, she'd glazed some pork chops with guava paste, telling him it was a new barbecue sauce from Hunt's.

Had any of it encouraged his appetites?

Wylie narrowed his eyes. "Sounds cheesy," he said.

"All ads sound cheesy." She turned herself to face him on the couch, put a hand on his knee. "This could be fun. Exotic. Just think of the things we could try."

"London broil?" He wrinkled his nose. "This sounds like a cafeteria."

"They list things that people will recognize," she said. "Some people are afraid to break from what they're comfortable with." She tried not to lace the last sentence with too much meaning.

Wylie had brought the *Dine-A-Mate* book from the kitchen.

"Lots of good restaurants still to try here," he said. "Good deals. You don't want it to go to waste, do you?"

"No. But don't you ever want to try something new? Branch out some?"

"We *have* branched out." He held up the book. "Lot of places we wouldn't have tried otherwise, right?"

However she tried to step up her proposal, he would escalate a counterargument—she'd learned that too. Insecurity at the root of it—his food hesitations and aversions, his fear of trying anything new. Or a control issue? That too in the mix—but recognizing it didn't make it easier to deal with. She braced herself for fresh frustration, tension, wondered whether to let it drop. But before she could, he slid his arm around her.

"C'mere, hon," he whispered, pulling her into a hug. She felt her body react despite herself. "Tell you what. Let's take a gamble. I'll open it up to any page at random, and whatever page we open it up to, we'll go there, no matter what. OK? Adventure *and* a bargain." His breath nuzzled her hair, a mix of heat against the coldness of his words. "A year of bargains, Sandra, more than we can use."

Wylie was an accountant. That was how they had met. Sandra had a question at tax time, and Wylie was manning a booth at the mall—free tax advice. It was his job to think in terms of balance sheets, payables and receivables, profit and loss, exacting down to the smallest detail. When they talked about their future, Wylie sometimes tallied up what was working in their relationship and what wasn't, weighing pros and cons. Once recently, he'd hinted that using the *Dine-A-Mate* book might help him save for something else someday—"something I may want to give to you," he said, "something special," raising his eyebrows. "I'm being practical for you. Practical in love." Wylie protected his assets. He hedged his bets. He calculated.

Snug in his embrace, Sandra felt his free hand caress her back, give her shoulder a squeeze. Further down, the corner of the *Dine-A-Mate* book pressed persistently into the small of her spine.

He released his grip, settled back on the couch. "Anything good on TV tonight?"

* * *

Was this the path all relationships took? Was it inevitably a question of practical matters? Monthly budgets and emotional economics? Did the passion vanish? And what if there hadn't been much passion to begin with?

Sandra had been in few relationships, had never dated widely. She was quick to fall in love, she knew—quick to have her heart broken if nothing developed, slow to end things if a relationship did develop but turned disappointing. Some days, Sandra hadn't known whether she was happy or not, what happiness even was. Too often, her twenties had seemed simply lonely.

She was in her thirties now. At least Wylie was there several nights each week.

The day after Wylie talked her out of the Royal International Buffet, Sandra found herself starting to share her concerns with Josie, a paralegal who worked down the hall. Sandra was taking her afternoon break on a bench outside the office, watching people passing by and the building renovations across the street. She flipped through some old magazines she'd picked up from the reception area. *Seven Ways to Spice Up Your Saturday Night* promised an article in *Cosmo*. Another asked *Stud of Your Dreams or Dud of the Month?* Advice columns echoed the same problems she'd read about in college, workout tips she should try but probably wouldn't. A horoscope promised Virgos that "Multiple men will vie for your affections this month"—patently untrue, even if the magazine hadn't been several months old.

She put the magazines aside when Josie sat down and lit up a cigarette.

"Do you ever get a craving for something new?" Sandra asked.

"Mm-hmm," Josie said, taking a long drag. "Like him." Across the street, a construction worker had pulled off his shirt. His torso glistened.

"That's not *quite* what I meant," Sandra said, but then wondered if that was entirely true. Often, she'd gotten the impression that she and Josie had little in common. Josie was small and feisty, with closely cropped brown hair and a tight figure that seemed even slimmer and sleeker beside Sandra's rounder frame. Josie had a pixie grin too, mischievous, conspiratorial—nothing like Sandra. Josie regularly came to work with dark circles rimming her eyes after long nights at the bars or the clubs in the warehouse district. But maybe they were just looking for the same thing in different ways.

"I thought you were still seeing Bob," Sandra added—a man Josie had recently begun dating regularly, ten years older, fresh out of a twenty-year marriage.

"Ugh," Josie said. "Don't get me started."

"Things not going well?" Sandra asked, and Josie waited until the construction worker had moved out of view before answering.

"He's started asking me how many men I've slept with," Josie said. "You know how they do." She nodded knowingly between drags of her cigarette, agreeing with her own statement. "I mean, he married his wife when they were right out of college—college sweethearts. One woman he's been with more than half his life. Did he expect that I was out there waiting for someone like him to come back on the market? That I just sat home night after night? I mean, I was out there looking. Who wouldn't be?" She sucked on the cigarette, the tip glowing red, then pulled it away, exhaled. "Let's say, what, three guys a year maybe I dated that might actually go somewhere? A few dates, you expect you're gonna sleep with them, right? Over ten years…well, that's fifty guys right there. How's he gonna take that?"

Sandra thought she had misheard. "Three guys a year over ten years is thirty."

Josie waved her cigarette in the air. "It's been more than ten years. Then, some one-night stands. Anyway, who cares about math? The point is I don't think it's any of his business. I don't think it's something he has a right to ask." She dropped the butt to the ground and smeared it against the concrete with her foot. "And he's not complaining about the benefits he's reaping from my experience, is he? What do you think he'd say if I said, 'You like that trick? Phil taught me that trick. You wanna thank Phil for that?'" She laughed bitterly. "Of course, him thinking he's had competition makes him try harder in bed, so I guess that's a plus."

Sandra nodded, still thinking she must have misheard. She could count her own list of lovers on one hand.

But it was true, the other thing Josie was saying: Wylie had wondered too, had asked—had nagged even. When she'd told him, he'd asked how he measured up, whether he was bigger or better—and what could you say to that?

Wylie's jealousy had reared its head before, too. The only man who had flirted with Sandra in months was an overweight process server who stopped by the office sometimes—an odd dumpling of a man, pear-shaped, bald as an egg. He called her Miss Williams or sometimes Ms. Sandra. Once, he complimented her on her dress, told her she looked pretty, and then immediately apologized for being too forward. When Sandra had told Wylie about it—funny story from work—he'd grown upset, started talking about harassment.

Wylie had been more attentive afterward, though—more... intense—after both her story about the man at work and her admission about her history of partners. His kisses, his touch, everything. Like he was trying to one-up her past, wipe it away. Maybe Josie was right. Maybe competition did make them try harder.

But Sandra lost the impulse to share any of this with Josie, and the two of them settled into silence. "See you inside," Josie said when she'd finished her cigarette. Sandra stayed out a bit more, moving from the *Cosmo* to an *Esquire* with tattered edges.

As she paged through, a picture caught her eye. A dark-haired Asian woman stretched naked on a long table. The length of her body was covered with food: tight spirals of sushi, thinly carved prosciutto, milky cheeses, mounds of grapes, layers of some tropical-looking fruit. *Tokyo Businessmen Pay Top Dollar to Satisfy Yens* read the headline. It was the new rage in Japan: lunchtime buffets served atop the nude bodies of beautiful women, businessmen in elegant suits paying big bucks to feast straight off their flesh. Even in the photograph, Sandra could sense the men's hunger, that devouring gaze. But she couldn't fathom what the young woman must be thinking; her eyes closed, her expression vacant, her body frozen in service, waiting.

* * *

Saturday night, Sandra dreamed about an international buffet of men.

Swarthy Italians with bare chests beckoned to her, waist-deep in a large metal bin. Mustachioed Spaniards sat atop silver platters, whistled, and kissed the air. Further down the line, a debonair Englishman raised a cup of tea while a Frenchman caressed the neck of a bottle of champagne.

"*Je t'aime*," he whispered to her, popping the cork. "Dom Pérignon. Beef Bourguignon. Blanquette de veal."

"Osso buco!" cried the Italians, bare-chested, waist-deep in their bins. "Veal parmesan! Veal Marsala! Chianti!"

Slim, mysterious Middle Eastern men clad in Bedouin robes glanced back and forth from the Frenchman to the Italians, stroked handlebar mustaches, cutting their eyes at Sandra as she passed. They held bowls of hummus and baba ghanoush along with small brushes, as if they might paint her with the dips if given the chance.

Shirtless construction workers strutted along the periphery, each of them like they'd stepped out of a Diet Coke commercial.

All around her drifted the breathy, eager whispers of faceless women. *I could eat him with a spoon.... Oh, yes, I'll take two helpings of that one.... The best thing about a buffet is you can sample a little of everything you want....*

"It all looks so scrumptious tonight," Josie said, nudging Sandra ahead as they moved down an oversized buffet line. She pointed to Sandra's empty tray. "Aren't you going to try anything, hon?"

Sandra woke with a start, feeling flushed and confused. And hungry. A stale, mealy flavor hung heavy in her mouth, some residue of spice. Where was she? Oh, yes, her own bed. Moonlight crept around the shades. On the bedside table, the digital clock glowed 3:16 a.m.

Wylie lay sleeping beside her, and she felt a rush of guilt, as if she had cheated on him in real life. Briefly, she felt certain she had, so strong was the desire at the dream's core—and the disappointment she felt toward Wylie, too.

They had been to FunWerks that night: Buy one go-cart ride, get one free. Dinner had been nachos at the snack bar. That's where the taste had come from, why she was hungry now. "Will one large order be enough to split?" Wylie had asked her, and she had agreed to avoid any argument.

There had been trouble at the snack bar too, Wylie taking offense at the way the guy behind the counter had been looking at Sandra—"leering," he'd said, leaning in, threatening to talk to the manager, his fists balled as if threatening worse, until Sandra talked him down. The server had turned pale, backed away. Wylie's insecurity again, Sandra thought, jealousy, but even more unexpected this time, the suddenness, the vehemence. Wylie had stewed as he munched through the platter of nachos, eating more than his half.

Then those nachos had given Wylie a stomachache—"the jalapeños," he said—and that had cut the night short. He apologized for his gaseousness as they went to bed. Sandra had kept her own body turned away.

And maybe the nachos had caused her dream, too. She could still hear the Frenchman calling to her: *pommes frites, biftek, jambon et fromage, les oeufs*—words that had lingered in her memory from college French. She laughed now at those men calling out to her, wooing her.

Josie's words echoed again—competition—and Sandra wondered whether she should wake Wylie, tell him about her dream.

He rolled away from her, a rumble under the bedspread—another bout of intestinal distress.

Sandra got up from the bed and went into the kitchen. She took a block of cheese from the refrigerator and cut a small cube, slicing away a hint of mold. She placed it on a cracker from a box in the pantry.

As she ate, she saw the newspaper on the counter. Closing her eyes, she leafed through the pages, picked one at random. Like an omen, the ad stood on exactly the page she'd chosen: *Swedish Meatballs! Jamaican Jerk Chicken! Yorkshire Pudding! Brussels Sprouts!* Each phrase had its own starburst.

The Whole Wide World Welcomes You Seven Days a Week.

Meanwhile, Wylie snored in her bed, deep in his gaseous oblivion.

* * *

After work Tuesday, Sandra looked over the clothes laid out on her bed. A white silk blouse with black cotton slacks seemed like a waitress's outfit. A knit dress with a fitted bodice seemed *too* dressy, and had she gained too much weight to fit into it? A navy skirt and a cream sweater? Black slingbacks? Not quite. But maybe with a white blouse instead...

As Sandra looked for wrinkles in the silk, her imagination roamed freely through the evening's possibilities. She would take a seat at the bar, not at a table—more cosmopolitan for someone eating alone, more mysterious, more alluring. She would order a glass of champagne, and as she sipped it, the bubbles pulsing, she would wonder if the other diners were watching. *Who is that woman?* they might wonder. *See how confident she seems, see how poised.* And she *would* be poised, and perhaps some woman might whisper to her husband, *Don't stare, dear, don't stare.*

You're dining alone tonight? a voice would ask then, a seductive accent, and she would turn to find him adjusting a cuff link on his shirt. *How fortunate for me*—he would smile, playful, intriguing, stroking his lapel—*that you are not waiting for an escort. But such is so difficult for me to believe, someone so lovely and...* Their tour of the Royal International would include escargot and caviar, goose liver pâté, glasses of sherry, a pot of chocolate fondue. He would dip a slice of banana into the creamy chocolate and feed it tenderly into her mouth, his fingers brushing her lips. They would dance, his body pressing against hers, urgent, insistent, and afterward...

But there was no escargot at the Royal International Buffet, no caviar or pâté, no dance floor. Cheap posters lined the walls—Paris, Rome, Istanbul. Stacks of chicken breasts and overcooked beef crowded against one another in the metal bins, surrounded by containers labeled Béarnaise, Béchamel, Hollandaise, Mornay—several covered with a thin film. Mexican and Chinese predominated—Wylie would've been pleased—but the chicken and black bean quesadilla tasted remarkably like the Chinese chicken in black bean sauce. The filling for the seafood crepes was indistinguishable from the pile of Lobster Newburg congealing in its pastry puff. The beef Bourguignon tasted like a Stouffer's pot roast. Everything had the same thick, greasy smell—old butter, leftover bacon fat, some half-dozen spices colliding and competing. Sandra pushed each dish aside, nearly uneaten, as she watched overweight men repeatedly trudge from one food station to the next, piling their plates high, their wives picking at their own plates. Children raced and squealed around the kids' buffet: chicken nuggets, spaghetti, tiny hot dogs in bite-sized buns. Gluttony and noise in all directions.

Sandra dreaded admitting it to Wylie, but except for the bar, the Royal International Buffet was indeed a cafeteria—and even the bar lacked any elegance or sophistication. No sharp-suited businessman waiting to seduce her, just two college boys at the other end of the bar, jeans and polo shirts, sampling rounds of beers from around the world.

Sandra had been ordering off the leather-bound *International Delegation of Drinks* menu, and empty glasses of various sizes now sat in front of her, the dregs of ouzo and grappa, a pale-green cocktail called a caipirinha, a small bottle of sake. With each new drink, she surrendered a little more of her fantasy about the evening, felt her resentment of Wylie grow all the stronger. Maybe she wouldn't tell him about it at all, wouldn't give him the pleasure of being right. After the caipirinha, she had slipped off the straps of her shoes, and the slingbacks now hung loosely from her feet, lolling around the metal rods of her stool. Her head had begun to ache.

"Don't tell me you're here alone?" said a voice near her shoulder, southern, drawling. She turned to see one of the college boys beside her. His head seemed out of focus somehow, his face fuzzy—her vision blurred from all the drinking? Not only that. His face wore more than a hint of five-o'clock shadow, almost as if he had cultivated it that way.

"I told my friend Bert that you were probably waiting for someone," he went on, in good-old-boy tones. At the other end of the bar, Bert aimed his finger like a gun, pulled the trigger, winked hello. "I thought maybe your date had just gone to the bathroom. But no one showed up. My name's Jack." He held out his hand.

Sandra hesitated and then offered her own hand, holding onto the edge of the bar with the other to keep her balance. "Sandra," she said, thinking of what she would tell Josie, how some twentysomething had hit on her. "No, my boyfriend didn't want to come."

"Lucky for me, I reckon." Jack smiled, sidled onto the next stool. "My friend and I just came over for a quick dinner. You get your money's worth here, and meeting you, well, that's even better than dessert."

She caught the gleam in his eye as he said it, deep-green eyes, hazel undertones. He looked away as if embarrassed. She couldn't tell whether he was blushing or not under that quarter inch of beard.

"I'm sorry." He laughed. "I don't do this often. I'm just not very good at it." He turned again to look at her. "How about if I buy you a drink?"

She hesitated, then pushed the *International Delegation of Drinks* toward him.

As he scanned the menu, Sandra looked him over. A few inches taller than her, thin and muscular, brown hair, a sharp slope to his nose, wide lips. Not conventionally handsome, but not that dumpling of a process server, not at all. For a moment, she remembered Wylie and felt another rush of guilt.

"What's a split of champagne?" Jack asked the bartender. "You split it two ways?"

"Single-serve bottle," the bartender said. "But it's Two for Tuesday on wine—buy one, get one."

Jack scratched his chin, mimicking deep thought. Sandra could hear the scrape of his fingers against his beard.

"Can't beat a good deal," he said finally.

He smiled at Sandra, and she answered with one of her own, but it felt torn. Two for one, a good deal, echoes of Wylie in another direction.

While they waited for the drinks, Jack told her again how ill-suited he felt when it came to meeting women. He joked about lame pickup lines he and his friend had come across in a magazine.

Do you believe in love at first sight, or should I walk by again?

If I could rearrange the alphabet, I'd put U and I together.

Your feet must be tired because you've been running through my mind all night long.

Each new line was worse than the last, but she found herself trying to play along. "Not sure what I'd say if someone tried a line like that on me!" She giggled.

The bartender brought two small bottles, two champagne flutes, and an unexpected plate of strawberries with a dollop of whipped cream. Jack poured the first glass of champagne, slid it her way. "Your drink, mademoiselle," he said, with a wave of his hand, and the *mademoiselle* stopped her short, the strawberries too, and her sudden desire for him to feed one to her—remnants of her dream, her guilt.

But he didn't pluck up a strawberry, didn't offer it to her mouth, just said, "Romantic, huh?" as he leaned in and laid an arm around the back of the barstool. That, too, left her thinking of Wylie, the way he hugged her with one arm because of the book in his other hand, and then about the nachos they'd shared, his clash with the server, and his stomach troubles.

"A girl appreciates a little romance." Sandra sipped the champagne. It tasted overly sweet.

"Aim to please." Jack's drawl had returned, a whisper now. "Look, I don't do this often, like I told you, but you… you're really attractive, and… Would you have any interest in coming back to my place for a drink?"

Shifting her weight back onto her stool, feeling her balance slipping, Sandra thought for a moment and then, despite herself, nodded yes.

Jack pushed his bottle of champagne away and pulled his stool closer to her, his leg brushing her knee. She could smell the beer on his breath for the first time, feel the bristles of his beard against her cheek.

"And how about Bert?" he whispered. "You know, he thought you were pretty hot, too." As she turned to look toward the far end of the bar, the other boy lifted one corner of his mouth in his own half-smile, opening his lips just slightly and fondling the end of his eyetooth with the tip of his tongue.

***

"I tried to call you last night," Wylie said the next evening. Another Wednesday, but not—Sandra knew—their standard Wednesday, not this time.

"I didn't get your message."

"I didn't leave one."

"Well, no wonder."

Wylie sat at the table behind her. Sandra sliced shallots at the counter. If he had asked, she wouldn't have bothered to pretend they were onions.

When she finished, she reached for a plastic container of fresh tarragon and began to mince it. Wylie would complain it was pungent, but she appreciated the flavor. And tonight, like last night, was going to be her night.

"Where were you?" Wylie asked.

"I went out to that buffet." She tried to seem casual, purposefully offhand. "The one I was telling you about. You weren't interested, so…"

"Oh." Surprise in his voice. "I don't remember you telling me." Surprise and…something else. Wariness? Uneasiness?

Even with her back turned, she could feel his eyes on her. Not just surprise or uneasiness but tension now. She turned on the burner under her skillet, added a tablespoon of butter.

"Your friend from work?" he went on.

"Josie?" she said. "No, just me."

"You went by yourself?" he asked, and he laughed—an anxious laugh, she thought. "That's a little odd, isn't it?"

"Well, you didn't want to go." She shrugged, watched the butter melt and puddle. "And since it was just me, no need for a coupon." She stirred in the shallots and the tarragon, stole a glance at him, and at the *Dine-A-Mate* book on the table near his elbow, same as always.

Wylie gave a snort. "Was it everything you dreamed it would be?"

"It was delicious," she said. "Amazing, really. They really must have chefs from each country back in the kitchen; it was all so… authentic. Some better than others, of course—and you had to plan right, moving from one cuisine to the next. But it was like little tastings—veal parmesan, veal Marsala, osso buco…" She remembered the Italians from her dream, wooing her with those same words, and then the boys from the night before. "Can you reach in the refrigerator and get that little bottle of champagne? Just a bit left from last night. I'm gonna add it to the sauce."

"You had champagne?"

"There were a couple of guys at the bar. One of them bought it for me." The slightest pause. She turned to watch him, curiosity getting the better of her—the effect of everything she was saying. "Businessmen. From France."

Wylie's eyes narrowed. "Frenchmen? Buying you champagne?"

"They were very elegant," she said. "Had the best accents, too. Jacques was the one who bought the champagne, and his friend was Albert." She pronounced it *Al-berr*, rolling the name off her tongue.

Wylie seemed to clench his jaw as he stepped over to the refrigerator and pulled out the bottle. He stared at the label.

With a spoon, she made nests in the shallots and slid some thinly sliced chicken breasts into each opening.

"I'm sorry I wasn't there," Wylie said, a hint of threat running under the words, the same tone he'd taken with the man at FunWerks.

"No. I don't think you'd have enjoyed it, not like I did."

The chicken breasts sizzled agreeably.

"You mean *you* wouldn't have enjoyed it if I'd been there." He banged the champagne bottle against the counter as he put it down. "Guys flirting with you."

"It was nice to be flirted with," she said. "A little harmless flirting—what difference could it make?"

Things were going to change—that's what Sandra had told herself. Last night had steeled her on that point. No more sneaking around with secret ingredients, no being held hostage to the *Dine-A-Mate* book—another glance its way. And Wylie needed to get past all his hesitations and insecurities and jealousies. Sandra needed to be more direct, more forceful. Maybe a little competition would push him to drop all that calculating and control—light a fire in him.

Either that or this would be the end of things. But she wasn't happy, couldn't be, not with the way things were going.

"How do you know it was harmless?" Wylie said.

Sandra squatted, peeked through the oven window: a mashed potato casserole, laced with leeks, almost browned on top. She didn't look at Wylie as she stood to flip the chicken breasts, but she could feel his stance beside her, rigid and tense.

"Just need to finish the sauce, and we'll be done," she said. "Do you want to get us some plates down? And set the table?"

Wylie lowered his voice. "I asked how you knew it was harmless." A sharper edge this time.

"Harmless," she repeated. "Well, that's what I thought. But then it turned more serious."

"What's that supposed to mean?" He hadn't moved toward the cabinets to get the plates, hadn't reached in the drawer for the silverware. She could feel his glower now, still not looking directly at him.

"Well, when Jacques ordered the champagne, he also ordered a plate of strawberries and cream." She poured the champagne over the shallots, added some chicken broth and a dollop of Dijon. "I started to pick one up, but he stopped me. 'Ah, but mademoiselle—' He called me *mademoiselle*. And then he plucked a strawberry, dipped it in the cream, and waved it back and forth in front of my lips."

"He did *what?*" Wylie said—over that edge now. "If I'd been there, I'd have—"

"You didn't want to go." Sandra focused on whisking the mixture in the pan. "Remember?"

"If I had known—" he sputtered. "I hope you left."

"It did make me uncomfortable for a moment," she said, "wondering what the other people in the restaurant might think. Thinking of you too, I mean." She watched the Dijon sauce bubble happily. "But no, I didn't leave. Jacques was so serious and so eager and… I don't know what came over me, but I leaned forward and ate it right out of his hand."

Wylie didn't speak, and she could feel that his anger had shifted somehow—the competition Josie had talked about, the way Sandra had glimpsed it a couple of times herself, now setting in again. It had simply been a matter of getting Wylie's jealousy to simmer a little, spicing things up—in a different way from what she'd first planned with the food so many weeks back. Her heart throbbed as she waited for all the ingredients to come together.

"Then, as I was chewing the strawberry"—she took a deep breath—"he asked me if I'd come back to his place for a drink. Share one with Albert too," she said, rolling those r's again on her tongue.

"What did you tell him?" Wylie said softly, back to a whisper.

Was he going to reach out and reclaim her? Or walk off in a huff? Either way, a decision was made.

Only a little further, Sandra thought, as she transferred the chicken breasts to their plates, ladled out the sauce. She worked slowly, methodically, in no rush now, weighing each step as she had thought it out, hoping that she could carry it through.

"I told him yes, of course," she said. "Two for—"

Two for one—that's what she was going to say next, slyly, the final touch. *A bargain, Wylie. How could I pass it up?*

But before she could get the words out, he'd whirled her around, the hot skillet spinning from her hand. Shallot and tarragon splattered the stove and the counter, specks of Dijon sauce scorched her skin. She could barely feel the burn, though, for his hands around her throat.

"I thought I knew you," he said through gritted teeth. "We were together, we were going somewhere."

He pushed her against the stove, his anger as hot as the burner searing her back. Her arms flailed, the plates jostled and fell from the counter, cracked as they landed.

I made it up, she wanted to say. *I made it all up.* She'd changed her mind at the last minute, turned down Jack's proposal, found herself alone at that bar, that extra split of champagne her only two-for-one of the evening.

No way to explain any of that now, no way to get the words out as her throat closed and her headache roared and her legs struggled to find their balance, her feet slipping through the shallots and sauce.

Not their standard Wednesday, not at all, but Wylie had indeed changed. No more weighing and planning, no more tallying the costs and calculating the consequences. All passion now, as his grip tightened in a new burst of control.

The *Dine-A-Mate* sat on the table in its usual spot, but its coupons would go unused, its thousands of dollars in savings wasted. No year of opportunity awaited anyone anymore.

Sandra could see it out of the corner of her eye—the last thing she saw, realizing too late that she herself had gotten more than she'd bargained for.

FLESH WOUNDS

By O'Neil De Noux

Anna is about to shout at the guy—*Close the damn door*—when he staggers, holds on to the doorframe, and carefully closes the door to the rain and howling wind. He looks at the wet floor for a moment and shivers.

"Sorry." He gives her a weak smile, runs his right hand through his wet hair to pull it away from his face. His left hand remains pressed against his side. His gray suit is drenched.

"We're closed."

"Oh. I uh— The lights are on, so I—"

"We closed early because of the storm. I was about to lock the door."

Anna stays behind the bar, pulls the white dishtowel off her shoulder.

He looks at her, his breathing labored. He tries another weak smile. If he wasn't so good-looking, Anna would run him up the street. But that curly black hair and face. Damn, he looks a lot like Tony Curtis.

"Can I? Can I sit a minute?" He raises a shaky right hand.

"We're closed. The bartenders are gone. I'm just cleaning up."

He looks over his shoulder at the rain, and Anna almost slaps her forehead. Why did she tell him she's alone? He moves forward, taking small, hesitant steps like a wounded bird.

"You have any coffee? Bars back home serve coffee."

Anna had made a pot around noon and was fixing to throw it out. She lets out a breath and points to the bar.

"Sit."

He goes around to the far side of the bar, away from the door, and gingerly climbs up on a stool with the phone booth behind him now. He looks out the windows. The music on the radio rises as a new song begins. Anna brings a cup of coffee, and he seems even younger up close. Almost as young as she.

"I'm Jimmy. What's your name?"

She tells him.

He sips his coffee, nods to the radio. "Tommy Dorsey."

Anna knows that. "I'll Never Smile Again" has been number one throughout this hot summer of 1940.

"Frank Sinatra singing."

She knows that as well.

He takes another sip of coffee and watches the windows. There's nothing outside to see but blurred lights beyond the heavy rain. Not even a passing car.

"You have any sugar?"

She brings cream and sugar and the coffee pot to refill his cup. As he puts his cup down, she spots a streak of blood under the left hand pressed against his side. He pushes his suit coat around to hide it.

He looks at her eyes, his smile shaky. The lights in the bar flicker as thunder booms.

"Pretty blue eyes." His voice comes raspy.

"You're bleeding."

He grimaces and lifts the coffee cup to his lips. Up close, she sees his eyes are green.

"But you're bleeding."

"Just a flesh wound."

Anna's throat clenches, and she feels her heart beat. She looks past him at the phone booth. She'll have to go around the bar and move past him. What if he has a gun? Lightning flashes and the lights flicker again.

"No need to worry, Blue Eyes. I'm as weak as a newborn kitten." He has trouble putting his coffee cup down, almost spills it as he misses the saucer. His eyes soften. Probably from the pain. No. No one's ever looked at her like this.

"You need an ambulance."

He shakes his head. "They'll find me if I go to a hospital."

"Are the police looking for you?"

"No." He winces. "Worse."

"Worse?"

"Gangsters." He tries to smile again. "I'm one, too."

Hard to imagine him a gangster. There's no scar on his face. And the soft eyes.

A bolt of lightning is instantly followed by a crash of thunder that rattles the windows of the old bar.

"I have to close up."

The rain washes against the windows in waves, and she sees the street's flooded.

"Any way you can lock me inside? I won't break up the place. I just need somewhere to rest."

"You mean hide."

He nods, his eyes flickering, and his right hand grips the counter.

Anna heads around the bar, keeping out of his reach, and pulls a nickel from the tip money in the right pocket of her skirt. She leaves the phone booth door open and deposits the nickel, thinking *ambulance*. She watches his head as it slowly sinks forward. He puts his elbow up on the counter and catches his head. She can't get a dial tone. She hits the receiver button, and the nickel comes out. She puts it in again, and still no dial tone.

The lights go out.

A blue-white flash of lightning is followed by concussive thunderclaps, and Anna checks to see the streetlights are still on. Slowly, the darkness in the bar gives way to a grayness, and she can make out Jimmy in the same position. She switches nickels, but the phone still doesn't work.

The rain changes direction outside in the heavy wind and a movement beyond the windows catches her eye. A big man in a long coat, his fedora pulled low over his eyes, moving just outside the windows. She hurries from the phone booth, almost running by the time she reaches the door, which opens before she can lock it. The man in the long coat steps in, a big silver automatic in his right hand, a cold smile on his wide face, eyes like dead pools of India ink.

He wipes the rain from his face and looks past Anna, his eyes growing sharp.

"Outta the way, sister."

A huge hand shoves her hard and she hits the bar and slides all the way to the wall and the man moves along the counter and she cannot see Jimmy now.

"Stop! Don't!"

The big man ignores her, raising his pistol as he steps away from the counter to get a bead on Jimmy. He hesitates, moving toward the side tables. Jimmy shoots him from the phone booth, and the man fires back, the gunshots exploding louder than thunder. The man staggers and shoots again, and so does Jimmy, and the man twists and falls.

One. Two. Three seconds before Anna can breathe, the acrid stench of gunpowder thick in the air, faint smoke in the room, the reverberations in her eardrums slowly subsiding. She struggles to move, her legs shaking, her knees weak. She falls away from the wall and takes a step toward the door, and another and another. Anna reaches for the door, looks over her shoulder, sees the big man's legs. He's not moving and she stops moving, knows she has to see.

He lies face up. Unmoving. He's not breathing, and she takes a deep breath and feels a cool wind on her face. The window beyond where the big man stood is shattered, and rain floats in. She stops, looks at him again, and he's still not moving. A cough freezes her, and she knows it's not from the big man.

"Jimmy?"

Another cough.

"Jimmy. I'm coming around the bar."

Jimmy sits on the floor, propped up against the phone booth, those large green eyes glistening. He blinks at her. Blood dots his face, and Anna sees his gun on the floor next to his right hand. There's a bloody hole in his chest, and he wheezes. She moves close, and he tries to smile. She kneels next to him and sees the pain in his eyes. Tears fill them, and she feels her eyes filling.

His eyes slowly close, and she covers her mouth. His chest rises and falls, rises again. He's struggling to breathe, and she has to get help. A scratching behind Anna turns her to see the big man struggling to sit up, his gun in his hand, his belly covered with blood.

She realizes Jimmy's automatic is next to her leg, and she slips it into her skirt pocket as the big man moves his eyes to her. He raises his gun and motions to the phone booth behind her.

"Call an ambulance." He grimaces, and blood drips from his mouth.

Anna tries to stand, but her legs won't move.

His eyes close, and he wheezes, coughs up a fine mist of blood. The eyes snap open, and he waves his gun at Jimmy.

"Is he dead?"

She nods.

"This is a .45, sister. Still got rounds in it." He points the barrel at her. "Call me a goddamn ambulance!"

She rises slowly, turns to the booth, right hand reaching into her pocket for a nickel, left hand gripping Jimmy's gun inside her other pocket. It's the same kind of gun only with a black barrel. A .45 the man says. Maybe Jimmy's still has bullets left in it.

She steps around Jimmy, hoping he's still alive, hoping he doesn't move. The nickel rings inside the phone, and there is still no dial tone. She dials the operator. Nothing but dead air.

"Hello. This is an emergency. We need an ambulance at..." Anna turns to watch the big man as she gives the name of the barroom and address to the nonexistent operator, explaining two men have been shot. She keeps talking as the big man leans back against a chair leg, his eyes closing again.

She hangs up, and his eyes flicker open. The gun shakes at her, motions her out of the phone booth. Anna inches out, turning her side toward him, feeling the beveled grips of the gun in her pocket. Her hand is wet, and the grip is slippery.

"They comin'?" The big man's eyes look red now, glowering at her.

"Yes. But the streets are flooded."

"Sit down. You make me nervous."

Anna moves up on the stool where Jimmy had been sitting. Her heart still slams in her chest, and her lips shake. She steals a look at Jimmy, and he's the same. When his chest rises, she looks away, hoping the big man doesn't see. He's busy looking at the door now. The seconds tick by, long, heart-stammering seconds, the rain still falling, lightning dancing in the distance, and the thunder not so loud now.

Anna hears it, and so does the big man.

Jimmy moans, and the silver gun rises as the big man closes his left eye and aims and Anna has the black gun in both hands and points it at the man and pulls the trigger and the gun jumps, and a bright red hole punches into the man's forehead, a cloud of bloody brains rising behind his head. The man's arm drops and his body collapses, and he rolls on his side.

Jimmy coughs. Anna drops the gun, turns to Jimmy, who's looking at her. He tries to raise a shaking hand, and she kneels next to him, takes his hand and it's hot.

"I'm going to get an ambulance."

He shakes his head and tries to talk. He won't let go of her hand. His lips move again, and she leans close.

"Too…too…late."

They look at each other, and she feels him trying to pull her closer.

"A kiss." His voice a faint whisper.

A kiss. Her mind runs through the lonely nights. All those lonely nights.

"A kiss," Jimmy says.

She slowly leans over and her lips hesitate and he tries to lift his head and she kisses him and feels the electric shock and his hand tenses and he kisses her back and then his lips go limp. She pulls back, and his eyes are half open, lips still parted. A long breath comes from him and then stillness. She presses shaking fingers against his throat. No pulse.

Anna sits back and holds his hand, watches his face.

Waits.

Eventually, someone will come.

She checks for a pulse again. Nothing.

Rainy mist floats through the broken window, and the rain outside falls straight down now. Not as hard. She will tell them they killed each another.

A tear rolls down her cheek. Then, another tear.

She looks at the man she killed and closes her eyes. Presses them shut tightly to drive out the memories, the visions, the torrent, the lightning, the thunder, the blood. Force herself to forget the feeling of the gun bucking in her hand.

Drive it all away. Every second. Everything.

Except the kiss.

NOT YO' MAMA'S IPA

By Kristin Kisska

Lynn

Pulsing like an emergency beacon, my cell phone's calendar app taunts me. Not today's date—June 21st. No, today Jack and I will celebrate. But it's the last day of the month that causes my stomach to churn.

Footsteps tromp down the stairs in the direction of the kitchen. I power off my phone, determined not to worry about *that* impending deadline for another nine days, or at least not right now.

"There you are." Jack shimmies up to me with a goofy smile, takes my hands, then twirls me into a deep back bend, complete with a kiss I know and love so well. We have a wedding reception photo framed in our living room with this exact pose. "Happy anniversary, babe."

Once I'm back upright, I look into my husband's eyes, snaking my arms around his neck. "You made twenty-five years feel like a couple months. When did we grow old?"

"Old? Speak for yourself. I feel as young as the day we met."

"So do I." Almost true, despite a few gray hairs, my struggling career in journalism, and two adult children launched from the nest. Not all our years have been user-friendly. How many miscarriages? How many health scares? Losing all but one of our parents. The layoff had been the scum skimming the surface of our pond of financial woes. So many loans. But no need to belabor our not-so-good moments. We're in a good place now. Better than good... I'd say perfect.

That our marriage survived the bad times and good is a testament to our unwavering commitment to each other. The girls refer to us by our couple's blended name, *JLy*.

"You look just as beautiful as when you walked down the aisle in your long white dress and veil." He rocks me side to side, slow dancing barefoot across the kitchen's tiled floor over to the coffee maker. I stand on his feet just like I did at our wedding reception—I'd ditched my heels after we cut the cake, then proceeded to dance the rest of the night atop his socks. "Any regrets?"

"None.... Well, maybe one or two itty bitty regrets." I feign seriousness. When he stops cold, his crooked smile fading, I wink and add, "Only that the years flew by too fast. And that I probably didn't tell you *I love you* as much as I should've."

"No time like the present to remind me." Jack kisses my neck, my chin, my lips. Suddenly we are honeymooners again, embarking on a fresh, new life journey together. We were naive children back then. "Let's celebrate tonight. Dinner. Someplace nice."

I don't override my instinctive wince in time. Jack notices.

"Don't worry, babe. Nothing too fancy or expensive. But twenty-five years is worth celebrating. Don't you trust me?"

"Of course." A white lie I've long since used to cover a multitude of sins, from irritations to painful frustration. Oh, but I learned since our early years that such little fibs are necessary to keep a marriage afloat. Like whenever I reminded him to take out the trash the fifth, sixth, and seventh time. Or whenever I discovered he applied for a new credit card.

"How about the Hops Along Brewery? Six o'clock? I'll make a reservation." He kisses me one more time, a lingering, delicious kiss with the promise of more. "Let's invite your dad to help us celebrate."

My dad? That wasn't quite the just-the-two-of-us romantic anniversary I'd hoped for. "Of course, babe."

Jack

With Lynn off to work for the day at the newspaper, I hop in my car as well. But instead of heading to the office, I cruise out to the coffee shop for a little caffeine pick-me-up. I took a personal day at work to run a few errands for our anniversary. You only hit twenty-five years of marriage once—a big milestone.

I'll head to the florist, the jewelry shop for a little anniversary bling, and then the bakery to pick up a miniature version of our wedding cake. Our daughters, Cici and Kitty, insisted I make today festive. I didn't tell Lynn I was taking the day off, so I'd have time to pull off something special.

Today is a huge day to celebrate, and not just our anniversary. Lynn's father—our only surviving parent—will be there. Given the awkward situation he put me in during our engagement, I'm glad he is around to witness today. Karma.

My making it this far was no guarantee, what with a couple of peanut allergy scares over the years. Especially that one time we were eating in a fast-food joint, and I'd forgotten to check whether the kitchen used peanut oil to fry their food. They did. I almost met my maker. But I can always count on Lynn to have an emergency EpiPen at the ready for me.

She's my rock. Always has been.

We met at college in a sociology seminar the last semester of our senior year. I couldn't take my eyes off of her. So smart and savvy. Way out of my league. The professor must've been just as enthralled because the two of them would go off on these heated debates about stuff that was way over my head. I kept calling her with homework questions. She was dating some other dude at the time, but my strategy paid off. After countless rejections of being too busy studying, she finally agreed to join me for beers after class—just friends.

That first night we went out, I ordered us both a new up-and-coming craft brew—Silent Arrow India pale ale. Lynn glanced at the pencil sketch on the chilled bottle's label and quirked her eyebrow, questioning me. "A bow and arrow? Should I be worried?"

"No subtext intended." For half a second, I thought she was legitimately concerned. But when her dimple twitched as she stared me down, I felt a glimmer of hope. "Besides, when you get to know me, you'll find I'm more Cupid than Wild West."

After assessing me for a hot minute, she tapped her amber longneck beer bottle against mine, then chugged half of it.

With that clink, I fell in love.

We talked until sunrise—her family, my family, life goals. Once the boyfriend was out of the picture, I swooped in and showed up at her sorority house holding a rose and a couple of IPAs. The rest is history.

Classmates who became friends and then lovers.

The one shadow across our relationship was that my future father-in-law didn't quite approve of me. We got along, but he suspected I was gold-digging. Trust me, the money didn't hurt her appeal as wife material.

I wonder if he even remembers.

Lynn didn't need to work after college but chose to follow her journalism career. She's a damned good investigative reporter too. Her income helped us early on in our marriage. As a real estate agent, I was commission-only, and it took years to build a customer base. Her job also kept her occupied, especially after we were young parents. Busy enough to keep her from noticing that my golf handicap improved, as did the quality of my custom-fit golf clubs. My latest hobby is fishing. I'm hiding my new rod, tackle, and boat charter fees on my new credit cards.

By the time my real estate commissions improved, I'd already amassed a hefty pile of secret debt, requiring creative accounting to hide it all from Lynn. But as soon as my father-in-law kicks the bucket, she'll inherit half of his estate, then boom—all my debt will be paid off. She'll be none the wiser.

I've been waiting for that golden day for twenty-five fucking years. Damned if the old geezer is still hanging on. Probably just to spite me.

When I asked for his blessing on our marriage, he insisted on a prenup. I was crazy in love with her, so I signed it. At least I had the foresight to add the sunset clause. He also insisted I take out a life insurance policy because he cut her off from any ongoing funding once she married me.

Cheap asshole.

Anyway, as of today—our twenty-fifth anniversary—the wait is over.

Last week, I paid my last-ever insurance premium. Hopefully, Lynn won't notice that the little stream of funds is newly available from her strict budgeting. In fact, I've already got a plan cooked up to spend those couple hundred bucks starting next month—dues for my new country club membership.

So, why wouldn't I celebrate?

After a quick meeting with some lawyers this morning, I may just head over for a bite of lunch at the brewery before running my anniversary errands—just me, myself, and I. Or not. Genna usually works the taps on Fridays. And a few years of healthy tipping have gotten me special attention: a heavy pour, a willing listener, a warm bed. I consider her my therapist.

There's a craft beer waiting for me with my name on it.

Lynn

Oh, good, Lord.

Jack's text messages this afternoon grew progressively unreadable with autocorrected mistakes. Huh. Apparently, he took the day off from work. The last one—a photo of his frothy beer on a bar top—came about an hour ago. If the empties behind it are any indication, he's been pre-gaming hard. One of us needs to be sober enough to drive home tonight.

I reply to him: *I'll Uber to the brewpub. See you in an hour. Save some beer for me.*

Jack doesn't know that I asked my dad for a rain check on tonight's events. It wasn't an issue, because we all had dinner together with the girls last weekend. I'm glad Jack is already celebrating. As long as he's sitting at a bar, he's not out spending too much money.

After zipping into my little black dress and touching up my makeup and hair, I spritz perfume on my wrists, then grab my wallet, phone, and lip gloss, and toss them into my wristlet.

The driver pings me that he's waiting in the driveway. The evening is balmy, just like the night of our wedding reception. Hopefully, he reserved a table outside on the brewery's patio under their string lights. I always loved how they reminded me of our honeymoon—dining alfresco in the piazzas of Italy. Back when love ran freely and hope for our future ran high.

"Hops Along Brewery, please." Slipping into the rear seat of the sedan, I let the moment of calmness wash over me. All may be fair in love and war, but I swear to God, no one prepares you for surviving decades of your spouse's quirks and habits. Not that I can claim to be fault-free.

Jack's shopping habit is the Niagara Falls of cash flowing out of our bank account. Dad forced him to sign a prenup, but I wish he hadn't cut me off from all funding from my family. It would've saved me so many sleepless nights worrying about whether or not I could keep a roof over our young family's heads with my meager—but, thank God, steady—salary.

Ten years ago, his gambling habit almost broke us, but I was able to intervene and get him into therapy. As far as I've been able to tell, the wagering stopped, but his spending continues.

Credit cards. Car loans. Second mortgages. Oh my!

Mom passed away two years after our wedding. I couldn't vent to Dad about our struggles. The one time I tried, his *I told you so* cut deep. Even my sister turned a deaf ear. Her advice was to send me the number of a divorce lawyer. Since then, I vowed to keep my tears and frustration to myself. The girls have no idea what their father has done to our financial stability. Maybe I should've left him for their sake, but I was determined to make that a last resort.

Plus, I loved the man. Still do, despite these struggles.

Over time, I learned not to take his shopping personally. He's an addict. Spending is his disease. He can't help himself. Regardless, he's been a loving spouse and a caring father to the girls. I've never once doubted his commitment to me. Or to our family.

Twenty-five years ago, we took our vows. Yes, I'm exhausted and drained. But I've gotten used to running circles around him, returning items he bought, and developing a system of checks and balances to help keep him in line.

As the driver pulls up in front of the brewery, I spot Jack's car in the parking lot.

Together, we fought hard for our family. For our girls. For our marriage.

That is what we are commemorating today. Our ongoing commitment to our vows: for better, for worse, for richer, for poorer, in sickness and in health, to love and cherish, until death do us part.

Jack

Leaning over to check my cell phone, I see Lynn's text from half an hour earlier. Shit.

"Genna, I have to get back to the brewery. Pronto." My pulse accelerates to sixty miles per hour. I rub her bare shoulder, gently waking her up, then slip my pants and shirt back on. "Can you drive me?"

She purrs her sexy little moan. "Sure." Instead of untangling herself from the sheets, she burrows deeper into the pillows.

"I'm not kidding, babe. We fell asleep. My wife is almost there." I toss her clothes at her to help shave a few minutes off our departure. "Hurry up. I could get busted."

"Seriously? My next shift doesn't start until later tonight." She stretches, then rolls over. "Besides, you promised to ask her for a divorce."

"Soon. Someday, very soon." Genna drove her car earlier because I wasn't sober, even though her loft is only a mile from the brewery. When I lean down to kiss her, she tries to tug me back into the bed. God, she's so hard to resist.

"That's what you always say."

"I mean it, babe. Today is a big day for you and me. It's my twenty-fifth wedding anniversary."

She rolls her eyes, then face-plants into her pillow with a groan.

"You don't understand. My prenup had a twenty-five-year sunset clause. It expired *today*. Now, when I divorce Lynn, I can claim her family's money."

Genna turns over to face me, blinking away her irritation into a smirk. She must know she owns me or at least my soul. "So, tomorrow, then."

"Not yet. We'll have to wait a little longer. My wife's family is loaded, but she was cut off when we were married. We need to wait until her old man pops off and she inherits the estate. Then I can divorce her. He's the payload. This is all part of my grand plan." She's not comprehending the gravity of my situation, probably not even listening. "Genna, babe, you won't have to tend bar at the brewery anymore. We're gonna be rich."

"Riiiiiiich." She reaches for my hand, tugging me toward her naked body and the promise of heaven. At least three brain cells must still be functioning because something stops me from diving back into the bed.

I can't screw up tonight by standing Lynn up. Especially not with her dad coming. I've been counting down the days—9,131 days to be exact—until I could witness the look on his face when he realizes what today means. This morning, I stopped by the lawyer's office to review the prenup language. They agree. I'm golden.

Tonight will be my victory lap. Shit, I might even help my father-in-law along into the grave.

But I can't gloat too much or let my guard down. If Lynn files for divorce before her dad dies, I'll be screwed. We have nothing to split between us except loans. Even our house is leveraged to the hilt with a second mortgage.

A quick glance at my watch proves that time is passing by at warp speed. "You stay here, babe. I'll hoof it to the brewery."

The evening air has turned a bit muggy, but I'll make it just in time, sweaty or not. As I jog down the street, I call the brewery to reserve a table for three on their patio. Lynn always liked the string lights creating a canopy with the dark nighttime sky hovering overhead. The courtyard reminds her of our honeymoon in Italy. "Oh, yeah. Can you have a few flights of beer waiting for us?"

Shit. I forgot all about stopping by the jewelry store and the bakery earlier today. Actually, there's a grocery store on the way. I can grab Lynn a bouquet of flowers. A big batch. All long-stem red roses. Plus, that'll give me a legit excuse for not being there when she arrives.

Leaning over, I huff and puff to catch my breath. This running crap is meant for guys younger than my fiftysomething crowd. After a minute, I text Lynn.

Me: *Hey, babe. Running an errand. Table reserved on the patio. Meet you all there in fifteen.*

Lynn

Sitting alone at an outdoor table set with three full flights of beers on wooden boards seems both awkward and excessive. Maybe I should've warned Jack I disinvited my dad, but it's too late now.

Half an hour later and still sitting alone, I feel downright self-conscious. I check my text messages for the umpteenth time, ready to call Jack. A few minutes later, he finally strolls in, sweaty and breathing hard, but gripping an armful of red roses wrapped in cellophane.

"Happy anniversary, babe." He hands me the bunch while kissing me on the top of my head. Sitting down opposite me at the table, he beams. "Twenty-five. One rose for each perfect year."

"You shouldn't have. That's so sweet." The scent of roses is intoxicating, as if they've been pumped up on floral steroids. I place them at the far end of the table.

"To us. Cheers." He picks up the lightest mini-beer in front of him, then chugs it down cold. Perspiration soaks his collar. "Where is your dad?"

"I asked him if we could reschedule. I thought tonight would be more romantic—just us." I switch seats, so we're sitting next to each other instead of across. Jack flinches as if I've just announced that I have lice. Doesn't he want to be alone with me? "Don't worry, babe. Dad and the girls are all planning to come over this weekend for another cookout."

"I guess that works too." He stares forlornly at the table.

"Here." I hand him the second mini-beer from his flight. He grabs the glass, raises it toward me, then chugs. As he slams it back on the wooden serving paddle, I'm surprised the glass doesn't shatter. What the hell is eating at him?

"Why don't you give me your car keys? I don't want you to go all rogue on me and try to drive us home drunk tonight."

Reaching into his pocket, his expression turns from wonder, to confusion, then to distress when he stands patting at all his pants pockets. He pulls out his wallet and cell phone, but no keys. "Shit. I must've dropped them somewhere. Maybe while I was jogging back from the store with your flowers."

Seriously? Our car is parked out front with no keys. This isn't the start to our anniversary celebration I had in mind. But I chalk it up to yet another benign Jack-ism. He could charm his way into a school of piranhas, but he'd lose his swimming trunks in the process.

"Work dragged on today, but at least I had tonight's celebration to look forward to. I wish I'd have known you decided to take a personal day." After waiting for him to sit back down, I reach across the table for his hand to lace our fingers together like we used to when we were young, and *to hell with the world* in love. "I would've joined you—maybe we could've even taken a long weekend getaway."

"It was a last-minute thing. Had a meeting. Stopped by here to make sure we could get a table. The usual stuff." He squeezes my hand but then slips his away to fidget with one of the cardboard coasters stacked on the table.

"Jack, good to see you back." A waitress hands us our menus. "We left your lunch tab open at the bar. Should I add it to your dinner check?"

"Uh, sure." Jack tugs at his collar, his cheeks flaming red. He's downing the extra flight meant for my dad. Then he slumps back in his chair. "Thanks."

After we order our appetizers, I take the first sip of my beer. The bitters in the cold brew resonate with my souring mood. Even now, on our anniversary evening, his eyes haven't met mine since I told him Dad wasn't coming.

At the rate tonight is going, it might take another hour before Jack breaks this awkward silence, so I try to lighten the mood. "By this time twenty-five years ago, we were probably cutting our wedding cake. Do you think—"

"Jack?" A shrill feminine voice slices the patio's ambiance like a razor. A stunning young woman slinks up to our table. She can hardly be five years older than our daughters. In one fluid swoop, she tosses him a set of keys, which he catches on instinct. "You left these on my nightstand, babe."

Babe?

I don't know what cuts deeper. The nickname or the obvious subtext of her message.

She struts inside the brewery as if she's on a catwalk. I twist in my seat to follow her as she walks through the glass doors, then behind the bar, tying an apron at her slim waist. The deep V in her tight top is the perfect depth for patrons to ogle while she runs the beer taps. When I turn back around, Jack's face has turned scarlet, his eyes as round as bullseyes.

"I'll take those." Leaning toward my two-timing husband, I swipe the keys from his paw. Yes, he should be scared. "So, I gather you're more than a regular here."

Jack chokes up some warbled excuse. While I can't quite understand his words, they tell me everything I need to know.

Holy crap. Dad had been right all along. Maybe not that Jack was a gold digger or that Jack didn't love me—at least, I believe he did in the beginning—but that our marriage never had staying power. We just experienced a twenty-five-year soft landing. The realization hits me like waking up with a wicked hangover.

Jack may have stuck it out with me through the years, but *JLy* has only been an illusion. It's always been that way with us. Me giving, him taking. Only, I'd let myself be deluded into thinking our relationship was balanced. Now I have proof he's not invested in me. In us. In our family. In our marriage. Do I even know my husband?

"Be right back." After swiping my wristlet, I dash inside, charging through the ladies' room just in time before losing what little I have in my stomach. Afterward, as I clean up, I'm reminded of the alert on my phone's calendar this morning. Though locking me out of my family's funds, my father had had the foresight to insist Jack take out a $5 million life insurance policy for the duration of our prenup. Thank you, Dad.

Despite years of scraping by paycheck-to-paycheck and minimum payments on credit cards, we diligently paid our monthly premiums. The policy expires at the end of the month.

For nine more days, Jack will be worth more dead than alive.

After rinsing my mouth, I touch up my lips, fluff my hair, and straighten my little black dress. I give myself a critical once-over in the mirror. Not bad for a jilted woman who learned her husband was cheating on her with an employee of the brewery. That he chose this very place to celebrate our anniversary is the salt in my proverbial wound. The gall.

On my way out to the patio, I swing by the bar to get a closer look at Jack's mistress. She's helping another male customer, and though her back is turned to me, I can see why Jack fell for her. Toned. Tanned. All that seductive, taut skin. Lush, long hair. Youth. And probably not a single stretch mark from childbirth. Top that off with her flirtatious sass, and the pieces fall into place. He just didn't factor in that she works for tips.

I notice several small bowls of complimentary salty snacks available on the bar top. They must have run out of their signature gourmet pretzels. This time, it's peanuts. An idea hatches.

After an awkward pause, Jack's *something-on-the-side* looks me up head to toe while pursing her lips. She knows exactly who I am. And she also knows I know. "Can I get you something?"

My pulse pounds in my ears, a cadence that grows louder and stronger with each passing moment. Ignoring her stare-down, I take my time while scanning the chalkboard listing today's beer specials. Nothing pops out until—yes. Perfect. "I'll take two of those, please."

While the bartender—Genna, according to her plastic nametag—steps away to fetch my order from their deep fridge, I swipe a pinch of peanut dust from a nearby snack bowl. Mentally tallying the exact contents of my wristlet, I steel myself. Jack's EpiPen is in my everyday purse back home. I won't have that crutch to fall back on once his writhing gets too bad, with him struggling for breath, his lips turning an unholy shade of gray-blue.

Not this time.

When Genna returns with the beers, I tell her to add it to Jack's tab. She's wearing diamond earrings. What are the odds those are the pair I misplaced a few months ago?

Under the guise of reaching for cocktail napkins, I stealth-sprinkle the peanut dust in each amber bottle. A couple larger crumbs take their time sinking through the beer, settling at the bottom. It doesn't matter which beer Jack chooses to drink. They'll both be contaminated. But only one of us is allergic.

Carrying the beers back to our table with my wristlet dangling, I sense a lightness to my being I haven't felt in years. Decades, really. Near freedom is intoxicating. I'm surprised my feet even touch the patio. The string lights illuminated overhead mask the darkened sky. The sunbaked pavers warm the night air. Beach tunes pulse in the background. All the patrons nearby are getting their Friday night partying on, ignoring us. They won't be for long.

When Jack sees me approach, he straightens his polo shirt, his eyelids reverting to half-mast. He's long past sloppy drunk, already having polished off most of the beer flights at our table.

I place the beers in front of him. Condensation beads invitingly on the sides of both bottles, encasing the promise of the bitter elixir, tempting him to pick one up.

Just like I knew he would.

"Tonight got off on the wrong foot. Let's take a mulligan. We deserve a do-over." As I slip into my chair, I keep my voice soft, soothing. Enabling. "Happy anniversary, babe."

He rotates the bottles to inspect the labels. When the grin breaks out over his face, I know he recognizes the symbolic, romantic gesture.

"*Silent Arrow*. Nice touch, babe." He closes his eyes for half a beat, relief evident in his relaxed brows. He raises his bottle up to mine. "To us."

This was the craft brew he ordered the very first time we went out. How fitting it'll also be our last. When I clink my beer to his I hold it there extra long while toasting him. "To our vows."

He raises his bottle to his lips, taking a long swig of the tainted IPA. Then he notices I have yet to sip mine. "Um… any vow in particular?"

"Till death do us part."

NOBLE ROT

By Robert Mangeot

They'd worn into Freilich, these drives from the Nashville airport to Mosh's winery. A pre-dawn summons this time, but Freilich had been anxious for the call, day or dark of night. Pines and cedars shading moonshiner knolls zipped by the car window. Mosh's peak scorcher, *Whip-or-Will*, was cranked on the rental's stereo. Freilich started at track one and let the album rage through like a whole supercell. Young Mosh, the guitar god, had shredded on his hand-built Duchess, a string ensemble beneath her electric roar and sludge. That session was thirty years gone, but when Freilich closed his eyes, young manager him still grooved in that LA sound booth and radiated sure-chart triumph. The album rocketed to double platinum—Mosh's only smash, as it happened.

October here, cold. Dusk had crept in, but Freilich knew the route even jet lagged from Ambien and Scotch. Take I-40 an hour east to the combo Exxon-Batter Hut, then through back-of-beyond meth central. Freilich stewed, as he did every frigging day, over when Mosh lost that edge. Not the eventual quicksand of industry trends, not his rehab stint. It'd been wife number five. Teca, the New Age sprite. Teca lured Mosh from Malibu to buy this godforsaken patch of nowhere.

Strings lilted again on the title cut. Mosh had insisted on a chamber orchestra. It shouldn't have clicked with his grungier-than-grunge metal, but it did. Its rhythmic flow and surprise poetry lent depth to Duchess and her distorted fury.

The thing was, Mosh had understood about Teca. One sunset, he'd summoned Freilich over to the beach compound for a veranda conference, the Pacific tide receding. Teca brought a syrup-sweet Hungarian wine, a Tokay she called it, and glided off to binge-read her gothic novels. Freilich said, "There goes Exhibit Five why I stopped at one divorce."

Mosh said, "You get this far, and a girl her age, you understand she's not sticking around." Mosh let Teca sell him on Tennessee anyhow. She split before he finished the mansion remodel.

The vineyard gate was shut, no wine drinkers of arguable palate around. A sign read *closed for special event*. Freilich buzzed the intercom. Faked a smile for the camera. A woman came on and said everyone was hanging out at the main house. She had a smooth voice, confident. A new applicant for Mosh's attentions, perhaps. With audible fumbling, she got the gate open, and Freilich eased up the hill, past the tasting room and picnic grounds. Rain had blown through, the creek at a surge. Fall leaves slicked the climb.

Jacked-up trucks crowded the chalet drive circle. Well, monster trucks proved Freilich's long-standing point. These were the core Pit Heads. Whip-or-Will brand whiskey—a licensed production deal with concert tie-ins and product placement—would have had more platform leverage with them.

Instead, Mosh had gone all in on wine. Now, his bankability lay on life support. Business had come down to last gasp, a standards-and-covers phase. Freilich had an agreement in principle to a three-album deal, with a low advance but upside if sales hit thresholds. The label didn't mind carrying Mosh as a Great American Songbook vanity project and duet partner for their rising stars.

Ms. Radio Voice answered the door while in mid-gulp of wine. Not a serious candidate for wife six, this one. Too put together, too self-actualized, her divinely angled chin held level.

"Man and myth," she said. "The great Ten P."

Meaning Freilich's ten percent of Mosh's gross. There was barely enough percentage left to cover rent on a Van Nuys office. It'd been Santa Monica Boulevard once. "You have me at a disadvantage."

"Sorry. Luana Simon. I was voted least drunk for the welcome wagon."

Luana made a show of waving Freilich inside. The house was a little warm, a lot dusty, the air laced with stale weed smoke. The same trophy Gibsons and Fenders and the same concert posters hung in the same spots. Laughter and garlic carried in from the kitchen.

"I did Mosh's knee," Luana said.

"Pardon?"

"His total arthroplasty last year. I mean, I'm not a random groupie."

"He could do worse."

"Don't think I missed that, California. Rock and roll never dies for you people, right? No, my boyfriend and I are limited partners in the vineyard."

"Wonderful," Freilich said.

"Mosh is so brave, how he powered through losing Shannon."

The last applicant for wife number six had exited the mortal coil. Shannon, the gold digger's gold digger. A hunting accident got her, some hick gunning for raccoon on Mosh's property. Mosh played her off with a memorial service jam and hadn't mentioned her since.

The only signs of Mosh in his wine bar or kitchen were his framed album covers, a *Whip-or-Will* LP in faux platinum. Searing kabobs at the chef's range was the gone-bald lead vocal for Sheetrock Rip. Musician types with dyed hair sniffed wine at the island bar, a few grizzled front men in black denim, and a power-ballad siren gone rhinestone. And Squirt, the bassist for Pendulate, with his tired man-bun look and a birthday hat on crooked. The lost-edgers really did find Nashville like elephants did a herd graveyard.

"Howdy," Freilich called, and back came drunken heys. "Anybody seen Mosh?"

"Yeah," Squirt said. "Where's Fingers?"

"He was here," Luana said. "Ten P., it's OK if I'm hitting the sauce. I'm not on call or anything."

"Glad to hear," Freilich said.

"My boyfriend is. He does geriatrics. Pay is lousy, but it's guaranteed volume."

"I'll try the deck."

There Mosh was, sipping wine in the twilight and staring at his woods. He'd lost his paunch since the funeral. Grayer, more leather to his skin.

"You rang?" Freilich said.

Mosh flickered in from wherever he'd been dreaming. "My dude. Mister Money. That was hotfooted getting here tonight."

"I aim to please. And tonight, buddy, I have something to please."

"Later," Mosh said. "We've got to move a commodity. Off property and quick."

"Commodity."

"Major bundle."

"What, you're dealing?" Freilich said. "Are you a moron?"

"Nothing like that. Honest." Mosh poured them each a white wine. "Drink with me. This Tokay is my prime stuff."

"Well, if you're using again, it's not out of grief. And screw you for roping me in. I've got a grandbaby."

"Drink. You're wigging, man. When have I lied to you?"

"When you were using."

"Can't dispute that," Mosh said. "This thing isn't junk. I'm strictly wine and medicinal herb."

Freilich drank and gritted through the wine's honey coating his tongue. With experience, he'd learned a surefire Mosh truth test. Mosh himself, the lines to his face. *Rolling Stone* described his wild expressions as the echo to his riffs coaxed from Duchess. Joy, abandon, whatever his momentary wellspring. Tonight, ache.

Mosh said, "You remember how Shannon was shot over by the woods?"

"I might've issued a press statement on it."

Mosh frowned. Mussed his gray shag. "This package, it's saying goodbye to that."

And good riddance. A Mosh back in the game was a Mosh up for recording, for a tour once the covers record dropped. Small venues, but historic, perfect for Pit Heads with disposable income now.

"We ride," Mosh said. He grabbed the Tokay bottle, and like that, they were tramping through the kitchen. The rhinestone siren had snuggled up to a studio drummer twirling butter knives for sticks. Luana had cozied next to Squirt. She grinned tipsily and toyed with his jacket fringe. Squirt was as dumb as ever, taking a knockout's attentions for granted. Nothing changed much at these parties. They just got sadder.

Mosh loped for the basement. His studio was there. Maybe he'd recorded demos for managerial feedback. Sure, his material had made a creative leap in his self-exile. Smarter, more soulful, but Freilich would be worm food before he'd let Mosh play new songs live. The Pit Heads shelled out for greatest hits—"Whip-or-Will," "Breaking It Down to Studs," "Your Nevermore"—though performed slower and bracketed with rocked-up throwbacks.

"Mosh," Freilich said, "there's a project I need you all over. It'll wow you silly."

Mosh kept loping past the studio toward the house vault, and Freilich's heart quickened above what his pacemaker specs might've preferred. Duchess was in that vault. Duchess, crafted that lifetime ago by Mosh in a Pomona garage. Freilich could close this standards album deal even if Mosh lost his fret hand—but only if his last good hand still held Duchess.

Freilich said, "Don't do it. She's no commodity."

"No, dude. It's done. That's what I'm attempting to relate."

Mosh jabbed at the vault keypad and tugged the door open. Wherever Duchess had been moved, she wasn't here. Mosh had turned the vault into a part panic room and part arsenal. Before Freilich could probe that, he had a scout rifle shoved on him.

"I need this?" Freilich said.

"For here after dark."

"But Duchess is alive and intact? You and her have a killer record to make."

Mosh didn't answer. Instead, he hustled Freilich out to the garage and a waiting ATV, a beast with black metal sheen and tactical spotlights. Next thing, Mosh had them jouncing out into his vineyard, his grimace framed by dash light.

"I hate guns," Freilich yelled over the engine.

"Don't be lame. Remember how us boys shot dynamite sticks in

Escondido?"

"As I recall, I was wrestling your guns away before someone got blasted to glory."

"Exactly. You're money when it counts."

The ATV bucked downhill and nearly dumped Freilich along the way. "This project I've scored us," he said. "It's bold."

"These guns are wiped," Mosh said. "A certain personage in Nash Vegas sells hardware with numbers filed."

Freilich braced against the crash bar. The ATV hopped a dirt mound, and he relived that faded childhood moment, that first school sing-along and him not able to clap in rhythm. Still couldn't.

Mosh juked them into the vineyard and skidded the ATV to a stop beside spent rose bushes flanking the vine rows.

Freilich needed a second. And another second after that. "About that project," he said. "Hear me out before you jump to no."

"Most reds we try, the wine is like fruit chalk. But this Tokay? Magic from the earth."

"We do this deal right; I'm talking concerts, TV bookings, possible bidders in a catalog sale."

Mosh stepped out onto the hillside. "Search pattern, my man. Find anything weird."

"This is weird. I mean, why the hell are we out here?"

Mosh kicked at the damp grass. "I might've left something best discovered by you and me. Rags or a casing."

"As in shell casings."

"I told you before. Birding has to happen, or crows take the harvest."

Freilich let out a familiar sigh. The soul-drainer. He'd done fast clean-up on hotel rooms, and Ferraris borrowed without permission. Tonight, they were after evidence—of what was best left alone until papers were signed.

Freilich followed out at a stumble. "So, winery investors."

"You finally want a piece of this?"

"I do not. But I'll admit, wine and laid-back vibes might be killer for this deal we've got simmering."

Mosh had vanished. That left Freilich to study grim fuzz blighting the grapes. Whatever funk had taken hold was turning the crop into diseased raisins.

"Nasty."

"What?" came Mosh from somewhere.

"You have a mold problem."

"That's the noble rot," Mosh said. "Teca hipped me to it. Swore this hill had the microclimate, and she nailed it. Leave Tokay to shrink for late picking. It gets that wicked fungus going. Concentrates the flavor. It's like an awesome held note, bro."

Teca. That sorceress and her grapes.

"She made you miserable," Freilich said. "And she's never stepping foot here again. Let her plague Europe already."

"Way off. Sometimes, she texts back. Wishes me the health and inner growth she's after. I can't explain it, but Teca misses this place bad. Spiritually bad."

"Christ."

"Don't diss that. Teca planted these vines, dude."

Freilich was watching grapes blotch and ruing that name in his marrow when the *thup-thup* beat of a helicopter broke over the hills. Its searchlight combed the woods.

Mosh appeared by the half-rotten vine. "Let's boogie. Five-oh will have seen our spots."

"What are you into? I can't help if you jive me."

"Deep," Mosh said. "I'm in deep. We've got to bounce."

Mosh bundled them into the ATV and put the hammer down. Freilich gripped on for dear life, a life tethered to a knee-replaced rocker stripped of edge and common damn sense.

"What is it?" Freilich shouted doubly hard. "Blow or horse? And Duchess. Did you smash our meal ticket?"

"Tokay," Mosh said.

Freilich's brain seized up trying to comprehend that. The breakneck speed didn't help. It wasn't until Mosh hid them in the darkened vintner's barn that Freilich could swig gone-warm Tokay and breathe. He said, "What the hell?"

"Stay in the zone" was all Mosh said. Regret hung on him, not fear of arrest.

Regret. Freilich could sell that. A lost man's relapse and bust. The devastation of losing Shannon wham-bang, the torture of her flings, and autopsy-confirmed China White dabbling. A deviant influence, Shannon. With 24/7 supervision from here out, Freilich saw a covers-album phase sparkling with redemptive press.

"I let local hunters on the land, yeah?" Mosh said. "Less birds at my grapes and keeps peace with some hardass cases out this far. Remember that guy, Ennis?"

"The shooter. I wrote your touching forgiveness in that grief-stricken tweet."

"Him. Redneck mafia. Cool about it at first. Huge Pit Head. Always asking about Duchess and how I cobbled her together. Said he'd seen me live umpteen times. So, I invited him around for tastings, neighbor-to-neighbor. What if, what if at a neighborly hour Ennis made it known that he pure hated Shannon?"

"Common sentiment."

"Easy odds he hit on her and struck out. Shannon dug guys more city." Mosh leaned against a stainless steel tank. "No probs on her side action. She was young, took her chance. But she was sticking around, man. Getting tight with those hard-ass rednecks. What if I told Ennis, on the QT, I abundantly hoped someone nudged Shannon along her way? That my gratitude would be abundant?"

"Nope," Freilich said. "Zip it. Leave me out of aiding and abetting."

"I did not aid or abet."

"Odd then how you broach this while dodging cops."

"No bodily harm suggested, either. I merely expressed aloud a desire for an epic discouragement scenario leading to her changing scene."

"Oh, in that case."

"Ennis, man. After Shannon went, he treated the chalet as his crib. Smoked my herb, bossed the vintners for gratis bottles. Started using my caves for his criminal storage. Then, he wanted to borrow Duchess. Show her around. You're feeling me? I know you are."

Freilich said, "Stop. Not another word of your Ten P. spiel."

"But this is a classic you moment. I told him Duchess wasn't happening, no chance. Took her apart to make sure, and he switched to hush money or else. Threatened to bring his buddies around."

Freilich drained his wine. "Good night, then."

"I had to get loose and give Shannon her rest. Full loose, for Teca. Someone in touch like her, she's warded off until this place has its spirit rebalanced."

Teca again, her name sliding airily from him. Mosh didn't need a talent manager. The fool needed an exorcist.

And high-priced defense counsel.

"Thanks for the memories," Freilich said, but he'd shambled into the vineyard before those words found his bones. After booking Mosh's dive-bar gigs and audition crash-and-burns, after shopping writers for a breakout hit, after the hair-metal years and grunge peak and slow fall into serviceable jam music, it was over.

Freilich trudged back through gray-funk vines, a feel of frost settling. It was dead quiet in these hills. Stars flecked a sky clear of light wash. Stars, not planes, circling LAX to the horizon, but he couldn't think of a wish worth believing in.

Freilich had reached the drive circle when Luana teetered down off the porch. "You're it," she called.

"Beg to differ."

"You most definitely are. The most sober individual on the premises. That's why you're talking to the deputy sheriff."

The night dropped icy. "Of course, a deputy."

"Here any momentito." Luana slinked Freilich's way. "Ten P., you are a suave bastard. I have to share a tip-top secret."

"Please don't."

Too late. Luana was draped on him. "I couldn't die having passed on a Squirt hookup. Nobody could. Dr. Geriatrics ought to be impressed, frankly."

Teca. This was Teca's conjuring, how Freilich stood freezing his keister off, how Luana whispered that Squirt was only seducing her for a free surgical consult, and, anyway, he'd passed out before his blue pill kicked in. Teca, how a deputy badge eased from a now-parked cruiser with its radio squawking away, Freilich thinking, *I only ever wanted to be around music.*

The deputy sauntered over. "Evening, folks."

"I made out with Squirt," Luana said.

"What? Like the bass player Squirt?"

"I'm not a tramp, if that's what you're assuming."

"Nobody is casting aspersions, ma'am. I'm here because Mr. Mosh isn't answering his contact number."

"I have a long drive to the airport," Freilich said.

"Roger that. But we could use some insight on some things. Sheriff has everyone hot on a missing-persons."

"Missing."

"Yes, sir. A full-bore ten fifty-seven."

"That's exciting," Luana said. "It's Squirt's birthday, is what I'm saying."

The deputy snuffled, rolled his shoulders. "What I mean…the missing gentleman resides in these parts and was last seen leaving to bag him a fall turkey. An Ennis Amburn. His phone pinged a tower from the vicinity of Mr. Mosh's fence line yonder. That was yesterday, seventeen hundred hours. We're fine-toothing this entire area."

"Smart," Freilich said.

"Procedure. We drill for it regular." The deputy flipped open his notebook. "Might you and Ennis be acquainted?"

"No-o," Freilich said. And at a higher octave, "But I recognize the name. He was involved in that death here. Mosh's girlfriend."

"Accidental death. Ennis is good people."

"Accident," Freilich said. "Totally."

"Trespasser," Luana said. "Trespasser and trouble is what our winery crew says about him. We equity investors get inside scoop."

"Good people," the deputy said. "He's a deacon."

"Haven't seen him," Freilich said. "Not hide nor hair, and that's the absolute truth."

"Write me down for likewise," Luana said.

"Hide nor hair," the deputy said, scribbling. "Hey, what was with Mosh and his four-wheeler? Our chopper spotted him and a Caucasian male tooling around here at speed."

"I'm your male," Freilich said on an octave rise. "I was getting a grape-mold tour."

"Mold?"

"Fungus," Luana said. "Natural inoculation. I'm in the medical arts."

Freilich shrugged. "A fungus. It completes the wine."

"Give me Jack straight any day," the deputy said. "I hate disturbing a host, but I do need Mr. Mosh's statement. Procedure."

"Once we find him," Freilich said. "Rockers, they wander off. Keeps his manager in work. But he won't leave town, bank on it."

"Appreciated. Hey, Squirt is here for reals? I guess I ought get his statement, too."

The deputy touched his cap brim and sidled toward the house. Freilich stood not quite ignoring his legs set to buckle, not quite ignoring Luana's nibbles at his ear.

"Squirt is a skunky dime bag," Luana said. "You, California, are the suave dog to finish the job."

Freilich removed himself from her wrap. "Do me a favor and keep Deputy Badge inside."

Luana turned a fake pout into another grin Freilich felt down to his toes. "YOLO, dirty dog. And fear not. I have held a thecal sac."

Take mine, Freilich thought, for the study of aged and cursed management. He trudged into the vineyard, a trudge even pumped full of adrenaline. Anyone with any sense ditched this train wreck quick, but here Freilich was on a frozen trudge in the wreck's direction.

Fresh ATV tracks veered away from the barn and over dewed grass up into a forest trail. Fair enough. Freilich plunged in and came upon Mosh hauling something heavy up from a narrow crevice.

Mosh glanced over, his expression numb. "Ten P."

"Is that what I think it is?"

"It's a situation, bro."

"A county badge wants a statement."

Mosh nodded. "Bound to. I'm sorry, man."

"Tell me anything," Freilich said. "Swear the guy shot first."

"Sure."

Weak. Forensics people would catch any lie, and that vacant look fixed on Mosh screamed of guilt and unstable artist. Ahead beckoned a mug shot gone viral and supermax stretch.

Freilich, though. Freilich could spin convenient facts. Ennis, a winery troublemaker and known danger. Blackmail attempts and bodily threats. Alleged criminal associates. Guys like that could disappear anywhere. They often did.

And Mosh, his heartbreak, he was ready for recording.

Freilich peered down into the crevice. "Let's face it. No one is crying over a trigger-happy crook. Was this his stash hole?"

"Think so," Mosh said. "He was moving stuff here when he might've got blackbirded."

"Outstanding. Caves tend to collapse."

"I guess."

"It's gravity," Freilich said. "And you never saw him here or recently, got it?"

"Yo."

"And what about his phone? It was traced here."

"Ten P., you know I can bust electronics. The parts might've gotten tossed into various regional cow ponds."

Freilich heard himself laugh. It'd come down to cow ponds. "Your wine. What kind doesn't sell?"

"Most any varietal, not Tokay. Zero ribbons."

"Cave-in or no, hounds can get a scent. We load dud wine with the jerk. Right on top of him. Dump that and whatever of your filed guns we can sneak." Freilich rubbed his hands together. "I imagine you keep dynamite?"

"Dude."

"Legally or obtained from certain personages?"

"Dude."

"Get it," Freilich said. "We blow the works before dawn after that badge takes off. We burn our clothes and whatever came near the Ennis jerk. That ATV catches fire and careens into the pool. You damn well know rocker party antics too."

Mosh surrendered a smile. "That is amped."

And also insane, but hey, cow ponds. "If hounds do find this mess, we lean into it. We're shocked and appalled at how Ennis stashed illegal items without your permission or awareness. We lament how he got wasted and blew himself to kingdom come."

"Here we go, brother. Spirits rebalanced."

"You really think she's coming back, don't you?"

"Watch," Mosh said. "She fits here. It's bigger than me."

The poor sucker. "That feeling you have? Put it into Duchess. And I've got your project. No better torch songs ever written."

"In the a.m.," Mosh said. "I'm too gone to sort business and get grilled both."

Morning, then. The cold had left Freilich. There was sweat and promise to his levering rocks loose at the crevice mouth, his pitching in dead branches. Freilich took a few pulls off Mosh's bottle. Moonlight broke slant through the pines, and the woods smelled dusty sweet. The vines practically glowed from that rot. Magic rippled here sure enough.

If that magic held, an investigation would yield zero on Mosh. If that magic held, Luana's YOLO motor was revved for sneaking out contraband ahead of a house search; maybe come around tomorrow for a *Whip-or-Will* listen and a washed-up manager's live commentary on landmark grunge. It wasn't like Freilich was leaving Tennessee soon. Mosh had this last music in him. Everyone was dying on their vine, Freilich supposed, but at least the lucky ones could pretend they hung on nobly.

RAZING THE BAR

By Leigh Lundin

"Barney, I ran glasses through the washer and counted down the drawer. Last call went down twenty minutes ago. All's left are three regulars and the morose guy in the alcove, table eleven."

"Morose?" I craned my neck. "The guy under the baseball cap?"

"I don't know if he prefers being alone or maybe he dislikes Black waitresses, but he talks *at me*, not *to me*. He left OK tips Monday and Tuesday, but he never looks me in the eye."

"Thanks, Grace. Catch your bus while you can. I'll lock up. Hurry now."

I appreciated her counting down the drawer. Grapes, grains, and guests, I understand. Numbers, not so much.

I turned to the taproom. "Gentlemen, time. See you tomorrow."

The baseball fan slid out of his booth and headed to the restroom. Jeffrey and Stevie pushed back their chairs and helped a less steady Rob Michaels to his feet. They side-shuffled Robbie outside.

A minute later, the morose man exited the restroom, head down, hands shoved deep in his pockets. I held the door for him.

"Good night, sir. Mind the step."

I didn't see it coming. Swiveling, he jabbed a compact automatic under my jaw.

"Lock...the damned...door."

I swallowed. "Uh, sir, not that much in the till. Everyone pays by credit card, see."

Yanking back the gun, he clubbed it hard against my temple, close enough to my left eye to pop loose retinal stars.

Crap. Three hours ago, I'd noticed the security cameras go offline. In their disabled state, they couldn't provide a recording, couldn't help to identify this guy.

He jammed the pistol under my nose. "If I tell you again, you'll be breathing out a *Chinatown* nostril."

Locking us in felt like a bad mistake. At this hour, traffic had abandoned the streets outside.

"Now, move to the bar. This time, pour me Glenfiddich."

How he knew I kept a bottle tucked away for my dad left me wondering. He couldn't expect we'd stock a whisky that good in a joint like this. I poured twenty dollars worth of liquid gold into a water glass.

He pulled out a cell phone and swept the room with it. I could see enough of the screen to recognize our security camera app. He laid his phone on the bar and drew on gloves.

My hand trembled as I pushed his drink across the mahogany. At that moment, my phone jangled, my wife's ringtone. The guy rapped his knuckles on the wood.

"Slide your cell to me. Jesus, a flip phone? Could you not find a cheaper model?"

He aligned my phone next to his. When he set down his little automatic, his hand never strayed far from its grip.

"Pour me another."

Armed theft could never feel right, but after three robberies in seventeen years, I'd gained a little perspective. Except for the ball cap, this guy was expensively dressed. He acted too unhurried, like this was planned, practiced, not a spur-of-the-moment thing. This felt worse than wrong. It didn't feel like a robbery at all.

He pulled back one glove to free a finger, poking at his phone. I couldn't tell if he was checking messages or the time.

I said, "Mister, the drawer's got less than a hundred bucks. It's all yours.

The safe down here… down behind the bar, see? Open and empty. Nothing of value here except the Glenfiddich. Please, take it, my compliments."

"Don't bother yanking out that sham shotgun under the bar. Pretty clever for a fake. In contrast, you'll discover this small but mighty pistol shoots real bullets."

This guy had somehow guessed the code to disable the cameras. He also knew the house kept a realistic combat shotgun that couldn't shoot anything deadlier than paintballs. Chills chainsawed my nerves. I might not emerge from this alive.

My phone rang again. He glanced at the display and ignored it, letting my wife's ringtone play out. Odd; she almost never phoned me on the job.

One scenario occurred to me.

"Mister, if this is about selling out, I already told your people I'm cool with that. I got lucky buying a dump that every developer wants gone to build skyscrapers. My wife understands finances, and she hired some shyster to wheel and deal. I don't know where negotiations stand, but we're not greedy."

The guy looked amused. "You're seventy percent right." He peeled off one glove to jab his phone again.

"So, what's the problem? Why send a thug? Why didn't someone call me and say, 'Hey, Barney, we want a better deal?'"

The man shook his head. Under his cap, his lips curled. "Four years BS, three more JD, and I get called a thug."

His constant checking of his phone gave a feeling time was running out. Certainty struck me; I wasn't meant to walk out of this barroom alive.

Quietly, I said, "I'm not sure who's BSing whom, but who wants me dead? And why?"

The man tapped his phone and peered at it again.

"You'll find out in eleven minutes."

"In this biz, I'm pretty good at reading people. Something's personal to you. What's going on?"

He compressed his lips the way women seal lipstick.

"You never quite hit the bullseye, but I'm impressed."

My brain finally kicked in. This guy knew too much—the off-line security cameras, their codes, and the app, the empty safe, Dad's secret cache of Glenfiddich, the fake sawed-off shotgun.

My eyes might have pointed directly at his, but my peripheral vision gauged, calculated, measured. Any grab for the gun, he'd have it in hand in milliseconds.

"That JD you mentioned, something to do with lawyering?"

"Yeah, Doctor of Jurisprudence."

"You're the attorney my wife hired."

He tipped his glass at me.

"Now you get it. You spend your evenings in this dump. She spends hers with me."

That explained the domestic chasm that gaped between Clara and me. My phone rang again; he glanced and ignored it.

I said, "She told you about the bar, the security code, the toy gun, all that. She visits here so seldom, I'm surprised she could give you the passcode for the system."

"She didn't, dumbass. Same code as your house."

"Oh. Well then, don't worry. I won't stand in the way of budding romance."

"You really are dense. She told you we're working oh-so-hard to squeeze maybe a couple hundred thousand for this septic tank of a tavern, but we're zeroing in on one-point-seven mil. No need to share that kind of loot with a soon-demised husband."

That news stunned me. A barman half hears hundreds of opinions an evening, each man a sports sage and seer, a political pundit, an armchair expert on any given topic. At my wake, customers would likely argue, "Poor Barney shoulda done this, he shoulda done that." They'd each be right.

Experts speak of fight or flight, but they overlook fright, the prayer that doing nothing could prolong a few moments of precious life. No sudden moves meant the tiger might not leap, the bear might not charge—not paralysis but deliberate inaction. Fear could fog the mind or focus it. This bastard relied on human nature's survival instinct. Any grab for the pistol or a dash to the door would undoubtedly end my life, but passive compliance allowed a forlorn hope rescue might arrive. Even though it wouldn't.

The man pulled back his glove to peek at his phone again.

I said, "What's with that? You checking messages from her?"

He snorted. "Police aren't stupid, and neither are we. Her texts will be among the first things they investigate. Nah, I'm clocking every step, checking she follows through exactly as planned, your meal in the oven, everything. We timed this exquisitely. That call at two twenty? That was Clara, concerned you haven't arrived home all safe and sound. She's been calling every ten minutes since. In precisely four tocks of the clock, your wife will phone the police, not frantic, but a little teary and concerned."

He whimpered in imitation of Clara. "Wah. My husband's always home by a quarter past two. He's never late. Never—except when he's been robbed. It's happened two, three times, and that neighborhood is going to hell. And he's not answering his phone. Please go check on him. Please!"

He swallowed his drink. "They'll find a body on the floor, the till empty, the safe likewise. She'll sobbingly tell the insurance company it was loaded with cash."

Resigned to the barrage of revelations regarding my wife, I fitted the pieces together.

"In her hour of need, her oh-so-solicitous solicitor hears the news and arrives to comfort her."

He chuckled. "Well put."

I stopped listening.

Visualize, coaches tell players. Picture slugging that ball, shooting that goal. I ran through it again, then twice more. *Visualize*.

Unsteadily, I poured a final nightcap for him. My hand trembled; the liquid splashed on his sleeve.

"Oh! Damn it!" he snapped, jerking back.

The bottle toppled from my fingers, slopping whiskey into his lap.

In the same motion, I snatched not his gun but his cell. I dropped to my knees behind the bar. Chucking his phone into the safe, I kicked shut its door.

A shot exploded inches from my ear.

I rolled under the bar. My shoulder oddly burned. I shouted up at him. "Stop. Don't shoot. Fingerprints. You can't shoot me."

"Stand up, hands up. Give me my phone."

"No."

"Give me my goddamn phone."

"Never going to happen. Your fingerprints are my life insurance. Within moments, you said, my wife will call the police. They'll swing by here, shine lights through the windows. After they find a body, investigators will eventually open the safe. You wore gloves for everything but accessing your phone. It won't take them long to drag you into the picture."

"Fuck all. I'm not leaving without my phone. Jesus. Damn you. Here's what you're going to do. Phone your wife, tell her don't call the cops. Tell her to get her ass down here to open the safe."

"That's just stupid. Even if she'd bothered to learn the combination, I'd be a fool to call."

"Fuck, fuck, fuck, fuck."

A lone flashlight beam raked the room. Abruptly, the barroom's interior burst into light. Strobes dazzled reflections in the mirrors. Through the front glass, spotlights swept the premises. Another police officer banged on the door.

"Sir? Sir? You OK? Your wife phoned."

Early for once in her life, bless her greedy impatience.

The saloon swayed. I felt light-headed. Holding up my hands, I wobbled to the door and unlocked it.

"Everything OK, sir? We got a call... Sir, you're bleeding. Sir?"

My mouth tasted funny, metallic. I said, "The guy behind me's got a twenty-five auto. He wants to kill me."

The officer pulled me outside as more cars drew up. "Sergeant!" she shouted. "Civvy wounded. Suspect inside, armed."

Blue uniforms swarmed past, all except a faraway cop poring over me. Her voice faded, small.

"...under the shoulder blade, out the clavicle.... Good God, I can't see how it missed the lung...if it missed it."

"I don't feel so good," I said before passing out.

***

Waking felt surreal. I couldn't tell if I lived or not. I couldn't comprehend why I lay on my back in a pastel room. I didn't understand my wife talking on television. Sobbing, she said she had no inkling her attorney would murder her poor, dearly departed husband.

Detectives didn't inform her I still lived, not until much later after she implicated her sleazy lawyer, and he, in turn, blamed her. The post-trial TV dramatizations struggled to capture the greedy glitter in both their eyes.

My limitations regarding high finance preclude counting down cash drawers. Grace is much better at that than I am. Two-point-two-million goes only so far, so I bought a modest pocket pub and winery.

Grains, grapes, and guests, I understand.

Lawyers and wives…not so much.

THE CATHERINE WHEEL

By Brian Thornton

"It was Heaven 17," Flippy said.

"Nope," Obie said. He looked down the Manhattan's long bar to where the band members congregated. The girlfriends and other hangers-on had begun to stir. "And we're not long for the end of this break."

Will downed his shot, then made a face. "It was Japan," he said. "One more before we're back across the street to 'beer and wine only'?"

"A band called 'Japan' had a song called 'Big in Japan'?" Flippy scoffed. "Get real."

A goth girl leaning against the bar a foot or so down from them looked over and said, "You guys shouldn't talk shit about those bands. They're gonzo."

"Black Sabbath," Will began to tick the names off on his fingers, one at a time. If he'd heard the goth trying to intrude on their music hatefest, he gave no sign. "Motörhead, Iron Maiden—"

Flippy did that thing where he closed his blind left eye and peered at the person he was talking to with his good one. "Your point?"

"All bands who did songs with their band name as the title, usually on their first album."

"Metal bands," Flippy said as he tipped back his already empty bottle of Kokanee. Then he shook it, as if to verify that it was, indeed, empty. "Have you heard 'Big in Japan'? This is synth-pop stuff we're talking about."

"Metal," the goth girl sighed and went back to her conversation.

Will looked from Flippy to Obie. "Is he right?"

"That's not how we play," Obie said patiently, as if to a small child. "And you know that."

"Hey Petey," Will waved over the bartender and then called loudly to be heard over the din of conversation, "Did Heaven 17 do 'Big in Japan'?"

"You need another?" Petey asked. Tall, skeletal, with wispy hair that floated about his skull like a gray halo, Petey had been owner/proprietor of the Manhattan since the Flood. As such, he hadn't listened to anything new since June 27, 1974—the last time he'd bothered to change out the 45s in the Manhattan's jukebox.

"Bourbon again," Will said.

"Sure thing, Eastwood," Petey said, using the nickname he'd given Will the previous year when a very drunk older woman, a tourist passing through town on the way from Billings to Seattle, had proclaimed that Will very much reminded her of a young Clint Eastwood. Then, as now, Will blushed to the roots of his ash-blond bi-level.

Petey looked at Obie and raised his eyebrows. Obie turned his empty shot glass over and gave a quick shake of the head.

"Ugh, you know the well drinks here are all Monarch, right?" Flippy said. He pointed each out as he ran his gaze along the bar's top shelf. "Monarch Bourbon, Monarch Gin, Monarch Vodka." He paused as he came to the wooden elephant carving that had sat in the center of the Manhattan's top shelf for at least as long as the three of them had been coming to the place. Then he said, "The really cool seated elephant that Petey flat refuses to sell to me, Monarch Tequila…"

"One sure way to get me to sell you my shit is to insult my selection," Petey said. "You want something or not?"

"Can I get another one of these?" Flippy said, holding up his empty bottle.

Petey quirked his mouth and fingered one of the three plastic leis that always hung incongruously about his neck. This time, it was the yellow one. Then he braced both hands palm-down on the bar and leveled a stare at Flippy. "Ask me that again," he grated, "and I'll have to cut you off."

It was as close as Obie had ever heard Petey come to making a joke. The Manhattan was not the kind of joint where anyone with money left to cover their tab had *ever* been cut off.

"You do remember," Obie used his patient tone again, "that you brought that Kokanee across the street with you from the Dipper, right?"

"It wasn't Depeche Mode, was it?" Will said.

"I got PBR on tap and Rainier bottles," Petey said. "Same as always."

"Rainier," Flippy said. "Hey, can I flip for it?"

"No pun intended," Obie said, as if to himself. "And no," he said to Will. "Not Depeche Mode. And not your turn. Now Flippy gets two."

Petey removed the red plastic lei from around his neck and extended it wordlessly.

"How about the green one?" Flippy said, pointing at the green lei where it still hung around Petey's neck.

"Whyn't you just use the red one, man?" Will said.

"Green's my lucky color," Flippy said.

Petey carefully placed the lei back around his neck and extended the green one in Flippy's direction. "Standard rules."

"Yeah, yeah, yeah, I get it to stay anywhere on the elephant, and my beer's free. If not—"

"You pay double," Petey said.

"And if I get three tosses in a row, it's mine for the night."

"And you drink for free all night, so long as King Jumbo doesn't leave the bar," Petey finished for him. And with that, he took two steps to his right and looked over his shoulder at the two-foot-tall carved wooden elephant where it sat on its wooden haunches in its accustomed spot between the Monarch Vodka and the Monarch Tequila there on the top shelf behind the Manhattan's bar. "Go nuts."

"And don't forget," Obie said, "It's also your guess for 'Name That Tune We All Hate.'"

"Wish that game was easy as this," Flippy said as he moved his wrist slowly back and forth, then back and forth again, a practiced move, like he was readying himself to pitch a horseshoe. "Because this"—he leaned forward and moved his wrist again, taking deliberate aim—"is easy as…" He paused, straightened up, and looked to Obie. "Wait, is it ABC?"

Obie opened his can of Copenhagen and took a dip. "Close, but no cigar."

"You're thinking of 'Look of Love,'" Will said. "Or maybe 'Poison Arrow.'"

Flippy sighed and leaned forward again, his gaze purposeful, locked on the painted crimson cap on the top of the elephant's painted gray head. "Yeah," he said, but distracted, his focus now diverted. "Still as easy as—" He flicked his wrist, and the green lei flew, landed on top of the elephant's head, spun around it three times like a Hula-Hoop around a seven-year-old's hips, then dropped down its torso to pool around its feet, as if they too belonged to a seven-year-old.

Flippy's hands doubled into fists and shot into the air. "Free beer!" he crowed. Every single person in the bar roared forth their approval.

"Yep, yep, yep," Flippy said. "Easy as ABC…wait…" He snapped his fingers. "Alphaville!" he said to Obie. "It's Alphaville."

"Give the man a cigar," Obie said.

"I'd rather have a dip of your snoose," Flippy said. And then to Petey, "Hey Petey, when you gonna sell me that elephant anyway?" Obie handed over the can.

Will muttered something under his breath, checking his watch while holding his other hand out, palm up, fingers motioning for a turn with the Copenhagen. "Better drink up," he said and gestured down the bar. "Band's drinkin' up. They gotta be back on in about five."

"So, can I get that in a traveler?" Flippy said to Petey.

* * *

Obie leaned over the soundboard and rechecked the dial settings while rewrapping the final cable.

"Hey, man, good gig." He heard Hoffman's voice behind him. "Sound was just what we wanted. Don't think 'Blues Inferno' has ever sounded better."

Obie turned and grinned at the sax player. "When you've got an epic name, you gotta live up to it. Glad I could help."

Hoffman slapped some bills in his outstretched hand. "Where are your argumentative friends?"

"They're around here somewhere. Gear ain't gonna load itself, and I know better than to pay either of them before we finish the gig." Obie looked around. From his perch overlooking the stage from the sound platform, he could easily look out over the heads of the rapidly dwindling crowd. For the first time, he noticed gumball lights strobing the upper parts of the Dipper's walls—light coming in through the club's floor-to-ceiling front windows.

He jutted his chin in the direction of the front doors. "Wonder what that's all about."

Hoffman shrugged. "Spokane's Finest," he said. "They show up around last call from time to time. 'Showing the flag,' and all that. Shoulda seen 'em a couple of months back. Mudhoney was here. Place was packed to the rafters. Fire marshal came and shut things down before the band even took the stage. Cops hauled in a lot of people on possession beefs that day."

"You were here for that?"

"Nah. A buddy of mine is their guitar tech. Heard about it from him. We had Blues Fest up at Winthrop that weekend. Plus, with us being out of Seattle now, don't get over here as often as I'd like. But I've seen them pull this kind of shit before. Plenty of times."

Obie said, "Doesn't really change, does it?"

Hoffman lit a cigarette. "What's that?"

"The cycle. The spinning wheel. What goes up must come down. Art pushes society. Society pushes back."

Hoffman nodded and offered the pack to Obie. Obie shook his head and jutted his chin again meaningfully. "Got one in, thanks."

Hoffman took a deep drag, blew a plume of smoke overhead, and said, "You sound like my girlfriend. She reads palms and shit." He called over his shoulder, "Hey! Kate! C'mere!"

A head went up from among the crowd of band backers and hangers-on where they huddled not far from the stage, and Obie recognized the black hair, the pale skin, the black lipstick from across the street earlier in the evening at the Manhattan.

She held up her forefinger, signaling for Hoffman to wait, while she slammed back the glass of wine she'd been working on. Of course, it was red. Then she started handing out hugs to the other band widows, as if she were saying goodbye before packing it in for the night.

"Goth girl dating a sax player in a blues band," Obie said. "Interesting."

Hoffman grinned. "That's why she's my girlfriend. She's interesting."

At that point, the aforementioned goth girl insinuated herself between the two of them and laid a scorching lip-lock on Hoffman. They made a striking contrast. Her gothed up, with powdered pale skin, jet black hair, short, tight, black leather dress, fishnets, and heavy makeup. He looked like a young Captain Picard, only with hair and a mustache: same lean, muscular build, same hooded eyes, same chin. A head taller than her, even in her spiked heels, wearing jeans and a Buddy Guy T-shirt.

The vamp and the off-duty Starfleet officer.

"Kate, Obie," Hoffman said once he'd come up for air. "Obie, Kate."

The girl—up close Obie could see she was much younger than he'd originally thought—extended her hand, limp at the wrist, as if expecting him to bow over it, like a French cavalry officer. He took it and shook it.

"Hekate," she said. "Nice to meet you, Obie." And then she turned her head sideways and said, "Unusual name."

"Thank you." Obie gave her his friendliest smile. "It's a family name. I assume yours is not, unless you happen to come from a long line of worshippers of the Greek goddess of magic."

Hekate looked to Hoffman. "You *see*! People *do* get the reference!"

"Tell that to your mom," Hoffman said. "She named you *Kate*."

"She named me *Catherine*," Hekate said. Then to Obie, "Thank you, Obie, for helping me make my point with this philistine."

Obie just inclined his head. No way was he getting even playfully involved in banter between the guy who had just paid him and his batty girlfriend. If he kept talking, he was afraid he might let slip that she was pronouncing "Hekate" all wrong.

He needn't have worried. Hoffman changed the subject. "This guy talks like you. I told him you read palms."

Hekate rolled her eyes. "I read *Tarot*," she said as she took Hoffman's cigarette and dragged deep off of it, then placed it back between his lips. "Say, weren't you hanging out with those two guys over at the murder bar earlier? The ones talking about synth-pop while not knowing shit about it?"

"What did you call it?"

"The murder bar."

Obie blinked uncomprehendingly at her. "The what?"

"We were all over there at the Manhattan earlier," Hoffman put in. "You mean the Manhattan?"

"I mean the dive bar across the street where the bartender wearing the fake plastic leis just got smoked." She looked from Obie to Hoffman and back again. "Didn't you hear about it yet? That's what's with all the cop cars out there."

"Wow," Obie said, suddenly dizzy. "We were just talking to him."

"About that elephant," Hekate said. "Right?"

"That was more Flippy's thing," Obie said. "But yes, I suppose so."

"Well, from what I hear, that elephant is what he got himself killed over."

* * *

Obie saw Sharpe out of the corner of his eye while he was schlepping his cables out back to the van. Sharpe, in uniform, looked at him and past him while ostensibly taking the statement of a drunken young blonde in a pleated, acid-washed denim skirt and an oversized hot-pink B.U.M. Equipment sweatshirt. Thus, Obie was not surprised to have Sharpe throw open the back of the van while he was stowing cables.

"My lucky day," Sharpe said without preamble.

"Officer Sharpe," Obie said.

"*Sergeant* Sharpe," the cop corrected him as he climbed in and shut the door behind him.

"Quite a party out front there," Obie went on as if he hadn't heard. "Five patrol units and, from the look of it, a crime-scene van?" He shook both hands out in front of his chest like he'd touched something hot and whistled, low and soft.

"You hear anything about that?"

Obie stowed the last of his wound cables. "I didn't know Spokane PD even had a forensics team."

Sharpe reached out suddenly and popped Obie with the flat of his open palm. Obie went with the shot, but it still stung, in more ways than one.

"How about I run you in for it?"

"Run me in for what?" Obie said. "What goes on over there?"

"Like you didn't know," Sharpe said. He removed his SPD uniform hat and scratched at his red-blond crew cut. "Like you weren't over there slamming down shots in between sets along with the rest of 'em."

"The Dipper only sells beer and wine." Obie shrugged. "I had lots of company. What happened?"

Sharpe's eyes narrowed. "That's not the way it works, shitbird. Or need I remind you, I *own* your ass?"

Obie sighed. "Nineteen eighty-six was a long time ago."

"Not so long." Sharpe shrugged expansively. "Five years. You can still be charged."

They stood staring silently at each other for a few heartbeats before Sharpe finally said, "Guy that runs the Manhattan. Know him?"

"Petey," Obie said. "A bit."

"He's dead."

Obie shook his head. "That's awful."

"You know anything about it?"

Obie didn't hesitate. "Not a thing."

"But you saw him when you were over there earlier."

"I thought we'd already established that."

They stared at each other some more. Finally, Sharpe said, "Know anything about that damned elephant?"

"The one on the top shelf, in amongst all those bottles of Monarch? The 'king in the middle of the Monarchs,' I've heard Petey call it. Just that stupid game he plays with it." Obie explained about the elephant and the three leis and the drinking for free all night while hugging the elephant.

Sharpe pulled off his hat and scratched his head again. Obie wondered whether he had dandruff, then decided he didn't want to get close enough to find out. No love lost with Sharpe, the cop who'd both saved and screwed him that night five years before.

"I need to get back to the bar," Sharpe said. "I need you to do something for me."

Obie gave an exaggerated frown rather than laugh out loud. "Are you asking?"

"This could be good for both of us," Sharpe said.

"Doing you favors now?" Obie said. "Don't make me laugh."

Sharpe sighed. "I need you to find that elephant for me. Think you could do that?"

Obie thought of Flippy and his ceaseless attempts to buy King Jumbo. "Why?"

Sharpe opened the van's back door and looked out, as if making sure they wouldn't be overheard. "It's missing, OK?" he hissed. "It's the only thing missing from the crime scene. They didn't even touch the register. No booze gone. Not a bottle even disturbed except for the one the guy was holding when they shot him."

"He was shot?"

Sharpe nodded. "Somebody emptied a Glock into him."

Obie stared blankly at him. "I don't know anything about guns."

"Right, right, right…" Sharpe smiled his unpleasant smile. "VCRs are more your thing."

"Who gives a shit about a carved wooden elephant?" Obie said.

"Find it, and you're off the hook."

Obie peered at Sharpe. "No more '86 this,' and 'VCR that'? No more twisting my arm about keeping my ear to the ground? No more leaning on me to snitch for you?"

"My word," Sharpe said.

"Your word means shit."

"Find this for me, and it's something you can use to block me from doing that sort of thing anymore."

"Mutually assured destruction?"

Sharpe smiled his unpleasant smile again. "Precisely."

***

It took Obie about five minutes to find Will. He was in the Dipper talking with Hoffman and a couple of the other members of Blues Inferno. "Where's Flippy?"

"He's around here somewhere," Will said. "We good to go on the gear or what?"

Obie handed him the van keys. "Cables are stowed. Start breaking down the stands, get the mics into their cases, and get them stowed and out to the van. Make *sure* to lock up between trips. Where's Flippy?" he said again, craning his neck to look around the rapidly emptying bar. "We can't budge the cabinets without him."

"Your other argumentative friend?" Hoffman, who had been listening to their exchange, chimed in. "Saw him head outside with Camino Suzy and her husband."

Obie had visions of Flippy going to smoke a bowl just around the corner from an ongoing police investigation. He swore under his breath. "Who's Camino Suzy?"

Hoffman grinned at him. "She's a huge fan. Comes out and sees us every time we blow through town for a gig."

"Drives an El Camino?"

"Red, 1978. Immaculate."

Obie turned back toward Will. "Get crackin', man. I want to get this gear broken down."

Will said, "Oh, come on, man. Was just talking with R.D. about his kit setup."

Will was a drummer. Talking about drumming. With another drummer. Obie pinched the bridge of his nose.

"You wanna get paid?" he said.

Will and R.D.—a squat, hairy, balding, muscular guy in his forties—

exchanged a look. And then Will held up both hands and said, "Okay, okay."

"You should hang after," R.D. said to Will. "A bunch of us are headed over to…" And Obie lost interest. He had a half-blind knucklehead to track down.

* * *

As it turned out, Hoffman wasn't exaggerating about El Camino Suzy being a "huge fan." The woman weighed at least four hundred pounds. And Flippy wasn't out in the back of her candy-apple-red El Camino, parked a block down from the Dipper—within sight of the cop cars with their lights still going out in front of the Manhattan—in pursuit of a shared joint. He was boozily negotiating what he termed "a date" with her.

And El Camino Suzy, who stood a *mean* six feet to go with her four hundred or so pounds and her hot-pink wig, was not interested in losing out on a chance to make some lucrative magic with 5 foot 2, 125-pound Flippy.

"Your friend's a grown-up," she said to Obie. "You're a grown-up, aren't you, Baby?" she said to Flippy.

Flippy just smiled at her for an answer.

"You know the drill," Obie said to Flippy. "You wanna get paid? You gotta help me with the cabinets. What, or who, you do after that, it's your business. Besides, whatcha gonna do? 'Date' right out here on the street in the back of this sweet, sweet ride of hers?"

"Hey, *fuck you*, man," Camino Suzy's husband called from the driver's seat. "My girl's just tryin' to *earn*."

Obie pinched the bridge of his nose again. "Alright, enough of this shit. Get out," he said to Flippy. Camino Suzy's old man apparently thought Obie was talking to him. He opened the driver's side door.

Obie met him there, kicking the door closed on the man's leg. Camino Suzy's husband/pimp howled in pain and reeled backward across the car's console.

***

"Jesus, Flippy!" Obie huffed as the two of them legged it up the street, back in the direction of the Dipper and the alley where Obie's van resided. "What's Pirta gonna say when she gets wind of this? A hooker?"

"Pirta's got her own troubles," Flippy said breathlessly, with his usual penchant for understatement. His half-Puerto Rican, half-Inuit girlfriend, always a deep breath at even the best of times, had only recently been released from Eastern State Hospital. Pirta, whose name in Inuit meant "blizzard," was not known for her live-and-let-live nature. "She just got tossed back into Eastern State."

"What for this time?"

"Bit a cop."

"What?"

They came to a halt next to Obie's van. Flippy, out of breath, hands on knees, held up a hand to signal for Obie to wait. And then he puked full on Obie's right rear tire.

"God dammit!" Obie shouted.

Flippy straightened, wiping his mouth with the back of his hand. "Sorry. Yeah, she bit a cop so they'd put her back in."

***

"Why'd you take it?" Obie peered at King Jumbo, where it sat on the console between the front two seats of his van.

"I didn't," Flippy said.

"Bullshit."

"Bullshit. I didn't. Why would I lie about that right after I told you where to find it?"

Obie just stared at Flippy for an answer.

"I didn't," Flippy repeated.

"Don't even try to tell me you bought it."

Flippy shook his head. "Petey wouldn't sell it."

Obie eyed King Jumbo again. "Why in hell would you even want it?"

"Memories," Flippy said. "Had one just like it when we lived at Clark, in the Philippines."

Obie sighed. "How'd you know where it was if you didn't steal it?"

"Because," Flippy said, "I saw Will hide it."

* * *

Will howled as he bounced off the side of the van. Obie tapped him again, this time on the nose, making a mental note to hold back. "Eastwood" had a delicate bone structure. Will sat down hard.

"Alright, alright! Yeah, I took it!" He covered his face clumsily with both arms, as if afraid Obie would pop him again. "Went back over during the final set. Place was empty! He was lying behind the bar. I took it! Impulse! He was *dead*!"

When no further blows were immediately forthcoming, Will began to awkwardly make his way to his feet. Obie noted, and not for the first time, that Will was grace made flesh behind a drum kit. Everything else he did with all the finesse of a newborn colt.

"Why?"

Will muttered something under his breath. Obie made to pop him again. "I wanted to know what the deal was with it! OK?"

"What deal?" Flippy said.

"Petey's bullshit game about people making three tosses and sitting with King Jumbo all night. I saw plenty of times when someone walked in one moment, and when no one was looking, Petey would just hand over King Jumbo."

"And?" Obie said.

"And I found something," Will said. "It's hollowed out. I'll show you."

While Flippy was retrieved the carving, Obie said, "That's why? You were curious? Something going on in a dive bar you visit maybe four times a year gave you an itch you couldn't scratch?"

"You guys are always the clever ones. You know stuff, and Flippy has that eidetic memory about music, and I can never be the guy who wins at shit like 'Name That Tune We All Hate.' I wanted to be the guy who figured something out for once."

"Why'd you stick it behind my wheel well?"

"You'll see once I open it," Will said.

Once he'd pried off the base, he handed the carving over to Obie. Obie reached in and retrieved a heavily taped, square parcel, about the size of his fist. Obie lifted the corner where Will had torn it.

White powder.

Obie tasted it. *Alkaline. Heroin.* "It ain't coke."

"You would know," Flippy said. Obie gave him a look. Flippy dropped his gaze, abashed.

"What do you think we should do with it?" Will said.

"Give it to the cops," Obie said.

"Or..." Will said.

"No 'or,'" Obie said, carefully rewrapping the parcel. "We give it to the cops."

"What's the 'or'?" Flippy said.

"There *is* no 'or,'" Obie said.

"*Or* we *sell* it ourselves," Will said. "There. I said it."

"Nope," Obie said. "No way."

"Why not?"

"Who do we sell it to? The type of people who traffic in shit this heavy aren't exactly known for being trustworthy business partners."

"You could sell it," Will said.

"Me?" Obie scoffed. "What do I know about selling drugs?"

"Says the guy who stuffed seventeen VCRs up his nose," said Flippy.

* * *

"This it?" Sharpe said.

Obie nodded.

"Base is loose. You look inside?"

Obie nodded again.

"Where'd you find it?"

"Does that really matter?"

Sharpe shrugged. "It's a cinch you didn't find it on his old lady."

Obie shook his head. "Nope. Why would you think that?" Obie didn't even know Petey'd had a girlfriend. He'd never mentioned one. Then again, all Petey really talked about was booze.

"She's the one who offed him, that's why. Had some slag show up at their front door, pregnant, saying Petey's the daddy."

Obie whistled low and soft. "Wow."

"Yep. Walked all the way from their place over in Brown's Addition. That's why she killed him so late. Took her a while to get here. Then she went down and waited in line at Central to turn herself in and confess. Even killed him with his own gun. Said the place was empty when she walked in and that was how she knew it was a sign from God she was s'posed to kill him."

Sharpe glanced at Obie. "I'm gonna take this. And the credit. We never had this conversation."

"What conversation?"

* * *

Hekate the Gothic Temptress leaned closer, across the van's central console. "It's really nice of you to give me a ride to my sister's."

"No problem," Obie said. She smelled surprisingly good after a night of smoking, drinking, and dancing. He couldn't quite place the scent, but it might have been lavender. Or maybe hyacinth.

"I just am not up for one of their all-night post-gig 'things,' you know? And we're off back to Seattle tomorrow, so…"

"Yeah," Obie said. "I get it."

"Wanna see my tattoo?"

Obie glanced sideways at her where she sat, looking like the cat that ate the canary. "I didn't think we knew each other that well."

She laughed and swatted playfully at Obie. "It's on my *shoulder*. Dirty boy." The way she said the last two words sounded like a lion licking its chops at feeding time. She tugged at the neckline of her little black dress. Obie got a peek at a lacey black bra strap, and then she bared her shoulder.

"Do you like it?" she said. "It's Hekate's Wheel."

The tattoo was about three inches in diameter. The black outline of a six-spoked wheel of the type Obie was all too familiar with. No color to it. "I do," he said. "And it's not."

Hekate pouted. "I don't get it."

"I do like it," Obie said. "But it's not Hekate's Wheel," without really intending to, he pronounced the name "Heh-Kah-Tee," in the *Koine* Greek fashion.

Hekate tugged at the neckline of her dress up and back over her shoulder. "Why do you say it like that? And what do you mean?"

"It's pronounced '*heh-kah-tee*,'" he said. "It's how the ancient Greeks said it, and they invented the word. And that design is nothing like the Hekate wheels I've seen. Those resemble a wheel-as-labyrinth. What you've got there is a punishment wheel. A Catherine Wheel."

Her eyes widened for a moment, then narrowed. Her glossy black lips hardened into a thin, straight line. "You're messing with me."

"Not on a bet," Obie said. "It's named after Saint Catherine of Alexandria, who was, as the story goes, intended to be its first victim. Also called the rack. I believe those little pinwheel fireworks that they sell for the Fourth of July also used to be called by the name."

She continued to peer at him. "It's just a coincidence?" She fairly spat.

Obie tried his best smile, the one that had paid such dividends earlier. "Well, like I was telling your boyfriend when we were settling up"—she winced when he said that—"life's a wheel, isn't it? The Great Circle? I think I said something about Art pushing Society and Society pushing back? But it's more than that. Nietzsche said that Life itself is suffering. But he was a syphilitic pessimist. It's more than that: it's circular. And sure, the wheel dips down and you find yourself on the bottom at certain points in your life, but what of it? Life continues, and the wheel carries you to undreamt of heights."

"Like a Catherine Wheel," she said, her voice barely above a whisper.

Obie thought of Flippy and the elephant and Pirta and Camino Suzy and her husband, and Will's drum envy and his strange jealousy over never being "the clever guy."

"Like a Catherine Wheel," he said.

BAD INFLUENCE

By Eve Fisher

The Norseman's Bar is the oldest in Laskin, South Dakota. That doesn't mean the building is old or impressive. The original Norseman's was a sod house, and when that finally collapsed, its replacement was a board shanty, which burned in the dirty '30s, and up went the cinderblock building. But it's always been in the same place, same name. As well as a lot of the same names sitting in the same place, being served by the same people year after year. Norwegian Lutherans don't like change. As Detective Jonasson once said, "The main similarity between the Norseman's and the Lutheran church is that everybody knows their pew and keeps to it."

So, when Orrin and Deb Dahlberg sold the bar to Ron, the bartender, and announced they were moving to South Padre Island, there was a farewell party that was…tame. Part of the reason was we all knew why they were moving: their only son, Josh, had bankrupted them with his endless legal troubles and was now in the pen for ten years for armed robbery. A good time to start anew elsewhere. Norwegian Lutherans also don't forget. And while nothing may be said, we have a variety of eyebrow movements that let you know we know and we haven't forgotten.

I admit, I'd toasted their farewell (moments after they'd left). "Good riddance to bad rubbish. I just wish I'd been the one to arrest Josh."

"*Grant*," Linda Thompson said, her eyebrows moving toward the kitchen door, where Karin Dahlberg, their only daughter, was cooling off between cooking orders.

"She didn't hear me," I replied.

"Don't count on it," Detective Jonasson said. "Everybody in Laskin has damn good hearing for anything that might offend them. Me included."

"Betcha five bucks you wish you'd arrested him too," Matt Stark, Linda's aunt, said.

Jonasson shook his head. "I don't like losing money." For once they laughed at the same time.

I watched Karin drinking her pop in her daily uniform of baggy clothes and apron, as well as the headscarf she'd worn ever since high school, when she came down with alopecia.

"Her hair ever grow back?" I asked.

"Yeah," Linda said. "Kind of thin, but it's back."

"Why on earth didn't Orrin and Deb take her with them?" I asked.

Matt said, "Couldn't be done. Children interfere with drinking."

"Plus, she just won't go anywhere," Linda added. "I used to try to get her to go on school trips and stuff. Anything to get her away from her brother." Linda and Josh had hated each other since high school when he'd tried to assault her. I'd heard that Gary Davison had rescued her, which might have been one of the reasons she married him. Why she divorced him later is up for debate. "Nope. No way could I get her to go anywhere." There was a long pause. "I suppose I should go over and see how she's doing." But she didn't sound too eager.

Matt shook her head. "Wait till tomorrow. It's always the day after they leave that the other person realizes how lonely they are."

***

We never saw Orrin and Deb again. But ten years later, at another farewell party, Josh was back at the Norseman's, fresh from the pen and thirsty.

"Is he allowed to be in here?" Matt Stark asked me.

"He did his time, so he's not on parole," I replied.

"How much of an asshole do you have to be to not get parole?" Matt wondered to her dog, Whisper, who went pretty much everywhere with her.

"Any chance that he's not too much of an asshole to get a trailer at the Koz-E Campground?" Linda Thompson asked, surprising us all, considering how much she hated Josh.

"Why would I want him as a renter?" Matt asked.

"To get him out of Karin's," Linda said. "He's moved in with her, and my bet is that he's going to stay until he finds a woman who will supply all his physical needs."

"Well, there's an image I could have damned well lived without," Matt said. "Not gonna rent to him. Not gonna happen."

"Besides, she's old enough to make her own decisions," I said. "If she wants to give him shelter—"

"I know, I know," Linda said. "But, he's gonna suck her dry. For some reason, she feels responsible for him."

Matt shook her head. "It's 'cause he tells her that he needs her, right? More damn fool women have fallen for that line than any other. Trouble is, when someone claims to need you, they almost never stop until they find someone with more money." Matt took a sip of her beer. "What do you care? You two haven't been friends for how long?"

"Oh, she dropped me as a friend when I married Gary," Linda said. "Of course, so did almost everyone in town. That's what happens when you marry into the Laskin Mafia. If I hadn't divorced him, I'd probably still be in the doghouse. But Karin—I can't help feeling sorry for her. Just because we're not tight doesn't mean I won't help her get Josh out of her life. Nobody deserves Josh."

Matt sighed. "Okay. I'll make nice."

So, the next time Josh went to the restroom, Matt flagged him down on his way back.

"So, Josh. How ya doing?"

"Glad to be out," he said, scanning the room. "Hell of a crowd here tonight. Bunch of old farts." He looked at Linda. "Not you and Grant, of course.

Quite a change from a Davison."

"That's all right," I said. "I don't like you any better than Gary did."

"You sure about that?" Josh sneered.

Matt changed the subject, saying, "The party's for Harriet. She's retiring."

"About time. Maybe they'll get someone worth looking at. Liven this place up a bit."

"Nothing keeping you here," I offered. "Squeegee's specializes in young and hot."

"Me and the owner don't get along," Josh said, his eyes still on Linda.

"I heard you were looking for a place to stay," Matt said.

"I'm staying with my sister."

"Yeah, well," Matt replied. "I can't see that lasting long. Man your age, just out of the pen. Looking for a good time. How much fun can you have with a sister always around?"

Josh looked directly at her for the first time. "What do you care?"

"Who says I care? I run a trailer park. I got vacancies. Rent's cheap."

"Not cheap enough. It's hard finding a job in Laskin. And I've earned a little R & R after being in. I deserve it."

"Well, if you change your mind. Or if Karin changes it for you—"

"If she does, it'll be because some old busybody bitch like you—"

"Josh." Her tone shut him up. "The last time you talked to me like that, I was subbing at the middle school, and I took you outside and kicked your ass. So, if you ever call me that again—*smile*."

He went to his barstool without another word.

"I'll buy you a beer for that one," I said and ordered another round.

"That goddam pissant toad," Matt said. "I wouldn't mind another crack at him."

"Don't worry," I said soothingly. "Something's bound to happen, and then one of us will get him."

When we were leaving, Josh pulled Linda aside and whispered to her. She laughed and went outside.

"What was that about?" Matt asked.

She laughed again. "He told me to leave him and his sister alone.

Apparently, I'm a *bad influence*. All us Stark women are." She skipped to her car, humming.

* * *

Harriet's replacement as waitress was short-lived, as were the next two.

"You don't pay enough, Ron," Matt said.

"And you don't tip enough," Ron replied. "The only reason I make any profit at all is 'cause I bartend every night."

"Please. You're just a cheap son of a bitch. For God's sake, give 'em minimum wage."

"And on a busy night, they'll make more than I will, what with tips and all. Nope, can't do it."

Well, that was an old quarrel, and it went down the usual ruts. A little while later, Ron hired Dana Telkamp, who was efficient, cool under pressure, had lots of experience, and also had a lot of buts to her. Like four bars in four small towns in four counties, which had, during her tenure, all experienced embezzlement. By one of the other waitresses.

Duneen. Orland. Homburg. Parker. And each and every time the other waitress confessed to stealing from the till. First time maybe. Second time, strange. Third time—the pattern was just screaming in front of your face: But why? How? And why did she keep getting hired? I mean, South Dakota's got such low population that the unemployment is always low, so employers (especially in small towns) learn to make do with what they can get, but still…

I knew one of the waitresses, Louise, who insisted she didn't do it, but paid back the money all the same. I tried to talk to her about it, and she practically got hysterical, telling me to just leave it alone. She'd gotten a new job out in Deadwood, and she didn't want to stir up trouble.

Anyway, Matt Stark went and warned Ron about Dana.

"I know Bonnie at the Duneen Bar," Matt told me, "and she never did it. She got set up. And Linda's worried that Karin will be the fall guy this time, and she very well might be, because Karin is God's own innocent. But it looks like we'll just have to wait and see."

I didn't tell her that Jonasson had tried, too. And I thought of trying, but when I went down to talk to Ron, there was Dana, taking orders. For a minute, I thought it was Linda talking to friends: there aren't that many women in Laskin with dark curly hair. But as I stared, Dana lifted her head from her pad and looked back at me with a little semi-smile that could have been an invitation or a challenge. And I turned around and left. I just didn't have the cojones to talk about that woman in front of her. And after all, it was all rumor and conjecture.

* * *

But all that didn't have a damn thing to do with why, as I drove by the Norseman's Bar on my afternoon rounds one day, I saw Josh pounding on Linda's car door. I turned the patrol car around and headed for the parking lot, but Matt Stark was already running out of the bar.

"Leave her alone, you son of a bitch!" Matt shouted. She pulled off her belt in one rip, twirled it like a lasso, buckle out, and let rip. It clipped Josh on the side of his head. Blood spurted out and down as he pawed at his face. Matt hit him again around the shoulders, then lower down. He stumbled and fell to his knees.

I scrambled out of my car and shouted, "Put it down, Matt!"

Matt glanced at me and nodded. Linda got out of her car on the passenger side and came over to Matt.

I grabbed Josh, hoisted him up, and started reciting his Miranda rights.

"What the—" Josh spluttered. "I'm the one that's been assaulted!"

Ron stood in the Norseman's door, holding up his cell phone, gesturing "should I?" I nodded.

"He said he was going to kill me," Linda offered. "Well, beat the crap out of me. Close enough. So I thought—"

"I want her arrested," Josh said. "Now."

By now Karin had replaced Ron in the doorway and was looking at us all with horror.

Linda continued, "He started pounding on the car door and said if he got his hands on me, he'd kill me."

"What was I supposed to do?" Matt asked. "Let him?"

"God damn it!" Josh cried. "Gimme something to stop this bleeding!"

"Sorry," I said and pulled out a handkerchief. "Press hard. So, did you threaten Miss Thompson?"

"She was—" He glared at me with his uncovered eye. "You don't know what she's been up to! Getting Karin all crazy."

"I just keep telling her she needs to boot your sorry ass out," Linda said.

"You do more than that. I've heard—" He stopped abruptly and switched gears. "And that old woman assaulted me, and I want her arrested."

Karin called out, "You press charges against either of them, and you're out of my house for good."

"You wouldn't," Josh said.

"Try me."

I saw the ambulance coming down the road, Officer Haugen's patrol car behind it.

"Well," I said, "you've got about a minute to make up your mind. I can charge Matt with assault and battery, but then I'd also have to charge you with simple assault against Linda. Or it could be you tripped and fell. Hit your head on the bumper."

"It's a goddam stinking crooked world," Josh said. He looked at Matt and Linda with his good eye. "I'll get—"

"I wouldn't threaten anyone else if I were you," I advised.

"Fine. I tripped and fell. Everyone happy?"

"Sure. Let's get you to a hospital and get you stitched up." And I waved the EMTs over.

* * *

Back at the station, I told Jonasson about the incident, and he agreed that letting everyone go was an unfortunate necessity.

"But if Matt kills him—"

"Or he kills Matt?" I interrupted.

"Then someone's going to get arrested."

I started filling out the paperwork, and after a while, Jonasson said, with longer pauses than usual between every sentence, "I wonder what got Josh so hot and bothered? Linda's hated him ever since I can remember. Never made any secret of it. So, why did he decide he had to assault her in broad daylight?"

"He's got a bad temper. Always has."

A few minutes later, Jonasson said, "He and Miss Telkamp are dating."

I stopped writing. "Really."

"Mm-hm. Paula heard it from the laundromat. Apparently, they were washing a comforter together. Kind of a dead giveaway."

"Well, I don't know what Josh's problem is, but speaking of Dana, it occurred to me last night that we need some extra security next week, not just around town but actually inside the Norseman's. You know. For the East River Poker Run."

"By damn," Jonasson said. "You're right."

* * *

Poker runs are frequent events in South Dakota. Bikers—whether from one chapter or many—get together and go from bar to bar over a more or less scenic route while hanging out with old friends, raising money for charity, and drinking. The East River Poker Run isn't as big as the Sturgis motorcycle rally, not by a long shot, but it's not a one-chapter fun run, either. Laskin could expect anywhere from three hundred to five hundred people. And this year Laskin was the last stop, with the dinner, live music, and a jackpot award, all at the Norseman's.

We were prepared for the usual trouble: DUIs, fights, D&Ds, simple assaults, and more. Some extra officers were coming up from Sioux Falls, and we would all be on duty, including Jonasson. I knew that Ron at the Norseman's had his backup bartenders and every waitress on mandatory overtime. Including Dana.

The night of the Run, the Norseman's Bar parking lot was packed and overflowing up and down the road. There was spillover to every other bar in town. It was a wild, hot, noisy night. We started making arrests around ten. We ignored the rowdies, yelling their way from bar to bar, and anyone that was passed out. We stuck with what would stick, and that kept us busy enough. The only thing that kept me going was knowing that the bars closed at two. If anyone wanted to keep on partying, they'd have to go to a farm party or to Wentworth, where the bar never closes.

And I could only hope that everything went well inside the Norseman's.

* * *

The next morning I got into work at eight, after five hours of sleep, and found Jonasson sitting at his desk. He was wide awake, with a face like grim death, making one of his paper clip nooses. A few other officers were there, yawning their heads off.

"Anybody here get any sleep last night?" I asked.

"Nope," Jonasson growled.

Stan Haugen cleared his throat and said, "Linda Thompson's in the hospital. Somebody knocked her out behind Squeegee's and then shot her."

I literally could not speak.

"At least we think that's the order of events," Jonasson said. "Whoever did it just clipped her hip, so we think they got scared off by somebody before they could kill her."

Stan said, "We've been up all night talking to everybody we could find in and around the bar. See if they'd heard anything, seen anything—"

"*Squeegee's*," I said. "Where's Josh?"

"He's in a holding cell right now," Jonasson said. "Drunk and disorderly, resisting arrest. His cell phone shows that he called Linda last night. I woke up Judge Dunn myself, and he agreed no bail."

"And Dana Telkamp?" I asked.

"She was at work all night," Carla Standing Bear said. "Never left once.

I kept an eye on her for, you know. See if I could spot any money going missing."

"Is Linda going to be OK?" I asked.

"Dahlberg better hope so," Jonasson said.

"Has anybody told Matt?" I asked.

"Yep," Jonasson said, tossing aside his noose. "She's at the hospital. Probably smuggled that damn dog in with her too."

The deputy clerk of courts came in with paperwork.

"Judge Dunn said to get these to you ASAP," she said. "They're the warrants you asked for."

"Thanks, Oona," Jonasson replied. "All right—Carla, you and Roger go see Miss Telkamp. Grant, you and Stan go over to Karin's and look through Josh's stuff."

* * *

Karin answered the door, looking awful. "Oh, Grant, I am in *shock* about Linda. I haven't been able to sleep—or eat. I don't know what to *do*."

"Karin, we've got a warrant to search the premises—"

"And Josh is in jail. Of course," she said. "Do whatever you need to do. I haven't been near his room. I didn't want to find anything and then have to…decide what to do. You don't think? Oh, God, if he did. What am I going to do?"

"Hire a lawyer," I replied.

Josh's room looked like no one had cleaned or straightened anything since he'd moved back in. It reeked of cigarettes and stale beer. There was dirty underwear lying around. I was glad to be wearing gloves.

There was a black backpack shoved underneath the bureau, hard to get to and harder to get out. Inside it was a pistol and a black travel shaving kit that had meth and pills in it. There was also a money belt between his mattress and box spring, full of cash, mostly twenties, along with a completed deposit slip for the Norseman's. And a second pistol under his pillow. Sweet dreams all the way around.

I went out to Karin and asked, "Does Josh have a laptop?"

"No. If he needs to use the internet, he either goes to the library or uses mine. Mostly, he uses his cell phone. Is there something I should know?"

"When was the last time he used yours?"

Karin gulped. "Maybe a week ago."

"Then I'm going to have to look at yours, Karin. Check the browsing history." Karin nodded. "Can I take it downtown?"

"Do you have to?"

"It would help."

Karin nodded.

As we were leaving, Karin asked, "How's Linda?"

"She's going to be OK," Stan told her.

"Thank God."

***

The browser history on Karin's laptop showed that Josh had a taste for mild Asian porn, poker runs, and real estate for sale or rent in Belize. Karin apparently went for cat videos, Pinterest, soap operas, and European river cruises. Or at least, that's how I decided who'd searched for what. There was also a significant absence of emails and personal files. Someone had been scrubbing.

"Did Josh have a gun on him when he was arrested?" I asked Jonasson.

"Nope. Probably threw it in the dumpster. I sent Roger and Lew over to search it."

"They're gonna love you. How about a cell phone?"

"Not on him. I told Roger and Lew to keep an eye out for that, too."

"Where's Linda's cell phone?"

"Evidence bag. From last night." Jonasson sat up straight and asked, "What's the bee in your bonnet?"

"Just thinking." I held up Linda's cell phone. "Anybody know the password?"

"Taped on the back. Matt knew it."

Stark 4G. Made sense. I opened it and looked through. There was the phone call from Josh, and oh, how I wished it had been a text. But there was a long history of texts from Karin, worried about Josh, finances, and the future. Linda's, however, weren't the texts of someone who was supposedly riling Karin up:

"Let him go.

"Quit enabling him.

"He'll find someone else to take care of him.

"Remember, take care of yourself first."

All boilerplate Al-Anon. The same stuff she told me whenever I got too worried about my brother Barry.

"Do we know yet what kind of gun Linda was shot with?" I asked.

"Nine millimeter. The bullet should be sent over any time now."

"I think we'd better see if the pistol we brought from Karin's was the one it was fired with."

I had the unique pleasure of seeing Jonasson surprised. *"What?"*

"Can we just run the test?"

"Sure."

***

Matt Stark called Jonasson the next morning, and soon, he and I drove up to Karin's. Matt's old junker was sitting outside. Whisper was pacing in the car—all the windows were open—but knew better than to jump out and greet us. Karin's windows were all open too, which made it possible for us to hear Matt:

"Cut the bullshit, Karin. Linda never went to Squeegee's, and she sure as shit would never have gone down there 'cause *Josh* asked her to." I reached for the doorknob, but Jonasson stopped me. "Hell, she wouldn't have spit on him if he was on fire. But she'd have gone to Squeegee's for you, because of how close you once were, and because you've been trying to help her lately. And if you said Josh was threatening you, or hurt you, and you needed help, Linda would have raced right on over. Little scared Karin, calling for help.

She'd never have dreamed that you wanted her to go up that alleyway to coldcock her. Shoot her. Just to set Josh up."

"What do you want from me?" I'd never heard Karin sound so hard. "Money? Drugs? Linda's going to be fine. I can give you—"

"Maybe I want to beat the crap out of you before you go to jail. How's that?"

"For God's sake, Matt," Karin screeched. "I didn't kill her!"

"You shot her. In cold blood. After or before you knocked her out?"

"*But I didn't kill her!* I just— I needed to make everyone believe that Josh was a serious threat. I needed to get rid of Josh. He wouldn't leave. I had to get him to leave. That's all! I'll pay all of Linda's medical bills! I'll—"

Jonasson opened the door, and I said, "Karin Dahlberg, I'm arresting you for the armed assault and attempted murder of Linda Thompson. You have the right to remain silent—"

Karin screamed, "No! You don't understand! No!"

But I cuffed her anyway, finished her Miranda rights, and took her out to the car.

Jonasson followed, saying, "I'll take her to the station and send Bob over to help you go through everything again. We need to find Josh's cell phone."

"I'll make sure I check the trash," I assured him.

Karin was in the backseat, crying. Whisper was sniffing the yard. Matt was smoking a cigarette.

"Matt!" Jonasson called, and she walked over. "Thanks for the tip. Tell your dog she can poop anywhere she wants."

Matt laughed as he drove away.

"When did you figure it out?" I asked Matt.

"Last night. Carla came by to see how Linda was doing. She told me about Josh's call on Linda's cell phone. When did you figure it out?"

"When I saw Josh's call on Linda's cell phone. I'd have been by last night, but Jonasson said we needed a ballistics test first. They ran it in record time."

* * *

The big question, of course, was why Karin was so desperate to get rid of Josh that she tried to send him back to prison. Why had she suddenly decided she needed her independence so badly? But she wasn't talking. Her attorney, Ulf Vegard, said she wouldn't even talk to him. Josh wasn't talking, either, especially after his fingerprints were found on the black shaving kit and the vials of drugs inside it.

Dana Telkamp gave us the answer under the watchful eye of her attorney, Jim Barnes.

"I have not spoken of this to anyone. Until now. The truth is, Karin thought we could have a future together. She and I." She took a sip of water. "I never encouraged the relationship. I…tolerated it. Karin is—was—an important part of the Norseman's personnel, and when she got upset, things did not go well. It was best to humor her."

"And what about when she found out about you and Josh?" I asked.

Dana's lips tightened. "I am not, nor have I ever been, nor will I ever be involved with Mr. Dahlberg. He helped me fold a large comforter one night at the laundromat, and I understand that some people took it to mean a relationship existed. And told others. *It was not true.*" She reached in her purse and pulled out a cell phone. "However, when Karin heard the gossip, she became upset. Inordinately jealous. You can read the texts for yourself. You can even make a transcript. I can buy another phone."

"Thank you, Miss Telkamp," Jonasson said. "I'm sorry that you were subjected to false reports."

"Thank you, Detective."

"At least about Dahlberg," Jonasson added.

"Are you implying something?" Dana asked.

Jonasson glanced at me. I sat up straight and said, "Duneen. Orland. Homburg. Parker." Dana didn't even blush. "And now, Laskin. All lonely women, no one to understand them, no one to—"

"That was not my fault."

"No, but it was your opportunity," Jonasson said. "I've heard of a lot of Lonely Hearts scams, but this is the first time I've ever heard of a woman pulling it."

"I'll ignore that," Dana said. "Is there anything further?"

I thought back to Josh banging on Linda's car. "Yes. You told Josh that Linda was what, fooling around with Karin?"

"I don't know what you're talking about."

"That's why he went after Linda that day," I said to Jonasson. "You remember. And why it would be believable that he shot Linda behind Squeegee's."

"I know nothing about any of that," Dana said. "And if you continue with this obvious campaign of slander, I will sue. Is that all?"

Jonasson nodded. As she left, we both sighed.

"The only way to stop her is to get someone to go on the record—" I said.

Jonasson interrupted. "They won't. You know what small towns are like up here. They'd never live it down. But at least we know how she did it. And why no one would talk."

THE BAR

By R.T. Lawton

The bar sat on a corner of the block, stuffed underneath the elevated train stop along one edge of the harbor. Not much to look at on the outside, it was the kind of place that attracted dock workers, ship captains of Third World countries, smugglers of people and goods, arms dealers, mercenaries, and low-level spies for clandestine meetings. In general, it was a momentary rest stop for those on the downward slide on the ladder of life. Its patrons made for a closed society where everyone minded their own business. Law enforcement, for its part, tended to avoid the establishment altogether. This enclave for criminals had long been known as a place where you took your life into your own hands every time you entered the door.

The rest of the buildings in this area were mostly warehouses servicing the harbor. At one time, the bar had a name painted above the front door, but now the wording had faded into oblivion and few remembered the original name. These days, the establishment was simply referred to as The Bar.

If anyone had been watching when the elevated train screeched to a slow stop shortly before dusk, they might have seen a slender man in a rumpled gray suit, pale-yellow shirt, and dark-orange tie, and wearing a black fedora get off at this station. Most of his clothing blended into the swirling fog as it wrapped around him. He stood patiently looking around while the train waited a few minutes before starting up again and pulling out. When it was gone, and the fog-muted sounds of the harbor had returned, the man walked to the metal stairs that led down to the street.

At his back, air horns from freighters moving in and out of the harbor blared their positions and intentions. Red lights, green lights, and strings of smaller white ones softened in the damp grayness, danced up and down above the water line. Air hung heavy with the scents of diesel fuel, salt, and dead fish. Seagulls squawked and fought over edible scraps wherever they could find them.

Coming down the stairs, the man's shoes made little noise except for the occasional small squeak of rubber treading on wet metal steps. He was halfway down when he noticed the man in a brown leather jacket and soft cap standing on the corner across the street. From time to time, the lit end of that man's cigarette would flare and light up portions of the man's broad, stolid face. *Thug* was the impression the facial features gave. That, or the type of people who did wet work for some of the Balkan intelligence agencies.

The man in the rubber-soled shoes took mental note of the man in the brown leather jacket, but otherwise ignored his presence as he descended the rest of the way to the sidewalk, walked to the front door of the bar, and went inside.

At the opening of the door, the lone bartender on the far side of the counter, plus those few patrons seated at various tables, glanced up for a moment, then went back to whatever they had been doing before the interruption.

The man sized up the room, walked over to the barman, placed his order, and indicated it was to be delivered outside to one of the tables in the small private courtyard behind the bar. The bartender nodded his acknowledgment of the request. He started arranging shot glasses on a round carrying tray.

After glancing around the interior of the bar once more, the man made his way to the rear exit, collected a couple of folded bar towels from the counter, and stepped into the enclosed courtyard out back. Four tables with an odd assortment of chairs sat devoid of customers. He chose a table and chair, giving him the best view of anyone entering the courtyard from the bar, and that was also positioned the farthest from that entrance.

To his left side, extending from the rear of the bar building, was a short section of nine-foot-high chain-link fence topped with concertina wire separating the courtyard from the edge of the harbor. To his back was a metal railing with a small gate and, beyond that, the open water itself. On his right, the brick wall of the warehouse next door ran from the back of the bar to the harbor's edge. Overhead, two strings of faded Chinese lanterns gave sparse light to the enclosed area. No windows from any of the buildings looked out into the courtyard.

The man used one of the towels to wipe the thin skin of moisture from the tabletop. The other towel dried the seat, arms, and back of the chair he chose to sit in. Finished, he tossed both damp towels onto an empty table nearby.

When the rear door to the bar next opened, it was the bartender carrying a tray in his other hand. He went to the man's table and placed a saucer and a cup of steaming black coffee in front of the man, who was now seated. Next, the bartender removed a slender silver tray containing a small cream pitcher, a sugar bowl, and a wrapped rectangle of chocolate from the bar tray. The silver tray went to the right of the coffee cup and saucer. Then, the barman placed two shot glasses of dark brown liqueur to the left of the cup. As the bartender lifted the third shot glass of liquid, the man in the rubber-soled shoes indicated a place on the other side of the table where any occupant would end up sitting with his back to the door. The third and fourth glasses went there.

Reaching into his inside suit coat pocket, the man in the rubber-soled shoes removed a black leather wallet, fingered out a fifty-dollar bill in US currency, and dropped it on the table near the silver tray. The waiter slowly picked up the bill and stared at his customer. The man returned the waiter's gaze with a Gallic shrug.

Surreptitiously, the waiter rubbed the bill between his thumb and fingers. The paper felt right. He risked a quick glance down. The ink had not smeared. He would wait until he got back inside before holding the fifty-dollar bill up to a light and looking for any anomalies.

"Keep the tab open," was all the customer said.

Mumbling to himself in reply, the waiter gathered up the two damp towels and returned to the bar.

To the man's left and behind him, waves of salt water slapped at the piers and pilings. Wisps of gray fog drifted across the courtyard. Off in the darkness, a Chinese freighter at a nearby dock loosed its moorings and was taken in charge by a pair of harbor tugs. Air horns gave notice of their movement while the seagulls continued to strut, squawk, and snipe at each other.

An hour later, the elevated train once more squealed to a stop at the harbor station above the bar. The doors slid open, and two men stepped out onto the platform. Both men wore suits, hats, and trench coats and carried furled umbrellas. The doors closed, and the train departed. Without a word, both men started for the stairs. Before they reached the bottom, one of the men touched the other lightly on the sleeve of his trench coat and subtly used the silver tip of his umbrella to point out the man in the brown leather jacket. The second man nodded slightly but never paused in his step. They continued down the stairs to the street and entered the bar. The last one to go through the front door glanced back over his shoulder, but the man in the brown leather jacket had now disappeared from his position on the corner.

Inside the bar, both men immediately moved to one side out of the doorway and looked around as if unfamiliar with these surroundings. When they unbuttoned their trench coats, the atmosphere inside the room seemed to stiffen until the men chose a table in the right front corner of the room and sat down. Only then did the other patrons relax from this new intrusion. The volume of low conversation returned to normal.

The bartender took his time before waiting on the two newcomers and taking them their drinks. He didn't recall seeing them in the bar before, but new customers were always coming in. He did notice that one of the men kept checking his watch and looking around as if expecting to see someone. After a couple of rounds, both men stood and left by the front door. The

THE BAR

bartender picked up their payment and the small tip they left, then wiped the table and cleaned up their discarded trash, including half of a torn postcard. The photo on the front of the card showed the ruins of an old castle; the back had no address, writing, or postage. He deposited the abandoned trash in a bin in the back corner of the bar and glanced at the clock on the wall.

With no more orders for drinks coming from the table outside in the courtyard, the bartender decided to close out the man's tab. The bartender had watched several people enter the bar, and several people leave the bar, but he had observed no one else go through the rear door to the courtyard nor come back into the bar from out back. Whoever was supposed to make the meeting with his sole customer on the patio had evidently been delayed or else wasn't coming at all.

Reaching into the cash box under the bar, the bartender stashed the fifty-dollar bill in US currency into a separate compartment and then made mental calculations as he counted out two short stacks of paper bills in the local currency. Too bad if his outside customer didn't like the way his change had been converted to that of the country he was currently in. The Bar did not keep American dollars for change. American money was always welcome in this establishment, but since local banks charged businesses a conversion fee, that cost must be paid by someone.

He locked the cash box, arranged the money neatly on a small plate, and placed the plate on a nearby bar tray. With the bar tray in hand, he opened the rear door and entered the courtyard. At first, he wasn't paying attention to where the customer was; however, as he drew nearer to the man's table, he realized the customer was absent from where he had been seated.

The bartender gingerly set the bar tray on the table and carefully looked around the courtyard. In fact, no one other than himself was to be seen.

The coffee cup on the saucer was empty, as were the two shot glasses closest to it.

At the bartender's feet, the customer's chair lay on its back on the patio. A few inches beyond the top of the chair back lay one rubber-soled shoe on its side, the laces still tied. The bartender glanced toward the harbor. Two drag marks leading to the harbor's edge showed in the moisture on the courtyard floor. Small puddles of water trailed on both sides of the drag marks.

Quickly, the bartender gathered up the cup, saucer, and empty shot glasses, placing them on the bar tray. He picked up the other two shot glasses, swallowed the dark liquid, and placed the empties on the tray. Bending over, he righted the fallen chair and straightened it in front of the table as if ready for the next customer. With one foot, he kicked the shoe lying on its side through the open railing and out of sight into the harbor. The tumbling of the loose shoe caused a piece of thin cardboard to flutter up from inside the footwear, catch a light breeze, and drift over the side and into the water. For one quick instance, the bartender thought it resembled half of a torn postcard with a picture on one side, but that made no difference to him.

Once more, he glanced at the two drag marks. Yes, he was curious, but no, he was not going to look over the edge to see if anything was or was not floating in the water. For one, it was not his concern; he merely worked at the bar. And second, he did not wish to appear as if intruding into someone else's business, especially in this place.

Having picked up the bar tray, the bartender walked to the back door and opened it. Pausing for a moment, he took the two thin stacks of currency off the small plate and slipped the bills into his pants pocket.

He closed the back door behind him and went immediately back to work.

DEEP TIME

By Lawrence Maddox

"Enjoying the show?" Youngman Fennel finally said. Though he was a heavy man who'd been imbibing nonstop for the last two hours, extra time standing at the wiz box wasn't his main source of discomfort. That honor went to the headphone-wearing man leaning against the sink, watching him. "If you stick around, I've been told my hand washing is a sight to behold."

"I'm not watching," Headphone Man said, turning away. "I'm waiting."

Youngman, stewed as he was on single malts, counted two unmanned urinals besides the one he was using. There were also two stalls, one of which was occupied. "Plenty of empty slots."

Headphone Man took a deep breath. "You don't get it. I don't expect anyone to get it. I haven't found a better way to launch into this, so here goes." He quickly glanced at his wristwatch. "I'm from the future. Three years from now, to be exact. And I need your help."

Youngman barked a laugh. As the founder of the alt-right conspiracy blog *Deep Time*, he was a self-proclaimed expert on "tracking the Deep State through time, space, and all dimensions in between." Time travel was his métier, even more than space aliens who'd been elected to political office in California.

"I love it. Who put you up to this? Was it Roger?"

"Nobody. It's not a joke. This is my last chance. You're everyone's last chance."

Youngman zipped his fly. "I'll play along. So you traveled all the way from three years in the future to watch me drain the weasel? And what is it that I, a humble citizen, can do? And what am I saving the world from?"

"Nuclear annihilation."

"Boring."

"And I'll be asking for five hundred thousand dollars."

Youngman erupted into more sea lion-like laughter. "This is delicious. I like a good prank, but let's make it snappy. A lovely barmaid I just met is waiting to be invited to my yacht." Youngman looked him over. "Those headphones are a nice near-futuristic touch. Or should I say headphone. It only covers one ear."

"It's not a prop. It plays an enhanced ultrasound synapse-linking loop."

"I'm intrigued. Why don't you start by telling me about your time machine?"

Headphone Man checked his watch again. "I have to talk fast. It's 2:04. I've only got eighteen minutes. At 2:22 exactly I'll be jumped forward to my time. I'd have more time with you, but it took you two minutes to pee."

"It takes what it takes." Youngman snapped his fingers impatiently. "Get on with it. I can't keep my hot barmaid waiting forever."

***

I can't believe that putz called me a barmaid. No, not just a barmaid. His *barmaid.*

The woman going by the name Rhonda Martinez put Youngman's Android into the pocket of her apron. *Handsy, arrogant, and drunk. Makes him a jerk customer but an easy-as-hell mark.*

Though Rhonda had to fight the urge to deliver a knife-hand strike to Youngman's throat, the grift was going just as she and Ken had planned.

After a month of R&D, Step One had been getting a waitressing gig at The Burke. The upscale Yorba Linda gastropub catered to those who spend top dollar on high-end whiskeys and imported cigars. The bar's free Macallan-and-Ashtons gravy train for a certain police captain ensured that The Burke could secretly remain open during the pandemic.

For three days, Rhonda had slung drinks and fought off entitled lechers. At the same time, her partner, Ken, rented a private booth for two hundred dollars an hour. Ken had told Chas, The Burke's day manager, that he needed a "new office with a full bar" since Covid had shut down his old office.

On the fourth day, Youngman finally made his waddling entrance.

Step Two. As she and Ken had already learned, Youngman was an afternoon regular who came in alone. He had a reserved corner table near one of the TV screens mounted above the bar. The barman switched the channel to the *Truth Rebel Patriot Power-Hour* and poured Youngman a shot of Balvenie.

Rhonda undid one more button on her tight-as-a-straitjacket bodice and zeroed in.

"I got this table," she said, pushing past Mindy, a skinny blond waitress.

"You can have him," Mindy said.

Youngman's eyes were glued to Rhonda's chest as soon as she arrived at his table. "You shall be my personal barmaid for the rest of the day," he announced.

"I'm flattered," Rhonda said, curling her lips into the shape of a smile.

After numerous rounds, he was showing her pictures of his yacht, the TARDIS Tomkat, on his cell phone. His phone case was bright red and emblazoned with the *Deep Time* logo: a flying saucer with a gun rack.

"You're throwing a yacht party, and *he's* coming?" Rhonda said, pointing to a photo of a morning news host aboard the Tomkat. Rhonda leaned into Youngman as much as gravity would allow. "For real?"

Youngman drained his glass. "Oh yeah, we're buds. Lots of celebs will be there. When I get back from the potty, perhaps I can make room on the guest list for one more?"

Rhonda grimaced. *What kind of grown-ass man calls a bathroom "the potty"?*

She handed the phone back, and he placed it in his tweed jacket's patch pocket. He got up to go, and she "accidentally" pressed into him. "Take your time," she said. "I'll wait for you."

He slid his hand down her backside. "I know you will."

Knee slam into groin! Head butt! Elbow slash across chin! Rhonda pictured various attacks, but refocused on the prize.

As Youngman walked away, a wet cocktail napkin stuck under his right loafer, his cell phone was back in Rhonda's hands. Rhonda pocketed Youngman's Android and pulled out her own cell phone. She texted Ken. *Step Three. Got his phone. It's 2:02, and the groper is on his way.*

Ken texted back. *Im in the bathroom waiting for him. Remember. I can stall him for 20 MINS TOPS.*

"Twenty minutes," Rhonda whispered to herself. *That should give me enough time to get what we need.*

* * *

"So, you were saying your brain is the time machine. Sounds like a library slogan to get slow kids to read books," Youngman said.

Headphone Man paced in a small circle. "You must know all about the Gateway Project and how sounds—"

"Can unify the brain's hemisphere."

"Exactly. It's the same infrasound said to have helped—"

"The ancients in building the pyramids. I know. I've interviewed both Bell and Landsburg for *Deep Time*."

"And like electrons—"

"Time is a wave. You can be both in the past and the present. So far, you're preaching to the choir. That also explains why you chose headphones as part of your costume for this little ruse."

"I have to keep the ultralow frequency running subliminally through my brain to stay here in the past."

A man in a Polo shirt with a turned-up collar walked into the bathroom. He briefly looked at Youngman and Headphone Man before heading over to the sink.

Youngman gently tapped the headphone with his index finger. "So, why meet me in a bathroom? Makes sense if you're pranking me. No sense if you're a time traveler seeking funds."

Headphone Man crossed his arms defensively. "That's not important."

"It's important to me. Or I can just leave."

"Fine! It's because I had a little accident during my very first time jump."

"Accident? What accident?"

Headphone Man sighed heavily. "I was nervous. I drank a lot of coffee that morning. Right before the jump, all I could think was, 'I need to use the bathroom.' When I time-jumped, that's when I suffered," Headphone Man cleared his throat, "accidental micturition."

Youngman nodded seriously. "It happens."

"To initially jump, one has to focus on a face, an object, something that forms the mold for all future jumps. From now on, mine is bathrooms. Ones that I've visited sometime in my life."

"That's limiting."

"Tell me about it. You know how hard it is to start up a conversation in a bathroom? I got into a fight in one at the Cinerama Dome when I jumped to 1998."

"What was playing?"

"*Armageddon*. What are the chances, right? There I was trying to talk with a rich studio exec about stopping the real Armageddon while the movie *Armageddon* is playing in the theater. He thought I was on drugs."

"Probably a lib-tard. They have no imagination."

Headphone Man brightened. "So you really believe me?"

"I believe you're entertaining. Why don't you just walk out of the bathroom? I'll even buy you a drink." Youngman looked toward the door. "But only I'm allowed to talk to my waitress, got it?"

"I can't leave. I'm confined to an eight-foot radius."

Youngman stroked his patchy goatee. "Makes sense. You don't want to go *4D Man* when you time-jump and end up fused to the walls like the sailors on the USS Eldridge."

"No. And *The Philadelphia Experiment* is total bullcrap."

"Whoa! Who knew Mr. Weak Bladder was all conspira-judgy?"

"I'm not conspira-judgy, and I have fourteen minutes."

Youngman studied him. "So, give me a name."

Headphone Man slowly nodded. "Someone involved in the Armageddon Project?"

"That's what you called your time-travel club? Even after the whole Cinerama Dome thing?"

"I'm not in charge, okay? That's what the powers-that-be, or will-be, called the project before I jumped to the Dome."

"Ahh, the TPTB. Can't wait to dig into *that* with you. First, give me *your* name. I'll look you up on ShadowPeopleFinder. That site can locate anyone." Youngman patted down his jacket. "I must have left my cell with the femoid servicing my whiskey needs. Guess I'm a wee bit buzzed."

"You don't have your phone?" Headphone Man panicked. "Can you check again?" He reached for Youngman's pockets.

Youngman slapped his hands away. "Back off, bucko! Nobody puts their hands on me."

Headphone Man stepped back. "If you don't have your phone, how are you going to transfer the money? This was all for nothing!"

"Pull yourself together. It's at my table. I'll be back in a jiff. Or maybe three jiffs. I might have to reignite loin fires in my waitress that have been extinguished by my absence."

"I failed again," Headphone Man said, burying his face in his hands. "We're all doomed!"

"Are you crying?" Youngman asked. "I hope Roger is paying you top dollar for this."

"You can't leave. If you go I'll jump back to my time before you're a zeptosecond out the door."

"Why?"

"I guess you wouldn't remember. You asked if you could hear what was in my headphone. I let you. Big mistake."

"What are you talking about?"

"Your eyes rolled into the back of your head. You fell into me, and we both hit the wall. It all took just a few seconds. Now we're on the same synaptic curve. You go, I go."

"No way! I'd remember that! Now I'm tempted to just wait here and see if you really do vanish."

"That will help no one." Headphone Man turned to the man with the turned-up collar standing at the sink. "Can I borrow your phone for just a minute?"

"There are private booths here if you two want to be alone. And a Radisson across the street." The man popped his collar and walked out.

"My waitress was hitting on me!" Youngman called after him.

A toilet flush sounded from the stall behind Youngman. He and Headphone Man turned to face it.

* * *

That was loud.

The man going by the name Ken Laslo recoiled from the flush button he'd just accidentally slammed his elbow into. He sat on the closed toilet seat lid and listened to the sudden silence on the other side of his stall door. He'd been sitting there for the past eight minutes as some actor pretending to be from the future corralled his intended mark.

Ken was fine letting this actor bozo eat up time while Rhonda did her thing. It was better than what he had planned for Youngman. He just wished that Rhonda would have returned some of his texts since she got Youngman's cell phone. He was dying to know if she was finding what they were after.

So, what's this actor's game? Just a practical joke by one of Youngman's rich right-wing friends? Or is he really working the guy for half a million dollars?

A powerful kick to the stall door startled Ken. "Hey, in there!" The voice sounded like the actor.

"It's occupied!" Ken called out.

"We need to borrow your cell phone."

"I'm busy in here!" Ken said.

"No, you're not."

Ken saw a man wearing one headphone, peering at him through the gap in the door. "You're just sitting on the closed toilet lid."

Youngman joined him. "His pants aren't even down."

"You're invading my privacy!"

"He was watching me take a leak just a few minutes ago, so get over it," Youngman said.

"I know how weird this all is," Headphone Man said. "But this is an emergency. Just a couple minutes with your phone is all I ask."

"I'm going to beat both your asses when I get out," Ken said.

Youngman shook his head. "This may be the final straw for me. It's been a fantastic dinner show, I'll admit."

Ken thought quickly. *It was only 2:12. Too early for Youngman to leave.* "It's really an emergency?"

"More than you could imagine!" Headphone Man said.

Ken opened the stall door and handed him his cell phone. "Fine. You seem desperate. But just a couple minutes."

Headphone Man quickly punched numbers.

That's when Ken's cell phone rang. Quacked, actually. Rhonda's ringtone was a quack.

* * *

Because the women's restroom had an unexpected plumbing issue, Rhonda had to resort to Plan B. She found a quiet spot in the cigar lounge and pretended to read a large hardcover edition of *Hunt's Guide to Cuban Cigars*. She had to hide Youngman's phone behind the book because The Burke didn't allow staff to use their cells while in the pub. *Makes sense. They're open illegally. No one's wearing a mask. Cops are getting comp'd left and right. A few pix could take this place down.*

For the same reasons, workers weren't allowed to leave before their shifts ended. It was a little hard-core, but with no other gigs around, who was going to argue?

Rhonda was certain she could easily handle Bruno at the door, but the off-duty police presence could be a problem. With her past, better to avoid too much police contact.

She focused on finding photos on Youngman's phone from the period leading up to October eighth. That's the date when an organized mob attacked the Delaware capital building and attempted to kidnap the Democratic governor. A small band of police officers saved the governor from the mob, but most of the attackers escaped.

"Youngman posts on Instagram over twenty times a day. I don't think it's a coincidence he went silent during the whole Delaware Debacle," Ken had surmised two months ago. He and Rhonda had just run a successful con involving a forged Klimt and were spending their ill-gotten gains in Tuscany. "Youngman's old man is worth a hundred million bucks. If we can prove Youngman was involved with Delaware, I'd bet the Fennels would pay big-time to keep Youngman out of the federal pen."

Rhonda had come up with the waitress angle after seeing a photo Youngman had posted of himself at The Burke. Now, as minutes went by, she couldn't find a single photo of Youngman connecting him to the mob attack. There were no photos at all for that entire time period.

She looked through the phone but didn't see any third-party apps for hiding photos. Youngman could have the Keepsafe Vault, which doesn't even show up as an app. Rhonda couldn't stand Youngman. Loathed him. She wanted to take him for every penny she could, but she was stumped. She couldn't email the pictures to the Google account they set up if she couldn't find them. *Damn! Maybe it's time to cut our losses and abort. We always knew there was a risk. I've only got less than five minutes anyway.*

"Rhonda!"

Rhonda looked up to see Chas, the day manager, standing at the top of the stairs that lead down to the cigar lounge. He was flanked by Bruno, as well as a police lieutenant she recognized as a regular. Behind them was Mindy, the smirking waitress she had body-checked earlier. Rhonda felt like the blood drained out of her body.

"Rhonda, I believe that's Mr. Fennel's cell phone that you're hiding behind that book," Chas said.

* * *

Youngman pressed the phone against his ear. "Whoever it was, they hung up."

Ken blinked. He grabbed his phone out of Youngman's hand. "I'm expecting an important business call. Better see if that was them." Ken hurried out of the restroom.

"Wait!" Headphone Man said. "Come back!"

"I believe that signals my exit too." Youngman glimpsed at his Roswell Moondust wristwatch. "You only have three minutes to go anyway, my entertaining friend. Sorry, but I can't keep my hot barmaid waiting—"

The bathroom door slammed open. Youngman and Headphone Man turned to see Rhonda rush in. She briefly clocked Headphone Man's one headphone before standing face to face with Youngman.

"I waited so long for you to come back," she said breathlessly. "I'll admit it. I got curious. I looked at more of your photos." She held out the phone. "Just so love the flying saucer logo on your phone case, by the way."

Youngman noticed that Rhonda's bodice was unbuttoned even more than before. He licked his suddenly dry lips. "Designed it myself."

Chas and Bruno came into the bathroom in time to see Rhonda easing the cell phone into Youngman's front pant pocket. "Excuse me, Mr. Fennel," Chas said. "We found our server here handling your phone. I was going to return it myself, but she ran in here with it."

"She already gave it back. And, of course, she had my phone," Youngman said, putting his arm around her waist and squeezing her close. "I allowed it. She's a fan."

Rhonda flushed red. "Yep. Big fan."

"Just checking, Mr. Fennel. We try to maintain the privacy of our guests during these trying times."

"Pfft. 'Trying times.' Just the lamestream media creating much ado about nothing. We'll all survive."

"No! We won't!"

Everyone turned to Headphone Man. "Are you OK, sir?" Chas said.

"We're all going to die in three years, so no, I'm not OK."

"He's fine," Youngman said. "A practical joke. Just give us a minute, Chas."

"I'll be waiting for you," Rhonda said to Youngman. She gave Headphone Man a curious look and left. Chas and Bruno followed her out.

Youngman patted Headphone Man on the shoulder. "According to your own rules, our time is almost up. Seriously, Roger is behind this, right?"

Headphone man looked at his watch. "One minute fifteen seconds!" He threw himself to the floor, wrapping his arms around Youngman's knees. "Please! You have your phone back! You can help me now!"

"Stop it! This is too much. And to think I was going to invite you to my yacht for a totally lit party."

Headphone Man jumped to his feet. "That's it! Your yacht! The TARDIS Tomkat! That's how I can prove it. It's going to be blown up! That little group you helped finance in Delaware—"

"Shut up!" Youngman glanced around the bathroom. "Keep it down. I can't believe Roger told you that story. That he made up. That's totally not true."

"They'll blow up your yacht. Today! It's to scare you into staying in line so you'll keep the money flowing."

"You tell Roger, or whoever is behind your little performance, that they have crossed a line. To think I was intrigued by all this bunk. I even thought we could hang."

"Give me a break! You've pretended to believe a heck of a lot worse."

Youngman turned to go.

"Keep your eye on the news, Youngman! Then you'll know I'm telling the truth." Headphone Man again checked his watch. "Oh boy. I'm almost out of time. Unfortunately, I may jump back to my time before your yacht goes kaboom. Hey!"

Youngman spun around.

"Remember this! Send five hundred thousand to Irving Thorson Research, and you save the world! You become a hero, not a talk-show punchline!"

"Wait, that's your name? Irving?"

"It's all going to come out, Youngman! You'll spend the rest of your life battling the Delaware charges in court. You won't go to prison, though."

Youngman cupped his ears. "I'm not listening!" After a brief pause, he dropped his hands. "Okay, why not?"

"Because we all die! Another group, one that your wacko father is financing, will launch a warhead at New York from an abandoned base in Alaska. That's how it starts."

Youngman pulled the door open. "Tell Roger he's going to pay for this charade. Revenge is going to be a brutal bitch!"

"Considering everything, you really ought to make it a million. Just to be safe."

Youngman walked out, the door slowly creeping shut behind him.

* * *

Rhonda and Ken hadn't come to Samoa to visit their money, though the bank that their offshore account was at was just a quick bus ride from their resort. Rather, they were vacationing at one of the warmest beaches they could fly to in December. They strolled hand in hand on the white sands of Lalomanu as tourists waited for the sunset and another round of taro cocktails.

"You did it, not me," Ken said.

"Did what?"

"You pulled the scam off. We would've walked out of The Burke with nada if it wasn't for your last-second sleight of hand in the cigar lounge."

Rhonda let Ken's words linger before answering. "Just realizing that now?"

"Nope. I knew it when Youngman's nine hundred thousand transferred to our account."

Rhonda smiled. "I wish I could've seen his face when it dawned on him I'd switched my cell phone case with his."

Ken chuckled. "Oh yeah."

"Actually, swapping phone cases was easy. Wiping my phone before handing it to him was the scary part. I hit 'Delete All' just before I ran into the bathroom."

"Cool-headed. Meanwhile you had Youngman's phone in *your* cell phone case, burning a hole in your back pocket. Funny what you can dig out of a cell phone if you pay the right expert twenty grand."

"Photos. That's what you can dig out. Incriminating photos."

"On top of that, the money we squeezed out of The Burke with the photos *you* took more than paid for the computer tech."

"Icing on the cake."

Ken scanned a group of beachgoers lounging near the waves. "We pulled it off. But it was humbling."

"Humbling?"

"Humbling. Remember that guy I told you about? The one in the bathroom?"

"Headphone Man," Rhonda said. "I saw him when I ran in."

"He was the ballsiest, smartest, no-limit, best-prepared grifter I'd ever met in my life. Really, if it wasn't for him, it might not have worked out for us."

"First, you say *I* pulled it off, then—"

"No, it was you. All the way. Full credit."

"Don't forget it."

Ken watched two boys throw a Frisbee back and forth. "It's just that, man, he was a total animal. Relentless. Unwavering. Even while claiming to be from the future. He almost had *me* convinced. And then to somehow arrange to have Youngman's yacht blown up. I wonder if he got his money."

"He couldn't have been working alone," she said, watching her toes step into sand.

"Yeah," Ken said ominously. "Deep state."

Rhonda punched his shoulder. "Please."

They walked in silence, enveloped in the sounds of the waves and gulls and distant laughter.

Ken suddenly stopped.

"What?" Rhonda said.

"There," he said, pointing to a group near the waves.

"'There' what?"

He looked up and down the beach. "It's just..." He threw up his hands and faced her. "Listen. I thought I saw someone sitting in a beach chair sipping a big fruity cocktail and wearing headphones."

"Headphones? Or do you mean 'headphone'? Not even funny."

"Not even funny," he repeated. "And now he's gone." He snapped his fingers. "Poof."

Rhonda laughed. "OK, I'll play along. It couldn't have been him because he only pops up in bathrooms. That's what you told me he said."

"Oh, Rhonda." Ken wrapped his arms around her and kissed her. "Haven't you ever peed in the ocean?"

GOLDEN PARACHUTE

By Travis Richardson

"You sure about this?" Clara asked, Scotch-taping five rolled hundred-dollar bills on each of my middle fingers.

"As certain as the day I started this company."

She started to respond but bit her lip instead. She was a good assistant like that. Knowing her place. I'd miss her.

"Hey, Ryan. You ready?"

The eager intern jumped up from his chair at the marble conference table, his eyes wide like a child getting a pony. "Yessir, Mr. Dorrett."

I realized I couldn't reach inside my pocket. "Clara, would you mind?"

I glanced down at my skinny jeans. She sighed, shook her head, and reached into my pants pocket, pulling out the black fob with a raging bull on it.

"Don't break it," she said, handing it to Ryan. He sprinted out the conference room door.

Clara picked up my gold-plated Zippo lighter from the table and read the word *Awesomepants* engraved on it.

"Really?"

"It's one of a kind."

She shook her head, opening the top and flicking the flame. "I'm going to miss you, idiot."

"I'll miss you too." I took a deep breath. No turning back. Ever. "Let's do this."

Clara walked out of the conference room into the main office full of caffeine-junkie geniuses busy logging code. She held up an air horn and pressed the button. I nearly jumped out of my skin as the blaring sound bounced off the polished concrete floor. And I knew the ear-splitting wail was coming. I bet a dozen lattes spilled across keyboards, a few bladders emptied, and, best yet, Ethan Lewis shit his pants.

"Attention, everybody," Clara shouted like a carnival barker. "Slammernet's founder and former CEO Alex Dorrett has a few words to say."

I walked out to the center lobby of a warehouse-converted-into-a-sprawling-open-office and saw a hundred-plus employee eyes watching me, mouths agape. Yesterday, they had been beneath me in the org chart. Now, my name had been deleted. They were like my children, all grown up, but instead of leaving the nest, they kicked me out.

"I wanted to say a few words before I leave. I started this company in my studio apartment six years ago. Just me, a computer, a ton of coffee, and a dream. I didn't go to Stanford or Harvard like most of you. Junior college, then a few years at Cal State…" I tapered off, studying my successor, Ethan's, paper-white shocked expression. Screw these silver-spooned bitches. "Anyhow, I created this company from nothing into a billion-dollar juggernaut. Of course, to get to a billion I had to sell portions of the company, which is how I ended up in the position where I am at today. Fired. Rich, yes, but unemployed. Sure, I made some mistakes…" A nervous laugh echoed off the floor and walls. "OK, some were bad. I've apologized several times in the media and to all of you. Regardless, you're in the hands of Ethan. Uptight and ubercareful Ethan." I shook my head, spitting out his name. We glared at each other. "All I can say is best of luck, suckers. I built this brand with high risk and balls, not over-the-top sensitivity. This company is a sinking ship. You should get out while you still can. And to Ethan, I have this special message for you."

I nodded to Clara. She flipped open the Zippo and lit the $100 bills. I raised my burning middle fingers to Ethan. "Sit and spin, asshole. I'm leavin' on top, unlike your sorry ass."

I proceeded to moonwalk across the floor and through the sliding glass door exit. The stunned silence blanketing the building was amazing. I rocked that farewell speech and then some.

My midnight-blue Lamborghini Aventador waited for me, rumbling a deep testosterone growl.

Ryan stood nearby with an orgasmic smile, holding the fob. As I reached for it, my fingers started searing. I tried to pull off the sizzling Franklins, but the heat was too intense.

"Fuck. Get these off now."

I shook my hands, fanning the flames. Ryan stood motionless with his mouth agape, totally useless. Clara ran out and pulled the bills off my fingers, stomping on the flaming currency. I looked at my blistered digits. Holy hell, they hurt.

"You need to go to the hospital, Alex," Clara said.

I glanced over at the building I had built as dozens of my former employees crowded by the windows, recording me on their cell phones. I held back my tears and straightened my back. I couldn't show weakness by getting into an ambulance or letting somebody drive me to the hospital.

"I'm fine."

"No, you're not," Clara said.

"Okay, maybe not. But I'll go to a hospital later. I just need to get out of here on my own and up to the winery."

Steering and shifting a twelve-cylinder beast without middle fingers is pretty damn hard. I proved that by scraping up my $300,000 machine against a light pole. That accident, unfortunately, was captured on video, too.

Twelve minutes later, I crossed the Golden Gate Bridge, cruising on the 101, leaving San Francisco behind in the rearview mirror. My objective was to keep driving north for an hour to a Sonoma County winery in Healdsburg I had purchased a few months earlier. There, I could drown my pain in barrels of pinot. Screw Silicon Valley; wineries were the future.

But that seventy-mile distance seemed too far. I needed something immediately to get me through the pain and humiliation of my less-than-slick departure. I turned off Sir Francis Drake Boulevard, incidentally the same exit folks take to visit friends and family at San Quentin prison. Clyde's looked like a biker bar catering to both six-figure Harley-owning wannabes and legitimate rejects who were down and out. I had the feeling I met both classifications, and believing the worst was behind me, I entered the bar.

"A cup of ice and a bottle of Jameson," I shouted to the busty, leather-clad bartender over the sound of Ozzy Osbourne's "Crazy Train" blaring through the sound system.

She eyed me for a few hard seconds as if wondering whether to throw me out. When she brought my order, I dunked my fingers in the ice. After a few swigs from the bottle, some of the self-inflicted injuries began to ease. Looking around, I took in the gloomy atmosphere. Several tables were occupied by gray-bearded dudes wearing scuffed leather boots and leather vests with similar patches. I was the only person wearing Chuck Taylors and skinny pants. Everybody pointedly ignored me, including the bartender. Fuck 'em. I'll let my Irish buddy Jameson keep me company.

People came and went, but I stopped paying attention, focusing on how Ethan did me wrong and all the ways I could get even.

An eighth into the bottle, a hand clasped my shoulder. I turned to see a plump man with unkempt, curly, reddish-brown hair.

"That your Italian Stallion out there?" he asked in a hoarse voice.

I nodded.

"Sweet, buddy. Listen, can I bum a ride? See, my wife just drained my bank account and took off with a car salesman."

The loser tried to give a dopey aw-shucks country-bumpkin smile, but his bad teeth and narrow, calculating eyes ruined his desired effect. He'd probably been released from Quentin a few hours ago. But I felt so damn lonely that I would've befriended a rabid porcupine. I pushed the bottle to him with my knuckles.

"Help me finish this. Sounds like we both need it. What's your name?"

"Chet. And you?"

I thought about giving him some BS name like Studs McGee, but fuck it. "Alex Dorrett."

His eyes widened in recognition of the name. "Aren't you—"

"Yes," I said, nodding to the bottle. "Drink up, buddy."

He did, and I did too. I talked nonstop, bitching about all the mistreatment and abuse that a billionaire like me had to endure from jerks like Ethan and others who harassed me about crap like ethics and decorum. It's the kind of BS that kills the innovative freedom necessary for a tech founder to thrive. Chet listened to me, nodding his head in sycophantic sympathy, even though I'm sure he didn't understand half of what I told him.

After a while, things got fuzzy. I remember lumbering to the john to puke, and vomiting on some biker's boots while he stood at a urinal. The biker shoved me against a wall and held a knife to my throat. I tried to apologize; maybe I cried, but Chet came in a few seconds later and got me out of there. I blacked out for a minute. Then I was inside the Lambo with Chet behind the wheel, giggling like a child. I tried to sober up using sheer willpower over the unhealthy amount of eighty-proof whiskey that saturated my bloodstream. Did we even finish the bottle? Regardless, I was drunk enough to believe I could make sobriety happen in the face of science.

Then I passed out again, and when I woke up, I found myself on a sagging spring bed in a small room full of cheap furniture. The wallpaper a faded pink-rose print that peeled around the corners. Definitely not my Healdsburg Victorian mansion full of high-tech gadgetry with a winery to boot. My head throbbed, but those FU fingers were worse. They looked like burnt hotdogs. I heard voices carrying beyond the door.

"This guy's like a billionaire. Started up Slammernet, sold shares of his company, and then got fired. They gave him a bunch of money to leave, too."

That voice sounded like Chet's.

"Did you see that video of him?" a woman's voice said. "Moonwalking with flaming middle fingers and then driving his Lamborghini into a light pole. The guy's a freakin' goofball."

"A rich goofball."

I stood on wobbly sea legs, making my way to the door. I planned on asking Chet why I was sleeping in this dump and not my winery palace.

"So how do we get his money?" a deeper, menacing third voice asked.

I froze, my hand hovering inches above the door handle.

"He burnt his middle fingers pretty bad," Chet said. "Maybe we can make him pay us to take him to the hospital."

"That won't get us millions," the deep voice said. "What about you, Christy? Think you could, you know, screw a bunch of money out of him?"

"I haven't been hookin' in years, and I don't know if you've noticed, but life hasn't been good to me lately. I'm not sure he'd go for me. He probably bangs supermodels."

Regular models, yes, but unfortunately, not supermodels. Alas, money can't buy everything.

"You still got a sweet ass, baby," Chet said, followed by the sound of a slap on her underside.

"You're all right with me fuckin' that freak?" Christy asked.

"For a million dollars? You betcha."

"Shit," the deep voice said.

"What?" Christy and Chet both asked.

"I still don't think you'd get much out of him offerin' sex. No offense, Christy. I think we oughta sit him down and offer him either his life or his money."

"And what? He's gonna write us a check for millions of dollars?" Chet asked.

"You got a better idea?"

In their silence, I crept over to a bedroom window. Looking through the filthy glass, I cringed when I saw my damaged Lamborghini parked next to a rusted truck. Some days I could be a true idiot. The yard made me think I'd been taken to a remote cabin surrounded by redwoods. Tucking in my middle digits, I tried lifting the window, but I couldn't get much leverage. I heard footsteps walking down the hall. I jumped into bed, burying my head in the pillow. The door squeaked open. Tobacco smoke wafted into the air. I felt the presence of people watching me, but I ignored them, feigning sleep. A boot kicked my foot. Once. Twice.

"Come on, Alex. Time to get up. You passed out, but you weren't drugged none. You've had a good three hours to sleep this off," Chet said.

I opened my eyes as slowly as possible. Three people looked down at me. Chet, some burly dude with a wild beard and long, greasy hair, and my supposed temptress, Christy. The dishwater blonde might've been some eye candy once, but age, hard times, and probable drug abuse made me think of a sponge dripping with venereal diseases.

I sat up, acting as refreshed as a fully charged lithium-ion battery.

"Thanks for letting me sleep that one off, Chet. I've gotta hit the road."

I started to stand, but the burly dude grabbed my middle finger. A million lightning bolts shot through my body, singeing every molecular cell. Falling to my knees, I screamed like a baby.

"Look, here's how it is, buddy," Chet said, bending down to my eye level. "You're going to give us five million, or my friend here is gonna keep squeezin' your fingers. And then I'll ask for ten or twenty million. You're worth what? A billion? That's what you told me."

I protectively tucked my fingers into my armpits. I blinked tears away and took a moment to size up my captors. They looked like idiots, people I could dominate in a board room or a spelling bee. But in my sorry state, they had a clear physical advantage over me. And while Chet was not wrong, my net worth fluctuates around the billion-dollar mark; it's mostly on paper…or digital lines of code. And then after taxes…

"How do you want it?" I said, trying to calm my voice and establish an ounce of authority.

Although the finger squeeze had felt awful, the intense pain had cleared the Jameson cobwebs from my brain.

"You for real?" the big guy said.

They looked at each other, surprised and confused, like I'd pulled a gold brick out of my pants. I took that moment to pick myself up and sit on the bed. Nobody should ever negotiate from their knees.

"I should warn you, cash is going to be the hardest thing for me to get," I said. "If you've got an open bank account, I can wire money to you right now."

Again, they looked at each other, this time their eyes wide with anticipation and savage hunger.

"And just how would you do that?" Chet asked.

"Give me your bank account number, and I'll—"

"Ain't no way I'm going to give you that," Christy said, pointing an accusing finger at me. "You'll drain what little money I've got. It's all you rich people know what to do. Screw over the poor."

"Plus, he'll know who you are," the big guy said, his narrow eyes boring into me.

"I don't care who you are. I just need to see a doctor and get on my way," I said, being the voice of reason. "We're all adults here. We can work together."

"Where's your final destination?" the big dude asked.

"What?" His choice of words threw me for a loop.

"A winery up in Sonoma," Chet said. "He bought the whole thing for cash."

"Well, damn," Christy said. She looked at me with a sparkle in her eye. Did alcohol have a stronger allure than money?

"I thought you said cash is hard to come by," the big guy said, standing over me. "How come you just bought a winery with it?"

"Cash means I didn't buy it with credit. The transfer of funds from me to the estate was still done electronically."

My three captors pondered this information quietly.

"You know anything about that Bitcoin shit?" Chet asked, breaking the silence.

"Sure. You can get it with different apps. Then you just log in and link it to your bank account. I can help you do it."

"You got money in there?" the big guy asked.

"Sure. A couple mil. But I mostly cashed out when it hit twenty-k." I laughed. "I know, I'm an idiot."

They looked at me, eyes glazed. I was starting to feel a little drunk again, but different this time. My intoxication was empowered off their stupid looks. I needed to pump the gas.

"What's the matter with you guys?" I said, standing. "I'm trying to give you money, and you're acting like you don't want it. Gawd."

All three of them flinched, cowed by my outburst.

"It's like, we need cash. That'd work the best," Christy said in a meek voice. "Even if it isn't five million."

"Christy," Chet hissed.

"What? You really think we can spend five million in cash without fucking up somehow?" She turned back to me. "How much can you get in cash right now, Little Man?"

I was taken aback by the "little man" comment. Sure, I'm not tall or physically imposing, but I make up for it in different ways. What should I call her? Scabby Whore? For that matter, the big guy could be Greasy Lumberjack, and Chet would be Inbred Judas.

"If I go up to a Chase bank and ask for all the money in my account, they might have a hundred k on hand. Maybe more, maybe less. Depends on the bank. Could you guys handle that?"

Chet's eyes lit up, and he clapped his hands.

"Well shit, what are we waiting for? Let's go to the bank. There's one in Petaluma."

His words helped orient me a little. We were somewhere near a quaint town halfway between San Francisco and Santa Rosa.

"But first these." I flipped them my pair of damaged birds. "They'd have a hard time believing I wasn't under duress if I'm bleeding all over the deposit slips."

The trio stepped out into the hallway and talked in hushed voices for a few minutes. Christy and Chet brought me a bottle of hydrogen peroxide, yellowed gauze, and a roll of duct tape. I was hoping for, but not expecting, a trip to urgent care. Their offering seemed barbaric.

"Any Neosporin?"

"How about an amputation?" the lumberjack said.

"How about you guys end up being a whole hell of a lot poorer than you already are."

"And why would that happen exactly?" Christy put her hands on her hips.

"People saw me leave with Chet from that bar. Other folks have seen my Lamborghini motor through whatever town we're in, and if I go missing for too long, they will remember seeing Chet in a machine he could never afford. Even if he made payments for the next two hundred years. In the meantime, you'll have to feed me—"

"We'd kill you first," the big man said.

"Then you'd have the trouble of getting rid of me and the car."

"Shit, man. We'd bury you and hide the car," Chet said. "Easy peasy Japanesey."

I raised my eyebrows. "You'd hide a three-hundred-thousand-dollar Lambo?"

"Sure." His eyes shifted as if wondering what else might happen with his simple plan.

"You think you or either of your partners would keep hiding that Italian supercar or even destroy it? It's worth too much money. I mean, you won't get anywhere near the value reselling it, considering it's stolen, but there are enough unethical dudes who would give you, I dunno, say fifty k."

Their eyes were just as wide as when I said five mil. Anything over a thousand bucks seemed like an amazing deal to them. Hell, they'd probably murder each other for a Benjamin. It's funny that when I was CEO, the board wanted me to have bodyguards and high-tech security at my house, even though there never were any credible threats or incidents the entire time. Yet, the day I got fired, I went to a bar and got myself kidnapped. Some things you can't predict. And that's when it hit me. I had so much more leverage than I realized.

"I say we just kill the fucker and sell the car," the big guy said, walking toward me.

I backed up against the wall.

"Chet or Christy. I'll give either of you a million bucks in untraceable bills if you kill this motherfucker. Right now," I shouted.

The big man stopped cold. His face scrunched in a perplexed *what-did-you-say?* expression.

"This is a once-in-a-lifetime opportunity. You both've made dumb mistakes in your life, but letting this opportunity slip through your fingers is really, really stupid."

"I'm going to rip your throat out, asshole," the lumberjack said, balling up his fists and taking a step forward.

"Great. And nobody gets my money. Brilliant move, dipshit. They'll end up killing you without any money."

He froze again. I looked at the other two, who were watching me as if trying to find a lie.

"You'll end up killing him one way or another," I said. "The question is, do you want a million dollars or not?"

He turned to them. "Seriously, guys, do you expect the little shit to—"

Christy bolted down the hall.

"Oh no," the big guy said, starting to run after her.

Chet tackled him from behind, and they tumbled to the dirty hardwood floor with a thud.

"What the hell, man?"

"Get the gun, Christy. I got 'im," Chet yelled.

The big guy grabbed Chet's head like a basketball and slammed it repeatedly into the hardwood floor.

Bam, bam! Half of the lumberjack's face disappeared in an explosion of blood and bone. I blinked, trying to comprehend what happened.

What I made happen.

For the past several years, people would jump through hoops to accommodate my demands—until this week when they turned against me—but never in my lifetime did I think I could ask anybody to murder for me. The power was both nauseating and thrilling.

Chet pulled himself out from under the big man's twitching body. Christy walked up to him, a smoking semi-automatic pistol in her hand.

"Thank you, baby," he said, rubbing the back of his head. "Now we can split that million between us."

"There ain't no we in *million*, Chet."

She raised the gun between his eyes.

"But Chris—"

A deafening explosion caused my eardrums to ring. I didn't see her kill him, but when I opened my eyes again, I saw Chet's remains splattered across the room. I felt sick. Fuck this power trip. Murder is horrible. She pointed the gun at me.

"You better have that million ready."

Unable to articulate words and fearing I might puke if I opened my mouth, I nodded instead. It was the best I could do.

We drove to a Rite Aid, where she bought Neosporin and patched me up. Then we went to the bank, and I deposited $950,000 into Christine McGinnis's account. She also took $50,000 in cash from my account. I assured the manager that I was making this transaction of my own free will in spite of my ragtag condition. Although the manager looked skeptical, she had to accept it. After all, I am Alex Dorrett.

I pulled up to a car dealership in Santa Rosa. Christy had a red Camaro in mind for her getaway. According to her, nobody visited the old house, and those who did wouldn't contact the police under any conditions.

"I'm expecting a good two to three months' lead time to disappear." She shot a pair of cold gray eyes at me. "That's assuming you keep your trap shut."

I brushed a bandaged finger across my lips like it was a zipper.

"I ain't saying a word."

She studied me for a minute before nodding.

"Where's the place you're headin' to again?"

I wasn't sure if she was issuing a threat to find me if the bodies were discovered or if she had genuine curiosity. Regardless, she could find out with a quick web search.

"An estate outside of Healdsburg. I bought a—"

"No, what's the name of it?"

I hesitated. A killer sat in my car. What would she think of the name? But then again, I'd issued a challenge, and she had answered the call without hesitation. Ruthless, focused, and unemotional. Damn, she'd have made a wonderful vice president. Might have saved my ass from getting canned.

"I'm renaming the place. Going to call it Golden Parachute Winery. Come by if you want a free bottle. The Zin is spectacular."

"What does golden parachute mean?"

"It's a term for execs and managers who get terminated but also get a tremendous payout on their way out the door."

"Rich losers who get even more money."

I chuckled. "I guess you could say that."

"And then somebody else comes in and cleans up their messes. Right?"

I shrugged. "Sure."

"Where I'm from, losers end up with bullets in their heads. But I guess you saw that firsthand, didn't you?"

I swallowed and nodded. I had witnessed a double homicide.

She raised the swing door and pulled herself out with a paper bag full of bills. Closing the door, she turned to me. I waved, not sure what she wanted. A lopsided smile crossed her face as she flipped me two birds and moonwalked backward through the Chevy dealership's sliding glass doors. Her moves were flawless.

They say imitation is the purest form of flattery. What does it mean when the imitator is a cold-blooded murderer? I felt a smile spread from ear to ear. It means I'm one badass motherfucker who shouldn't be trifled with. I sat up straighter, knowing I would go up to my winery, drink a few barrels of wine, and map out ways to avenge myself against Ethan and everyone else who had ever crossed me. I let out a maniacal laugh, put the Italian beast in gear, stomped on the gas, leaving smoke and burnt rubber in my wake…and immediately T-boned a passing police cruiser.

That's how I learned some situations are harder to get out of than others.

NEVER HAVE I EVER

By Barb Goffman

March 1989

I kept watching him across the room, his easy smile, his twinkling eye, but he never gave me a second glance.

"Here you go." The petite waitress set two more pitchers of golden beer on our round wooden table. Working here at Carlo's, carrying endless trays of food and drink, must have made her strong enough for the Olympics. The bar was hopping, as always.

"Put them on my tab," my friend Maury said in his usual friendly tone as he lifted the pitcher closest to him to refill some of our glasses. My friend Clark handled the rest.

As they poured, my gaze wandered again until I heard "Tamara." Maury had said my name loudly to catch my attention, perhaps not for the first time, then handed my glass over. Guns N' Roses's latest, "Paradise City," came on, and he began bopping his head. His dark-brown hair—curly on the top, short on the sides—swished to the beat.

The conversation about our college's chance of winning this year's national basketball championship continued between Maury and the rest of my pals. I didn't care about basketball, and I didn't even really like beer—I was much more of a strawberry wine-cooler girl—but I loved my friends, and I loved getting out of the dorm on Thursday nights to blow off steam. I used to be a Stepford student, studying all the time. But since the start of this semester, I'd been going out partying every Thursday night. We always came to Carlo's.

He did, too—Dustin, the guy I couldn't stop thinking about. My friend Jasmine introduced us a couple of months ago, right after the semester began. It had been stifling in here, between the heat from the vents and off all the bodies crammed together. When my hand brushed against his, it felt like a jolt of electricity all the way down to my pink-painted toenails. I was thrilled I'd worn a tight tank top that night. As my friend Laine often said, "You've got the goods, baby. Show 'em off." So, pretending someone had bumped into me from behind, I'd leaned forward, giving him a good look. He'd waggled his black eyebrows, then we'd exchanged some small talk before he got dragged away by one of his frat brothers. But that twinkle in his eye had stayed with me and left a smile on my lips.

"Enough about b-ball," Eileen said, pulling me from my reverie. She usually had pale skin, but she'd gotten a deep tan during spring break in Cancun two weeks ago. I'd planned to go with her and the rest of the gang, but a family matter had come up, and I'd had to bow out.

"Not talk about b-ball? Sacrilege!" Clark's chapped lips curled into a goofy grin.

Eileen rolled her eyes. "Let's play Never Have I Ever." She loved the secrets-revealing drinking game.

"Since when do you need a game to get drunk?" Kelly said, laughing.

"Shut up!" Eileen swatted Kelly's arm. "It's fun."

"Can't argue with that." Kelly's large mismatched earrings—a sun and a moon—dangled out from beneath her wavy auburn hair, which cascaded past her shoulders. I wished my dark-brown hair had body like that, but it had always been stick straight. No amount of fluffing ever made a difference.

"Okay, I'll start," Eileen said. "Never have I ever…drunk so much that I blacked out."

The six of us at the table all looked at each other, then Maury lifted his glass with an amused smile and took a large gulp. He'd blacked out last year, having partied way too hard after midterms. Somehow, he hadn't gotten a terrible hangover, and he treated his memory gap like a badge of honor. Too bad every blackout didn't turn out as well.

"You're not drinking for this one?" Kelly asked her roommate, Laine.

Laine's blue eyes grew so big they reminded me of a pond back home that overflowed every spring, the excess water streaming over the banks like a mother's tears.

"No, I've *never* blacked out," Laine said.

"Yeah, right," Kelly said. "Does the name Señor Frog's ring a bell?"

"No." Laine appeared confused.

"My point exactly," Kelly said. "Anyway, my turn. Never have I ever…taken a pregnancy test."

"That rules me out," Clark said, leaning his beefy arms against the table and taking a drink anyway.

We all laughed, but I was astonished at the intimate nature of the question. Then Laine sipped her beer, and Eileen's eyebrows flew to her chestnut hairline.

"What?" Laine said. "Like you've never had a false alarm."

Shivering as if he'd been served stale beer, Maury said, "This is getting way too serious. Time to change the subject. Never have I ever cheated on an exam."

Clark tossed back the rest of his beer. When Kelly's mouth dropped open in surprise, he said, "What? It was in high school."

When no one else drank, he tilted his head at Eileen. "You're not drinking because…?"

"What are you talking about?" she said. "I've never cheated on a test."

"That's not what you told me," he said.

Eileen's hazel eyes bugged out. "That was my sister, not me. I was the valedictorian for God's sake."

"And now we know why." Laine smirked. "Okay, never have I ever…lied while playing Never Have I Ever." She looked pointedly at Eileen, who broke into a huge grin before taking a drink, and we all nearly fell off our chairs in laughter.

"But I wasn't lying about not cheating," Eileen said, slapping the table with her hand. "I swear."

"Sure you weren't," Clark said.

"Like none of you have ever lied during this game." She stared around the table, and eventually, everyone else laughed and drank, too. Everyone but me. I was the good girl of the group.

The game went on for a few more rounds. They all got buzzed—me, not as much—while I kept glancing about for Dustin. To be truthful, he was why I came here every Thursday night. Despite myself, I kept trying to catch his eye, but it was like I was invisible.

It had been different the night we met. An hour after Dustin's friend dragged him off, the six of us had been sitting at a nearby table, deep into our third—or was it fourth?—pitcher of beer. Out of nowhere Dustin had leaned over me, asking if he could pull up a chair. Emboldened by my buzz, I'd said, "Hell yeah." I'd introduced him to everyone and explained he was a friend of Jasmine's. His frat was paired with her sorority, and they did lots of stuff together. None of my close friends were into that scene, but they all knew Jasmine. She'd lived in our dorm first year. Dustin fit into our group well, matching us drink for drink as the night went on. Soon, he and I had been holding hands under the table. Then he'd started rubbing my thigh through my jeans.

"I'm never going to attract the waitress's attention," Clark said, catapulting me back to the present. "I'm getting food from the bar. Any requests?"

"Nachos," Laine said.

"And wings," Maury said.

"Bathroom?" I suggested after Clark walked off.

"Good idea," Kelly said.

We pushed through the pulsing crowd as "She Drives Me Crazy" by Fine Young Cannibals came over the speakers. Boy, could I identify with the song's obsessed singer, who was stuck on a girl like she was superglue. I spent all my time these days thinking about Dustin, no matter how hard I tried not to.

When Kelly and I finally neared the women's restroom, we found a line running out into the hallway, of course. Construction-paper green shamrocks decorated the maroon walls, left over from St. Patrick's Day last Friday. As we waited, I spotted Dustin again. He was making out with some blonde. Every week, he hooked up with somebody new.

"What are you looking at?" Kelly yelled over the music.

"Nothing." I hated I'd been obvious. Dustin hadn't been a topic of conversation since the day after that fateful night we met in January. He'd been one and done, as far as my crew was concerned. They had no idea how I really felt.

By the time Kelly and I made it back to our table, Clark had returned with the food. We dug in. As always, the buffalo wings were extra hot, their spice making my face flush. I loved that feeling. Craved it, in fact. Sometimes, lately, I felt so forlorn I feared I'd never feel anything else.

Things sure had been different that night in January. It's hard to remember everything that happened, but at some point, Dustin and I had begun making out at the table, and I heard Maury say, "Geez, get a room."

Dustin pulled away. "Want me to walk you home?"

I knew what that meant, and I beamed. It had been way too long since my last relationship. Since my last anything. Then, I had a moment of sanity. "Hold on."

I staggered from the table, my shoes repeatedly sticking to the floor. Probably spilled beer. Clark would call it "a damn shame." I found Jasmine dancing and led her to a quieter spot.

"Dustin offered to walk me home," I told her. "Is he safe?"

Jasmine smiled, dimples popping on her brown cheeks. "Yeah, he's a nice guy. You don't have to worry."

"Excellent." While I wanted to fool around with him, I didn't want him to be pushy. Unlike all my other friends, I'd never gone all the way.

When I got back to the table, Dustin grabbed me and kissed me. I leaned into him, reveling in how he made me feel petite in his thick arms, instead of like the tall girl who always avoided heels. Finally, we broke apart. "Let's go," I said loudly, tugging my wool coat off my chair.

"Tamara." Laine leaped up and yanked me aside. "Don't leave with this guy."

"Why? He's scnise," I slurred, then giggled. "I mean nice. I like him."

"Well, I don't. He's smarmy."

I waved her off. Jasmine had given him the thumbs-up, and she knew him better than Laine did. "I'll be fine. See you later." As the rap song "Wild Thing" spilled out of the speakers, we stumbled down the long staircase and out into the frigid night.

"Tamara, are you in?" Kelly snapped her fingers in front of my face, rousing my attention. I reached for another hot wing. "Movies? Tomorrow?" she said. We all often went to the movies on Friday nights.

"Which one?" I shouldn't go—I was way behind on my reading for every class—but the distraction was tempting.

"She wants to see that new chick flick." Maury rolled his eyes. "*Chances Are*. Stars Robert Downey Jr."

"Oh, from *Saturday Night Live*," I said.

"And *Weird Science*," Clark added.

"Love John Hughes movies," Eileen said. "*Pretty in Pink* was awesome."

"And *Ferris Bueller*," Maury said.

"Hell yeah." Clark gave him a high five. "Bueller, Bueller, Bueller."

While everybody laughed—Clark's imitation of the monotone teacher in the movie was spot on—Kelly sighed. "Yeah, love John Hughes too. But this isn't a John Hughes movie. It's about a pregnant woman whose husband is killed in an accident, then he gets reincarnated. Twenty years later he's dating their daughter—until he remembers his past."

Lordy. I gulped down some beer.

"I still think it sounds weird," Laine said.

"More like gross," Clark said.

"It sounds fun to me," Eileen said. "We discussed reincarnation in my world religions course. If you have good karma, you come back to a better life."

A better life did sound appealing. But I didn't believe in reincarnation. We only had this one life. It was up to us to make the best of it.

"Are you in?" Kelly asked me.

"Sorry. I have a paper due Monday," I lied. That movie wasn't for me.

"This is why I take engineering courses," Maury said. "Noooo papers."

I sipped my beer, thinking about the idea of a better life. I'd tried to improve mine back in January. I'd been tired of studying so much, having little time for my friends. No time for romance. So, when Dustin and I arrived back at the dorm that night, I invited him up to my room. There weren't many single rooms in my dorm. I'd lucked out with one this year, but I hadn't put it to good use. Yet.

Before I knew it, we were side by side on my bed, partly undressed. I was kissing his neck, breathing in his woody scent. Really turned on. But I had to do what was right for me. Mustering my courage, I eased away from his embrace and told him I was a virgin. "No oral, no sex, not tonight." Not until we were more of a couple, I thought, assuming things went as I hoped they would.

"Got it." He kissed me again. Damn, he was a good kisser. I practically melted in his arms.

Suddenly, I opened my eyes. A sharp pain in my groin made me gasp. What was going on? Had I fallen asleep? And then I realized Dustin was on top of me. Inside me. "No!" I tried to push him away. "Stop it! No!"

He lay on top of me like a dead weight. "What's wrong?"

Was he kidding? "I told you I wouldn't have sex with you."

He caressed my cheek. "Come on. You're enjoying it." He started nibbling my ear, and I must have passed out once more because, when I woke up, he was grunting over and over before he stopped in a rush.

Dizzy, I tried to push him off again. "Why did you do that? I told you I didn't want to. I was a virgin."

"You were serious about that?" He rolled off me and sat on the edge of my bed. "Wow. I'm sorry." Except he didn't sound sorry—or surprised. He started getting dressed.

"You're leaving?" Despite being furious and upset, I didn't want him to go. I wanted him to stay and hold me and make my first time everything it was supposed to be in some stupid fairy-tale world.

"I have an early class. But I'll call you." He kissed me, grabbed his jacket, and left.

It wasn't until a few hours later, after I'd puked my guts out, that I realized I'd never given him my number.

Looking at Laine now as she ate another cheese-smothered nacho chip, I thought about how my life would be different if I'd listened to her that night in January. She'd sure had Dustin's number.

I hadn't told anyone he'd raped me. I was too embarrassed at how stupid I'd been, so I'd made up a story that we fooled around a little before I sent him packing. I hated how much I thought about him. Didn't want to think about him at all. But I found myself coming to Carlo's every Thursday night now. I wanted him to see that he hadn't hurt me by nailing me while I was unconscious. That I could have a good time without him. That he didn't matter to me at all.

Even though he did.

Jasmine had mentioned him when we had lunch a few weeks ago, right before spring break. Apparently, I was the first of Dustin's "conquests." He'd gotten himself quite the reputation among his frat brothers as a "stud." I don't know if his friends knew exactly what happened between us—probably not, who'd admit to rape?—but I was the first girl he'd had a one-night stand with, Jasmine had said. It had become a regular thing for him.

That hadn't been news to me. Every Thursday night, I watched him hook up with a different girl here at Carlo's, and then, when they were plastered, they'd leave together. I didn't know if any of those girls were virgins before they left with Dustin, but I was certain none of them were the next morning.

In a weird way, it felt like my fault. If I hadn't drunk like a fish that January night, if I hadn't passed out on my bed, I might have been able to fight him off before it was too late. Two days ago, I went to a lecture on date rape. The counselor running it said the victim was never at fault. That made sense in my head. My heart was having a harder time with the concept. My heart felt like I should have done something more. Like I still should do something more.

Across the room, Dustin and the blonde were putting on their jackets. She wobbled and tipped into him. He whispered into her ear, and she flashed a flirty grin his way. She looked like a nice girl. Even if she wasn't, she deserved better than him.

We all did—she and I and the rest of Dustin's "conquests."

"I don't feel well," I said, standing up. "I need to go home."

Maury set down his beer and nodded. "It's getting late. Let me pay the bill." He knew everyone would cover their share tomorrow.

Dustin and the blonde were shuffling toward the long staircase.

"I really need some fresh air now," I said. "I'll meet you all outside."

I stumbled and swayed toward the stairs, tottering into some people who commented on how wasted I was. Just as Dustin was about to walk down, I reached the stairwell and fell against him hard. While the blonde screamed, he tumbled down the long, steep steps, his head banging over and over, until he landed with a thud on the concrete floor below. Blood flowed from his nose and scalp, pooling beneath him.

"Oh my God," I cried, gripping the gummy railing to steady myself. I prayed I looked sorry to anyone watching. I was, in a way. I was sorry Dustin had raped me. I was sorry for the aftermath. I was sorry for so many things.

But I wasn't sorry he was dead—or at least that I wanted him to be. This was the plan that had sprung fully formed in my mind as I left the date-rape lecture on Tuesday. I'd needed to do something to make things right. I didn't want one more girl waking in a haze to find Dustin pumping away on top of her. Not one more girl wishing she would die, thanks to him.

As the blonde ran down the stairs, a guy leaned close to Dustin and yelled, "He's not breathing!"

Bon Jovi's "Born to Be My Baby" was streaming from the speakers. It felt perverse, listening to this song about a guy professing his love to his girl, his "baby," whom he'd never let go. And suddenly, I was back in that cold clinic while my friends were on the warm sands of Cancun, and I was making the hardest choice of my life—the only choice I could make—about my own baby. Letting it go. I couldn't have survived having a part of Dustin grow inside me.

I was barely surviving now.

Dustin had taken so many things from me, my virginity the least of them. I'd lost my drive. Bombed my midterms. I woke up regularly from nightmares in which I tried to push him off me, but he laughed and kept going. More than once, I'd considered throwing *myself* down this flight of stairs. And I'd become the best liar of all in Never Have I Ever. Guaranteed, none of my friends realized I should have drunk in response to every single question tonight.

I needed it to be that way. To preserve my good-girl image. Otherwise, I'd have motive. Now, people would think this simply was a horrible accident.

Horrible but oh so necessary.

I couldn't help the other girls, Dustin's "conquests" since his night with me. But I'd saved the blonde. And I'd saved his future conquests, girls who would've meant nothing more to him than a notch on his bedpost.

Maybe one day I'd feel as if I'd saved myself, too. It was hard to imagine that day. Right now, I felt as lonely as ever, having committed this horrendous crime and needing to keep so many secrets.

That's what Dustin had done to me. He'd turned me into a guarded, secretive person. Into a liar. And now, into a killer. I was glad I didn't believe in reincarnation, because I prayed he'd rot in hell.

Kelly appeared at my side, staring down the stairs with her mouth open as someone said, "Holy shit. He's dead."

Thank you, God. I let out a breath so deep it was as if I'd been holding it since that bitter January night.

"What happened?" Kelly asked, wide-eyed.

"I tripped into him," I said, my voice shaky, "and he fell down the stairs."

"Oh my God." She hugged me, then pulled back. "Are you OK?"

"Yeah."

It was true. I was. For the first time in months, I felt something in addition to shame and loneliness and sadness deep inside my soul.

Finally, at long last, I felt hope.

Contributors

Melodie Campbell, called the "Queen of Comedy" by the *Toronto Sun*, was also named the "Canadian literary heir to Donald Westlake" by *Ellery Queen's Mystery Magazine*. Winner of ten awards, including the Derringer and the Crime Writers of Canada Award of Excellence, she has multiple bestsellers and was featured in *USA Today*. Her publications include more than one hundred comedy credits, sixteen novels, and sixty short stories, but she's best known for The Goddaughter mob caper series.

Joseph D'Agnese (JosephDAgnese.com) is the Derringer-winning author of more than twenty short stories that have appeared in *Ellery Queen's Mystery Magazine, Alfred Hitchcock's Mystery Magazine, Mystery Weekly*, and *The Best American Mystery Stories*.

O'Neil De Noux (oneildenoux.com), a retired police officer and former homicide detective, has authored forty-five books and more than four hundred short stories, which have been awarded the Shamus Award twice, the Derringer Award, and Police Book of the Year (awarded by PoliceWriters.com). Two of his stories have been featured in *The Best American Mystery Stories* annual anthology (2003 and 2013). He is a past vice president of the Private Eye Writers of America.

David Dean's short stories have appeared regularly in *Ellery Queen's Mystery Magazine* as well as several anthologies, including *The Best American Mystery Stories*, since 1990. His stories have been nominated for the Shamus, Barry, Derringer, and Edgar awards, and have received the *Ellery Queen's Mystery Magazine*'s Readers Award on two occasions.

Eve Fisher (evefishermysteries.com) is the author of nearly one hundred short stories. Her work appears regularly in *Alfred Hitchcock's Mystery Magazine*, *The Bould Awards*, *Murderous Ink Press's Crimeucopia*, and *Black Cat Weekly* as well as many other publications and anthologies. Her novel *The Best Is Yet To Be* is part of the Guideposts series Mystery and the Minister's Wife. Her short story "A Time to Mourn" (*Alfred Hitchcock's Mystery Magazine*) received Honorable Mention in *The Best American Mystery Stories 2012*.

John M. Floyd (johnmfloyd.com) has written for more than three-hundred-fifty different publications, including *Alfred Hitchcock's Mystery Magazine*, *Ellery Queen's Mystery Magazine*, *Strand Magazine*, *The Saturday Evening Post*, *The Best Mystery Stories of the Year*, *Best Crime Stories of the Year*, and three editions of The *Best American Mystery Stories*. He is an Edgar finalist, a Shamus Award winner, a five-time Derringer Award winner, a three-time Pushcart Prize nominee, the 2018 recipient of the Golden Derringer Award for lifetime achievement, and the author of nine books.

David Edgerley Gates is the author of the Placido Geist bounty hunter stories, a series of noir Westerns. His short fiction is widely anthologized and has been nominated for the Edgar, the Shamus, and the International Thriller Writers awards. His spy fiction includes the novels *Black Traffic* and *The Bone Harvest* and the novellas *Cover of Darkness*, *Viper*, and *The Kingdom of Wolves*.

Kristin Kisska (kristinkisska.com) is the author of a dozen short stories published in mystery anthologies, including two that won the Anthony Award for Best Anthology.

Janice Law (janicelaw.com) is an Edgar finalist and a Lambda award winner who regularly appears in *Alfred Hitchcock's Mystery Magazine*, *Ellery Queen's Mystery Magazine*, *Black Cat Mystery Magazine*, and *Sherlock Holmes Mystery Magazine* as well as anthologies, including *The Best American Mystery Stories* and *The Best Mystery Stories of the Year*. In addition, Law has published the Anna Peters and the Francis Bacon mystery series, historical and contemporary novels, several history books, and numerous popular and scholarly articles.

R.T. Lawton (amazon.com/author/r.t.lawton) is a retired federal law-enforcement agent, a past member of the Board of Directors of the Mystery Writers of America, and the 2022 winner of the Edgar Award for Best Short Story. He has more than one-hundred-sixty short stories in various publications, including forty-nine sold to *Alfred Hitchcock's Mystery Magazine*. He also has seven story collections on Amazon in paperback and e-format, with two more collections in production.

Steve Liskow (steveliskow.com) is a mentor and panelist for both Mystery Writers of America and Sisters in Crime. He has published sixteen novels and forty short stories in *Alfred Hitchcock's Mystery Magazine, Black Cat Mystery Magazine, Tough, Mystery Magazine*, and various anthologies. He has been a finalist for both the Edgar Award and the Shamus Award, has won Honorable Mention for the Al Blanchard Award four times, and was the first two-time winner of the Black Orchid Novella Award.

Robert Lopresti (roblopresti.com) has had eighty-plus stories published, almost half in *Alfred Hitchcock's Mystery Magazine*. He has appeared in *Ellery Queen's Mystery Magazine, Strand Magazine, Sherlock Holmes Mystery Magazine*, and *Black Cat Mystery Magazine*. He has been a finalist for the Derringer Award five times, winning thrice. He is a winner of the Black Orchid Novella Award and an Anthony Award nominee. He has been reprinted in *The Best American Mystery Stories* and *Year's Best Dark Fantasy and Horror*.

Leigh Lundin has been published by *Ellery Queen's Mystery Magazine, Alfred Hitchcock's Mystery Magazine*, Mystery Writers of America, and *Ficta Fabula*, among others. He won *Ellery Queen's Mystery Magazine's* Readers Award, the first time a first-story writer won first place. He's a founding member of SleuthSayers.

Lawrence Maddox is the author of the novellas *Fast Bang Booze* and *The Down and Out (A Grifter's Song Vol. 16)*. His stories appear in the anthologies *Orange County Noir* and *44 Caliber Funk*.

Robert Mangeot (robertmangeot.com) is the author of nearly forty published short stories. His work regularly appears in *Alfred Hitchcock's Mystery Magazine* and *Mystery Magazine*, and he has contributed to the Bouchercon and Mystery Writers of America anthology series. His stories have three times been named a Derringer Award finalist.

Travis Richardson (tsrichardson.com) has published more than fifty short stories. He won a Derringer flash fiction award and has been a three-time nominee for the Macavity and a two-time nominee for the Anthony short story awards. He has two novellas, *Lost in Clover* and *Keeping the Record*, and his short story collection, *Bloodshot and Bruised*, came out in late 2018. He reviewed Anton Chekhov short stories in the public domain at chekhovshorts.com.

Stephen Ross (StephenRoss.net) is the author of over thirty short stories, has won the Rose Trophy (Crime & Mystery, New Zealand), and has been nominated for Edgar, Derringer, and Thriller awards. His work appears in *Alfred Hitchcock's Mystery Magazine*, *Ellery Queen's Mystery Magazine*, and many other magazines and anthologies. His most recent story appears in *Dark Deeds Down Under*, the first ever anthology of New Zealand and Australian crime fiction.

Art Taylor (arttaylorwriter.com) is the author most recently of *The Boy Detective & The Summer of '74 and Other Tales of Suspense*. His fiction has earned numerous honors, including the Agatha, Anthony, Derringer, Edgar, and Macavity awards.

Mark Thielman (markthielman.com) is a two-time Black Orchid Novella Award winner and the author of more than twenty published short stories. His short fiction has appeared in *Alfred Hitchcock's Mystery Magazine, Black Cat Weekly, Mystery Magazine,* and several anthologies.

Brian Thornton (BrianThorntonWriter.com) is the author of twelve books and a whole bunch of novellas and short stories. His work has appeared in *Alfred Hitchcock's Mystery Magazine, Seattle Noir, Shred of Evidence, BulletUK, The Big Click,* and a host of other publications.

Jim Winter is the author of numerous short stories, the Nick Kepler series, and *Holland Bay,* inspired by 87th Precinct and *The Wire.* Since 2001, his short stories have appeared in the late, lamented *Plots With Guns* and *Thrilling Detective.* Additionally, he contributed to the Steely Dan-themed *A Beast Without a Name* and Colin Conway's *A Bag of Dick's.* Tell no one, but he is the secret identity of science fiction writer TS Hottle.

Elizabeth Zelvin (elizabethzelvin.com) is the author of the long-running Bruce Kohler Mystery series and the Jewish historical Mendoza Family Saga. Her short stories appear in *Ellery Queen's Mystery Magazine, Alfred Hitchcock's Mystery Magazine,* and *Black Cat Mystery Magazine.* They have been nominated three times each for the Derringer and Agatha awards for Best Short Story and have been shortlisted for *The Best American Mystery Stories.* The editor of *Ellery Queen's Mystery Magazine* has called Zelvin "one of our genre's most celebrated short story writers."

About the Editor

Michael Bracken

Michael Bracken is the editor or co-editor of twenty-eight published or forthcoming anthologies, including the Anthony Award-nominated *The Eyes of Texas: Private Eyes from the Panhandle to the Piney Woods*. Editor of *Black Cat Mystery Magazine* and an associate editor of *Black Cat Weekly*, he is also the Edgar Award- and Shamus Award-nominated, Derringer Award-winning author of more than twelve hundred short stories.

SOCIAL MEDIA HANDLES:
　Facebook: https://www.facebook.com/michael.bracken.908
　Twitter: @CrimeFicWriter
　Instagram: crimefictionwriter

AUTHOR WEBSITE:

http://www.CrimeFictionWriter.com

BOOKS BY MICHAEL BRACKEN

All White Girls
Bad Girls
Deadly Campaign
Psi Cops
Tequila Sunrise
Yesterday in Blood and Bone

As Editor
Fedora
Fedora II
Fedora III
Groovy Gumshoes
More Groovy Gumshoes
Hardbroiled
Mickey Finn
Mickey Finn 2
Mickey Finn 3
Mickey Finn 4
Prohibition Peepers
Small Crimes
The Eyes of Texas

Edited with Gary Phillips
Jukes & Tonks

Edited with Trey R. Barker
The *Guns + Tacos* series

About the Editor

Barb Goffman

Barb Goffman is the editor or co-editor of fifteen published or forthcoming anthologies, including the Anthony Award-nominated *Crime Travel*. An associate editor of *Black Cat Weekly*, she has also won Agatha, Macavity, Silver Falchion, and Ellery Queen Readers Awards for her short stories and has been a finalist for major crime-writing awards forty-one times.

SOCIAL MEDIA HANDLES:
   Facebook: https://www.facebook.com/barb.goffman/

AUTHOR WEBSITE:
   http://www.barbgoffman.com/

BOOKS BY BARB GOFFMAN

Don't Get Mad, Get Even

As Editor
Crime Travel

Edited with Donna Andrews and Marcia Talley
Chesapeake Crimes: They Had It Comin'
Chesapeake Crimes: This Job Is Murder
Chesapeake Crimes: Homicidal Holidays
Chesapeake Crimes: Storm Warning
Chesapeake Crimes: Fur, Feathers, and Felonies
Chesapeake Crimes: Invitation to Murder
Chesapeake Crimes: Magic is Murder

Edited with Rita Owen and Verena Rose
Malice Domestic 11: Murder Most Conventional

Printed in the USA
CPSIA information can be obtained
at www.ICGtesting.com
LVHW020312090324
773950LV00001B/188